BOOK 1

JOLETTE'S DREAMS

BOOK 2

DREAM RIVER

Joletta's Dreams

The Story of a Young Woman's Journey Home

KAREN CRAKER FORESTER

My Very Best Wishes!

Karen Craker Forester

JOLETTA'S DREAMS
COPYRIGHT PENDING 2019
KAREN CRAKER FORESTER

BOOK 1
JOLETTA'S DREAMS

Chapter 1
TRIBULATIONS / October 2000

Joletta sat on the edge of the bed with her head between her hands. Even though the room was beginning to grow dark she didn't bother to get up and switch the light on.

Her mom was on the couch, her head back and her eyes closed. Passed out cold, she still held a half-empty beer in her hand. On the coffee table sat several empty cans; one had fallen to the floor and spilled onto the carpet. Biting her lip, Jo reached over and placed the can with the others. She realized this was the least of her problems; the carpet was old and dirty already, and one more spill would make little difference.

Still dealing with anger because of the incident last week, Jo had decided that, instead of going home immediately after school, she would first walk to the library because she had a geography assignment that needed to be done. However, the real reason was she just did not want to deal with her Mother! Joletta did not usually do things without first getting permission, but she needed some time alone.

Closing her books, she sighed and put everything into her backpack as she prepared to head home. She was dreading the confrontation ahead and she walked the six blocks slowly. Having decided to try, once again, to get Mom to listen to reason, Joletta knew it would not be easy. She knew some programs helped people who drank too much. Her school counselor, Miss Lee, had talked with her about "Alcoholics Anonymous," explaining that it could prove helpful, but only "if" someone was willing to participate. She pointed out that many people needing the most help are unwilling to admit there even is a problem. It could be difficult to get them to attend meetings, no matter how much you want it or think they could benefit from it. She also explained to Joletta about

1

the support program for teens whose parents were problem drinkers.

Miss Lee had kindly offered to come home with Jo and speak with her mother, but Jo knew her Mom would likely be angry when she realized that she had been talking with a stranger about their personal problems.

Instead, Jo decided that she would try, once again, to talk with Mom. Perhaps this time, if she explained it right—that it could really help – she might agree to attend some of the meetings.

"So much for meetings!" Jo spoke aloud as her anger flared. She surveyed the room and sarcastically said, "Did you think that just because I came home a little late, it should give you permission to get drunk again?" The room was so cluttered that you could not walk without climbing over books, clothes, and dirty dishes. Jo carefully stepped over and took the beer from her mother's hand, causing her to shift her position, but she did not wake.

Annie was crying from the crib in the corner of the room, and Jo wondered how long she had been awake and trying to get attention. Poor baby! She sounded so sad and lonesome. "It's ok, Hon. Jo-Jo's here now."

The entire place smelled terrible: a mixture of the baby's unchanged diaper, stale beer, cigarettes, and dirty clothing.

As Jo picked her up, Annie's little body was shaking with emotion, her tiny nose running, and her face streaked with tears. "I'm so sorry, Sweetie. Sissy should have come home sooner." Holding her close, Jo continued to whisper softly in Annie's ear as she looked around the cluttered room, sifting through dirty clothes and old newspapers, hoping to find a diaper and some clean clothing that she could put on the baby.

Several minutes into the search, Jo found a diaper in an old diaper bag under the couch. After bathing her sister Jo opened a can of vegetable soup, smashed the veggies, and fed Annie. With a full tummy and a bottle of warm milk, the baby played happily on the bed beside her older sibling. Eventually, she fell back to sleep and snuggled against Joletta. Listening to her little sister's soft breathing, Jo gently touched Annie's cheek, and drawing her knees up to her chest, she stared out at the darkening evening, contemplating what to do next. She was just so confused!

Jo knew her mother loved them. At least she always said she did. Sandi told them often how much they meant to her. However, to Joletta, her mother's actions did not feel much like love. Some days her Mom would just lay around the house, hardly paying attention to anything or anybody. Her mind seemed to be far away. She was drinking more than ever before, although she would not acknowledge it. Once she started drinking, one beer would lead to another, and then another.

Jo was scared, and she felt utterly helpless. Mom used to go out occasionally, but she had never acted like this, and never brought alcohol home before. Joletta felt like she did not know this woman. She did not even like coming home after school anymore, and now she was worried. What if something terrible happened to Annie? The house could catch on fire and Mom might not even realize something was wrong! This was the last straw! This was not right, and Jo knew it!

It had not even been a week since the last blow-up. Mom had said she was going to the grocery store. However, rather than doing what she was supposed to do and buying the food they needed, she had instead stopped at the bar and spent everything they had on alcohol! Even worse was the fact that they were completely out of baby food for Baby Annie!

Usually, when they used their food stamps and with the WIC program, (Women, Infants, and Children, a government-sponsored feeding program), they were able to get by pretty good. But Mom had forgotten her last appointment at "WIC" and, as a result, she did not get her allotment for the month. Although she had scheduled another appointment for the following week, that would not help the current situation!

Luckily, Jo had found some oatmeal in the cupboard and a can of applesauce. She and her mother could make do for another week with what was there, but the baby needed milk, and she could not eat peanut butter or hot dogs!

Jo's anger was evident as she told her mother that they had no milk for Annie. At first, Sandi just stood and looked at Jo, confused, but then she began crying. "It's gone, Jo! The money is all gone! What are we going to do now?"

Joletta rolled her eyes angrily. "You're drunk Mom! You need to get up and go take care of Annie! She's hungry! I made her some oatmeal. It's on the table. Feed her, and I'll be back. Since you don't seem to know what to do, I'll take care of it myself!"

Jo knew she was being disrespectful, but turned and walked out of the house, slamming the door behind her! She would not admit to herself that she really didn't know what to do either. She would just have to figure it out on her own. Stuffing her hands into the pockets of her worn-out denim jacket, she walked morosely down the sidewalk.

After pacing up and down the block several times, she slowed and stopped in front of their neighbor's house. "Mrs. Taylor. That's it!" Jo would ask Mrs. Taylor if she could borrow some money from her!

The old lady liked to sit outside on her porch, and whenever Jo walked by her house she would always smile and wave. She seemed like a really nice lady and besides, Jo couldn't think of anyone else to ask; surely Mrs. Taylor would be willing to help.

Within minutes, Joletta had decided exactly what she should say. She would just tell her that Mom's check from Social Services had gotten lost in the mail or something and had never arrived. Later, she could figure out a way to pay the money back, but she wouldn't think about that now. There was enough to worry about for today.

She knew, of course, that lying wasn't right, but she couldn't tell Mrs. Taylor that Mom had spent all their money on drinking instead of getting the needed baby food.

Luckily, with little questioning, Mrs. Taylor gave the money to the girl that she had requested. "Now my dear, don't you worry your little head about a thing. There is absolutely no hurry in returning the $10.00. I'm sure your mother will take care of it as soon as she is able."

Although the kind neighbor offered Joletta some cookies and a glass of milk, the girl turned her down and hurried off. Mrs. Taylor thoughtfully shook her head as she watched Jo quickly cross the street and walk around the corner. Sighing, she turned and picked up her book, then settled herself, once again, in her favorite overstuffed chair and began to read.

The next morning Jo had confronted her mother. Sandi, who was now sober, could not clearly remember the day before and listened in horror as her daughter retold the story. Reaching out to draw her daughter to her, Jo's body stiffened. "Oh, Sweetheart! I am so sorry. Darling, I just don't know what to say. What would I ever do without you?" Jo looked at her mom but gave no response.

Her mom had screwed up, again! Had she completely forgotten last week's incident? She had promised Joletta at the time, it wouldn't happen again. The girl was absolutely at her wit's end! What would happen next?

"I'm only 13! I should not have to take care of you and Annie too!" Joletta wanted to have a temper tantrum, like she did when she was little. She thought it would feel good to just fall down on the floor and kick and scream to her heart's content!

Although her mom was passed out cold, and unable to hear her words, Jo again spoke aloud, "Why are you doing this to us?" Tears of frustration were running down the girl's face. "Momma---Annie, and I need you! We need you so much!" Joletta then curled up next to Baby Annie. Her head hurt, and her heart was broken. Finally, the tears stopped coming, and with a long soft sigh, Jo fell asleep.

Several hours later Sandi Breese awoke with a throbbing headache and her stomach doing flip-flops.

Wondering why the room was so dark, she looked at the clock on the opposite wall. It was 6:15. Almost dawn, the sun would be coming up soon. On good days Sandi loved this time of the morning. Waking early to the magical unearthly glow of morning can be a breathtaking experience. Not today. Today she could barely hold her head up and gave no thought to the glorious breaking of the new day.

Feeling confused and disoriented, she tried organizing her thoughts, and as the fog in her head began to clear, she suddenly remembered her children. In a panic, she pulled herself to her feet, steadying herself on a wall. Where were her girls? Stumbling toward the bedroom, she saw Joletta and the baby curled up against each other, asleep on the only bed in the apartment. Thank goodness! Wisps of the baby's soft golden curls contrasted with Joletta's dark shining hair.

Shaken and nauseous, she stumbled to the bathroom and became violently sick in the toilet. She then turned on the faucet and splashed cold water on her face and, bracing both hands on the sink, stared at her own bedraggled image in the small mirror of the medicine cabinet.

Bit by bit, she began to remember. Obviously. She had screwed up badly. Again--- and---not only that, she had broken the promise that she had made to Joletta.

As she pulled off her jeans and sweatshirt, she shivered, but not from the cool room. Stepping into the tub, she turned on the faucet and let the shower run hot and full force over her body, hoping it would clear her head. The flow of the water was so strong that it stung her skin, but instead of adjusting it, she let it continue to run as it was. It was only a small penance for her sin. She needed to think, for she had no clue what she would say to Joletta this time. There was no excuse for her behavior, and she knew it. Feeling helpless and trapped, Sandi closed her eyes and her tears suddenly mixed with the hot water running over her body.

Sandi had tried explaining to Jo how the situation from last week had started.

She had not meant to get drunk. It was not as though she planned it! The reason she went to Jen's in the first place was to ask her if she could baby-sit for Annie. She wanted to start job hunting that day and stopped over to ask Jen if she would watch the baby for a while. She had forgotten that Jen would be busy preparing for a birthday party later that evening for her boyfriend Robert. He was the newest of her friend's long line of ever-changing male companions.

Jen said if Sandi could wait until Wednesday, she would then be glad to babysit. So, without anyone else, she knew well enough to ask. Jen agreed. Since she now had no immediate plans, she offered to stay a while and help. While Annie played on the kitchen floor, the two women visited as they worked, and the morning passed quickly.

Jen had not been stretching the truth when she told Sandi she needed help getting things ready for the party.

7

Jen was in the manic cycle of her bi-polar disorder, "hyper" and unorganized. She thought they didn't have enough nametags made, or the planned decorations were not sufficient, or --- whatever else happened to pop into her busy brain.

Sandi had actually enjoyed working and laughing with her friend, and the two of them spent the remainder of the morning busy cooking and making plans.

Annie napped as they continued with their work. Later, after eating a sandwich for lunch and drinking several beers, Sandi did take Annie and go home. She was only a little tipsy when her older child arrived home from school, certainly not drunk. But shortly after Jo came home, Sandi had told her she was going out to pick up some things they needed.

The trouble started when Sandi decided to go to the store. Driving to Food City, she noticed Jen's car already parked outside of Tony's. She pulled over and went in to see if Robert was there yet. She would not be able to go to the party and only planned to stay long enough to say "Happy Birthday." Afterward, she would go on to the store.

Unfortunately, it was hours later, when she returned home, this time more than a little tipsy. Sandi now remembered why. . .She remembered feeling completely overwhelmed and helpless as Jen told her about the encounter with Sam, Annie's father and Sandi's ex live-in boyfriend.

Sam was back, and he was looking for Sandi. Jen had pretended she was busy, but Sam wasn't taking any hints. He hung out for over an hour, trying to get her to tell him where Sandi and the girls were living. Insisting he had changed and that he was sorry for everything that had happened between him and Sandi, he became emotional and cried as he told her that all he wanted was another chance. He wanted to get back together. He wanted to have his family back. He begged Jen for her help, telling

8

her that she was his last hope of finding Sandi and the girls. Eventually, just to get rid of him, Jen agreed to take his cell-phone number, saying she would deliver the message, but that was all.

"I think he was high on something, and I think you would be crazy if you even consider taking him back. I didn't give him any information, but I figure it's your life and your decision to make."

Sandi knew her friend was probably right. Sam did not have a good track record, but she also wasn't sure that Jen really understood how hard it had been for her! Being on your own and trying to take care of two children, especially when you have no job or any money most of the time. Most of all, it hurt being alone; it hurt when you had no one to love you.

Of course, she knew Jen was also a single mom. She had her own things to deal with, but at that moment, Sandi wasn't thinking about anyone but "herself and her problems."

There had been a time when Sam had been pretty good to her. Well, at least for a while he had. She had experienced his bad temper, and of course he wasn't dependable. When he took off, he had taken what little cash they had and left her with a stack of unpaid bills. If she allowed him to come back, the likelihood was that he would end up hurting her once more.

She sighed. The only thing she wanted to do was to go somewhere and crawl in a dark hole and hide from everything – a place where no one could find her, and she didn't have responsibilities. She wanted to stop hurting, and she had no one who understood. Although she didn't necessarily like alcohol, it numbed the pain, and after she drank a couple of beers, she could forget about her unhappiness and everything else she didn't want to think of---at least for a while.

Joletta was such a good girl. She had always been Sandi's "shining star." Sandi knew she depended on her

9

more than she should, but she felt like without Joletta she couldn't cope at all.

Unfortunately, after last week's incident, Joletta had become cool and withdrawn, retreating, and barely speaking to Sandi. She knew that this was not going to help matters at all. Then, there was sweet little Annie. Beautiful, happy little Annie-bell! It was just too much! "Damn!" she thought. "Damn, it all!"

The following morning a very angry daughter had confronted her mother. "How could you, Mom?" Joletta had screamed at her when Sandi tried to explain. "How could you just forget about Annie like that? We deserve more than that, Mom!" Jo ran out of the room and Sandi had not followed for she had no answer.

"Mom?" Joletta's voice came through the closed bathroom door, interrupting Sandi's thoughts. "Mom, are you all right? Annie needs a diaper, and I can't find any."

"I'm fine, Jo. I'll be out in just a second." Sandi dried herself quickly on her discarded clothes. Wrapping an oversized sweater around her still damp body, she walked into the front room to help Jo look for a diaper. After several minutes of searching, they found some behind the bed, buried under blankets.

A good thing too, since Sandi had no cash until their check from the State arrived next week. There was hardly any food at all left in the fridge.

She could hardly believe that she had sunk so low. Spending all of their money buying alcohol was unforgivable! She felt like the worst mother in the world!

Chapter 2
NOT FORGOTTEN / Susan Taylor

Mrs. Taylor sat with a cup of hot coffee on the open porch of the old Victorian house and watched as the young family which had recently moved across the street came out of their duplex and prepared to leave.

The mother opened the back door and buckled the little one, Annie, into a car seat, and the older girl climbed in beside her. Mom then got into the rusty old Chevy and drove away.

Susan wondered about them.

The mother looked very young, but of course to Susan just about everyone looked like kids these days. She sighed and stretched, remembering she was barely out of her teens when Ted Jr. was born.

Susan had met Joletta, the older girl, a couple of weeks before. She was pretty and slim, with dark shining hair that fell loosely around her shoulders. She had dark eyes and olive skin, in sharp contrast to the little one with bright blue eyes and blonde ringlets that went "every which way." The child did not look like she could be a year old yet and the older girl was perhaps 13 or 14. Joletta had a warm, friendly smile but seemed quite serious and quiet-natured.

Closing her eyes, Susan's memories involuntarily went to the time, so long ago, when her own children were small---the time that tragedy had changed their lives---forever. It came without warning, the memory of her husband's death.

Ted had died in a tragic car accident on a beautiful summer day. That day Susan was left alone, with three small children to protect and care for. His death left her with responsibilities that she never thought she would have to face. Without the help and support of the only man she had or would ever love, she simply did not think she would survive. She was only 25 at the time and could not believe she was now a widow and a single mother.

After all the years, it still hurt her to remember, but remember she did. What triggered the memory she did not know, perhaps little Annie's golden curls that reminded her of her own little girl at the same age, or the older sister's serious face. She remembered so well her oldest son, Ted, how he tried so hard to be a man when he was not even in primary school yet. Memories are strange like that. They pop into your head when you least expect them and, good or bad, they take you back----

After the devastating news, there were several days that she could feel little, except a deep numbness. She lived in a kind of limbo, simply doing whatever her family told her to do. Others took on most of the necessary preparations for her husband's burial. That first week remained a blank for many years. Eventually, she did remember some things, but for the most part, those first few days were nothing but a dark blot.

As time passed, she began to process what had befallen her family. She wanted nothing more than to run away. She wanted to draw her children close to her and hide far, far, away from reality. But there was no place she could hide; it was not in her power to protect her children from the bitter reality of their loss.

She was angry with everyone, including her gentle-natured Ted. Frequently she would dissolve into tears and beg God, "Please wake me up! Please make this all a terrible nightmare!" Susan soon realized she would now have to deal with everything on her own. Although she understood, it didn't make things better to blame Ted. Somehow it was easier to feel anger at him than to accept the cold fact that he was gone. He would not be coming home again.

Both she and Ted were from large families, and although she did not see it until much later, many of them stepped in to support and help her get through what seemed like a long unending abyss.

Parents, brothers, sisters, and so many others willingly and happily pitched in, bringing food, bathing children, and cleaning the house. So many of the small things we do daily without a second thought were done for her when she was not mentally able to do them for herself.

Eventually things did start to get a little easier, and after what seemed like an eternity, a time came when she began to see the "light at the end of the tunnel." She began to believe they were going to make it through, and life would go on. Realizing this, she knew it was time for her to find a way to support her children and herself. What kind of work she would do was something of a problem, Susan had married right after graduation and had not been employed since working as a grocery cashier the year before graduation. She did not have a college degree or any particular skills that she could market, so how would she support herself and her children?

There were insurance forms that had to be filed and processed and lawyers to consult with, but any money from insurance would be months or possibly years away.

After several weeks of putting in applications, she got a seasonal job at a canning plant, and shortly after that she started working at a restaurant not far from where she lived. She worked at "Celia's Roadhouse" for the next several years as a waitress and even though the job at Binder Cannery was hard, hot work, it made a huge difference when the first of the month and bill-paying time arrived. Although the job at Celia's did not pay much, she was a popular waitress and did quite well with generous tips. She was efficient and friendly, and knowing that she was doing a good job gave her real satisfaction.

Eventually, she did receive the insurance settlement from Ted's accident. With some of the money she decided to attend a local college, and the remainder she put in savings for her children's education. After much hard work, she proudly earned her business degree.

Susan realized she would never have been able to accomplish all this had it not been for her supportive family who had given so much after Ted died.

Not long after she got her degree, Susan, along with her other siblings, received a surprising, and sizable inheritance when their grandmother, Penelope Ames, passed away. That money was to play a major role in the future of her family.

She could now afford to stay home with the children full-time, but although she considered quitting her job at the Roadhouse, she enjoyed the work and the people there. If she quit her job, she knew she would miss them. By now, the children were happy and well settled into their own routines, one in preschool, the other two at daycare for two days each week; then grandpa's and grandma's house the other three days. Under the circumstances, Susan felt no great need to change so she chose to continue working at the Roadhouse.

She did decide not to go back to the factory again. That job was a blessing at the time because she still needed the paycheck. However, the factory work was hard and left her with very little energy to give to her children. She decided it would be best not to return the following Spring.

One day at work, Celia came over and told Susan she needed to speak with her in the office. Susan had no idea what the reason could be, but she followed Celia into the small office behind the kitchen.

As Celia closed the office door Susan saw that Mr. Bollinger, a frequent customer, was sitting in the room as if waiting for them. He had always been kind to Susan, and she had actually visited his law office recently to ask for advice about the money left to her in her grandmother's will. However, Susan was completely confused as to why Celia had singled her out and why Mr. Bollinger was here.

Celia offered Susan a seat and began to explain the reason for the meeting. Speaking softly, she told Susan that she had recently been diagnosed with a serious heart condition. She explained that there was little the doctors could do, except offer moral support and advise her that she would need to severely cut back on her activities. She would soon be putting the "Roadhouse" up for sale...

As sympathetic as Susan was when told of her employer's condition, she still had no idea what the reason for a private meeting could be. Celia could have easily told her this along with the rest of the staff, but as Celia continued Susan began to understand more clearly.

Celia said Mr. Bollinger had suggested to her that Susan might be interested in purchasing her business. As her story continued, Celia told Susan that Mr. Bollinger was her sister's husband. His wife was no longer living, but he was still close to his extended family. When Cilia told Walt of her circumstances and her plans to sell, he suggested that she should consider asking Susan if she was interested in becoming the owner. Not divulging all of Susan's private information, he had told Celia she should ask Susan about possibly purchasing the business.

At first, Susan could not believe that Celia was serious. Opportunities like this don't just happen, do they? However, weeks later, after a lot of prayers and much thought, she decided she very much liked the idea. It felt like the right thing to do, and she soon found herself in the middle of contracts and plans for this new venture. It took a couple of months, but after making the decision and with the encouragement of her family and friends Susan bought and indeed became the new owner and manager of Celia's Roadhouse.

The very first thing she did as a new landowner was to rename the business. Celia's Roadhouse officially became "Penelope's Place" in June of 1968 in honor of her grandmother Penelope Ames. Susan made few changes to the business the first year, keeping not only the former staff but the building's original look too, other than adding a beautiful new lighted sign mounted on a tall pole, proudly proclaiming, "Penelope's Diner, Open for Business."

For the next thirty years, the restaurant continued to support Susan, and though she was no longer actively involved in the business, she still carried an interest in Penelope's. She and her family lived happily and well. They bought this beautiful home; both of her sons had eventually completed college and gone on to become lawyers. Susan's daughter became a lay minister.

Five years ago, Jillian had married Thomas Turner, a handsome young preacher and they were now living and doing missionary work in Malawi, Africa.

Bill and his wife Mary blessed her with two beautiful granddaughters: Tiffany, at 14, was the eldest and Samantha was almost 11.

Ted, her youngest son, was unmarried and resided in a beautiful high-rise in the city. He loved his un-encumbered, bachelor existence.

Things could have been so different for us, Susan thought. *What if we had not had a family to help us out so many years ago? What if Grandma had not left us the money to buy the restaurant? Could I have ever managed if I had been left all on my own?* Luckily, those were questions that Susan had never needed to ask. Life had not always been easy for them but there had always been someone, family or friends, that had reached out with helping hands whenever it was most needed.

Susan began watching in the late afternoons for Joletta and her little sister. The weather had been beautiful the past week, and Joletta would bring the baby outside to play or take her in the stroller and walk around the block. Susan would wave at them, and Joletta would respond with a cheerful "Hi, Mrs. Taylor! Annie wanted to go for a walk. What are you doing today?"

Last week was a different story though. Joletta had shyly knocked on the door and asked for a loan. Susan invited her into the house, but she refused.

Instinctively Susan knew that the story the girl told was probably not completely true... Susan could tell by Joletta's nervous appearance that something was not quite right. The girl looked as if she believed Susan would send her away and refused to come into the house.

Without asking for any further information, she gave the money to Joletta. She would have even offered more but she was aware that her sons would not approve, as it were. Not wanting to embarrass the child, she let her go her way. Obviously, there was a problem of some sort. Perhaps later she would find out what it was, but at that moment the reason did not seem as important as giving the child what she apparently needed.

As Susan's mind slowly came back to the moment, she made a decision. If ever given a chance to help this young family, she would like to do just that. It seemed obvious that they had no family support. She had not ever noticed anyone other than the three of them at the house near hers. They lived in the old Bellamy place, directly across the street from Susan's home. Of course, she had already met the children, but hadn't had an opportunity to introduce herself to their mother. Perhaps she would invite them over for iced tea and cookies one afternoon soon.

Susan slowly lifted herself out of the wicker rocker she had been sitting in and went inside to make herself some lunch.

Chapter 3
WINDS OF CHANGE

"Mom," said Joletta quietly. "Would you tell me about my dad?"

Sandi's head turned sharply toward her daughter. "Just what more do you want to know? You know the jerk left me when I was six months pregnant with you. He ran out on us and never came back. That really is all there is to tell. He was a jerk and he probably still is a jerk!"

"I just thought," stammered the girl, "I thought maybe he could help us out or something." Joletta went silent, and her head dropped.

"Jo, I'm so sorry! Sweetheart, I didn't mean to hurt your feelings." Sandi had realized too late that she had spoken harshly, and she felt ashamed of herself for her quick, bitter reply. "Joletta, your father has never even seen you. I'm sure after all these years he isn't likely to show up now and start helping us out! I am sorry to disappoint you Dear, but that isn't the way it usually works."

"That's all right, Mom." Joletta paused. "What about Sam? Maybe he'll come back."

Sam was Annie's father. They had lived with him for almost a year, but a few months ago Sandi and Joletta returned home from a shopping trip and found him and a half-naked blonde girl, not much older than Joletta, making out on the couch.

Sandi and Sam had argued loudly until Sam ended up throwing a few of his things into the back of his old work truck, grabbing the speechless blonde teeny bopper who was still trying to get her clothes fastened, and driving out of their lives, leaving black tire marks for half a block down the road.

He did not come back that night, and he did not return the following week. He never even said good-bye to Joletta or to baby Annie!

A couple of weeks after the incident he called, saying he wanted the rest of his things.

Sandi stuffed everything into several garbage bags. She tossed the bags outside by the curb and left with the girls. When he arrived, the house was empty, and the lock on both the front and back doors had been changed.

Sandi and her daughters stayed in Sam's house until the first of the month when the property owner threatened to throw them out on the street if they didn't give him the money Sam owed for the last two months. That's when they ended up at the State Welfare Agency.

Mr. Benning was the social worker assigned to them. He worked with Sandi, doing the paperwork that needed to be done before they could begin receiving State assistance. He also helped them find the place they were now living in.

They were on their way to see Mr. Benning now. Their standing appointment was on the third Monday of each month. They were required to keep appointments and follow a case plan in order to continue receiving benefits. Sandi did not want to do anything that could jeopardize getting the check that they so badly needed, so they dutifully walked into the office at 2 o'clock sharp.

Mr. Benning was sitting at his desk in the small office he shared with another caseworker. He smiled as they entered the room. "Hello, Ms. Breese. Hi, Joletta. How is little Annie doing today?" He leaned over and touched the baby's cheek, and she smiled, showing her new tooth which was her very first.

Joletta thought he seemed nice, but she knew how her mother hated coming to see him. Momma said he asked too many questions that were none of his business!

"How are the girls doing?" he asked. "Joletta, did you get settled in your new school?" "Did you get Annie's D.T.P. vaccination yet? How's the job hunt going?" On and on the questions went, with Momma answering each in a low voice and Mr. B. writing

19

everything down on a sheet of yellow paper lying upon the desk in front of him. When Sandi told him she still did not have a job, he looked at her sternly over the top of his wire-rimmed glasses. "Ms. Breese," he said, "you do realize that if you are not employed within 90 days of beginning State assistance, it could be denied meaning you would be unable to maintain the rent on your apartment." He paused and continued, "It could even create a possibility that your children would be placed into foster care until you are better able to support them."

Sandi put her hand on Joletta's and clung tightly to the baby. "Mr. Benning," Sandi said with a tremor in her voice. "I've been trying. I will have a job soon. I promise I will. You just can't take my kids away from me! They're all I have!"

Sometimes Jim Benning did not like his job very much. He heard raw terror in Sandi's voice, and he felt compassion deep in his heart. Perhaps, he should not have spoken so harshly. Joletta was now holding her mother's hand tightly, her fingers turning purple.

For a few moments no one spoke, and he tried to think of something that could ease the tension.

Sandi Breese seemed like a nice enough woman; the kids appeared to be well cared for. At least they were clean and looked healthy. Joletta, the older girl, always seemed a little nervous and worried, and she very seldom smiled. *I guess it isn't any wonder,* he thought. *It's probably not been easy moving to a new town, and they apparently don't have family or friends who live within this area.* He sighed and then remembered something. "Perhaps, there is something I can do to help," he said. "There is an organization over on Fifth Street that does job placement and counseling. The manager is a friend of mine. I should have thought of this before," he continued, "but it is still a new enterprise in our community, and we have just recently started doing referrals. If you would like, I could call him and tell him you'll stop in to see him

20

tomorrow. Perhaps he could help you find something that would be suitable. Would that be O.K?"

"Oh, yes. Thank you, Mr. Benning. I would appreciate that." He handed Sandi a slip of paper with an address on it as she stood to leave.

"Oh, Momma," Joletta said as they got into the car. "Do you think they will be able to get you a job at that place? Mom, they couldn't really take me and Annie away from you, could they?"

"Joletta, could you please be quiet for a minute! Of course, they won't take you away!" Truthfully, Sandi was still shaking inside from what he had said to them, but she didn't want to frighten her little girl further. *He had already done enough damage!* Sandi's mouth was dry, and her hands were shaking. *What she needed was a good stiff drink.* She was could hardly believe her own thoughts! "Dear God! What is wrong with me? What can I be thinking?"

The baby whimpered from the car seat in the back, and she looked into her rearview mirror. As she watched Joletta gently comfort Annie, she thought, *My girls are the world to me. They are the only thing I have that is worth living for! Somehow, I just have to get my life together.*

Chapter 4
JOB HUNTING

The following day Sandi put on a gray linen skirt and a simple white pullover with a matching cardigan and black pumps. After pulling her light brown hair back into a classic twist, she picked up Annie and headed out the door. "Are you going to wish Mommy luck, sweet baby? Mommy's going to take you over to play with Jen for a little while, but I'll be back soon."

Fifth Street was in an older section of town. Many old brick buildings stood with dirty, broken windows, sad and neglected. However, there were also signs of urban renewal. Brave young urbanites were buying property and lovingly renovating the worn houses, turning them into family homes, while old factories were now converted into beautiful uptown loft apartment buildings.

After circling the block without finding a parking space, Sandi gave up and pulled into a lot. Giving the attendant her last $5 bill, she then walked around the corner where a sign on the front of an old brownstone stated. . . "Fifth Street Center," and on a second line— "Job Placement and Counseling Services."

Opening the door, she spoke to a young woman sitting behind a glass panel that separated her from the outer room.

"Excuse me, I'm supposed to see a Mr. Landers."

The girl at the desk smiled. "He's on the phone right now, but he will be with you in just a couple of minutes. You're welcome to have a chair while you wait. I will let him know that you are here."

Sandi sat down in one of several upholstered chairs that filled the outer area and picked up a magazine. She didn't have long to wait before an older man with gray hair and piercing blue eyes came from behind a closed door.

Wearing a somewhat rumpled gray flannel suit which had seen better days, a bright blue shirt, and a black tie, Sandi thought he looked more like a "Grandpa" than the stiff businessman she had expected to meet. "Well, Ms. Breese," he said after introducing himself and shaking her hand. Sandi was an attractive young woman, a fact that Mr. Landers noticed. She held her head high and gave the appearance of confidence. He liked that even though he realized she was likely more nervous than she appeared. His friend and colleague Jim Benning had given him some information about her situation. He was hopeful the organization would be a good resource to help her.

"Sit down Miss-err–Sandi, is it? Yes, please do sit down and make yourself at home. Let me see here," he said, picking up a notebook and flipping several pages before stopping to read from one of them. "Yes, of course, Sandi. Jim Benning tells me that you are looking for employment. If that is the case, I think you may have come to just the right place."

He handed Sandi some papers and explained to her that he would get whatever information she could give him now, and if she needed to finish, she could take what remained with her and finish at home. "We need your work history and educational background." He then explained that the placement center was a pilot program, funded by State money and that it was the first of its kind in the state of Pennsylvania. "Our focus is not only to help with job placement, but it is a mentorship program. Our goal is helping people become financially independent."

Sandi nodded and listened carefully, responding when necessary, although Mr. Landers did the majority of the talking.

"Now let's see here. We have a number of options for our clients. Some folks take advantage of our Basic Education Classes, and we offer an English Skills class. Furthermore, we will assist with resume' preparation, and

23

we also coordinate with employers that are willing to do hands-on training. Last but not least, we keep a running list of businesses in our area that are currently hiring. In order to keep our facility operational, we are required to keep the State updated with whatever information we gather that will show the program is working as it should. We also help those that have special needs, mental and physical, and are unable to find a job on their own."

He stopped and looked at Sandi with a smile on his face. "I know it seems like a lot. What we need to do right now is to determine your needs and see what we have to help you meet your personal goal. Once you are employed, we continue to follow your progress, using all pertinent data. This will then, hopefully, help us renew our grant."

Pausing again, he said, "It is a lot of babble, but we want our clients to understand how important our program is to our community. The follow-up is not intrusive at all. You have the option of either stopping at the office once a month, or we will mail you a questionnaire that you can send back to us. It only takes about 10 minutes or so to fill out."

It was almost an hour later when the paperwork and discussion with Mr. Landers was finished, and Sandi left the office.

He had been correct about the fact that it was all quite overwhelming. Nevertheless, she felt like a burden had been lifted off her shoulders and that perhaps there might be a brighter time coming. She left the office with the addresses of two businesses and a nursing home that Mr. Landers suggested she visit...and all three gave on-the-job training.

Sandi stopped first at a business downtown, a photography shop not far from the placement agency. They were looking for a receptionist. It appeared to be a pleasant enough place to work, but Sandi worried that her car would not last another winter as it was. Driving an

24

extra 40 miles a day would be a huge problem. In addition, she didn't know how she could handle childcare. She decided this would not work.

Her next stop and the last she would have time for today was "Maryville Home for the Elderly," a privately-operated facility with beautiful landscaping. It was quite close to where she and the children were now living.

She would stop and put in an application before she picked the baby up from Jen's house.

Pulling into a parking place in front of the nursing home, Sandi watched several older people and two young women who were sitting on a covered veranda in front of the long brick building. They were talking and laughing and appeared to be enjoying the sunny afternoon.

A brilliant red cardinal was happily hopping around in a flowerbed full of colorful late-summer flowers, and the smell of newly mowed grass hung in the air.

Sandi stepped out of the car and went through the double glass doors into the front entry area. Inside, she walked down the hall passing several people, some sitting quietly in wheelchairs looking at nothing in particular and others watching TV or visiting in pleasant community areas near the nurses' station. Off to one side, an ancient looking man sat with a heavy blanket wrapped tightly around his shoulders although it was almost 80 degrees outside. Next to him was a silver-haired lady holding a stuffed teddy bear. The bear was worn and tattered. It looked almost as old as she did. Reaching out her thin hand to Sandi, she asked "Where's my Mommy?" Sandi smiled and patted her on the shoulder. "I think she'll be here soon, honey." Seemingly satisfied, the old woman went back to rocking her teddy, humming a tune that only she and her little friend knew.

"Hi." A woman working at the reception area interrupted Sandi's thoughts. "Can I be of assistance?

"Oh, yes. Please, may I speak with someone about the job opening you have?"

25

Two hours later, Sandi was in the kitchen when she heard the door open. "Joletta, Honey, is that you?" Sandi turned from the stove, a smile on her face as her daughter entered the kitchen. Sandi was so excited that she could barely wait for Jo to put her things in the other room. "I've got news!"

"News? What is it, Mom?" Joletta's voice came from the bedroom where she carelessly tossed her light jacket and book bag. She came around the door into the kitchen...

"Honey, I have a job! I start working tomorrow evening at the nursing home over on Valley Drive. Can you believe that? I stopped there a while ago, just to get an application, and the person in the office was not an employee--- She was the owner!" She waited for a response from her daughter, but since none came, she continued. "She invited me to come into the office, and before I knew what was happening, I had a job! Can you believe that?" Sandi turned from the stove toward Jo.

"Joletta, I will have to be at work at 8:00 in the evening, and I won't be off work until around 3:00 a.m. You are going to have to take care of your little sister while I'm working. We'll make up a plan for you; things should work out pretty well...

There was still no response from her daughter, and Sandi began to feel a little uncomfortable... "I'm really sorry, baby. I know it isn't ideal, but I don't know what else to do." Sandi put down the large spoon that she was using and stepped across the room to put her arm around her daughter. "Before I leave, I'll have Annie all ready for bed so that all you will have to do is give her a bottle and tuck her in for the night. After you get her down, you can read or watch TV for a while."

"That is, as long as you have your homework done. I know that's really late honey, and I don't like asking you to take on so much, but other girls your age baby-sit, don't they? You just need to make sure that the doors are

26

locked, and the curtains are drawn. I'm sure everything will be ok."

"Do you think you can do that? Of course, if you get nervous or need me, you can call me at work." Sandi was getting concerned because Joletta was still quiet. "Honey, this way I'll be home with you girls in the afternoon." Her eyes searched Joletta's face. "The best thing is, their pay is better than most nursing homes because it is privately funded, and as long as I continue to work with the Job Placement Agency, I will also be getting a supplemental check. Mrs. Hardy, that's the owner's name...even called Mr. Landers and promised she would have my application processed immediately, so I will be able to start tomorrow evening."

The girl looked at her mother with her serious dark eyes. Then, her face lit up, and she smiled. "Wow, Mom, that's just great!" She turned and threw her arms around Sandi. "Of course, we'll be just fine, Momma. I'm not afraid to stay alone," she said.

Sandi's heart was about to burst! It had been days since Joletta had willingly hugged her. Although she was not entirely happy about putting so much responsibility on Joletta, she could not think of any other options. Joletta had turned 13 in May. She was a very responsible girl.

"I thought we would celebrate," she said. "I'm making spaghetti.... Oh! I'd better stir the sauce before I burn it and we don't have anything to eat! There is brownie mix in the cupboard if you would like to make some. I already have the oven preheated."

Chapter 5
NEW RESPONSIBILITIES

Sandi's first few weeks on the job were busy. She was a fast learner and quickly found that she loved working with the elderly people she helped, which impressed the supervisors. She was consistent and always patient and willing to take the time needed to listen to confused or lonely residents.

The first few weeks she worked with housekeeping, cleaning and doing laundry. When returning clothing to the residents, she would always stop and speak a few kind words as she checked to see if anything was amiss. It was not long before Zelda, the head nurse, asked if Sandi would like to take training so she could work directly with the patients.

Ina had been a resident at Maryville for almost 10 years, and until a year or so ago, she had been able to participate in the activities provided for residents. Sadly, she now suffered from dementia and was no longer able to talk or communicate with others effectively. She understood very little of what was happening around her, although occasionally she became lucid for a brief period. Her eyes would open, and she would quietly observe whoever happened to be in the small room which had become her entire world. She would watch but never spoke.

As long as no one touched her, she sat quietly waiting for her days to pass. Sadly, her dementia caused her to be frightened of physical touch. When someone needed to work with Ina, she would cry pitifully, making it hard for the nurse's aides who daily had to help dress and clean her.

One evening, while getting Ina ready for the night, one of the aides called for Sandi who was passing by the door. Two aides were already there, but the elderly woman was struggling. Crying and pushing at them, her arms were waving wildly about in a panic. Frustration and irritation showed in the faces of the two workers, and as Sandi came in, she saw Ina's panicked struggle. It was not the first time she had heard Ina crying, and she had heard stories from others about how hard it was to take care of her. It seemed that no one liked working with Ina. Sandi had not yet been certified as a nurse's aide, so she was not able to physically help patients, but she came into the room and walked over to Ina's bed.

She had been in and out of her room now daily to clean and return clothing without any problems. Speaking softly, she asked, "Ina, what is wrong? Can I help? These ladies are only trying to help you, Hon. It's going to be ok." Amazingly, something about Sandi's voice quieted Ina. She stopped waving her arms around and sat very still.

Everyone in the room waited--- for only a moment, Ina's clouded eyes cleared, and she looked directly at Sandi. Reaching her long crooked fingers out, she gently touched the younger woman's cheek. The two other women in the room could not believe what had just taken place.

Soon they had Ina dressed and settled, hopefully for the rest of the night. "What on earth did you do?" one of them asked.

Sandi smiled and shrugged her shoulders. "Not sure. But I'm glad it worked." She continued smiling as she returned to her housekeeping duties. It felt good knowing she had done something to help the sweet old woman and the two young aides, even if she wasn't quite sure what it was that she had done.

The next evening the Floor Supervisor called for Sandi to stop into the staff office. As they passed in the hall, Rachel the night nurse assured her that there was no reason to be concerned.

Entering the office, Mrs. Booth explained the reason she wanted to speak with her. "It seems that Ina likes you, Sandi. Nan has been telling how she reacted when you came into her room."

"Yes, she did seem to relax while I was there, but I didn't really do anything special. I just talked to her like I do any of the other residents while I am in their rooms."

"Well, Ina certainly seemed to appreciate what you did. As I think you are aware, the nurse's aides have had a continuing problem with her and if you are willing, we would like to try having you spend some time during the evenings with Ina before she has to be dressed for the night. Unfortunately, because she is unable to understand that we are only trying to care for her, it is quite a problem for the staff when she gets so upset, and although she cannot verbalize her feelings, I am sure the trauma is not good for her. The nurses and aides do the best they can, but she is very fragile, and it causes much concern for her safety. I know that under the circumstances, it has been a long time since Ina has had a friend. She has no family left except a great-nephew that lives out west. If she responds well to your visits it could make things much easier for everyone involved, especially, for Ina."

Although Sandi was unsure that she could really make a difference, her heart went out to the elderly lady, and she agreed to try. In the weeks that followed, she spent part of her shift each evening in Ina's room. Every night she sat with her and would talk or do whatever seemed to be pleasurable or comforting to the old woman. Sandi read short stories aloud to her, combed her thin silver hair and put lotion on her hands and arms. One evening as Sandi was humming an old song, one she didn't even remember the words to, Ina opened her eyes and looked directly at her.

"Do you remember this song?" Sandi asked. Ina's eyes closed again, but the corners of her mouth curled slightly. That was the only time Sandi ever saw Ina display any emotion other than fear. Sandi continued humming until Ina was peacefully asleep.

30

Ina passed away only a few short weeks after Sandi started working at Maryville. Sandi cried off and on her entire shift that night. She had not thought about becoming attached to these people, but Ina had outlived her family, there was no one left to grieve her loss. It broke Sandi's heart. She had come to love this precious soul, and she would certainly miss her, although Ina had never spoken as much as one word to her. She believed that somehow, Ina understood the love she had offered.

Later that night, Sandi was in the employee break room when she happened to overhear a conversation between several of the employees. She could hardly believe what she was hearing when one of the aides commented "Well, at least that is one less "old crow" we have to worry about." Sandi stood up, and with both hands clenched, walked directly over to where they were talking. She felt like slapping the aide right in the face, but in response, she only said "Ina couldn't help herself. You should be ashamed!" Then with her hand over her mouth, choking back her emotion, she walked out of the room, leaving the three girls with embarrassment and shame on their faces. *How could some people be so heartless?*

As Sandi's confidence slowly began to grow, weeks became months, and she actually began to feel hope that her life was going in a better direction. It had been a long time since she had dared to believe in anything except bad luck. Although it was not always easy, she kept up pretty well with the house and spent as much time as she could with her children. She faithfully went to work each day and even developed several new friendships.

There was very little extra time for socializing, but she did find a few hours a week to read or do something she enjoyed.

Each morning, if you can call 3:30 a.m. "morning," when she finished work, she would go home and collapse on her bed. Her alarm went off at 8:00 a.m., barely four hours later, and she would then get up to fix breakfast and eat with Joletta and Annie. It was soon time to take Joletta to school after which Sandi and the baby would return home. She spent the early day with Annie and working around the house doing whatever needed to be done. Paying bills, doing laundry, housecleaning, and caring for the baby filled most of her time while she was not working. Annie was ready for a nap shortly after lunch and Sandi would then lie down once again and sleep, if possible, until Annie woke up or whenever Jo got home from school.

Their evening routine would then begin. It was a crazy schedule, but for now, it was how they were getting by. Actually, it was not so bad. In many ways, the busier she was, the happier she felt.

Sandi felt good to once again have a real job. Her check wasn't large, but she still received some state assistance, and that added to the small stipend from the job placement grant. It gave them enough extra that they went to the local resale shop, where Sandi bought both girls much-needed coats and clothing for the upcoming winter.

Joletta had been walking home from school with her new friend Tina, who lived just around the corner.

Tina and Jo met the very first day of school and soon became "fast friends." Tina had first noticed Jo sitting alone at lunchtime, and she asked her if she wanted company. Before lunch was over, they realized they not only shared lunch period but the same homeroom and study hall. Also, they found out they lived practically next door to each other.

Jo had not had a real friend for a long time. Keeping friends was not an easy job when you moved two or three times a year. She and Tina made an agreement that they would be friends forever, even if they moved far away from each other.

In the evening, after waking her mother up, Joletta had about an hour that she could visit or do pretty much as she pleased. It wasn't a lot of time, but so far, Jo had not complained. Mom wanted her home by 6:30 so they could eat dinner together. After the meal was over and the dishes were done, Joletta did homework while Sandi got ready to leave for work.

Mom would bathe Annie, put her pajamas on, then read to her or sing her little songs, and after hugs and kisses, she would leave for work. Joletta would play with Annie for a while or rock her as the baby took her last bottle. After checking to make sure that she didn't need her diaper changed, she would tuck her into the crib.

Mom had given her permission that after Annie was in bed, and after double-checking to see that the doors and windows were locked, Jo could read or watch TV, unless she still had homework to finish. Her lights were to be out at 10:00.

Chapter 6
ASKING FOR HELP

Sandi's life was now so busy that she had very little time to think about anything much, except for her job and the girls.

There were times she considered stopping at the bar. If she left for work a little early, she would have been able to visit her old friends beforehand. Months ago, she had spent a lot of time at the bar, but she now realized what a bad choice that had been.

After the terrible incident with Joletta, Sandi had begun to realize that her life had gotten completely out of control. She had certainly not seen it coming, but in hindsight she could understand why it ended so badly. *No, she could not and would not risk it!*

Even though things were now going along fairly well, she still felt there was something more she needed to do. Thinking of how awful it was for Joletta to come home and find her little sister crying and their mother passed out made an ugly, disgusting picture. It frightened the "living daylights" out of Sandi.

Another thought slipped into her mind – seeing a small girl, standing beside an unresponsive person, and not understanding. After a moment, she realized that her thought was not just random, but it was a memory, long forgotten, and she was the child. The person lying on the floor was her own mother. She felt a cold chill run through her body. She had never considered that her past might be still affecting her and her children. *Could there be a reason for the memory?* Tears streamed down her face as the painful feelings from so long ago filled her being. Sandi now could see that she had unknowingly transferred that hurt from her childhood to her own girls. She knew now what she must do. She must prove to Joletta that she would do everything she could to keep her promises and take care of her and Annie.

The guidance counselor at school had suggested to Jo that her mother probably needed help. She had even offered to come to their home and talk with Sandi about Alcoholics Anonymous. At that time, Sandi had totally rejected the idea. She did not believe that she had a problem, and furthermore, it certainly was none of the school's business! Unfortunately, she was not so sure about anything now.

Deciding the time was "now or never," Sandi picked up the phone and dialed a number she had found listed in the yellow pages. She nervously waited for an answer.

"Addiction Services Hotline," spoke a friendly but businesslike voice on the other end. "May I be of help?"

Sandi's voice quivered, and her hands were shaking as she said, "I think. . ." She took a deep breath and continued, "I think I have a drinking problem. I'm afraid I may be an alcoholic!"

The person on the phone assured her they would try to help if she would let them and began to explain the procedure for setting an appointment.

Sandi's first appointment was a needs evaluation, and an introduction to the caseworker who introduced herself only as Lynn, a young woman about the same age as Sandi with a pleasant voice and a warm smile.

After the initial interview and the never-ending paperwork, Lynn suggested that, before they set up another appointment, she felt Sandi should make an appointment and see her physician. Sandi had admitted to Lynn that she had not seen a physician since shortly after the baby was born. Lynn asked if Sandi had ever suffered from depression in the past. Rolling her eyes, she said, "Well, if you would call a person that cries almost every day---." Sandi had never thought that some of her problems might be treatable.

At her gynecologist appointment a few weeks later, the doctor did both a thorough examination and blood work. After receiving the test results, Dr. Preston was able to rule out several possible disorders and eventually diagnosed Sandi as suffering from severe post-partum depression. Sandi had heard of this before, but believing her personal problems were to blame for the way she felt, she had never suspected that hormones could be playing a part in her overwhelming sadness. The doctor prescribed an appropriate anti-depressant, and after several days she did begin to feel some better. The constant tightness in her chest disappeared, and she did not toss and turn every time she tried to sleep. Amazingly, she no longer felt a desire for beer or alcohol of any kind.

In the following weeks, as her therapy continued with Lynn, they talked about how Sandi's relationships "always ended in disaster." Each break-up only served to confirm her lack of self-worth.

She talked about when Sam left her, which was when she began to spend more time at Tony's where she worked before Annie was born. Sandi was so lonely, she was desperate for friendship, and since the baby was still very young, she would either sit in her stroller and play or nap while Sandi visited. Except to go to the grocery or laundromat, she went out very little.

She had become friends with Jen, who also worked for Tony. They shared a common life experience, tough childhoods, both had babies while they were teenagers, and now, both were raising children on their own. Jen's kids were several years older than Jo and Annie, but both women struggled just trying to keep their heads above water.

Tony had a thing for Sandi, and sometimes he even provided her with drinks. He liked playing "Mr. Nice Guy," thinking that at some point he might benefit personally. As long as everyone got his or her work done, he was happy that Sandi was there. He liked to watch her and fantasize about what it would be like to be with her. Afternoons were slow, and he didn't even mind the kid.

36

She wasn't much of a problem, as long as no one expected him to mess with her.

Sandi slowly began to understand that she had been using the alcohol as a crutch. When she drank, she didn't have to think. It numbed the anger and almost made her forget, if only for a short time, the hurt, the loneliness, and the stress that she was suffering from.

As time went by, Sandi began to feel much better, but Lynn felt she should continue their weekly appointments, at least for the next few months. Lynn encouraged her to consider how seriously her childhood experiences had shaped her present life experience.

Sandi had only recently begun to understand that she still carried pain buried deep in her mind. Shadowy figures sometimes danced through her thoughts, thoughts mixed with angry voices and her daddy kneeling with her gathered into his arms. Feeling his rough coat against her face was the last memory she had of her father.

She was only seven at the time, and she never knew why he left. She tried her best to be a good girl but her Momma was always angry. Once, Sandi asked why her daddy didn't come home and her mother said that she was the reason he left! Sandi cried, but the little girl's misery seemed to give her mom cruel pleasure.

Why did he hold her so close on the day he left if he didn't love her? Her mom never made any effort to comfort the sad little girl, and as time went on, Sandi decided her mother must have been right all along. He never did come home, no matter how long she waited.

Within months her mother remarried, and by the time Sandi reached her 12th birthday she had three younger siblings.

The summer she turned 16, Sandi fell madly in love with Joe. Tall, good-looking, and the quarterback of the football team, he was every girl's dream! He treated Sandi like a princess, and she felt that there had never been a happier girl.

They dated for several months before she realized that she was pregnant. Of course, they had certainly not planned this, but she couldn't help feeling excited. They were young but they loved each other, didn't they? She was sure it would all work out.

At first, Joe was loving and supportive. He said things would be ok, that Sandi could move in with his family and they would get married. For the next few weeks Sandi lived her rose-colored dream.

Things began to change shortly after classes started in the fall. At school, Joe started to avoid her, and when they did spend time together, he was restless and moody. She gently asked several times what it was that was troubling him. He finally told her that they needed to have a serious talk.

He picked her up on Friday and they drove in silence until he pulled over by the river and parked in a gravel area that was a fisherman's access. By this time Sandi was feeling sick and nauseous, and Joe was acting so strange that she did not know what to think.

An hour later, Sandi sat in her room, shaken and heartbroken. She could hardly believe what had just happened. Joe had actually questioned her, suggesting that the baby might not be his at all. She knew better and she was sure that he did too!

They argued, and finally he admitted that his parents were the ones that put the idea in his head, but that was not all. He said he was not ready to be a father and he didn't see how they could get married anyway. He had plans to start college the following fall, and there was no way they could take care of school and a family.

Then he dropped the bombshell! He told Sandi she should go to a doctor and get rid of the pregnancy!

She was truly sick now. Feeling faint and was shaking like a leaf, all she could do was tell him to take her home. She couldn't think; they would have to talk

38

later. He couldn't mean what he was saying. This was his baby! Their baby!

At school the following week, he would not even make eye contact with her. She tried to believe it was all a mistake, even after calling more times than she cared to admit. At first, his mother answered the phone, telling her that he was busy or not at home. However, after about a week she informed Sandi that Joe no longer wanted anything to do with her. She said to stop harassing them or they would have to call the police!

Sandi tried to believe he still loved her. She tried to believe he would come back and rescue her, but as the weeks and months went by, she slowly began to accept the facts. It had all been a dream. Now, the dream had become a nightmare!

When Sandi's mother found out about the pregnancy, she was furious. She had never shown affection for her oldest daughter, just constantly complained about what a burden she was. Many times, she would say hurtful things such as telling her the only reason they kept her around was to have someone to take care of the kids! She would laugh and pretend she was joking, but it was not funny to Sandi, not at all. Her stepfather, Dan, would sometimes scold her mother, telling her she needed to stop picking on the girl, but her mom would just light up another cigarette, roll her eyes, and walk away.

Sandi suffered severe morning sickness, leaving her tired and depressed most days, but it made very little difference to her mother, who insisted that she keep up with her schoolwork, and expected Sandi to keep the house clean and babysit for her younger siblings. Sandi's mom told her, "As long as you are living in *my* house, you are expected to help!"

Actually, the time spent caring for her little sister and brothers was her one "saving grace." She loved them so very much. They willingly returned her affection.

A week before summer break was to begin, Sandi went into labor, and after twenty-one long hours, little Joletta Caroline Breese made her appearance. She was tiny, only 18 inches long and not quite 6 pounds, but she was beautiful. Even Sandi's mother had to smile when she saw her granddaughter.

Sandi watched her mother's face soften when she looked at the baby. It made her wonder once more what it was that caused the distance between them. She would never understand it. Sandi loved this tiny baby girl with her whole heart and soul, and she knew that would never change! With or without her mother's approval or Joe Lenders in their lives, she knew this precious child was meant to be.

Mrs. Meeker, the school counselor, had arranged for Sandi to take her final exams early, making it possible for her to complete 11th grade on schedule. The following year Sandi attended a local vocational school which offered childcare as part of its curriculum, making it possible for her to graduate in June of 1988.

The weeks following graduation were not easy ones. Her mother's drinking was creating problems in her marriage, causing frequent outbursts of anger. Dan had become quiet and moody and was threatening to leave and take the children with him if their mother did not get help. Their arguments concerned Sandi. It seemed like nothing ever got better in her family. She did not have the power to change that situation between her parents, but for the past weeks she had been quietly making plans for herself and her little daughter.

She had a folding stroller, a bag with diapers, clothing, powdered formula, and the necessary items little Joletta would need. She also included a change of clothing and a few personal items, a picture she had found once.

Finally, a day came when everyone was going to be away. Taking a deep breath, she boldly went into her stepfather's office, and into the lowest desk drawer. Lifting the papers on top, she found what she was looking for. Taking $250 from the stack of bills in the cream-colored folder, she replaced it with a note telling her stepfather that she was sorry for taking the money. She said she had to leave and she promised to return the money when she could.

Having purchased a bus ticket earlier, she had a plan to meet and stay temporarily with cousins of a friend. After that, she did not know exactly where she would go or what she would do. She was determined she would never return, and she did not believe anyone would come looking for her.

Mr. and Mrs. Maxim were wonderful people in their early forties. They had never had children of their own and fell in love with the young mother and little "Jo-go," a nick-name she earned the week they arrived when she rolled and scooted her little body all the way across the living room.

Sandi and Joletta ended up staying in their home for several months. Sandi often wondered about her sister and the two baby brothers she left behind. She loved and missed them. But she believed she had done what she had to do. How different her life could have been if her mother had only loved her.

The more she talked about her life experiences, the more she remembered, and although many of the memories were heartbreaking or sad, Sandi was surprised when she began to feel less stress. Amazingly, she felt as if she had physically put down a heavy weight!

Lynn told Sandi, "I really think you are doing well. I think we can wait a few weeks before I see you again. I want you to continue with your meds but let's wait a few weeks before your next appointment. I am confident that you are going to do well, but we want to make sure you are completely comfortable on your own. Remember, you can always call if you need me."

Their neighbor, Mrs. Taylor, and Joletta had now become fast friends. Joletta would stop over every afternoon to visit before she went to Tina's. Sometimes she preferred staying at Mrs. Taylor's and never even went to visit her young friends at all.

In addition, on Saturday she would spend hours there when Mom did not want her to stay home. She usually took Annie over with her and let Mom get some extra sleep.

Mrs. Taylor always told the most wonderful stories about when she was a young girl. She had nine brothers and sisters, and she loved telling stories about their childhood adventures. She told of the trouble she and her siblings had gotten into, and then she would tell more stories about her children and grandchildren!

It all sounded so fantastic! Joletta wondered if anyone could really live like that. To Joletta, it really didn't even matter because it was wonderful just hearing about it all.

The last week of October, Mrs. Kiley, the night nurse, came into the room where Sandi was working. "Excuse me, Sandi, someone from Lakeview Hospital is on the phone and needs to talk with you."

Sandi immediately thought of the children, and her heart started to throb. "Hello, this is Sandi Breese," she said when she picked up the phone at the nurse's station.

"This is Lakeview Hospital E.R... I'm afraid there has been an accident involving your daughter. You will need to come in as soon as possible."

Sandi rushed through the emergency-room doors and saw Joletta and Mrs. Taylor sitting in the waiting area. Joletta's eyes were red and puffy, and Mrs. Taylor had a protective arm around her.

"Oh, Momma! I'm so sorry!" She ran to the door and into her mother's arm. "The doctor is examining her now. I only turned around to get the baby wipes, and she fell off the bed! Mom, I couldn't get her to stop crying, so I ran over to Mrs. Taylor. She brought us here!"

A young doctor stepped from behind the curtained area. "Are you the mother of the Breese baby?"

"I am," she said. "Please tell me, is she all right?"

"My name is Dr. McCauley," he continued. "Your baby was lucky this time. Her fall was not bad enough to break the arm, but she apparently twisted it under her. It will probably be uncomfortable for a few days. Your older daughter tells me that she was babysitting while you were at work?"

A nurse carried Annie from the examination area, and when the baby saw her mother, she began to cry loudly. Sandi reached for her and held her closely. "It's all right now, Pumpkin," she soothed. "Momma's got you." Annie's trusting blue eyes looked into her mother's face and studied it for a moment. She then stuck her thumb in her mouth and sighed contentedly. All was "well with her world" once again.

Dr. McCauley cleared his throat and spoke. "In circumstances like this, you understand, we must contact Children's Services. Your daughter is quite young to be expected to take on the care of such a small child. A social worker will need to make a visit to your house tomorrow to talk with you." The Doctor's voice was cool and impersonal. "You will have to excuse me now. I have other patients I need to see. The nurse will have papers you must sign, and she will talk with you about the medication you should give her if she has any discomfort, then she may go home."

The older woman gathered up their coats, and they walked out of the hospital together. As she started to get into her car, she turned and gave Joletta a hug and smiled at Sandi.

43

Sandi tried to tell her how much she appreciated her help. "Mrs. Taylor," she began, but she could go no further. She bursts into tears. "I am so sorry! I should have been there! What if Annie had been seriously injured?"

"There, there, it'll be OK," comforted Mrs. Taylor, patting Sandi on the arm.

"What am I going to do now?" Sandi sobbed, "I'm afraid they will try to take my children from me!" She was shaking as she tried to wipe the tears from her face with the sleeve of her sweater. Many months of frustration and worry spilled out right there in the hospital parking lot. "I was only trying to make a living for us! That is what they told me I had to do! I was doing the best I could. I have no one else to help. Dear God, what am I going to do?"

Mrs. Taylor's hand was on her shoulder, and she spoke between Sandi's sobs. "I would like to help. Perhaps the girls could stay with me while you are at work."

"What?" Sandi blew her nose on a tissue Susan handed her. "What are you saying?"

"I enjoy the company the girls give me so much, and I'm just a lonely old lady in a great big empty house. I do wish you would at least consider it, my Dear. I know you don't know much about me, but I assure you I would do my best to care for them. I could even get you references if you would like."

"But... but, I have no money," stuttered Sandi.

"No, no, my Dear, there is no need to worry about money. What does an old lady like me need with money? You don't need to make any decisions tonight, just go home and think about it, Dear. We can talk tomorrow, but right now you need to get your family home, and you should try to get some rest."

44

On Sunday, Bill and Mary drove up and parked the new Lincoln in front of his childhood home. The large yard was now mostly brown and covered in leaves of red and gold, the maples bare. Only the big oak out back still had leaves clinging to its branches. The gardener had been raking, and piles of colorful leaves lay along the edge of the road waiting for the fall cleanup crew to pick them up. It was a wonderful old house.

Bill remembered all the good times he and his brother and sister had while growing up in the sheltering shade of these huge old trees. The old Victorian in Summerset Hills was the only home he could remember, and he loved it, but Mother was getting older, and he felt she needed to realize this. He felt she would be better off living somewhere closer to them, in a nice little condo. There were also some pleasant assisted-living communities within the area. They offered many planned activities, and employees were there twenty-four hours a day to handle whatever residents needed. It was beyond reason why she adamantly refused to talk about the possibility.

This house was much too large for her now, and the neighborhood was becoming quite dilapidated. Some of the old houses had been converted into apartments or duplexes which would soon affect home values, and probably already had. His mother was a wonderful person and he only wanted the best for her. It was hard to understand why she was so stubborn. *She definitely had a mind of her own!* Soon Bill was to see that his ideas for what was good for Susan were certainly entirely different from hers.

The family was just sitting down to eat when Bill's mother first mentioned the crib. "You need me to do what, Mom?"

"I need you to go up into the attic and bring down Teddy's crib and set it up in Jillian's bedroom."

"What on earth would you need the crib for?"

45

"Are we having a baby," interrupted 8-year-old Samantha. "Is it a girl or a boy?"

"A girl, Sweetie." Answered her grandmother.

"Have you gone daft, Mother? What on earth are you talking about?"

Mary watched in silence as her husband and his mother glared at each other. She always enjoyed watching them spar. They were so much alike, a fact that at least Bill would vehemently deny, but their arguments never went very far, for Bill's soft heart for his mother usually swayed any situation in her favor.

After considerable discussion and much frustration on Bill's part, the crib that Ted had slept in some 38 years earlier was set up next to the bed that had once belonged to his sister Jillian.

Bill's daughters did not stop asking questions for the next two hours, and though he strongly disapproved of his mother's plan, her stubbornness had, as usual, prevailed.

As they were driving away, the sun was setting behind the old Victorian house.

"What can she be thinking?" Bill spoke as he turned the corner of the old town square.

"You know, Bill, your mother has always been a very good judge of character. I'm sure it will be all right." She smiled and squeezed his hand.

"But Mary, she's too old to be caring for children."

"Now, Bill, she's only 67 and she is in very good health. I think it is her decision to make."

"You still can't convince me she hasn't gone completely mad! The very thought!"

Mary smiled and said nothing more.

Chapter 7
HOLIDAYS

Thanksgiving had arrived, and there had been no more disasters in the past few weeks. A light snowfall had covered the ground in the night and the air was clear and brisk. As the sun rose, it looked as if someone had sprinkled glitter over the frozen ground. Susan's family would be arriving soon. Sandi and Joletta were already in the kitchen, helping to prepare the food.

Joan, Susan's part-time cook and housekeeper, had been offered the day off but had chosen to work, saying the extra money would be handy with Christmas coming. She would go home to her own family once she decided everything was under control and Susan and the girls would finish up.

Warm holiday smells drifted throughout the house as Susan walked into the dining room where Joletta was beginning to set the table.

It had been several weeks now since the girls had been staying with her, and what a joy they were. Susan had never thought about being lonely before, but now her life seemed so much fuller. It felt wonderful having children in the house again. She was now feeling younger than she had in years.

She had to admit though, today would be the first time Bill and Mary would be meeting her new friends and she certainly hoped that the day would turn out well.

After Annie's accident, Social Services came to the house and interviewed Sandi and Joletta. Since the girls would now be staying at Susan's, no further action would be needed. Unless there was another incident, the girls would remain with their mother.

Susan watched Joletta with a smile on her face. "My! Everything looks so nice, Joletta."

The girl smiled. "Thanks, Mrs. Taylor. I never knew anyone that had such fancy dishes before."

"They were my grandmothers. You know, Joletta, I told you that you could call me Susan."

"Oh, I'm sorry! It's just that Momma says that it isn't very respectful to call older people by their first name."

"Oh, poppycock! I'll have to talk to your mom about that." Susan patted Jo on the cheek and turned toward the living area. "Oh, they've arrived. I hear the car door."

"Mom?" She heard Bill's voice as the heavy oak door opened.

"We're here, Grandma!" Samantha's excited voice was right behind and only a moment later, Susan's youngest granddaughter came running through the door, practically knocking Susan off her feet as she was smothered in hugs and kisses. "Look, Grandma, look what I have!" In her arms, she carried a small bundle of golden fur. "She's a puppy, Grandma! I got her for my birthday! Remember? I told you I wanted a puppy, and I got one!"

"Yes, I do remember when you told me, Samantha. Here let me see what she looks like."

"Oh, Grandma, remember she's still just a baby. No one knows how to hold her except me!"

"Now, Sam. What were you told?" Her father spoke firmly but gently.

"Oh, ok, I forgot. Just be careful, Grandma. Her name is Stubby because she has a stubby nose."

"Happy Thanksgiving!" Susan laughed, "I am so happy you are all here, my dears, including Stubby."

She greeted Mary and their older daughter Tiffany with a hug as they entered the room.

Mary carried a large bouquet of chrysanthemums. "I thought these would look nice on the table," she said as she handed them to Susan.

"Oh, Mary, they are just lovely. Thank you so much, Darling. Come on in girls. We will go and find a vase for the flowers and get them in some water. Grandma has a surprise for you. There is someone here I want you to meet."

"Samantha, remember the puppy can only be out for a few minutes for you to show everybody. We will need to put her into her crate in a little while."

Tiffany and Samantha did not know that Sandi and her girls were going to be joining them for the day, but it didn't take long before the three young girls were chatting away as if they had known each other their entire lives. At the very beginning, Jo seemed a little embarrassed by all the questions the others were asking, but soon she relaxed and was now giggling along with the other two, more animated than Susan had ever seen her before.

The new puppy had been taken outside to do her "business" and then tucked into a small wire cage and was now sleeping away on her own little pillow.

It was so good to see the girls having a good time together, and she could hear Joan and Sandi talking and laughing from the kitchen. She smiled to herself and thought *It is going to be a good day.* She headed back to the front room where Bill and Mary had just finished putting away coats when the phone rang.

Bill picked it up, "Oh, hi, Jill. Yes. We just arrived. Ted hasn't gotten here yet but should be here soon. Mom's new friends are here also. I'm sure she will tell you all about them when you talk to her. Sure, Hon, Happy Thanksgiving, to you, also. Yes, of course, I'll talk to you later." He handed the phone to Susan. "She wants to talk to you for a few minutes, Mom. I think she's home-sick."

Ted, Susan's younger son, soon arrived with his newest love interest, a pretty girl with green eyes and thick auburn hair that fell loosely in a shining mass around her face. Her name was Julie and with her came her 4-year-old son. The very busy youngster's name was Danny. He had his mother's eyes, freckles across an upturned nose, and he sported a brilliant crop of wild copper-colored ringlets framing his angelic face.

Susan noted that this was a major deviation from her youngest son's normal behavior. Ted, up until now, had never involved himself with any woman who had children, or any kind of baggage. He said the last thing he needed in his life were women who had complications in their lives. Most of the previous women he dated were the professional type, tall, slim and sophisticated, and usually blonde. He seldom brought any women home to meet the family.

Soon, everyone gathered around the table which was full to overflowing with all the wonderful foods of the season. As had always been their tradition, Susan, as head of the household, reached out and took the hand of her eldest son who in turn took Mary's hand. When everyone at the table had joined hands and bowed their heads, Susan prayed.

"Dear Heavenly Father, we thank You with all our hearts for this gathering of family and friends. We thank You for this bounty and ask that You bless it to the nourishment of our bodies. We thank You for those who are unable to be here and ask that You bless and protect them from harm and give them a good day. Also, we humbly ask that You watch over and bless those that are in need. We gratefully acknowledge that You are our Lord and Savior and ask Your continued blessing on this very special Thanksgiving Day. Amen."

All in all, the day turned out to be a great success. The girls ended the day as good friends, making big plans for the next time they would get together, and the adults, after an afternoon of eating, visiting, and then eating some more, were happy to go home and sit beside the fire or read a good book.

Later that evening, after Annie had been tucked into her bed for the night, Joletta came in and plopped herself down on the couch beside her mom. Snuggling up against her, she laid her head on Sandi's shoulder.

"Mom, do you ever pray?"

Sandi was somewhat taken by surprise by the seriousness in Joletta's voice. "Why do you ask honey? Is there something wrong?"

"No, Mom, I was just wondering. When Susan prayed today, I thought it was nice, and it just made me wonder."

"Well, I guess I do pray sometimes. But not exactly the way Susan prays. I don't really know. I guess I never thought about it much."

"I liked it, Mom. Did you know Susan goes to church every week? She says being with other believers and learning more about Him brings her closer to God.

"She told me that Jesus died for our sins and that we need to ask him into our hearts."

"My goodness, Joletta. It sounds like you are taking what Susan says very seriously. I'm sorry I can't be of much help. Our family never went to church as far as I can remember, and I just don't know if I believe what she says. Don't get me wrong. I don't mean that Susan would tell you a lie. I just don't know what to tell you about God or Jesus, or even if there is a God."

"Aren't you afraid that if you don't believe in God that you will go to Hell? I know I don't want to go to Hell!"

"Oh, Honey, you are certainly not going to go to Hell! In fact, you are not going anywhere for a very long time, except to bed!"

"I don't know Mom. I just know the way it makes me feel when Susan talks to me about God and that when I die, I do want to go to Heaven!"

Sandi sighed. She was tired and didn't quite know how to respond so she said to her daughter, "It's really getting late, and we need to get some sleep. You may not have school tomorrow, but I have a lot to do before going to work tomorrow night."

"Oh, all right, Mom. I will go to bed, but I am going to pray tonight. I am going to pray that Jesus will come into my heart and save me from my sins!"

"Darling, you couldn't possibly have enough sins to need to be forgiven! You haven't lived long enough! On top of that, you are already my angel. Now go to bed and stop worrying."

"I will Momma. I love you."

Sandi smiled, "I love you more! Goodnight Sweetheart."

An hour later Sandi started to turn off her light and noticed the Bible recently given to Joletta by Susan was lying on her pillow. Wondering why her daughter had put it there, she picked it up. There was a blue ribbon placed between the pages and as she opened the book to the highlighted page, several verses were circled and Sandi began to read.

John 10:9-11" I am the gate; whoever enters through me will be saved. They will come in and go out and find pasture. [10] The thief comes only to steal and kill and destroy; I have come that they may have life and have it to the full. I am the good shepherd. The good shepherd lays down his life for the sheep."

Sandi closed the book and sat quietly for a few moments before switching off the lamp on top of the night-stand. Pulling the light blanket up around her shoulders, she realized the time had come to talk with Susan. Unsure about any of this Bible stuff, she could not believe that Susan would purposely tell Jo things that were not true. Sandi had always sensed something different in their sweet older neighbor; perhaps she would have the answers Sandi needed. She had never really considered that the Bible could be anything more than just an old book full of old stories. Maybe she would ask Susan to tell her more. As she drifted off to sleep, she thought *She sure has Jo convinced!*

"Do you know what today is, little one?" Sandi smiled as she reached into the crib and picked up the baby. She lifted her in the air and whirled her around. "Today is little Annie's very first birthday, and Mommy has the day off!"

Annie watched her momma with a quizzical look but broke into a big grin after another spin around the room. "Sissy has to go to school today, but we are going to make you a pretty cake, and when Jo-Jo gets home, we will go to Grandma Susan's and blow out your candle and sing 'Happy Birthday to You'! Mommy and Jo-Jo got you a present, but we have to wait. Then we will go to Grandma Susan's!"

Sandi was happy that one of her co-workers agreed to trade shifts for the week. It worked out well for both girls. Everyone at work liked being allowed to make temporary changes to their schedules if both workers agreed.

Sandi and Annie happily spent the entire morning playing and cooking. They made a teddy bear cake in a special pan Sandi found at the Goodwill store. It would make an adorable birthday cake for the baby. Even though Sandi had never baked fancy cakes before, she didn't think Annie would care. It was fun doing the project while Annie watched from the highchair.

"There! I think we're all done!" She held the chocolate-covered bear with a pink icing bow up for Annie's inspection. The baby squealed with delight and clapped her hands on her tray in approval. . . at least Sandi decided she would accept that as her approval. "Well, now we had better get some lunch and put you down for your nap. It won't be long, and Joletta will be home to help Annie have a birthday party!"

It didn't seem possible that a year had passed since Annie's arrival. Many things were different now. The past year held some painful memories. However, Sandi felt that for once, her life was going in the right direction.

It had been a long time since Sandi had dared to feel anything, but as she tucked little Annie into her crib for a nap, she smiled and realized that she actually felt happy. She laughed aloud. "Happy Birthday, my little Sweetheart."

Christmas came, although it was less hectic than Thanksgiving. Bill's family had gone out west to spend the holiday with Mary's family, and Ted and Julie were in Vermont on a ski trip. Sandi and the girls invited Susan over on Christmas Eve to share in their more modest Christmas.

They did a wonderful job of making their apartment look festive. They had obviously gone to a lot of trouble to make it lovely. They had trays of cookies sitting around the room, and Christmas music played on an old cassette player.

As they were opening packages, baby Annie gave them her own special gift. Letting go of the couch, she proceeded to take several toddling steps across the room to her big sister. Everyone laughed and clapped as she showed off her very first steps without assistance! Annie knew she was the star of the show and was passed from Joletta to Sandi and then to Susan and given kisses and bear hugs to celebrate the occasion as she squealed with delight.

After opening their gifts, they sat down to eat the pot roast that Sandi had prepared in the slow cooker, while she worked the night before. Susan brought some homemade hot rolls, and Joletta made a tossed green salad.

As the food was passed and everyone was preparing to begin, Joletta said "Mom, I want to pray before we start."

"Ok, Dear, that will be fine."

Joletta reached out and took little Annie's chubby little fingers and then her mothers. Susan repeated the action on the other side connecting the four of them as Joletta prayed.

"Dear God, I am not very good at this yet, but I am going to get better. Thank you for Christmas and Baby Jesus and my family. Thank you for the sweater from Mom and the watch that Susan gave me and thanks for my family. Amen. Oh, and I'm sorry! Thank you for the food. Amen!"

Sandi looked at her daughter with warmth rising in her cheeks. "That was very sweet, Jo, thank you."

Joletta and Susan exchanged glances and smiled at each other. "Mom, we were wondering—that is Grandma Susan and I, if we could all go to church tonight?" she paused and waited.

A few months before, Sandi would have given her a simple no for an answer, but now everything was different. "Joletta, I think that would be just perfect. I think we *should* all go to church tonight. It is Christmas after all."

Chapter 8
CAR TROUBLE

With the holidays over, the winter of 2001 set in with a vengeance. No sooner would they dig out from one storm than the next would hit.

If it had not been for Mr. Jennings, a kind man who had been friends with Susan for many years, Sandi's car would have stayed buried until mid-June. He called it his hobby, getting out in the early-morning hours and using his big snow blower to clear drives in the neighborhood. Sandi did not even know who he was the first time she found him digging out her driveway, and he totally refused to let her give him money. She was very grateful because she had little to give. He had already cleared the path for them a half-dozen times, and it did not appear that the storms were going to let up any time soon.

It was not even mid-February, and it felt like winter had been in full force for months on end instead of only weeks. Each time they bundled up to go out the door, it seemed like Spring would never arrive!

On Friday, Sandi went in for her appointment with Mr. Benning, leaving the girls with Susan. It was very cold and the weather was worsening. After only a short visit, he suggested she needed to head home. She left the office and walked the half block in the biting wind to her icy vehicle. Putting the key in the ignition, she turned it with no results. The car refused to start no matter how many times she took the key out and repeated the exercise.

Her teeth were chattering and her hands in her thin gloves were numb. Almost in tears, she started to step out of the car and begin the long cold walk back to the office in hopes of finding someone who would help. With her hand on the door handle, Jim Benning himself knocked on the frozen window.

"Need a jump?" he asked.

"I don't know what's wrong with it. It started ok this morning."

"Let me see if we can get it going for you." Soon it became evident that, at least for now, the old car was going nowhere.

Sandi hesitantly accepted his offer for a ride home. He insisted it would be no trouble since his day was officially over. It was still early, but because of the weather, his last appointment had been canceled. "The weather most likely," he said. "I was really surprised when you made it in."

After getting into his black and silver pickup, Jim reached behind the seat and pulled out a plaid stadium blanket. "Here, wrap this around you, you are half frozen!" Sandi gratefully accepted the blanket and wrapped it tightly around her shoulders. By now, she was shaking uncontrollably, and she could not blink back the tears.

He spoke gently. "The truck doesn't take long to warm up. Maybe we should stop and get you a cup of something hot to drink before I take you on home."

"Oh, no. Please." She said through her chattering teeth. "You have done more than enough already, and my family will be worried if I don't get home soon."

"Well, if you are sure you're all right."

Sandi nodded, and for the next several minutes, they were both quiet. Their hands had touched when she took the blanket, and though she was indeed very cold, warmth had sparked within her, and for only a moment their eyes locked. The relationship between the two had been slowly changing over the past months. Because of his obvious good intentions, Sandi's initial resentment had slowly disappeared. Today was different though. She felt confused and a little shaken.

He interrupted her thoughts. "How would it be if I pick you up tomorrow around 11:00? We can go get you a new battery then. That should get you back on the road."

"Oh, I can't thank you enough, but I'm sure I can get it taken care of without you wasting your Saturday on me!"

"Tell you what," he smiled. "You let me help out, and you can repay me by going into the city with me afterward! Tomorrow, they are predicting sunshine and much more pleasant weather, if you can believe that." Glancing at her, he laughed, "I know what you are thinking. You think I'm crazy, to even consider spending the day outside, aren't you?" Not giving her a chance to answer, he continued.

"The girls can come along, and we'll make a day of it. Winter Carnival is taking place over at Greenbrier Park this weekend. It would be a great afternoon! Please say you'll go.

There are plenty of warming stations, and if it is too cold, we will leave. I promise."

Jim knew he was crossing a line here. He understood the rules concerning caseworker-client relationships, but for weeks Sandi and her two little girls had been constantly on his mind. At first, he tried to stay professional, brushing his feelings aside, but as time went on, they were becoming harder and harder to ignore.

Joletta was looking out of the window when the black pickup drove up in front of Susan's house. Her mom opened the door and got out.

"Look, Annie, Momma's with Mr. B." "Mommy, Mommy," chimed the baby, clapping her hands.

Sandi walked toward the house, turning to wave good-bye to Jim, a grateful smile on her face. As she stepped through the door, Joletta immediately started to question her mother.

"Mom, what were you doing with Mr. B.? Where is our car? Where have you been? We were worried about you."

"Joletta," Susan spoke softly but firmly from the overstuffed chair in the corner of the room. "You might

58

try to give your mother a chance to take off her coat and warm up a bit before she starts answering so many questions."

"Oh, I'm sorry, Mom. I'm glad you're home."

Sandi smiled and kissed her elder daughter on the cheek as she scooped little Annie into her arms and hugged her close, breathing in the sweet fragrance of her soft baby skin. Later in the evening, after the baby was in her bed, Joletta sat curled up on the couch next to Sandi.

"Mom, I just think it's so weird that you're going out on a date with our social worker!"

"Joletta, I already told you this is not a date. He's just trying to be nice to us." Strangely, she did feel this was different. Perhaps it was more, but she wasn't ready to go there yet. There were just too many complications.

Chapter 9
NIGHTMARE

Later that night, Joletta had a dream about her daddy. He was tall and dark like her, but she couldn't quite see his face. She knew she needed to see his face, but as she moved closer to him, he started yelling at her. "What do mean, I'm your father? I don't have a daughter!" Mist rolled around him, and when he turned, he was wearing Sam's angry face!

"No!" she cried. "You aren't my daddy! Where's my daddy?"

He jeered at her, "Joletta doesn't have a daddy! Joletta's daddy is a jerk!"

She could see her mother and Annie. They were with Mr. B. They were holding hands and laughing. First, they stood beside her but did not invite her to hold hands with them and the, they all started walking away from her, leaving her standing alone.

"Wait! Where are you going?" Now they were not walking. They were running; faster and faster they went until they were out of sight. She could hear them laughing as they disappeared into the mists. "Momma, come back! Please! Come back!"

"Joletta, Honey, what is it? Are you ill?"

Joletta, who was sitting up in her bed, slowly became aware of her surroundings and her mother beside her. "Oh, Mommy," she said as Sandi gathered her shaking daughter into her arms.

"Was it another bad dream, darling?" Sandi soothed her and wiped away a tear that slipped from Joletta's eye. "You're right here with me. Everything is all right."

"Yeah, Mom, it was only a dream though. I'm OK now, I really am." Joletta's voice was quiet. "You can go back to bed. It was nothing. It's all right now."

"Are you sure?" Sandi's voice was full of concern. Recently Joletta had had dreams, more frequently than

Sandi felt was normal. She knew that kids have active imaginations, but it just didn't feel right.

Jo refused to talk to her about what her dreams were about, and it was obviously very upsetting to her. Most times she claimed she was fine and seemed to be ok the next day, but it worried Sandi, nonetheless. "You know I'm right in the other room if you need me."

"Yes, Mom. I do know. Thanks, I love you."

"I love you more." Sandi squeezed her daughter's hand before she left the room. It took Sandi some time before she could fall asleep. For weeks, she had been worried about Joletta. Perhaps she would talk to Jim the next day and see if he might have any suggestions.

The storm was gone the next morning, and as Jim had predicted, it was sunny. There was no wind; it was still cold, but it was not the biting hard cold of the day before. Sandi stepped into the girls' room, watching them as they slept. They were so beautiful and growing so quickly. *How will I ever protect them?* Sandi thought as the baby opened her blue eyes and reached her chubby arms into the air expecting her Mommy to pick her up. "It's time to get up, Sweetheart," Sandi said as she touched Joletta's arm. Joletta seemed no worse for the wear after last night's disturbance.

None of them had ever been to Winterfest before. As morning passed, Jo kept her mom busy asking questions and Sandi felt a little bit like a teenager going on her first date, even though this certainly was not a "real date!" "Do you think this sweater looks OK Honey? What do you think about my hair?"

Only little Annie was calm, watching her momma and big sister get ready to go bye-bye! They already had her bundled in her fat pink snowsuit when Mr. B. came to the door.

"Hello, ladies!" Jim arrived wearing a bright red hat and scarf that he later told Sandi his mother had made. "Is everyone ready?" Once the new battery was installed in

61

the car, they were ready to start their Winterfest adventure.

"We'll pick it up on the way home this evening," Jim said.

As they entered the gate, a giant snowman and two full-sized unicorns carved out of ice greeted them. The air smelled of hot chocolate and cinnamon bread. Everything was made of ice or snow. Snow bears, snow bunnies, snowmen, and snow monsters were strategically placed throughout the display area, while competitors were busy carving ice into fantastic shapes.

Joletta and Jim, with baby Annie squealing between his legs, slid down a slide made entirely of packed snow. People were participating in winter games and contests of all kinds, and there were souvenir stands selling all manner of things.

Before the day was over Jim won Annie a soft white bear almost as big as she was, and he bought Joletta a snow globe with a tiny glass unicorn inside.

After everyone was buckled into the car, Jim handed Sandi a small package. "I thought you might like this. It is a hand-cut Austrian crystal. If you hang it in the sun, it makes rainbows. It will remind you to be happy."

"Oh, Jim, you didn't have to do that---"He put his fingers to her lips. "Hush."

"That is so sweet. Thank-you."

Joletta could not remember the last time her mom had seemed so relaxed. She was always so busy with work and taking care of her and Annie. It felt good to see her having a good time.

Over the past several months their lives had gotten so much better. Although she hadn't minded taking care of Annie, she was glad they were now staying with Susan. Best of all, mom was better. Even though she was sometimes tired or grumpy, she never drank anymore. Jo wasn't sure why but was just glad she had quit.

The baby, who was quickly adding to her vocabulary, had spent the day pointing and saying her favorite word in her sweet baby voice. "Piddy!" she would say, and with encouragement from the others, she would giggle then point at something else, and once again say "Piddy!" – her own special version of the word pretty!

By mid-afternoon Annie went to sleep in her stroller, and since the temperature was also dropping, they decided it was time to "call it a day." Jim took them to their car and insisted on following them all the way home, just to make sure that it did not quit on them again. He carried a very sleepy Annie to the door for Sandi. He took her free hand in his. "Sandi, thank you so much for today." With that, he kissed the baby on the top of her head, reached out, gave Joletta a friendly pat on the cheek, and then turned to leave.

"We had a good time too, Jim... "

He turned once again to face her. Sandi could tell that he wanted to kiss her. However, instead he said, "I'll talk to you tomorrow." Then he turned and quietly shut the door behind him.

Chapter 10
LATE WINTER

After the winter festival Jim and Sandi continued seeing each other, but only on a friendly basis.

Both were aware of the problems their relationship could have on their lives. His job could be at risk.

Sandi was still unsure of how she felt about their relationship. She was undeniably attracted to him but continued to hold him at arm's length. When she was with him, he was so gentle and sensitive to her feelings, but when they were apart, she would worry.

This is all wrong, she thought. *He can't really want me. He's a college graduate. I barely finished high school! He would never stay. He would just end up walking out on me and the girls! Men always walk out on me! I just can't do that to my girls again!*

She planned to tell him that he should stop calling, but every time she started, something inside of her would keep her from actually saying anything to him.

Sandi continued to see Lynn. Even though she was feeling much more confident about her life in general, this was a new and unexpected concern.

Lynn had helped her understand that even if she experienced a setback, it did not mean she was a failure. She must acknowledge her mistake and vow to try again. In the last few months she had not touched alcohol of any kind, nor had she accepted any invitations to go out with her former friends. She was proud of that fact but was very afraid of backsliding. Then there was Joletta, who continued to have nightmares.

Jim did talk with Jo some about what might be troubling her, but he had felt that she would be better off talking with someone whose specialty was in the field of Adolescent Behavior. Sandi at first resisted the idea, but after seeing how upsetting the dreams continued to be to Joletta, she made an appointment with a child psychologist Jim had suggested. Her name was Dr. Kathleen Heller and she had been working directly with youth for over a decade. Jo was scheduled for her first appointment with Dr. Heller the following Monday after school.

The doctor came into the waiting area and introduced herself to Sandi and Joletta.

Asking Sandi to remain in the waiting room, she invited Joletta into her office, indicating that she would speak with Sandi a little later.

"I am so glad to meet you, Jo! Is it all right if I call you Jo? Or do you prefer Joletta?" Joletta shrugged, and Dr. Heller continued. "My name is Kathleen Heller. Most of the time, my young friends call me Dr. Kathy. Would you like to have a seat?"

The girl shyly sat down on the chair that Dr. Heller offered.

"I've spoken with your mom on the phone. She tells me you've been having some nightmares. Would you feel ok talking a little while with me? Perhaps you could tell me what your dreams are like and what they might mean to you."

"I guess I could," said Joletta, "But really, they're no big deal."

"Well I'm glad to hear that, but perhaps we could explore them some. You might be surprised. Sometimes we can find out things about ourselves that we never knew by exploring our dreams."

"OK, I guess that would be all right, but I don't see what good it will do. I keep telling Mom that I'm all right." She rolled her eyes toward the ceiling. "But she doesn't always listen to me! Well--, you know what I mean."

Dr. Heller grinned at Jo. "Well, Jo, I am a mother myself, and I think I do know what you mean. My own daughter has, on occasion, told me pretty much the same."

"Maybe we can just spend a little time getting acquainted. What school do you go to? I understand you're almost finished with the 8th grade? I have a daughter in 7th grade. She goes to Fallen Timbers Middle School over in New Junction." As the hour-long appointment ended, it was apparent that Joletta and Dr. Kathy were getting along quite well.

Dr. Heller came highly recommended with Doctorates in Child Psychology and Adolescent Behavior. Besides seeing private clients, she also worked with children referred through Children's Services. Having a wonderful rapport with the young people she had a special empathy for girls Joletta's age, having experienced trauma and abuse in her own life.

Jim called Sandi Thursday afternoon before she left for work. "Sandi, could we go out to supper and a movie tomorrow night? You told me the girls were staying the weekend with Susan, and I need to talk to you about something."

"I'll have to be at work at 11:30, but if we are back in time for me to get ready, I guess it would be OK."

Jim drove up at 6:30 sharp, and Sandi grabbed her coat and met him at the door. "Hi, Shivers!" He had been calling her that ever since the afternoon her car wouldn't start, and she had gotten so cold she couldn't stop shivering. "I've got something special planned for tonight. Are you interested?"

Sandi smiled and nodded as he kissed her on the cheek. His hand slid around her waist, and she could feel the warmth of his breath on her neck. She gently, but firmly pushed him away. It was getting harder and harder to resist his advances.

Why does this have to be so hard? She thought. *If I let him have his way, he'll just be gone, and I don't think I could stand it.*

"Sandi," he said, "What is it you're so afraid of? You know I would never hurt you."

"You just don't understand, Jim. I have to be sure the next time. I have hurt my girls too many times. I don't ever want to hurt them again." Suddenly, Sandi was in tears.

Sometimes it felt like she cried more than anyone else she had ever known before. *No one understands! How can they? I don't even understand myself.*

Jim reached out, and this time, he pulled her close to him and would not let her go as she made a weak attempt to push him away. "Sandi, Darling, you are killing me! You are going to have to trust someone, sometime. I have come to care so much for you and the girls, and you barely let me touch you."

"But Jim, don't you see how impossible it all is? You are my social worker! Who ever heard of a social worker going out with their client before? It would never work, and you know it! You would lose your job, and pretty soon you would lose interest and leave me."

"I know of no such thing, Sandi. All I know is that I love you, and I want to be with you always!"

"No, Jim, you aren't listening. You aren't thinking. No one ever stays! You'll leave me just like all the other times." She pushed hard against his chest. "Jim, don't you see? First my daddy left, then Joletta's dad, and then Sam. Men never stay!"

Holding her shoulders firmly, he shook his head and said, "You have me all wrong, little girl. This is one guy that you're going to have a hard time getting rid of." He pulled her to him, more roughly this time and held her tightly against his wool jacket.

"Now say it!" he demanded. "I want to hear you say it. Tell me that you love me too! I can feel that you do, no

67

matter how hard you push me away!" Winding his fingers into her hair, he tilted her head back and then his lips were pressing hers. As he kissed her, the whole world began to spin. "Now! Are you going to say it, Sandi? Say you love me!"

Sandi could hardly breathe, partially because he was holding her so closely, but mostly because the warmth of his body and the smell of his cologne overwhelmed her. "I do, Jim. I do. I've tried so hard not to, but I do."

Once again, Jim pulled her to him, and this time she did not resist.

Later, as they parked outside of Sandi's and he held her in his arms, he quietly said "Sandi, have you ever heard of the J.R. Benning Company?"

"Well, I do remember there is a building downtown that has J.R. Benning across the front. Is that what you are talking about?" She paused and looked up into his face. "You don't mean that you have anything to do with that, do you?"

"J.R. is my dad. The business has been in the family for the past three generations."

Sandi could not speak. The implications of what he had just revealed were more than she could handle. Her face flushed, and she felt slightly sick.

"It's OK, Honey. We don't bite. I just thought you needed to know since I plan to keep you around for a long while." He put his finger under her chin and kissed her gently. Sandi sat in stunned silence, not knowing what to say. "Jim, I have to go in. It's almost 11:30. I have to work tomorrow.

Chapter 11

A VISIT WITH DR. KATHY

"Come right on in Joletta," Dr. Heller said with a friendly smile. "How have you been doing?"

"OK, I guess." The girl seemed somewhat agitated. Dr. Kathy stood and stepped over to the window. Sometimes it was easier for patients to talk when you were not sitting directly across from them.

This was Jo's third visit to see the psychologist, and although she liked Dr. Kathy, she still thought it was "kind of creepy" talking to a complete stranger about herself. Mom had always said family problems are no one else's business! Now it seemed like she was saying just the opposite!

"What have you been up to this week, Jo? Have you thought any more about what we were discussing last week? Any more dreams?" The doctor continued to look out the window. "You know, it is not long now before Spring. I'm really looking forward to a change. It's been quite a winter." She said nothing for a couple of minutes, "Oh, I'm sorry. What did I ask? Oh yes, did you get a chance to give some thought to what we had talked about the last time you were here?"

"Well," started Joletta. "My new friend down the street invited me to come over and spend the night with her Saturday, but I couldn't. I had to stay with Mrs. Taylor. That's our neighbor. We stay with her while Mom works. Anyway, I couldn't go because Mom had to work all weekend, and I needed to stay at Susan's house and help out with Annie."

"How did you feel about that? Were you very disappointed you didn't get to spend the night with your friend?" Dr. Kathy paused and watched the girl's face as she waited for a response.

"Not too much. My baby sister Annie sometimes gets upset when I'm not with her even though Susan is really great and takes good care of her. I like taking care of Annie. She depends on me a lot. Susan, that's Mrs. Taylor's first name, said I should have told Tina to come over and stay with us, but Mom says that would have been asking too much. She says we have already asked too much of Susan. It's ok. Mom said, maybe next time."

"Do you and Tina see much of each other?"

"She and I walk home from school together when the weather is not too bad. Recently, her dad has been driving us or Mom takes us when she can. Sometimes we get together for a while before supper, and if Mom isn't working, I can go over to her house. She came over to my house last week and ate supper with us. Mom made some hot dogs while Tina and I made cookies afterwards."

"That sounds like a lot of fun."

"Yeah, Tina is fun to be with. She is really funny sometimes. She says when she grows up, she is going to be a comedienne."

"That sounds like quite a goal. What about you, do you have any dreams? Have you ever thought of what you might like to do when you are grown up?"

"Not really." Joletta was thoughtful for a minute. "Well, I think that maybe I might like to be a teacher or something. I want to help other people, especially little kids who have a lot of trouble."

"Ok, I think that sounds like a good plan to me," Dr. Kathy observed. "Have you had any more of those bad dreams recently?"

"Well, yeah." Joletta became restless, her fingers making patterns on the tabletop, and she grew quiet.

"Do you feel like talking about it?"

Jo shrugged and said nothing for several seconds, but then she began her story.

"I dreamed about my dad again the other night. Well, I knew it was my dad. I never saw his face. He had a little girl with him, and he was swinging her."

70

Another pause--- "She started crying because she was scared to go so high, but then she turned and looked back, and he wasn't there anymore. After a minute she fell off the swing. That's when I woke up!"

"What do you think the dream meant? Any ideas?"

"I don't know, Dr. Kathy, but it was really scary. I always feel so alone afterward."

"Are you afraid of losing someone in your family? Or that you will be left alone? Do you think the child with him could have been you?"

"Maybe, I never really thought about it and I've never, even been with my Daddy, so I don't know how it could have been me."

"Would you like to see your dad sometime?"

"I think I would. I would just like to know what he looks like, and I'd like to ask him why he didn't want me. It feels sad not to have a daddy. Momma and Annie don't have daddy's either. Well, there's Sam. He's Annie's daddy, but he took off last year and no one knows where he is. I'm really kind of glad anyway; he was not very nice to Mom. He drank all the time and cussed and yelled whenever I didn't do something, he wanted me to do. One time, he even hit Mom, right in the face, but he told her he was sorry the next morning after he had sobered up."

"That was definitely not a good thing. I can see why you feel the way you do. Have you ever thought the reasons your Dad isn't with you might not have anything to do with him not wanting you? Perhaps there were other reasons."

"Well, what Mom says is that they were really young, and he wasn't ready to handle the responsibility of a baby. But I don't know. If I had a baby, I would never ever leave it." Joletta's voice was full of emotion, and her eyes misted.

Her counselor reached over and laid her hand on Joletta's shoulder. "Well, Sweetie, maybe if you try to realize that people make many mistakes in life and often

71

never realize just how their decisions affect others. . . in your case, you've spent a long time wondering about your father. I don't know if I have any answers for you, but I do know it is a good thing that you've been able to acknowledge the fact that you miss having a father in your life."

"Would you like to go down to the cafeteria and have a soda? It's almost 5:00 and I told your mom that we would meet her out front. It's a lovely day out, don't you think?"

Sandi drove up in front of the clinic a few minutes before the hour and watched as her daughter walked down the path with Dr. Heller. She was laughing and talking.

Perhaps these appointments were going to help her in some way. Sandi certainly hoped so. It hurt her that Joletta didn't seem able to open up to her about her dreams, but the important thing was having someone she felt she could trust, to talk to, and Jim seemed sure Katherine Heller could be that person.

"Hi, Mom. What's up?" Joletta waved a good-bye to Dr. Heller and gave her mom a tight hug before she climbed in the seat beside her. "Where's Annie?"

"Susan called and asked if I could bring her over so Bill and Mary could see how much she's growing. They're all going out to get a pizza after a while, and she asked if we wanted to go?"

"Oh Mom, that sounds like a great idea!" Joletta was all smiles as she and her mother drove through the old part of town on the way to meet their friends.

Chapter 12
A BREATH OF SPRING

It was hard to believe it had been almost six months since Joletta and Annie had been staying with Susan while their mother worked.

The winter had been long and bitter, but signs of spring were now everywhere.

Finally, the snow had all but disappeared. Crocus, tulips, and yellow daffodils were in bloom, and the creeping phlox would soon follow. Soft green moss and tendrils of new spring grass now were beginning to cover the brown winter ground. The air had now taken on a gentle warm fragrance as Spring breezes replaced the long biting winter chill.

Although the girls stayed with her most days now, Susan still adamantly refused to accept any money or payment of any sort. The best that Sandi could get by with was making cookies or special little treats for her, which she did as often as possible. One week it might be homemade fudge or chocolate-chip cookies, another time it might be fresh, warm, whole-wheat bread.

Sandi had learned to cook when she was quite young, and she still enjoyed making things from scratch when she had the time. It wasn't very often that she had time, but she willingly put in extra effort when cooking for their wonderful neighbor, for Susan was special. It sometimes felt like she was more of a mother to Sandi than her own mom had ever been to her. Joletta and the baby loved Susan like the grandmother they had never had.

Bill and Mary were sitting on the beautiful oak porch swing that had been a gift from Ted several years ago. At one time he enjoyed woodworking, and he had made the swing for Susan as a birthday gift. He now lived in the city and his woodworking tools were in storage.

Susan was sitting with a wiggling Annie on the worn wicker rocker. Samantha and Tiffany, who had been playing a game of pitch and catch in front of the house, ran to meet Joletta and her mom.

"Hi girls, how are you?" Sandi came around the side of the Chevy and patted Sammy's head.

"Hey, Joletta! We get to go have pizza! Want to come?"

"Yeah! Mom said we get to! What are you guys doing here in the middle of the week?"

"I don't know exactly, something about dropping off some things that Granny needed." All three girls started giggling. Tiffany knew very well that she wasn't supposed to call Susan Granny, but did it anyway just to get a reaction from the grown-ups.

"One of these days you are going to get swatted on the backside for that, young lady!" Her Grandmother smiled as the three of them headed for the backyard.

"Don't go far girls," Mary smiled. "We'll have to be leaving in a short time, or we won't get back to Avondale before bedtime."

As the girls headed around the side of the house, Bill said, "You know, Mom. It won't be long before your birthday."

"As if I wouldn't know! People won't let me forget, for even a moment, how old I'm getting!"

"What would you like to do to celebrate? Would you like to go over to Belleview and eat at Lovella Lounge?" Bill waited for his mother's response. Lovella's was where his father had taken her when they were first married, and as small children, he remembered going there on special occasions. It had sort of become a family tradition to celebrate his mother's birthday at Lovella's.

"Thanks, Bill. You know how I've always loved going there, but this year I think, if it's OK with you young people, I would like to do something different."

"And what would that be, Mother?"

74

"I think a picnic would be heavenly. Do you know how long it's been since we've gone out on a real picnic?"

"Oh, I think a picnic would be lovely." Mary spoke with enthusiasm. "Don't you think a picnic is a wonderful idea, Sandi?"

Bill gave his wife one of those looks but knew he had already lost the battle. It was bad enough when his mother got one of her hare-brained ideas, but when Mary got in on it, there was little hope left. It would just be so much simpler if she would stick with what they had done in the past. He saw no reason to change things that already worked. All you would need to worry about would be making reservations. The waiters were always great and the steaks spectacular.

Bill just could not see a reason to change. However, here they were with Mary now sticking her nose into it!"

Sandi wasn't sure what to say. "I think a picnic would be great, but you certainly don't have to include us. This is your family occasion."

"Oh, don't be silly! Of course, you'll go!" Susan's voice did not invite argument. "I wouldn't have it any other way! The children will have a grand time! Anyway, you have become part of this family. Of course, you'll have to be there. Surely you know how I feel about you and the girls. Just consider yourselves "adopted." If anyone asks, just tell them you are one of us."

Bill and Sandi were speechless!

Mary laughed and said, "Well, I think we had better round up those wild little girls and go get that pizza! It's getting late." Susan put her arm around Sandi's waist as they walked to the cars.

"Can Joletta ride with us, Mom?" suggested Tiffany.

"Sure, honey, I'll ride with Aunt Sandi and Grandma."

"Aunt Sandi?" The three girls started giggling and climbed into the car with Bill. Tiffany said to Joletta, "Cool! That makes you and Annie our cousins!"

Sandi had taken a moment to regain her composure after Susan's comment. No one else could possibly know how much it meant to her when Susan said she was part of her family, even if she did not really mean it. She knew Susan had only said it to make her feel better, but it was nice to hear her say it.

They had all been so kind to her and the girls. Someday she hoped she could do something special for them. It seemed impossible that last year at this time, she had been alone, without anyone to count on. Back then she thought it would be easier to just give it all up and die--- if it had not been for her girls--- her entire life had changed in the past year, and it just kept changing. She wondered what would come next!

"What was Mom talking about when she called Sandi our Aunt, Dad?"

"Ask your Grandmother, Tiffany. She seems to have answers to everything!"

They did not get back to Susan's until almost 9:00. It was later than usual for a school night, but they were all enjoying the evening so much, time had just slipped away.

Sandi was tucking little Annie to bed when Joletta came out of the bathroom with her toothbrush still in her hand. "Wasn't it fun tonight, Mom? Tiffany and Sammy are so sweet, and their parents are really nice, too."

"It sure was, Sweetheart." Sandi, still remembering Susan's comment, went on to say "They are very nice indeed."

Chapter 13
THE FACTS OF LIFE

The next day Sandi did not have to work so after Joletta left for school, she and the baby walked over to Susan's house. She had made some oatmeal muffins and wanted to take them over and share them while they had a cup of hot coffee. It had been almost two weeks since she and Jim had admitted their love for one another, and he had dropped the bomb about his heritage. She had not breathed a word of it to anyone, but she just had to talk to someone.

At first Sandi considered talking with Lynn but ruled that out, fearing what she would think. Of course, Lynn would only listen. She would not come out and say anything. Even if she did not think it was right, she would leave it to Sandi to think it through. Still, this was just too personal. Sandi wanted someone she felt close to, that would not be judgmental or condescending. Yes, she decided, Susan would be the better choice. Sandi knew she would listen carefully and respect whatever decisions she and Jim might make, whether she agreed with them or not.

"Sandi!" Susan hugged the young woman. "What a nice surprise. I didn't think I would get to see you today."

"Well," stuttered Sandi, "I wonder if I could talk to you about something."

"Of course, you can, my dear girl. My goodness, something sure does smell good. What is it that you have there?"

Two hours later, Sandi and Annie were preparing to leave. Susan gave the baby a final pat on top of her head. "Bye-bye, little one."

"Now remember Sandi, you be sure to tell that young man that I expect him at my birthday celebration. I think it's about time he met all of us. And don't you worry about anything. You are a wonderful young woman. I have no doubt you will fit in just fine. As for Joletta. . .she will be OK. From everything you have told me about Jim, he sounds like the kind of person Joletta and Annie need to have around."

"Thank you so much, Susan." Sandi reached out to the older woman and hugged her tightly. "I don't know what we would ever do without you. I only wish you had been in our lives a long time ago."

"Everything happens for a reason, Dear. Sometimes we just don't know what those reasons are at the time. You know Sandi, I have been praying for some time that the right person would come along and make you happy. Now, it looks like my prayers are going to be answered."

"Susan, you don't really believe that, do you?"

"My darling young woman, any time the Lord wants to answer my prayers, I certainly have no objections. One of these days we'll talk more about that, but I know you have to go now. Just give me a big hug, and I'll let you get on with your day, Dear."

Jim came by the house when he got off work at 5:00.

"Hey there, little Peaches!" He picked up Annie and kissed the top of her golden head. "Where's Joletta?"

"She and Tina walked down to the store. I think Tina's dad gave them a couple of dollars for cleaning out the flower beds last week, and it was burning a hole in their pockets."

"Good." He laughed, pulling Sandi to him, kissing her hard on the lips. "That will give us a few minutes to do this. Annie won't tell on us, will she?"

"Annie, now you remember. This is a big secret! Don't you dare tell on your Momma and Jim-boy here!"

"Oh, Jim! You are so silly!" Sandi's face pressed into the front of his shirt. She could still smell the aftershave that he had used this morning before leaving for work.

Every fiber of her body tingled, and she felt like she might faint dead away!

"Got anything to drink?" he asked as he scooped Annie into his arms. "Come on, Cutie-Patootie. Let's go out back and swing. I have something to tell your Momma." He laughed as he swung the little girl around in a circle on the way outside. "Meet you out back, Shivers!" he called over his shoulder, and he carried a giggling Annie out the back door.

Sandi watched Jim through the kitchen window as he deposited the baby into the little blue plastic swing he had given on her birthday. She squealed with delight as he started swinging her and tickling the bottoms of her bare feet. Every time the swing came toward him, he would grab at her tiny toes and tickle them. A long-ago memory of another little girl and another swing came to Sandi's mind. "Oh Daddy," she thought, "why did you leave?"

He leaned around and kissed the back of her neck as Sandi handed him the glass of iced tea.

"What did you want to tell me, Jim?" Sandi asked as she took a sip of her own cool drink.

"Well, you remember me telling you that my major in college was not in the field of social work, but that I had originally planned on a career teaching special education?"

"Yes, I remember."

"Anyway, I've made a decision. I have decided that it is time for a change. I've already talked with Dean Matthews out at Crowder College, and he says there are only a couple of refresher courses that I will have to take in order to make it happen. If I decide to go forward with it, I will start classes later this summer. It will take a few months before my credentials are in order. After that, we will just have to wait and see. I already did a year of student teaching at Good Samaritan before I started working with the agency. I'm still not sure if I want to work in the school system or what."

"But Jim. . . what about your job at Family Services?"

"Sandi, you know I will have to quit that job. I couldn't continue working there anyway, once Mr. Herman finds out that I plan to marry you. There are strict rules against client/ worker relationships, and I believe we have broken all of them!"

Sandi gasped, and her mouth fell open. "Jim! What are you talking about? We can't get married! My life has been a mess for so long." She paused, her heart pounding. "I can't ask you to marry me!"

"Exactly where did you think we were going with this relationship, darling? Also, I don't recall you asking me anything! –and when are you going to stop saying, "I can't?" Sandi, I have known for a long time that I would change fields one of these days. Of course, I didn't know I was going to fall in love first. Guess it has just served to get me thinking about what's really important!"

She was still in his arms when the two young girls came out the back door.

"Mom, are you out here? Mom!"

Sandi and Jim jumped and backed away from each other as the girls stood looking at them with wide eyes.

Jim was the first to speak. "Joletta, your mom and I have something we want to tell you."

"Joletta, wait!" Her mother called as the girl ran into the house.

"What's the matter with her?" Joletta's friend asked, looking totally confused. "Is there something wrong?"

"It'll be alright, Tina. Joletta and her mom are just going to have to have a few minutes to themselves. Maybe you should go on home for the time being. I'm sure Jo will call you after a while."

"Are you sure she's OK?"

"I'm sure she is going to be just fine, Sweetie." Jim assured the girl as he patted her on the shoulder and sent her on her way.

"Mom!" Joletta sobbed, "How could you? Everything has been going so good! You were kissing him!"

Sandi was not at all sure what to say to Joletta. "I didn't realize you would be so upset, Sweetheart. I thought you liked Jim."

"I guess I do Mom, but we're doing just fine on our own. I suppose you think you're in love with him." There was anger in the girl's voice. "You're just going to mess everything up!"

"Joletta, be reasonable. Jim and I have come to realize that we do love each other, but we aren't going to do anything that will mess things up! Joletta, Jim cares for you and Annie also, very much, and he wants all of us to be happy."

Joletta did not answer but sat on the edge of the bed, refusing to look at her mother.

"Can I come in?" Jim spoke from behind the partially opened door.

"Is it OK, Joletta?" Jo shrugged her shoulders and gave her mom a resigned look.

"It's OK, Jim. Where's Annie?"

"I thought maybe it would be better if she visited with Susan for a little while. I told her we would be over to get her soon." "What's the problem with this young lady here?" He reached over and gently poked Joletta on the arm.

She sniffled and pulled slightly away, still unwilling to let go of her anger.

"Come on, Joletta. It was only a kiss. Not the end of the world! You know, kisses aren't meant to make other people unhappy."

"Yeah, right!" Joletta rolled her eyes, but a slight smile touched her lips. She could envision the first time her mother found out she had kissed a boy.

Her mom didn't know it, but she had kissed Tina's brother, Jacob just a few weeks ago. He was 15, and his friend Tommy dared her to do it. He had walked right up to her and said, "I am going to kiss you," and he did! Actually, she sort of liked it. Little sparks of electricity had made her feel funny inside, and she thought she might like to do it with him again sometime, but then he had laughed at her and said she was just a kid. Then he told her to go back and play with her Barbie's!

Boy! That made her mad! She'd show him someday that she wasn't "just a kid!"

"One of these days, your mom is going to have to deal with you kissing boys. I'm sure that will make her happy!" Jim was grinning as his voice brought her back to the present. "There, that's better. Seriously, Jo, your mom and I love each other, but we love you girls, too! We just have to take things one step at a time. It's going to all work out for all of us."

"Now, how about if we go and get little Peaches? I think we all could go for some ice cream about now!"

"Can Tina come? Was she mad at me for going in the house?"

"No, she isn't mad. I told her you would call her later. But I think just the four of us should go this evening."

"We'll have to get a sandwich or something before treats, Jim. None of us have had anything for supper."

"Yes, boss! Haven't you ever heard the saying "Life is short, eat dessert first!"?

Sandi laughed as she hugged Joletta close to her side. "You might want to go wash those tears off of your face before we go." She patted her daughter and kissed her on the cheek.

Chapter 14
THE GIFT

Where do you suppose I put those darn paints? Sandi spoke to herself as she pushed aside several containers of out of season clothing, *I just know I put them in here somewhere.* Sandi had finally decided what she was going to do for Susan's birthday gift.

It had been almost two years since she had gotten out her paint supplies, but, with little money to work with, she had to do something, and she wanted it to be special.

When she was in high school her art teachers told her she was quite talented. She even won a statewide competition her Junior year, winning a blue ribbon and a gift certificate for an oil painting of her little sister Beth and brothers Tyler and Jacob. She had done the painting for her mother, trying to please her, but she told Sandi it didn't even look like the kids and before long her mother had put it in the back of a closet.

Sandi never let on how much it had hurt her feelings. She always tried so hard to make her mom happy, but nothing she ever did was good enough! Sandi had thought the painting would be something special. That was the last time she had even tried pleasing her mother.

She hoped this time it would be different...

Finally! Sandi pulled out a box filled with tubes of paint and brushes of different sizes and shapes. Behind the box were several canvas-covered boards. She picked out the largest and, pushing other things aside, she made her way out of the dark attic and back down the ladder that she had propped against the opening in the bedroom ceiling.

Sandi stepped into the small bedroom the girls had been sharing and checked on Annie, who was napping peacefully. Yawning herself, she headed back into the other room to start her project. Naps would be out for the next couple of weeks. She set her canvas on a kitchen chair and contemplated where to start.

She knew exactly what she would paint. It was a matter of getting it done, in just the right way, and it excited her just to think which colors she would use as well as which brushes would give her the effects she wanted.

The first day of June dawned bright and cloudless. The smell of the climbing rose bush outside Susan's window was intoxicating. Today was her birthday, and she could not remember feeling so good. Not in a long while, anyway. She felt giddy, almost like when she was a girl.

Jill and the boys had always been good about doing something special for her on her birthdays, which usually culminated in going out to supper at Lovella's, but today was going to be extra special. It had been a very long time since the family had gone on a real picnic! She did wish that Jillian and Tom could have been there, but that couldn't be helped. They were doing what they felt called to do, and that was ok with her.

Teddy was planning to pick her up at 11:00, and they would meet the others at the park a short time later. The picnic was at a beautiful little park about 20 minutes from home. There were exquisitely maintained flower gardens and a small lake, and in case it showered, there was a large shelter house right next to the playground area.

Her brother Will was coming from Pittsburg and her younger sister Anna would be there, along with her family and friends from nearby. Will and Anna were the only siblings living a reasonable driving distance from Summerset Hills. The others lived out of state, except her sister Pauline, who now lived at a full-time nursing facility.

Susan had always been close to Pauline, and it was hard accepting the fact that after her stroke a year ago, she would never be able to live on her own again. Occasionally she did get to go on outings, but recently she had been sick and was unable to come. Susan would visit later in the week and tell her all about the day.

Susan was next to the youngest of nine siblings. It had been a number of years since she had even seen some of them. Sadly, the last time they had all been together was at the funeral of their sister Elizabeth four years ago.

She decided that today she would not let the world and its problems get her down. Today would be a day of happiness.

It appeared that everyone was already waiting when Bill and Susan pulled into the gravel parking area of Willow Brook Park. Bill's Lincoln was parked close to the shelter house with the trunk open. Her brother's Caddie and Julie's little red Corvette was there as was the black Silverado that belonged to Sandi's special friend. Several small children were chasing around picnic tables setting around in the lush spring grass.

A tall, distinguished-looking man with silver-white hair walked toward the car, an arm around Samantha. "Uncle William!" Bill said as he reached out to shake the older man's hand. "It's so good to see you. It certainly has been a long time."

"Too long I'm afraid, young man. Aunt Molly and I were just talking about that the other day."

He pulled his sister to him and gave her a hug. "Happy Birthday, Sis! How is my prettiest little sister doing? Have you discovered the fountain of youth? You look younger every time I see you!"

Susan laughed. "Right! You are so silly, Will. I guess brothers never change?"

"I must say, you look lovely in gray hair, Sis!" He laughed and holding her hand, they headed together over to the shelter house where everyone was waiting for the "Guest of Honor" to arrive.

Soon the entire group of people was surrounding Susan, and for the next two hours, the laughter and visiting never let up for a minute. The food was delicious, and there was so much of it! Everyone thought they were going to burst before they quit eating!

Three long tables covered with colorful cloths had been set with plates and platters of good things to eat. It seemed like every person there had brought at least one of their favorite picnic foods and some had brought several things. The hardest part was choosing among the fried chicken, grilled hamburgers, or the taco salad. There were scalloped potatoes and potato salads. There was fresh fruit, pies, cookies, and of course, a large birthday cake that Mary and Susan's cook Joan had collaborated to design. To top everything off, Mary had pestered Bill until he finally dug the old hand-cranked ice-cream freezer out and dusted it off so the girls could make ice cream.

It was a grand party indeed!

Bill really didn't object as much as he let on. One of the last memories he had of his father was when he was five years old, cranking the same-old freezer, standing between his dad's legs, his small hand covered by the larger hand of his father. It was a special memory that he would always hold close to his heart.

"Come on over here and sit down, Mom. It's time to open presents!"

"My, oh my! This is my favorite part!" Susan clapped her hands like a little girl, and everyone laughed.

The children gathered in a semicircle in front of Susan while the adults sat in lawn chairs and on picnic benches to watch the festivities.

First, there was a beautiful antique brooch; this was from Ted and Julie. Little Danny presented her with a picture he had colored of a very old lady in a rocking chair. "This is for you, Grandmother Susan."

"Why Danny, I think it's lovely. She has very pretty purple hair."

"I know," said Danny proudly. "Purple is my favorite color. I told Mommy it was yours too."

"Open this one next Grandma. It's from us," said Sammy, handing another package to Susan. It was a beautiful pillow, done in counted-cross-stitch. "Tiffany and I helped. Do you like it?"

For the next half hour, Susan continued to open packages and read beautiful cards carefully chosen by her loved ones.

At last, there was only one gift left. Sandi's painting was propped in a lawn chair, unwrapped but covered with a pretty piece of old lace she had found in the attic.

Moving the chair next to Susan, Jim dramatically lifted the lace from the picture.

"Oh, my goodness! Sandi, it is beautiful!" Tears sprung to Susan's eyes as she looked at the painting.

The painting showed a summer scene with white puffy clouds and rays of sunshine filtering through lush green trees. There were morning glories climbing the trellis of the wrap-around porch and a wooden swing hanging from an oak tree. Three little children were romping in the big yard. Their mother, in a blue cotton dress, stood and watched the children from the open back door.

"Oh, Sandi, it looks just like it did when the children were small! However, did you know we used to have morning glory vines?"

Looking closer, she exclaimed, "Why, I had a dress that looked just like that! How on earth could you have known that?"

"I have to admit that Mary showed me some photos. There's one in front of the house, and you had that dress on. The rest I got from the stories you've been telling Joletta. I could just see it in my mind, and I wanted you to see it again."

"Oh, Darling! Thank you! Thank you so much--- and everyone else, thank you! I love you all very much. This has been the very best of all birthdays!"

Chapter 15
BRUSHSTROKES

"Sandi, do you have any idea just how talented you are? This painting is absolutely beautiful." Mary stood back and looked at Susan's birthday present. "The light in it just seems to glow. And the flowers, they look like you could reach out and pick one. I envy you your talent. Do you know what people pay for paintings of this quality?"

"Thank you, Mary. I'm glad everyone thinks it's a nice picture. I did the best I could, but I'm not really very good."

"Sandi, you are wrong. This is much more than just a nice picture."

Sandi appreciated the praise Mary was giving her, but still she could not see anything out of the ordinary. She had worked hard to make the painting special for Susan; other than that, it was just one of the many that she had painted over the past years. Some were better, but most were in the attic gathering dust. . . like the picture she had done for her mother so many years ago.

"Sandi," Mary interrupted her thoughts, "would it be all right if I have a friend of mine come and look at this? She was my roommate at college, and she's going to be here for the weekend. Do you have any more paintings?"

"I have some things in the attic, but they've been there since we moved last summer. I don't think there's anything anyone would be interested in. Why do you want her to see this?"

She has a little shop in Manhattan. She sells a variety of unique things there, and I believe she might be interested in your paintings. Of course, she would have to see what you have, but I know she will love this one. What do you think? It couldn't hurt, could it?"

"Well, I guess not, but I can't imagine that anyone would pay for them. I never thought about selling them. I just paint because I enjoy it.

Several days later, as Sandi was cleaning up after supper, the phone rang. "Sandi, my friend Eleanor is here. Do you have time to meet us over at Mom's?"

"I guess if you can give me a few minutes to finish up here."

"Sure, see you in a few minutes then."

Sandi hung up the phone. She wondered about what Mary's friend would say about the painting that she had given Susan. She had never shown her work to anyone, other than family and a few friends. She was not sure how she would feel if this woman didn't like it. *Oh well*, she thought, *I guess I'm going to find out. It doesn't really matter anyway. Mary is just being nice to me.*

As Sandi walked across the freshly mowed grass she could hear laughter and friendly voices coming from Susan's open windows. An unfamiliar, very expensive looking silver car was sitting on the street in front of her friend's home.

"Come right on in, Dear," Susan greeted as Sandi came up the porch steps. Susan put her arm around Sandi's shoulder and guided her inside. "Come in and meet Eleanor."

A tall, elegant woman stood and extended her hand to Sandi. She was breathtakingly beautiful with eyes and skin the color of a strong cup of coffee. "It is so nice to meet you, Sandi. Mary has been telling me about you and your little girls. They sound absolutely charming."

Sandi, feeling completely out of her league, spoke as she reached out and shook the other woman's hand. "The girls are my pride and joy, but I'm not sure charming is the word I would use. They walked over to visit Tina for a little while. Tina is a friend of my older daughter, Joletta. My little one is Annie," she explained to the newcomer.

After several moments of small talk about Mary and Eleanor's college days, Susan invited them to come into the formal dining room where she had a tray of fresh cookies and iced tea already sitting on the large mahogany table. There was a smaller sunny sitting room next to this – Susan's favorite room in the whole house. She had spent many happy hours enjoying the warm sunlight that filtered through the sheer curtains. Here, on the wall above a white, brick fireplace, was where Susan proudly displayed her "birthday painting."

The exotic woman from New York City walked over and stood several feet away, quietly focused upon the artwork.

Now the painting was in a wonderful handcrafted wood frame and matted with sky blue. A narrow outline of soft yellow to match the floral print of the room's wall border finished the presentation.

"How long did it take you to paint this, Sandi? I can certainly see why Mary was enthusiastic when she called me the other day. It is simply enchanting. Did Mary tell you about my business?"

"She told me you had a shop in Manhattan and that you sometimes sell paintings."

"Well, I do have a small shop, but most of my sales are special orders. My clientele come from all over the country, and I sell internationally. Not only do I buy and sell paintings, but I also have glasswork and antiques. I travel and find my inventory in many different places. I focus on unique handcrafted items. Jack, my husband, takes care of the business end of things while I take care of buying new art and contracting with my craftspeople. When Mary saw how wonderfully you painted, she knew I would like your work."

"I am definitely interested, but I would like to see more. Mary tells me you have others. Perhaps I could take one or two to display in the shop and see what customer response will be. We would need to wait and see."

Sandi was flabbergasted! Never, not in a million years, had she ever fantasized about selling her works. "The ones I have are up in my attic, and they are not framed. I can't imagine that they are worth going to any trouble over."

"If the others are even close to as well done as this one, then I think you have been severely underestimating yourself. If you are interested at all, you should get them down and let me look them over. Framing would not be a problem as we can have them framed before putting them on display and would just subtract any cost, after the picture is sold, from your earnings."

"Mary, I hate to rush, but I have that charity affair tonight, and if we're going to go get a bite to eat first, then we need to go."

"Sandi, call Mary tomorrow, and let her know when a convenient time would be to see your works. That is, if you decide you want to bother with it." Eleanor extended her hand, and Sandi took it in her own and shook it. She smiled with a still unbelieving look on her face.

Mary walked over to her with a triumphant look. "See, I told you. I'll talk to you later, O.K?" She hugged Sandi.

"I'll be ready in just a minute, El. I need to get my things."

They waved Eleanor and Mary off a few minutes later and watched as the car disappeared around the corner.

Joletta and Annie were just walking out the front of their house when Sandi started across the green lawn. "What have you been doing, Mom?"

"Oh, Joletta. You aren't going to believe what just happened," Sandi said as the three of them re-entered the house. "I'm not sure I believe it myself."

Chapter 16
SUMMERTIME!

What a busy month it had been. . .

First Susan's party, then everything going on with Sandi and Jim, and now it was only one more week until Joletta would be graduating from the 8th grade.

Sandi was planning a small reception for her. She was so proud of her daughter. Even with all the problems her family had faced in the past year, Joletta had still qualified for the Junior National Honor Society.

Although Sandi had been an above-average student, no one had ever acknowledged her efforts. Sandi wanted to make sure Joletta never felt the same rejection.

Jo had helped Sandi plant flowers in the backyard, and Jim recently brought over a picnic table crafted by his father. Susan's church would be providing folding chairs. Joan, Susan's cook, was making a special cake and Sandi's friend Trisha from the nursing home had offered to help make sandwiches and vegetable trays.

"Now, if only the weather cooperates," Sandi thought.

Graduation day did start out cloudy and cool, but it actually worked to their advantage. Since the ceremony was outside, the clouds kept the early afternoon sun from getting too hot for the 40 graduates and their guests. Joletta was having a wonderful day and reveled in all the attention and gifts.

Sandi almost cried as she watched her daughter and their many new friends. She could still hardly believe it all. Their lives had changed a lot in the past year. They now had plenty of loving people as friends, and Jim who cherished her and her children more than anyone else she had ever known - her heart was truly overflowing.

"Mom," Joletta came running over with Tiffany, her voice full of excitement. "Mom, Tiffany wants me to go to summer camp with her! Please, Mom, could I?"

"Oh, Joletta, I don' know honey. Camp costs money. I don't know how it would be possible." Sandi's voice trailed off as Mary and Susan walked over to where the three of them were standing. They had smiles on their faces.

"Sandi, we planned to talk to you ourselves before the girls let the "cat out of the bag" Susan said with a grin. "We were hoping you would let us pay for the trip as part of her graduation gift."

"Oh, my! I don't know. I had never--- I don't think---"

"Mom! Please, please! If I don't go, Tiffany will have to go by herself! Samantha is still too young to go, and Tiff doesn't want to go alone."

"Girls, why don't you go for a walk or something? We need to talk things over with Joletta's mom. I promise we'll let you know what's going on later." Mary waved her hand, indicating they were to leave.

She immediately turned to her friend. "Now Sandi, Mom and I have talked about this for a while, and we really think it would be a good idea, not only for the girls but for you also. It will give you and Jim a little break and it truly is a wonderful camp. It is only for three weeks, and parents can even come to visit on the weekends. Tiffany went last summer and had an absolutely wonderful time.

Mary continued. "You know the money is not the issue here, but if it would make you feel better, Mom said Joletta and Tiffany could help Joan with the spring-cleaning, and she would pay them."

"But three weeks? Joletta's never stayed away from home more than a night in her life!"

"She's growing up, Dear. She needs to be allowed some room to grow."

"Oh, Susan, do you think I don't give her enough freedom?"

"Not at all dear, I think you've been trying very hard and have been doing an excellent job, but you and the girls have had a lot of changes recently. I just feel it's time for a breather. It will be good for Joletta. I hope you will say yes." Susan smiled.

"Now go talk it over with Jim, before the girls get back. We'll take care of your guests for a while."

Sandi smiled and reached out and touched her friend's hand. "You are really too good to us, you know? Something tells me I have already lost this battle. You know as well as I do what Jim is going to say."

Hours later, Joletta curled up on the couch and scooted close to her mother's side. "Oh, Mom, this has been the very best day of my life! I love, love, loved my party and I can't believe you are letting me go to camp! No one could ever have a better Momma than I do." Sandi's arm tightened around Jo. As she kissed the top of the girl's head and smelled the sweet scent of her freshly bathed child, she said nothing, but a tear silently escaped and slowly continued down her cheek.

The week before camp Joletta packed and repacked her things at least a dozen times. She and Tiffany had spent countless hours on the phone talking about what they would be doing once they got there.

The camp, located in the Pocono Mountains, was almost three hours away from home. Tiffany's dad told them they would need to be ready bright and early. He had an early morning meeting the following day and needed to be home again before it got too late. So, as promised, the Lincoln pulled into the driveway at 8:00 a.m.

"They're here, Mom!" Joletta was about to bounce off the walls with excitement.

Sandi and a very sleepy Annie came into the front room. "Do you have everything?" A large lump was forming in Sandi's throat making it hard to talk.

Jo was waiting impatiently, loaded down with a backpack, suitcase, and duffel bag. She was dressed in shorts, high tops, and a rather tight-fitting pink t-shirt with her dark hair pulled into two pigtails, reminding Sandi of when Joletta was little. *Oh, how she hated to have her hair combed.* Smiling at the memory, Sandi reached for the larger of Joletta's suitcases and headed for the door to meet Bill and Tiffany.

"Call me as soon as you get there. Jim and I will be coming up this weekend. Are you sure you're ready for this?"

"Oh, Mom, I don't know why you're making it such a big deal! You would think I was only a little kid!" Sandi knew all too well that Joletta's days as a little kid were becoming a thing of the past. *Where had the years gone?*

Susan came out and kissed Jo and Tiffany goodbye. "Now you girls have a wonderful time and stay out of mischief. Do you hear?"

"Hi, Joletta! Ya ready? Mom says don't forget your paperwork!"

A smiling Mary waved from the window. "Don't worry Sandi. We'll let you know as soon as we get them settled."

"Yep!" Joletta turned and reached out for Annie. "Peaches, I sure am going to miss you. Be good and take care of Momma, OK?"

"Love you, Mom! Tell Jim I said good-bye!" She sat Annie down and grabbed her mother in a bear hug.

"Thanks, Mom! I'll write to ya!" "Bye, Susan, I love you too!"

"I love you more!" Sandi stood for several minutes, watching as the big car disappeared down the tree-lined street. She already missed Joletta.

Susan interrupted her thoughts. "It's OK dear. They are going to have the best time of their young lives!"

Sandi jumped. "Oh! I didn't know you were still here, Susan!"

Susan laughed. "Come on over and have a glass of orange juice and a fresh muffin. Joan just finished making them." She reached out and took Annie's little hand, and they walked up the steps onto Susan's front porch and into the welcoming old house.

LETTER FROM CAMP #1
Dear Mom,
Hi! How are things going?

Good for me. Camp is GREAT! I was a little homesick the first couple of days, but it's not so bad now.

You wouldn't believe how busy we've been. We get up at 7:00 in the morning and go for a hike first thing and have breakfast at a different place almost every morning!

Then we go back to the main shelter and get our assignments for the day. One day it's soccer or volleyball and the next it's baseball or tennis. We get to choose as long as the teams aren't too big.

That's after breakfast, and then we have free time before lunch for an hour.

Oh! I forgot. We have an hour before leaving for our hike to get ready, make up beds, and have everything in order. We go swimming every afternoon at two and have another break between three and four. At 4:30, we get to ride horses or go canoeing. Supper is at 6:00 and campfire at 8:30. We have to be in our bunks by 10:00 and lights out at 10:15. Some of the girls gripe about having a "baby bedtime," but I'm so tired by then I really am glad when the lights go out. Can you believe it's already been almost a week?

How are Annie and Susan doing? Oh, I forgot Jim. Is he doing OK? Tell everyone I miss them lots and be sure to give a kiss to Annie.

Mom, I hope you don't mind, but I think I miss Annie most of all. Do you think she misses me?

Everyone is excited about this weekend. We're planning something special for the parents that will be visiting.

The cabins are cool. Our counselors are Gretchen and Tammy. They are both kind of crazy, but a lot of fun.

Oh, and the food is great. The other night we grilled bananas on the campfire with Hershey bars and marshmallows melted on top of them. They were yummy!

By the way! I got a little sunburned, but it's better now. I'll remember to use my sunblock from now on.

LOTS OF XOXOX's,
Your daughter, Joletta

LETTER FROM CAMP #2
Hi Mom!

Just thought I better write, or you might wring my neck when I get home next week. I'm sorry I haven't written in a while, but we just stay so busy.

I know. I can just hear you saying, "That is no excuse, young lady!"

One of the girls from our cabin fell and hit her head yesterday and had to be taken to the hospital. Her name is Callie. I hadn't talked to her very many times, but I hope she is going to be all right.

She slipped on a rock while we were hiking and fell down the hill! When we got to her, she was all bloody and skinned up, and two of the counselors had to carry her to an open area so a rescue helicopter could pick her up. It was a really bad scene.

Guess what? You'll never guess. Oh, all right, I'll tell you. I met a boy! He is so cool, and he is cute, too! He is a cousin of my new friend Jessi.

We all went to campfire together Monday night. His name is Alex, and he has black hair and blue eyes! It is sooo cool! He's going to be a basketball star I think because he is really, really tall!

Ha! Anyway, you will like him. He lives in Richmond, Va. And when we go home, we are going to write to each other!

He says if we get a computer, he can send me emails! I really think we need to get a computer, Mom. What do you think? Everyone else I know has one!

What have you and Annie been up to?

Has Tina called? I sent her a postcard the other day.

Did you get the picture of me riding Starlight? I thought it was a good picture. I sure am going to miss not getting to ride horses. It is a lot of fun and Starlight is such a beautiful horse. Do you think there is any place close to home where I could ride?

Mom, I just wanted to tell you thanks for letting me come to camp! I am having such a great time. Tiff and I are going to be best friends FOREVER!!!!

Did you and Jim like coming and staying at camp? I liked having you here, but I sure wish Annie could have come, too! I am going to be so glad to see all of you next week. I guess I'm getting kind of homesick, but I hope I'll get to come again next year!

Lots and Lots of Love, Joletta

Chapter 17
TWISTER

Sandi woke to the sound of rain hitting the windows and the howling of the wind. She sat straight up in bed and knew immediately that something was wrong, very wrong. A roaring ominous sound, like nothing she had ever heard before, sent chills up her spine! Suddenly, there was a loud crash, and the windows in the front room came shattering to the floor.

Sandi screamed and ran to Annie's crib. Grabbing the little girl up in her arms, she literally dived into a closet as the wind roared through the house tearing pictures off the walls and tossing heavy furniture around. Crouching down low and as far into the back of the closet as she could get, she tried calming the hysterical child. "It'll be alright, Sweetie. Mommy's right here." The noise was deafening, and she could barely hear the sounds of Annie's voice as she cried into her mother's breast. Sandi was far from calm herself; shaking like a leaf, she held her frightened baby, praying there in the darkness in a way she had never prayed before!

The tornado hit without warning in the early morning hours while the normally peaceful little community was still sleeping. It was stiflingly hot, and it felt like there was no air to breathe. Sandi's nightgown and long hair clung to her warm skin.

As she huddled in the dark space she thought, *Thank God that Joletta is not here, at least she is safe.* "Oh, please, dear Jesus, if you are out there, please, please, protect us." *Joletta will not know what to do if something happens to us. She would have nobody to love her.* "God, Please! Help me!"

Suddenly, Sandi began to feel an odd sense of calm. The wind still howled, screaming and screeching its way through the small town, but Sandi no longer felt the fear of just a few short moments ago. It was almost as if a warm arm was holding her and little Annie. She heard a voice that whispered in the wind. "It is all right, my child. Do not fear."

"What? Who are you?" She could not see, and there was no response. The tiny room was so dark. She could not even see her hand in front of her face. On the other side of the door, the storm raged. Minutes felt like hours and as Annie's cries quieted, there was one final crash and then total unbroken silence. Silence so complete you could have heard a pin drop.

When she tried to open the door, it would not budge. She pushed with both her feet and still it refused to budge. Sandi had no other choice than to stay huddled on the floor of the closet for what seemed an eternity, hoping beyond hope that someone would come to their rescue. She dared not move, fearing the walls might collapse around them.

Within minutes there were new sounds in the distance, the high-pitched sounds of sirens and dogs barking. Several times she thought she could hear voices calling out, but no one responded to her calls for help. No one knew she and Annie were there.

Realizing the storm was over and that they were still in one piece, she sat in shocked silence and thought about the warm feeling of comfort and the voice in the wind. *Could it have really happened?* Nothing felt quite real, but still, she had heard something. *There was a voice...* Something or perhaps, someone, had been with her in those terrifying moments. *Could it be possible?* She didn't know exactly what it was that had happened, but she breathed a small prayer of gratitude, still not sure who she was praying to.

Surely this was just a terrible nightmare and she would wake soon. If only it were a nightmare, but Sandi knew she was already awake, and the nightmare was real!

"Annie, my precious baby. Is Momma's little Sweetheart OK?" She felt Annie's arms and legs, her

101

head and body, to make sure she had truly not been hurt, kissing her over and over, and telling her again and again that she loved her and that everything was OK now.

When she tried to get up, she felt dizzy and realized her head had a large gash on it and sticky warm blood was running down her forehead. Something must have hit her as she ran to get the baby. It had all happened so fast she had not been aware of anything hitting her at all, but the blood continued to ooze down her face and into her eyes.

As she listened to the sirens in the distance, she began to assess their situation. By now, she realized they were not alone in their plight. She wondered about Jim and Susan and their other neighbors.

It was so dark. She had never feared the dark, but she longed for the bright sunshine. She tried to push the door once again, but no matter how she tried, it would not open.

"Help! Please, someone, help us!" She cried into the night. Finally, leaning back exhausted against the wall, she let tears flow freely down her cheeks. Holding Annie tightly, she prayed once more that someone would find them soon.

Eventually, Annie slept, secure in her mother's arms and Sandi dozed fitfully, waking several times with a jerk, thinking every noise she heard was another storm coming.

"Sandi, are you there? Where are you?" It was Jim's voice--- and the sound of others that woke her. Although it was still very dark in the closet, Sandi could see sunlight creeping under the door. Hearing the sound of voices and debris being moved out of the way by the rescue workers, she called out.

"Jim! Oh, God! Jim, we are here! In the closet. I can't get the door opened. Please, come help us." Tears were flowing again, but this time they were tears of joy and hope.

"We're coming, Darling! We're coming!"

It took another several minutes to get through the rubble of what had been their home and then a crowbar to pry open the door, but, at last, they were safe in Jim's strong arms.

"Oh, my Darling! I was so frightened. So afraid, of what we would find!" Jim's voice was thick, and his own tears flowed. He held tightly to the woman he loved with all his mind, body, and soul.

As they stepped into the bright sunlight, Sandi's hand went to her mouth---"Oh my! Oh, Jim, this is horrible, just horrible!" She clung to him, afraid to ask the next question.

Finally, she was able to speak. "Susan? What has happened to everyone?" Her voice was tight and barely audible.

The devastation was complete. Not a single home in the neighborhood was standing without major damage. The beautiful community of Summerset Hills was gone, just a jumble of downed trees and badly damaged homes.

"No one was killed in this neighborhood, that's the good news, my Darling, if there is such a thing right now. There were quite a few injuries and unfortunately there were three people over at Tall Trees trailer park that didn't make it."

"Oh, Jim! How terrible--- what about Susan and Joan? Are they OK? What about the neighbors?"

Jim stepped away and put his hand on her shoulder. "Susan has multiple injuries, but nothing life-threatening, she's going to be OK. They took her to the hospital over at Vernon. It could have been much worse."

"She managed to get herself into the basement, but not before the windows started blowing out. She was hit by parts of the framing as it blew in." Gathering Sandi into his arms again, Jim continued, "She really is going to be OK, Hon. She's more worried about you and Annie than herself!"

103

"What about everyone else?"

"Well, Joan wasn't working, her neighborhood wasn't affected, so they are all right. Johnsons down the street are both in the hospital."

"Beck's house was destroyed; no one in the family was injured, but Tina's dog was found dead."

"Oh, poor Tina, she loved that dog!" Burying her face in his chest, Sandi sobbed. "What is everyone going to do?"

"We'll get through this, my Love. I promise. The main thing right now is to get you and Annie checked out."

Sandi looked dazed as Jim led her to the waiting ambulance that would take her to the hospital. She had a large gash running from her forehead down the side of her face that would need stitches, and the paramedics would make sure that she and Annie had no other injuries.

Leaves, tree branches, and debris of every kind covered the green grass. The roof of someone else's house, upside down but still intact, was in the middle of the road and a giant maple tree lay across the roof of Susan's beautiful veranda. It would be a huge challenge, trying to figure out what to do first.

Families without anywhere to go were being housed in local churches until other arrangements could be made. The Red Cross had already set up food lines. Bedding, water, and other emergency supplies were already on the way.

The terrible storm was over, but there would be much to do in the weeks ahead.

As the ambulance drove around fallen trees and debris, people wandered aimlessly around the broken neighborhood, wondering what would happen to them now.

Chapter 18
AFTER THE STORM

Joletta walked into the camp director's office shortly after 10:00 in the morning, wondering what could be so important that she needed to miss recreation time. She had planned to play tennis with Tiffany and two other friends that morning. Maybe if she hurried, she would still have time. Hopefully, he wouldn't need her for long.

Mr. Willard's face looked worried as the girl walked in the door. He smiled and came to meet her. Putting his hand on her shoulder, he said, "Please have a seat Joletta. I need to tell you something." He indicated a chair beside the window. The sun shone brightly through the light curtains as Joletta did as he asked. "I just talked with your mom on the phone." He hesitated, and then continued. "I'm afraid I have some bad news."

Joletta could hardly believe what he was telling her. It just couldn't be true. "I don't understand," she said. "I talked to Mom just the other day. Everything was OK then."

"Are you sure that they are all right?" Her mind was a whirlwind of thoughts. *Where would they go now? What would happen to them?* At least, her mom and Annie were OK, but it was hard to imagine having no home. Tears gently slipped down her cheeks as Mr. Willard kept a hand on her trembling shoulder.

She was still crying when Tiffany and her new friend Alex came into the room.

Mr. Willard hardly knew how to comfort the girl. This was only his second year as camp director, and he had not had to handle this sort of thing before. He was a young man with good intentions but not a lot of experience.

"Oh, Joletta, they just told us about the tornado!" Tiffany's words tumbled out as she ran to her friend's side. "Mom called and told me everything. Grandma's in

105

the hospital! Did you know that? She broke her leg in three places, but they said she's going to be OK."

"Are your mom and Annie all right? Mom told me it was terrible, and there were even people who were killed! Oh, Joletta, do you think your friend Tina and her family are OK too?"

"I don't know," Joletta said. She had not thought of this before, and the tears started flowing again. "Mr. Willard said he only had information about Mom and Annie and Grandma Susan."

The director of the camp stood slightly away from the young people. Watching them, he felt sorry for both girls. Tiffany, always precocious and talkative, and Joletta, a quiet, sensitive girl, they made quite a pair. What an awful way to be ending what was, for the most part, a wonderful three weeks of camp.

Suddenly, he felt very tired. He had already been gone from home for the major part of the summer, and although his home was nowhere near the area hit by the bad storms, it made him wonder if everything was all right there. It would be good to get home to his own family when camp wrapped up in a few days.

The following Saturday, Bill picked up his daughter and Joletta. Joletta would be staying with them at least until the beginning of school, which would start the last week of the month. Sandi needed some time to decide what she and the girls would now be doing.

For the time being, she and Annie were staying with Jim. That presented its own set of problems because she did not want Jo to get the idea that they were co-habituating. She was done with that type of relationship forever.

Jim wasn't about to let them out of his sight any longer than necessary. Those long hours, when he didn't know where Sandi and Annie were, or if they had even survived the terrible storm, had been the most excruciatingly painful hours of his life!

"Your mom said to tell you how sorry she was that she couldn't come to pick you up, Joletta." Bill was putting the last of the girl's things into the trunk of the Lincoln. "Your mom's car was badly damaged in the storm. I think she will have to get another one after the insurance is all straightened out. She said to tell you she would be with Grandma Susan today. Your mom's been helping to take care of her."

"Mom called me last night and told me. Where's Annie? I thought she would be with you." Joletta's voice was full of concern.

"Mary has her, Sweetie. You'll see her when we get home. Try not to worry. Your mom and Jim will be there later this evening. Wild horses couldn't keep them away."

As they rode through the beautiful wooded mountains, the girls talked quietly in the back seat about all their adventures of the past few weeks. They talked about the changes that would take place in their lives in the coming year. Both would be starting their first year of senior high.

Joletta wondered aloud where her family would be and what they would do now.

"Oh, Jo! I wish you could just come and live with us forever!"

Bill, listening from the driver's seat, wished there was some way to protect them from the hurts that life would hand them through the years. He wished he could just stop time and keep them little girls. In her young life, Joletta had already experienced far too many heartaches. He smiled to himself, wondering how Jo's family had managed to move into the hearts of every one of his family members! Moved right into their hearts to stay.

Chapter 19
BETH

The young woman with the long blond ponytail hung up the phone. She had dialed the number off, and on all day, and had no luck at all getting an answer. Sometimes it would ring over and over, and then go dead. Twice now, when she dialed all she got was a recorded message saying the line was out of order. It was so frustrating. She had waited a very long time to make this call; surely if she tried enough times, it would go through.

Beth sat down in an old-fashioned high back chair that had come from her mother's house. She wondered what to do now. She guessed she didn't have much choice except try again later. Probably the phone lines just weren't working properly. She looked at the clock on the wall. It was already almost 5 o'clock. Darrel would soon be home from the plant where he worked as an engineer.

She should probably go and start something for supper. Mentally, she went over what she might have in the cupboard. She knew she had a package of ground hamburger and some cheeses in the refrigerator, so she decided on lasagna. It was one of Darrel's favorites, and she had ice cream in the freezer for dessert. A short time later Beth's husband of three months came in the door.

"Oh, my goodness! You're smelly," she laughed while trying to hold her nose as he grabbed her in a bear hug.

"Didn't you even miss me today?" he said. "You mean I have to be clean before you're even willing to let me touch you? Can't you at least appreciate the fact that I have been slaving away all day just for you? I can't believe a guy can't even get a simple little hug!" In mock disgust, he headed down the hall and into the tiny bathroom. He turned his head and called over his shoulder, "By the way, what's for supper? Will I have enough time to watch the news before we eat?"

"I don't think I'll even tell you, Mr. Smarty-pants!"
She laughed and said, "I can wait a little longer before I
put things in the oven." Forty minutes later, Beth almost
had dinner ready when Darrel called from the other room.

"Honey, didn't you say your sister lived in
Summerset Hills, Pennsylvania?"

"Yeah. Why?" Beth wiped her hands on a kitchen
towel as she stepped into the living room.

"Look at this! There was a really bad tornado there
last night. It says there were a number of injuries and
several people killed". The television was showing a
large area of land with many houses that looked more like
"pick-up sticks" than homes. The trailer court they
showed was completely beyond recognition, and there
was literally nothing left of it.

Beth's face turned ashen.

"Oh, Darrel, I've been trying to call there all day.
That must be the reason I couldn't get through."

He reached for her hand, "It's OK, Hon. Just because
the phones aren't working doesn't mean they aren't all
right."

Beth barely ate the lasagna she had made that
evening. She had been so excited about finally finding out
where Sandi and Joletta were, and now this! Surely God
wouldn't let anything bad happen now.

She slept fitfully that night, and when her husband
got up at 6:30 the next morning, he found Beth in the front
room, just sitting and looking at the large painting on the
wall – a painting of two small boys and a smiling blond-
haired girl. The painting her sister did so many years
earlier.

"I have to go there, Darrel. I have to go and find
them," she said quietly.

He sat down and put his arm around her. "I know,"
he said.

Three days later, Darrel picked Beth up from her job and drove her to the airport. She barely said a word during the 40-minute drive downtown. She had said very little in the past several days, and her husband was concerned.

"Call me when you get checked into your hotel," he said.

He held her close. "I am really going to miss you, babe. Are you sure you're going to be all right? I'm sorry, Hon. I wish I could have gotten off work." He put his finger under her chin and lifted her face to his. "I really tried but the boss said we are just too busy right now."

"I'm fine," she paused, "at least right now I am. I'm just dreading what I might find." She held tight to him and said into his chest, "Oh, I wish you could go too, but I'll be all right, really I will." Her bravado slipped a bit as her voice caught in

her throat. Squeezing his hand once more, she turned to wave as she walked down the chute to the waiting 747. "I'll see you next week, Sweetheart. I love you!"

"I love you too. I'll talk to you tonight."

Chapter 20
A VISITOR FROM THE PAST

Sandi was in the kitchen fixing supper when the doorbell rang. "Get that, will you, Joletta?" she called. It had been close to two weeks since the storm and Sandi and the girls were now staying with Susan.

Jim tried to get them to continue staying with him, but Joletta wanted to start school with her friends, and Sandi planned to stay and care for Susan when she came home from the hospital. She felt that now she had a way to give back, at least partially, the many months of support her friend had given her and her children.

"Can I help you?" Joletta said as she pushed open the old-fashioned screen door.

Signs of the cleanup effort were evident all around them. Joletta spoke above the noise of a chain saw as workers attempted to repair the damage done by the tree that had fallen on Susan's front porch. Part of the roof and floor remained, leaving a huge gaping hole. The sun reflected on scattered shards of glass and broken pieces of the porch swing. The wicker furniture that had looked so lovely only a short time ago lay mangled and unusable further out in the yard, and two large potted geraniums lay on their sides, dirt spilling across the floor, the flowers lying limp and forgotten in the late-summer sun.

"Hi, I'm looking for Sandi Breese. I was told she might be staying here?"

Joletta stared at the young woman standing in the doorway. "Mom, I think you might want to come in here." There was little doubt that the woman at the door was Joletta's Aunt Beth. A framed 8x10 inch of Sandi hung on her bedroom wall, and although this young woman had darker hair, she could have easily been mistaken for the same person. The two stood contemplating each other, Joletta backing away slightly as her mom came into the room.

"What is it that you want, Joletta? I'm busy right now." As Sandi walked through the kitchen door, her eyes went past her daughter. She paused for a moment, staring in disbelief. "Oh my! Oh, my Dear God!" Her hand went over her mouth as she looked into the eyes of her long-lost younger sister. "Beth? How can this be?" Sandi hurried across the room. "Is it really you? Where did you come from? What are you doing here?" The two women that were so much alike reached out for each other, laughing and crying at the same time. "Oh! My precious little Beth! I never thought I would see you again!"

Joletta, not knowing quite what to do next, observed from several feet away, wondering where this long-lost relative had come from and what she wanted. She had always known that her mother had younger siblings and even asked once if they could go and visit them, but now she was actually standing in the same room with one of them. It all seemed unreal.

Beth's gaze finally moved from Sandi to Joletta. "Hello! You have to be Joletta. I am your Aunt Elizabeth."

Joletta did not know what to say, but she smiled shyly and accepted the hug offered by the older girl with the large green eyes.

"What a beauty you are! You were a beautiful baby, so I guess I'm not surprised. Do you know I used to rock you to sleep at night?"

It took several minutes for Sandi to calm down enough to make any sense of what had just taken place. She had not seen any of her family since she had left with Joletta almost 14 years ago. There had been a time that Sandi had tried finding where they were, but had come up blank. . . She had gone back to the town she had grown up in and found their old house, but it stood empty and neglected, the grass tall and the yard full of weeds and trash. After that, she could find no trace of where they had gone. Finally, she had just given up. She believed her mother would not have welcomed the visit, anyway, perhaps not even allowing her into the house. "I tried to find you, Beth. Where did you go? It was just like you had fallen off the face of the earth. Oh, Beth, I just can't believe you are here. I've missed you so much! Tell me, where are the boys? Where is Mom?"

"Sandi, there is so much to tell. I'm just so glad we finally found you. What a terrible thing to have happened. It is beyond weird the way it all worked. I was trying to call you the same day of the storm! I had been trying all day, and then we heard about the storm on the news. I was so afraid that something terrible had happened to you. Are you sure you're all right? Is this your house?"

A timer sounded from the other room. "Oh, my gosh! I have cookies in the oven. I completely forgot! Come on in the kitchen, and we'll talk in there."

"I was just getting some supper ready. Jim, that's my fiancée', he will be here soon. He is going to be so surprised." After Sandi took the cookies out of the oven and cooled them on a rack, she sat down to continue catching up with the past.

"Sandi, we've been looking for you too," Beth said and then hesitated, wondering how her sister would handle what she had to tell her next. "Sandi, I have some news, and I'm afraid it isn't good news." She took a deep breath and said. "Sandi, Mom's dead." She fell silent for a moment and then continued, "She was killed in a car accident last winter."

Joletta watched her mother's reaction, shock and disbelief written all over her face.

"Mom's dead?" A choking sound came from Sandi's throat. "It can't be true." Beth reached across the table and put a comforting hand on that of her older sister. "I'm so sorry, Sandi."

"There was a storm last spring, and while driving home from work, she hit the ice and lost control. The car

113

went over the side of the mountain, and she was killed instantly. She should never have been driving in that kind of weather, but I suppose she didn't realize how bad it was."

Beth continued. "Sandi when I was going through her things, I found a journal of hers. It talks about her feelings and a lot of other things. There are entries in it where she wrote about you, Sandi. It said she was sorry she pushed you and Joletta out of our lives. She never talked much about you. We didn't really know what happened to you or why you went away. We kids were just so little. I guess we never asked any questions. Or at least, if we did, I don't remember." Pausing, Beth looked pensive. "There are some things though that I do remember, Sandi. You used to sing to me at bedtime. Do you remember singing to me?"

Sandi nodded silently. Memories so long pushed to the deep recesses of her mind, now were almost overwhelming. "Hush, little baby. . . You loved to be rocked, and that was your favorite. . ."

"And I remember crying because I didn't know where you had gone. I've brought the journal for you to read. I thought it might make you feel a little better about her. I know how hurt you must have been. Actually, it was when I found the journal that I got serious about looking for you again."

"Oh, Beth, I just didn't know how else to do it. I missed you all too, so very much. I wanted to take you away with me, but I knew I could not. I couldn't have taken care of you, and I would not have done that to Mom anyway. I was so angry with her. I felt like leaving was my only choice."

"Sandi," Beth paused, "there's more." Sandi waited, wondering how much more she could take. "There is a letter in it from Joe." Beth stopped talking, giving Sandi a moment to process the full impact of what she was hearing. "It was right there with Mom's journal. I guess

114

he sent it to our house several years ago hoping Mother would get it to you."

Sandi began shaking uncontrollably, and Joletta put her arms around her mom, trying to comfort her. She didn't understand at all what was going on. She always thought Sandi hated her mother, and... *who the heck was Joe?*

Oh, my gosh! She thought. Joletta suddenly realized that the Joe that Beth was talking about had to be her father. A strange, unfamiliar feeling ran through her body. *A letter from her father?* She wondered what the letter said and if she would get to read it. She was brought back to the moment when her mom spoke.

"What about the boys?" It was as though she had not even heard about Joe's letter. "Where are they? Are they O.K? Do they even remember me?"

"They live with a cousin of ours in Pittsburg. They want to see you. Tyler says he remembers when you would sit him on the counter and let him help make cookies. He just graduated from high school, and Jacob will be a senior this coming year. Tyler has already been accepted at Penn State this Fall. I've brought pictures with me. Actually, it was Tyler that found you."

"When we were going through Mom's things, we found your social security number and a copy of your birth certificate. The next day he looked and found you on the Internet. Isn't that amazing? All these years, and it was as simple as typing in a few words and numbers on a computer keyboard. We just couldn't believe it!"

Sandi sat down on the couch; she felt as if she had been hit in the head with a two by four! In fact, she was beginning to wonder if something had happened to her in the storm! Maybe she had been "hit on the head" and none of this was real! It was all too much to comprehend at one time.

"Are they good boys? Did Mom treat you OK?"

At this, Beth laughed. "Oh, Sandi, they're just great! Tyler was at the top of his class last year. I think he has the I.Q. of a genius! I spent hours studying every night, all the way through high school, but not Tyler. He seems to know the answers even before the teacher asks the question! He's been given a full ride to college and plans to be a pediatrician." Can you believe that? .... A doctor! In our family! Of course, that is a very long way off, but I know Tyler, and he will do it. He always does what he sets his mind on."

"Jacob is more into sports and girls than lessons, but he's a good kid and stays out of trouble, for the most part. Sandi, our dad and mom divorced the year after you left, and Mom never remarried. I know she treated us a lot differently than you. I think when you left, she finally realized what she had done. By that time, she thought it was too late. She told me once that if you hadn't walked away, she might never have gotten the nerve to leave Dad. She said he was abusive and used to hurt her. A lot! They were very secretive about it, and he never hurt her where the bruises would show. She lived in fear of him. He would threaten to hurt us if she ever left or told anyone about what he was doing to her. He lives out in Nebraska somewhere now, but I haven't seen him for a long time."

"Oh, Beth, I never knew any of that. How could I have not known?"

"I don't know. I guess you had your own problems at the time, and as I said, she never told anyone. She was afraid of him. She was afraid of what he might do."

"Mommy!" Annie was waking up from her nap and calling out to be picked up. The baby's call brought Sandi back to the present, and she stood.

"Mommy, Mommy. Mommy!" the little voice from the next room continued.

"Sandi! Do you have another child?"

"Oh, yes! Come meet our little Annie. Come in and see. She looks like you did as a baby!

116

Chapter 21
AFTERMATH

A few minutes later, the women heard the sound of Jim's Silverado pulling into the driveway.

As he walked up the steps, he could hear laughter from inside. He smiled. Laughter was something there had been very little of in the past few days.

Late the following evening Beth told Sandi and Joletta she must leave soon for her motel. Her flight home was scheduled for 6:00 the next morning.

"Oh, Beth, no! You can't leave so soon! We have had hardly any time at all! We still have so many things to talk about. All this time, and I know so little! Please, can't you just stay a few days?"

Beth reached for her sister's hand. "I wish I could. I only have a week. I have to be back at work on Thursday, and I was actually lucky to get this time off. Also, I talked to Darrel this afternoon; he sounded pretty lost." Taking her sister's hand, she said, "I promise, though, I'll call, and we can write to each other. I want you to meet Darrel and the boys. They are not going to give me a minute's peace until they get a chance to come and see you."

It was hard letting her sister go, but Sandi knew there was no other choice. Sandi knew her younger sister had to be just as anxious to get home to her husband as he was to have her home again. There would be more visits with her sister. She just wished this one could last longer! Once again, they hugged, cried, and then reluctantly moved away from each other. Beth waved as she got in the waiting cab; it had been a long day for everyone.

Joletta sat down on the couch beside her mom, who looked exhausted. "Are you OK, Mom?"

"Sure honey. It's been quite a day, hasn't it? We all need to be thinking about getting to bed. I will have to work tomorrow. What do you think of your Aunt Beth?"

117

"Oh, Mom, I think she's beautiful. Do you think that she really will bring Tyler and Jacob to see us? I think that would be so cool."

"I'm sure of it, Honey. Now if you don't mind too much, I believe I'll turn in. I have some things I need to think over and Jim will be calling soon. In all the excitement, I forgot to ask him what time he planned to pick you girls up. I need to know if Joan should come over for a couple of hours or if he can get away from work by noon. It won't hurt your feelings, will it, Sweetheart?"

"No, it won't hurt my feelings. Mom," Joletta paused, "I'm really sorry about your mom. I never thought much about my grandmother, but now it seems sad that we never saw her."

"Oh, Jo, it is sad, Darling. She missed so much. I wish things could have turned out another way, but sometimes we just have to take what life gives us." Sandi's voice caught, and she cleared her throat. "I don't know. Maybe if I had stayed, things would have changed. But at the time, I didn't know what else to do. I really don't know why she felt the way she did. I guess she blamed me because Daddy left us, but I never knew what it was I did." She reached out and gave the girl a tight hug.

"You were just a little girl when your daddy left, weren't you? I don't know how it could have been your fault."

"Thank-you, Sweetheart, but I guess we won't ever know now. I'm just sorry that she never got to watch you grow up. You need to get on to bed now, Sweetie, so you'll be rested for tomorrow. I should be home from work at around 8:30. We'll talk more about everything then. OK? I love you, Sweetheart. I'll see you in the morning." Joletta yawned and smiled as Sandi turned to go into her bedroom, shutting the door behind her.

Later as Joletta lay in her bed, she thought of the events of the last two days. She had liked her mother's

118

sister and couldn't help but wonder about her uncles. Also, even more than that, she wondered about the letter from Joe, the man that was her father. She had not dared to ask her mother about it, although she imagined by now her mom had read it. She wondered, *What did the letter say?* Perhaps he wanted to come and take her from Sandi, or maybe he would tell her about a family he had that no one knew anything about. She might even have brothers and sisters she didn't know. Joletta wondered if she would ever get to sleep. She wondered, *Was he rich? Did he live in a big house or a small house? Was he a good man or maybe a drunk, or even worse someone who would hurt little children?* So very many things she thought about that night before she drifted off to sleep. Several hours later, in the deep of the night, Joletta woke. She had been dreaming about her father again. Recently, the dreams had not been happening as frequently as in the past, but they were always quite upsetting. They seemed so real, and it would take her several minutes to realize that once again, it was only a dream.

Her mother and Jim had been there in this dream, and as she thought about it, she remembered that Susan and all of Joletta's friends were there also. *Goodbye, everyone!* She was saying. There was a tall, handsome man standing next to her, leading her away. She could not remember where he was taking her, just away. Away from her family, away from her friends, away from the life she knew and the home she had come to cherish so much. *No!* her mind said, *I can't go with you! I don't have a home! Wait!* She pulled her hand away from the man and started running. *I can't go. I can't leave my mom! She needs me, and Annie needs me too. I'm so sorry!* Joletta was running back, back to the family she knew and loved, back to the ones she knew loved and needed her.

Joletta slowly came awake. What did it all mean? Sleepily she tried to recall what else had been in the dream, but it had already become a blur and was no

119

longer clear. *Maybe we don't have a home*, she thought, *but we do have a place to stay, and people that love us. I will never let anyone take that away from me.*

Perhaps it didn't really matter what the letter from the man called Joe said. Joletta was beginning to realize that no matter what it said, there were people in her life that would care for her and love her always. Somehow, this dream felt different, and she was strangely comforted. She curled up hugging her old teddy to her heart and was soon back to sleep.

Chapter 22
YOU'VE GOT MAIL

Sandi held the wrinkled envelope in her hand for several minutes, looking at the still familiar handwriting. It seemed to her that after all these years, she should be able to think about Joe without hurting, but her hands shook as she slowly tore it open. The date at the top of the page was nearly five years ago. As she unfolded the letter, a business card and a picture of two golden-haired toddlers fell into her lap. She read the information on the card – "Joseph Lenders, Attorney at Law." There was an address and phone number listed on the reverse side.

Looking at the photo, she immediately saw the resemblance. There was no doubt these children belonged to the man she had once believed she loved; she realized these little girls were half-sisters to his first child, the child who spent her entire life without knowing who her father was!

LETTER FROM JOE

My dear, sweet Sandi,

I have tried for several years to reach you and tell you just how sorry I am for all that I   put you through so long ago.

I do not know what your life has been like or where you are, but I continue to hope that someday we will meet again. I was told that we had a little girl and I am hoping that there could come a time when I may meet her, perhaps a time when I might become someone special to her. I'm sure that if she is like her mother, she is smart and very beautiful.

Sandi, I will never forget your soft skin and how your hair fell around your shoulders, and you had the most beautiful eyes.

Oh, Sandi, how I loved you. I think that perhaps I still do. Why, oh why did things have to get so complicated?

Sandi thought sarcastically, Complicated! You think your life was complicated! You and your safe little world! You, and your wonderful life, with Momma and Daddy catering to your every whim! The letter continued. . .

I thought I could go on with my life, but I have never forgotten the times we had together.

After you told me about your condition, I was very confused and decided I needed to talk to my parents about the situation we had gotten ourselves into.

Well Sandi, they convinced me that you probably got pregnant on purpose. They said you thought that way I would marry you! They insisted that I had to think ahead, that Law School would be hard enough, and a kid and a wife would almost guarantee failure. I know now that it was wrong, but I was just so young, and I thought they knew best.

I hope you can understand getting married would have ruined all of our plans. Ever since I was small, I knew exactly what was expected of me. I was already registered to start college in the fall and they said not to trust you, it was probably not even my child!

I know that was a mistake, Sandi, and I know you were never with anyone else. I always did, I think.

That first year at college was very hard on me. For months after we broke up I couldn't stop thinking about you and I couldn't concentrate on my classes. It was so bad that I almost flunked out that first semester.

I thought about calling or writing, but I was so ashamed of myself that I never could work up the nerve, so I did nothing.

I want you to know that I am sincerely sorry for the way I left you. I believed you would have understood how important college was. It would have broken my parent's hearts if I had not gone. You probably remember that Dad was a third-generation lawyer, and I always knew I was expected to follow in his footsteps.

Anyway, we were very young. I don't know if we could have made it together, but I do know that just walking out on you was a terrible thing to do.

I should have explained how important it was for me to continue my education. Of course, I would have helped you financially, maybe later we could have gotten back together, but then you just disappeared!

Well, I hope when you read this you will understand how much I regret the way we handled things.

Please, if you ever read this letter, try to forgive me.

Also, the enclosed photo is of my two daughters, Amy and Molly, our daughter's half- sisters.

Their mother, Monica, was a partner in my law firm; we married six years ago but sadly, we lost her to cancer last Spring, and we are now alone.

We knew for some months that she was losing ground with the cancer, but it still came as a terrible shock when she finally passed on.

It is still hard knowing she is gone.

I am now raising the children with the help of their Aunt Paige, who lives in our home. She has been with us for close to a year now. I don't know what I would do without her. She loves the girls with all her heart and they love her equally.

Sandi, If this letter ever finds its way to you, I hope you will tell my daughter that I love her and would like to meet her and perhaps be part of her life.

I know you probably don't think I deserve to know her, but perhaps you will change your mind. I have enclosed a business card and my personal address.

With Much Love and Many Regrets, Joe Lenders

The enclosure at the back of the few pages was what Sandi had been dreading.

The final page was a short note written directly to Joletta, though, of course it did not contain her name. *He had never taken the time to find out her name.*

"You self-centered bastard!" Sandi put her hand over her mouth and swallowed hard. She had cleaned up her language a long time ago, but she could think of nothing else to say---

Sandi was exhausted! How was she ever going to get any sleep?

Joe Lenders had no idea what she and Joletta had been through in the past 14 and a half years*! As if he would really care anyway! It might have interfered with the "grand ambitions" he and his parents thought were so important!*

She wished for a moment that she had something stronger than Cola in the house. Of course, by now she knew beyond any doubt that alcohol was not the answer to her problems. It had never been anything but a temporary fix and had never really made her feel anything but miserable!

She thought of her sister and her younger brothers that she had not seen since they were small boys. She thought of her girls and her mother. She thought of the many changes in her life since she had left her mother's home, and she thought of Jim.

It was Jim that she needed to talk to. He would be home now and calling soon, as he did every night when she was not working.

She laid her head down on the soft pillow, tears of angry frustration, hurt and loss running down her cheeks, as she waited for the anticipated ringing of the phone.

Chapter 23
A TRIP TO THE ZOO

Jim picked the girls up the next day as planned. The air was cool and crisp, a sign of early Fall, but the sun was bright with the promise of a beautiful day, and fortunately, there had been virtually no damage done to the zoo by last month's storm.

Off they went, big Jim, Joletta and little Annie. They all loved the zoo and went frequently as it was only a short drive to the park complex, and the cost to go was minimal. The giraffes were, hands down, Annie's favorite, and so they were the very first of their animal friends to get visited by the little group. The baby could hardly be contained as she struggled in Jim's arms to get closer to the long-necked beast with the soft brown eyes, not in the least bit frightened by them, although the difference in their size was great.

"I guess it's been a pretty exciting week for you and your mom and Annie, hasn't it, Joletta?" Jim spoke as he held Annie on his shoulders for a better view. "Would you like to talk about it?"

"I just couldn't believe it when I answered the door the other day. My aunt looks so much like Mom. She's pretty don't you think. She's smart too! She writes a column for a newspaper, and she's a real photographer. She's even had pictures published in magazines. She photographs a lot of different things. She told me that the next time she comes to see us, she's going to bring her equipment with her and take pictures of us."

"Did she tell you my grandmother had been killed in a car accident?"

"She did, Joletta. I'm so sorry to hear that. Are you doing, OK? I know you didn't know your grandma, but I'm sure it is really sad for you anyway."

"Yeah, I guess it is. I don't know exactly how I feel about it. I'm really worried about Mom though. She cried

125

when Beth told her about it. I didn't even think she liked her mom, but I guess she did." Joletta's voice trailed off, and she turned her head away from Jim as she rubbed her hand across her eye to keep a tear from escaping.

"It'll be all right, Sweetheart. Your mom is a strong person, and so are you." He swung Annie down from his shoulders. Joletta slipped her hand into his. He smiled and squeezed it gently as they walked down the manicured pathway to see the seals.

"Did she tell you about the letter?" Joletta hesitated. "The one from Joe. My real dad."

"She sure did honey. I think she is pretty concerned about how it could affect you. She's never really had to share you before, at least in the way you would with another parent."

"Oh, Jim, Mom shouldn't ever worry. I could never love anyone more than I love her."

It was nice talking to Jim. He always seemed interested in whatever Joletta wanted to talk about. Things had changed a lot since Joletta had first found out about Jim and her mom.

She realized that just because they had fallen in love, it didn't mean the end of the world. Things were even better now than before. In ways, he was easier to talk to than Mom. Mom was always so worried that Joletta might make mistakes, and sometimes she treated her like a baby.

Jim treated her almost like an adult. Well, not quite, but he was fun to do things with, and he always respected her opinions on things.

Jim interrupted her thoughts.

"How is the school year going so far? High school is a really big step, isn't it?"

"It was really scary the first week, but now I'm getting used to it. There are so many more students at Central, and I don't know many of the kids. Tina is only

126

in one of my classes, and I don't even get to have lunch at the same time with her."

"Is she the only friend you have? I thought the rest of the eighth graders graduated, also."

"Well, yeah. She is just the only best friend I have there. I wish Tiffany went there too. Tina's brothers, Jacob and Derrick, go there, but they're older and don't know I'm alive."

"I bet you'll make a lot of new friends. It'll be fun. Are you planning to play any sports? Or are you going to try out to be a cheerleader?"

"I'm going to join the choir and probably run track in the spring. Mom says it will be OK, as long as I keep my grades up."

"That would be a lot of fun for you."

Jim smiled and leaned down to tickle Annie under the chin. "Want to go get some hot dogs and a milkshake?"

"We're going to have to get Annie home before long for a nap, or she will be a bear this evening and Mom wouldn't be too happy about that."

Joletta laughed and nodded her head. "Wave bye-bye to the monkeys, Annie. We're going to get something to eat." Joletta pushed the stroller along as Annie waved and clapped her hands.

"Your mom tells me that Susan is coming home from the hospital the day after tomorrow."

"Yeah, Mom and I are fixing a special supper, and everyone will be coming over."

"I know. I'm invited too."

The cheerful conversation continued until they arrived at the hot dog stand.

Jim smiled as he watched Joletta helping her little sister. He was so proud of these girls and hoped it would not be long until he could make them a part of his family. It was becoming increasingly hard each time he had to leave them and go to his lonely apartment.

Chapter 24
SEPTEMBER 11, 2001

Sandi stared in disbelief at the television screen. It was close to 9:30 on the morning of September 11, 2001.

Sandi had been working an extra shift for a friend of hers whose child was ill and was on her way to take some linens down to one of the rooms before she left to go home for the day. As she walked past a lounge area, she noticed several co-workers standing quietly looking at the TV.

At first, she didn't know what to make of the scene that everyone was watching so intently. It looked like some disaster movie. There were a lot of people in the street covered in a black substance. They didn't seem to know where to go, and there was a lot of confusion. The video feed switched to a scene of a plane crashing into a tall building. It was obviously the New York skyline as the photographer at one point switched the focus to the Statue of Liberty and then to another shot of a second plane crashing into another building.

She didn't remember seeing anything about a new movie of that sort recently and wondered why so many people were standing around watching television when there was so much work to be done.

Sandi paused for a moment and watched. It was so realistic.

Smoke and flames were everywhere. People covered with gray ash ran between the tall buildings, as huge billows of smoke blackened the sky!

Everyone looked shocked and terrified. Some were crying, some were coughing and rubbing soot from their faces. Everyone was hurrying as quickly as they could go, trying to get away from the disaster.

As Sandi looked around, she began to realize this was not a movie. Every person that could stand on their own was watching the events unfold, with looks of horror and disbelief on their faces. Not one of them said a word or smiled, and as reality began to register, she heard the newscaster's voice.

This was a real news program. The people on the screen were actually running for their lives, some with their clothing in flames. People were jumping from windows several stories above the ground! It was a horrible, devastating scene.

Sandi wanted to believe that she was having a nightmare, but as she joined the group and began to listen, she realized that this was all too real.

The reporter repeated what he had said only moments before. He said our own planes had been hijacked with hundreds of passengers aboard and crashed into the twin towers of the World Trade Center where thousands of people were reporting for their daily shifts. There were other planes still unaccounted for; no one yet knew who was responsible for hijacking the planes or why this was happening.

"Oh, my dear God!" A voice beside her spoke as the first of the two towers began to collapse. There was a collective gasp as the tower crumbled to the ground! Sandi felt like she was going to be sick. No one seemed to know what to do. Barb, the night nurse and Sandi's friend, touched her on the arm. "Are you all right, Sandi?"

Sandi's face was chalk white. Her hand was clasped tightly over her mouth. It took a few moments to realize that Barb was speaking to her and looking at her with concern.

"Oh, Barb! What is happening? This is so terrible." Her voice trailed off, and after a few seconds, she said. "Oh, my! Lou Ellen needed these linens. I have to get them to her. I need to get home and see if the girls are all right." Sandi left Barb standing with the others and hurried down the hall.

Workers were pushing wheelchairs and escorting the residents back to their rooms after the morning meal.

Others were standing in small groups talking quietly. Everyone was discussing the events unfolding in New York City and other parts of our country. Everyone dreaded what might happen next.

The next hour seemed more like a week. Sandi had called and talked to Joletta, but the only thing she could think of was getting home. She needed to see her girls and know they were safe. She knew the terrible things that were happening were many miles away, but Sandi felt the primal urge of a mother to protect her children and to hold them in her arms, and she needed to talk to Jim. She wanted him to hold her and reassure her that she was safe and that he would take care of her.

Sandi punched out at 11:00 and walked into the bright September sunshine. The air was cool, and the sky was brilliant blue without a cloud to be seen. She took a deep breath as she walked to the parking lot and got into the new Dodge Durango Jim had given her, an early birthday gift after her car had been ruined by the storm only weeks before.

It was just too much. Her life had been going so well, and in a matter of minutes, everything had changed forever.

There were just so many things happening --- first, the storm that had frightened her so badly. For a while, she wasn't sure she and Annie were going to get out with their lives, and then there was Beth after so long – her little sister, coming to tell her about their mother's death.

Now, this! What a horrible thing! Sandi simply could not comprehend it all. So, she did what many other people did on the morning of September 11, 2001. She went home to be with her family.

She was now glad that Joletta had stayed home from school that morning, suffering from a headache. Jim had spent the night at Susan's with the girls, but, would have already left.

Joan, Susan's housekeeper, and friend would be with them now. Sandi needed to get there so Joan could go and be with her own family.

As Sandi drove up to the curb in front of the house, Joletta came running out of the door and down the steps.

"Oh, Mom, did you see? What's going to happen? Oh, Momma, all those people, I don't understand any of it. Why would anyone do something like that?"

Sandi didn't have any answers because she could not understand it herself, but she held her daughter and tried to tell her it would all be alright. Sadly, she was not a bit sure that things would ever be all right again. She was much more frightened right now than she had ever been in her whole life, the uncertainty of their future was more than she could bear.

"Let's go inside and find your little sister. How is your headache? If you feel like it, I think we should just take the morning and go to the park."

"But, Mom, you haven't had any sleep."

"It'll be all right, Sweetheart; all I want to do right now is be with you and Annie. Jim will be here in a couple of hours, and I can lay down for a while then."

Mother and daughter went into the house where they were met with the innocent and blissfully unaware giggles and hugs of the youngest member of their family.

Chapter 25
JILLIANS SURPRISE

A brisk wind whipped Sandi's scarf as she walked from the car to the house with her arms full of groceries for the following week. Autumn was coming to an end, and the holidays were fast approaching, with Thanksgiving just a week away. Sandi and the girls were going to spend Thanksgiving Day with Jim's parents.

Sandi was more than a little nervous about it. She had only met the senior Mr. Benning twice and had never met Jim's stepmother.

Mr. J. R. Benning, who's close friends called him Jay, was a tall good-looking man with a pleasant personality.

Little Annie had taken to him immediately, surprising her mom when she willingly let him hold her. Not only was it the first time she had ever seen him, but she had just woken up. She normally liked to be cuddled by someone she knew and trusted, while making the transition from naptime to playtime.

Gloria Benning, on the other hand, according to Jim, was somewhat of a challenge to get acquainted with. She was younger than her husband by almost a decade and had been married twice before marrying Jim's father.

Although they had now been together for close to 12 years, the marriage had created a distance between father and son that had only recently begun to heal.

Jim still did not feel particularly close to his stepmother, but he wanted Sandi and the girls to meet the family of which they were to become a part.

Thanksgiving dinner was to be a catered affair served at 2 o'clock sharp at the Benning estate and Sandi had no idea what she and the girls were going to wear, much less how to act in such a grand house.

They had been living with Susan for close to four months, and although Susan lived a comfortable life in a beautiful old house, it surely would not compare with the kind of wealth that Jay Benning controlled.

Jim told her to stop worrying so much; he said if Gloria got too full of her high and mighty self, he would talk his father into cutting her out of his will! Of course, he was joking. Jim always thought he was so funny. Sandi just shook her head and kept on worrying.

The phone was ringing as Sandi walked in the door and she reached for it as she put the groceries on the kitchen table.

"Taylor residence."

"Hello, is this Sandi?" the voice at the other end of the phone inquired.

"This is Jillian, Susan's daughter."

"Hello, Jillian. How are you? I'm sorry, but your mom isn't here right now; she had an appointment with the doctor this afternoon. Bill picked her up an hour ago. I'm not really sure what time they will be home. He usually takes her out for lunch after her appointment."

"Oh, that's all right, I can call her later. I wanted to fill her in on our news. I think she'll be happy to hear it. How is she doing anyway?"

"She's so much better, Jillian. The doctor says she will probably be able to get rid of the walker in a few weeks. She is so looking forward to that and says she hopes to give it to the garbage man as a Christmas present."

Jillian laughed. "Does that ever sound like Mother. I do know it has been a challenge for her these past months. By the way Sandi, I just wanted to let you know how much we have appreciated all the time you have spent helping her this last year. All she ever talks about is you and the girls. I am so anxious to meet you. In fact, if you promise not to tell Mom, I'll fill you in on a secret. Bill and Ted don't even know about it yet."

"Oh, Jillian, maybe you should wait to tell your family first. It might hurt their feelings if you tell me before you tell them."

"Oh, don't be silly, I'm just dying to tell someone, and no one will be mad, we don't even have to tell them you knew first if you don't want to."

"Well, it's up to you, I guess then."

"OK. Here it is. Tom and I are being sent back to the States in a few weeks. We will be home for Christmas!"

"Oh, Jillian! Your family is going to be so excited, your mom especially. She has missed you so much. I'm sure that is going to be the best Christmas present you could ever give her."

"That's not everything, Sandi. We have an even bigger surprise for her; I'm just not sure how she is going to react to it when I tell her. We have adopted three little boys. We will be bringing them home with us!"

"Oh, really? Oh, my goodness! That really is wonderful news! Oh, Jillian, I knew you should not have told me first. You had better tell them soon because it's going to be hard to keep quiet. Seriously though, that is just so wonderful! Your mother is going to be thrilled when she finds out. Do you know yet when you'll be arriving?"

"I'm not absolutely sure, but, if everything goes according to schedule, we should be leaving Johannesburg on the 18th of December. Tell Mom I will call her later this evening, OK?"

"Oh, Sandi it was good to talk with you, and thanks for listening. You don't know how much I needed to tell someone."

Sandi hung up the phone with a smile on her face. What a wonderful day it was! Not only was Susan's daughter coming home after being away so long, but she was bringing her husband and three brand new grandchildren along with her!

Sandi had no doubt that they would be welcomed into the family as if they had always been there.

After all, she and her girls had once been all alone. Susan had taken them under her wing, making them feel they belonged when there had been absolutely no family connection at all.

Chapter 26
EXTENDED FAMILY

Thanksgiving Day arrived, and Sandi and the girls were almost ready when Jim pulled up to the curb outside of Susan's house.

Sandi was wearing the ice blue sweater that Susan had gotten her for her 31st birthday last month and navy-blue dress pants. Around her neck, she wore a diamond pendant that had belonged to Jim's mother.

She still could not believe they were actually going to become a part of the Benning family.

Joletta and Annie looked so pretty in the new dresses Sandi had bought them a few days before. Sandi wanted them to look their very best today, and even though she had spent more than originally planned, she decided it had been worth every penny of it.

At first, Joletta argued that she did not want to wear a dress. She insisted that jeans and a sweater would be fine, but she eventually agreed to go with her mom shopping, as long as she got to help choose.

It had taken them awhile before they both agreed on one that suited mom and daughter both. But now, as Jo came down the stairs, you could see both the sweet little girl and the beautiful young woman she was becoming.

Little Annie, even without the frilly holiday dress, could melt the hearts of just about everyone. Even the coolest of Sandi's acquaintances soon fell victim to her sunny personality.

Hopefully Jim's stepmother would be equally charmed by Sandi's daughters.

She was excited and nervous about the day ahead, but she also knew that to Jim, it would make no difference in the way he felt about her. Whether his stepmother was impressed or not, he loved her and her girls just as they were.

As Jim stepped in the door, he let out a long, low whistle as he pulled her to him.

"Hey, Sexy Lady, how about you and I, and these lovely young things take a little trip to the country? I know an elegant place where we can dine on roast pheasant and caviar."

"Jim! Will you never quit with your silliness? I am so nervous, and all you can do is joke!"

He held her at arm's length and smiled. "Oh, Shivers, how can I convince you there is nothing to be worried about? Dad already has told me he thinks you are something special and, well, you'll see. Gloria doesn't bite. She is just a bit stiff, if you know what I mean."

Laughing once again, he kissed her hard on the lips and ran his hand down the length of her back, ending with a solid smack on her backside.

Turning to Joletta, he said, "Jo, if you get any prettier, your mom is going to have to lock you up in a closet."

Joletta blushed and giggled.

"By the way, Dad's brother Cliff and his family are going to be there today. I think you will like them. Do you remember me telling you about the twins, Jo? They're just a year older than you. Anyway, Tim and Tammy are a lot of fun. They are always pulling something."

"Last year at Christmas they put a rubber snake on Gloria's plate just before we sat down to eat! Talk about a ruckus! I'm not sure that she has forgiven them yet. I'm shocked she is letting them within 50 miles of the place!"

"By the way, Joletta, Dad said to tell you to bring some riding clothes. The twins keep their horses stabled on the ranch, and after we eat, you kids can go out and ride awhile if you want. I told him how much you enjoyed horseback riding last summer at camp. You can ride either Lady Love or Golden Boy."

"Oh, Mom, could I? Please!" Joletta was practically jumping up and down in her excitement.

"I don't know, Joletta." She paused and looked at Jim. "If Jim thinks it is safe, I guess it would be all right!"

"Sandi, Dad has had Golden Boy for longer than he's had Gloria, and Lady is the sweetest little mare on the property. Even Annie could ride her without a problem.

Jim had the usual twinkle in his eye and Sandi gave him a warning look

"Annie is definitely not ready to start riding yet, so don't get any big ideas."

"I rode Golden Boy a lot before I went to college, but I don't think he's ridden very much now. Old Mac, our stable keeper, puts him out daily, but, I'm sure he would love having a young person to exercise him."

"Tim and Tammy come out to Dad's on weekends in the summer and ride quite frequently."

"Oh, Mom, that sounds like so much fun."

If Joletta had not been fully enthusiastic about this Thanksgiving before, she had now done a complete 360-degree turn around.

"I'll go and get some things together, Mom." Joletta whirled around and danced all the way up the worn staircase before disappearing along the upper hallway.

"Don't forget to bring a heavy jacket and your high tops! It's only 40 degrees out there," Sandi called after her daughter and shook her head.

"I hope she doesn't catch her death of pneumonia."

There were almost 30 of Jim's extended family in attendance, and though things were more formal than it was at home, everyone was warm and friendly.

Sandi believed that the day had gone well.

At first, she had felt quite uncomfortable, fearing she and the girls might not fit in, but as the afternoon passed without incident, she relaxed and began to enjoy herself.

138

Gloria was kind and gracious. Obviously not new to the job, she was an accomplished hostess, keeping her guests happy and occupied.

She was a truly beautiful woman. Slim and graceful, she looked stunning in her royal blue satin top, and tight black leggings. Her dark shining hair was pulled back on one side with a diamond-studded comb.

Before the day was over, Sandi decided that she liked the woman. At first, Gloria did come across as somewhat aloof, but after having the chance to get better acquainted, Sandi realized that perhaps she had judged too quickly.

Another thing Sandi observed was the gentle way Jim's father treated his wife. There was obviously much love between the two of them.

As Jim drove them home later that evening, snow began to fall, fast and thick, and soon they were driving in a world of pure glistening white.

With both the baby and the big girl sound asleep in the back seat, Jim and Sandi drove silently through the dark swirling wonderland.

What a wonderful way to end the day.

They pulled into the drive of Susan's house, and Jim put the car in park, keeping the engine running.

Pulling Sandi close, he whispered in her ear, "I love you, and I want you to be my wife." He reached into the pocket of his pants and drew out a small velvet box. Inside was a beautiful solitaire diamond ring. "This was my mother's. My precious Sandi, please say that you will be mine forever."

Large tears rolled down her face as he slipped the ring onto her finger, making their engagement official.

"Oh, my Darling, I love you so much. It is beautiful, and yes, I so want to belong to no one else."

Chapter 27
A FAMILY AFFAIR

Jillian and Tom's plane was due to arrive in less than two hours, and Susan was impatient to get there, but today the traffic had a mind of its own. Of course, it didn't help that the east coast weather was horrible, or that their arrival time was at the height of rush hour.

It seemed like they would never get to the airport.

She was not usually a person that let things get on her nerves, but today was special, and she was anxious to be there the minute they stepped off the ramp.

Of course, Ted had factored in time for the extra traffic and road hazards, but it was hard to be patient. Her children were finally going to be home again, and with them would be the three beautiful little darlings who were now her own grandchildren.

She had only recently received a picture of Tom, Jill, and the children in front of a small house with a thatched roof. It had served as their home for the past two years.

The photo was only a snapshot and not a very good one at that. The two toddlers had short-cropped hair and large dark eyes; they were each wearing a brightly colored scarf that wrapped around the middle of their bodies. Standing close to Tom, the little boys looked very serious. Jillian held a tiny sleeping baby.

The young mother looked exhausted but had a wide smile on her face. Tom was watching his wife and the three little ones, with a look of protective love. He was also smiling.

It thrilled Samantha and Tiffany when they were told they had permission to go with their grandmother and Uncle Ted to the airport. They had not seen their aunt and uncle for almost three years, but their excitement was mostly because of the three little boys that were now their new cousins!

Living in a community that was predominately white, the girls really had never known anyone that was black.

Once when Samantha was younger, a man had come to see their daddy and brought his little girl with him. She was about the same age as Sammy, and they played while the grownups conducted their business.

They had a good time playing together and later that day a tired Samantha cried when her momma wouldn't fix her hair the same way as the other little girl.

"Mommy," she begged. "She has so many pretty ribbons and ponytail holders."

She did not even remember the little girl's name anymore, but she would never forget how much she wanted to have braids and ponytails.

That was the only time she ever remembered playing with a child that was not white, like her family.

She wondered if it would be OK to ask her new cousins questions because they were family.

"Of course, they were little boys and "practically babies at that," so she guessed they wouldn't be able to tell her much anyway.

Her grandmother patted her on the knee. "I'm so glad you got to come with us today, Sweetie. It won't be long now. We are almost there."

"Look, another plane is coming in. Maybe that is the one they are on!"

"Grandma!" Tiffany laughed from her seat in the front of the car. "You know it is still almost a half-hour before they will get here."

Susan laughed back. "Well, I was hoping it would get here early."

"Right! A few minutes ago, you were worried about us being late!"

The four of them walked through the airport's revolving doors, and Ted looked at the flight schedule on the large lighted billboard above their heads. It listed names of airlines and cities in rows, with flashing lights that were constantly changing planes' times and status, according to whatever was currently going on, and where each one was coming from or heading to.

"It looks like it's running about 10 minutes behind schedule, so we should have enough time to go and get something to drink or to take a bathroom break if you need to, and then we'll wait by the baggage area. They will be coming down that escalator to pick up their luggage, but since they are arriving from another country, they will have to go through customs, so it may take a while."

Since Ted traveled a lot, he knew just where to go and what to do when it came to navigating around large airports. Susan, on the other hand, would not have had a clue where to start. It had been many years since she had gone anywhere outside of her home State. She was glad to have raised a family that had knowledge and confidence when it came to complicated places and situations.

As far as she was concerned, there was plenty of excitement, much more than she needed at times, right here where she had spent the major part of her life. She had always been a homebody. Even as a young woman before her husband died, she preferred to stay close to home.

Finally, the anticipated announcement came over the airport speaker. "Flight 1434 will be arriving at gate 3, in 5 minutes."

First, they saw their Uncle Tom with one little boy on each hip and then Aunt Jillian walking slightly behind carrying a small bundle in a blue blanket.

"Aunt Jill-O! Uncle Tom! It's us! We're over here!"

Sammy was jumping up and down and waving her arms wildly. As soon as Tom and Jill stepped off the escalator, she gleefully ran to them with the others not far behind.

Jill laughed aloud as Uncle Tom knelt and sat two little boys down on the highly polished floor, and her family surrounded them and immediately smothered them in long-awaited hugs.

The children had beautiful dark skin and wide brown eyes rimmed with thick black lashes. The older of the two looked up at his father then back again at these noisy people. He put several of his fingers into his mouth and leaned his head against Tom's pant leg, waiting and observing everything while the smaller boy began to cry, and reached out to be held in the safe arms of his new "Da."

"Let me see. Let me see!" An excited Samantha, who had now seen two of her new cousins, was now determined to see the baby that Aunt Jillian was holding.

"Sam! You need to be patient," her dad scolded. "Let them breathe." He sounded stern, but not one in the group could really blame her.

Everyone wanted to see the tiny new members of their growing clan. No one could stop smiling.

"It's OK. Honey, if you give them a little time. They will get used to everyone," Jill spoke kindly. "You have to remember that everything here is new and different; they are tired, and it is going to take some time."

Tom and Jillian were exhausted. The fact was they were still new parents and adjusting to, not one baby, but three children. Flying many hours with babies that had been traumatized was not an easy undertaking. Jabral and Omari were restless and cried frequently, not understanding what was going on and why they were in this strange place.

Luckily, the baby Ajani was happy as long as he was given his bottle regularly. Every one of them was suffering from time and climate changes.

It was hard to know how to comfort the little ones. So, Jillian and Tom just held them close and talked or sang softly to them in the language of their heritage.

They were so grateful that no one on the plane complained; the other passengers and attendants were kind and helpful. It renewed the faith of the tired parents when a seatmate offered to hold the baby and feed him. The flight steward warmed his bottles and brought small treats to the older boys, and another young mother several seats away shared the small toys she had brought for her own little one.

The next evening sitting in Susan's living room, Jillian and Tom told them the children's story.

It had been only three months ago that these little boys had been brought to them. Tom told the family, "Their grandfather walked with these children for miles before he got to the mission. He came to us after he was told that we could help him. When he realized that we did not have an operating orphanage, he begged Jillian to take the boys and "love them as her own."

"His daughter had died only a few days after the baby was born. Their father had died recently, and they have no living grandmothers or aunts to care for them."

"Jabral is three, and Omari is two, and they are doing well, but we have been very worried about Ajani, he was so tiny and sick when he came to us." Jillian's voice was sad. "We were so afraid he would die."

"This only goes to show how urgent the need is, for a place where these little ones can be properly cared for. There are so many of them. Alone, hungry, sick and without love."

"It's no wonder so many die so young."

Tom continued the story. "Jillian could not refuse the old man's pleas. No one in their village could feed them, so the men of the village encouraged their grandfather to bring them to us. Somehow, they knew that we were building an orphan home, but although we had not

144

officially opened, that made little difference to them. They believed we would take them, and Jillian believed that it was God's hand that sent these desperate people to us. There was no other plan, and it was meant to be."

"Once we agreed, the grandfather gave little Ajani to Jill, and they left."

"We couldn't send them back. The baby would have died!" Jill's voice broke.

Tom reached over, putting his arm around his wife's shoulder. "It is OK, Hon, they are safe now."

"Poor Jillian, although we both always wanted children of our own, and had pretty much accepted that God had other plans for us, we thought once we got the funding settled for building the orphanage, things would progress from there."

"We certainly never thought we would get children before we had an orphanage!"

Not only were the children a full-time responsibility, the littlest was very sick, weak and needed constant attention. They had to go all the way to Johannesburg in order to see a pediatrician and get a special formula to help meet his nutritional needs. When the doctor examined Ajani, he discovered what appeared to be a possible problem with his heart. If further testing confirmed his suspicions, he would need treatment by specialists.

Of course, they knew there were many other children with unmet needs, but, at least for now, she must focus on these three God-given miracles. She needed to see that these little ones were taken care of.

The women of their village did their best to help Jillian, teaching her about caring for the baby, and sharing what little they had. One family even brought them a skinny goat so they would have fresh milk for the children.

The women were glad that they now were able to be of some help to these wonderful people. They were grateful for "Pastor" Tom and his sweet wife, who had come to teach them of Jesus who died on a cross for our sins. Many had been amazed to find out that God loves all people, no matter where they are or what they have done in the past.

After a very long month of soul-searching, Jillian and Tom decided that they should return to the States for a time. They hoped they could resolve the children's physical needs while there. Ajani was not gaining weight, and the pediatrician felt he needed to see a heart specialist as soon as possible.

Arrangements were made as quickly as possible with Mission headquarters to arrange a replacement for Tom, and they were then ready to make the long trip back to their homeland.

While they were in America, they planned to see a cardiologist for Ajani. Also, they needed to consult an orthopedist for Jabral. The Lord had been good to them, and the baby now was healthy and happy.

They were looking forward to attending their home church, and it had been a long while since they had seen many of their friends.

They were also hoping this would be the right time to raise money, and recruit workers willing to go to Africa when work was to begin on the orphanage that they had been praying about for so long.

Chapter 28
SONG OF SPRING

Joletta stood looking out of what would be the window of her bedroom. Not that it was a bedroom yet. It was actually only an unfinished floor surrounded with framework with a partially completed roof above it.

The room was large, nearly 15-foot-wide and 12-foot-deep. She would even have her own bathroom connected to the room and a closet that looked almost as big as the bedroom they had all shared in at the little duplex across from Susan's.

Of course, since the storm had destroyed that house, her family had all been living with Susan. Although that house was much bigger than the apartment, it was old and had small closets and only one full bathroom. There was also a half bath, which helped, but in comparison, this house felt like a mansion.

For Jo, it was not going to be easy. It was somewhat sad moving away from Summerset Hills. She had made friends that she would miss after she moved, and she would miss some of her school activities. In the past she had never participated in any of the "extras" at school because of their frequent moves, but her friend Tina had encouraged her to try out for a part in the school play. It did not take very long until she realized how much she enjoyed it. She had always loved music but found it exciting to see how everything, the script, music, costuming, set, and acting, all fit together.

She would especially miss seeing Tina and all the things they did together. She and Tina were best friends and had spent a lot of time with each other, especially in the past several months. It was easier since Grandma Susan (as they now called her) had taken on much more of the responsibility for Annie.

Tina's brother Jacob had even been flirting with her the past few weeks, but so far, she had totally ignored him. He used to tease her about playing with Barbie dolls, and she still got mad when she thought of it. *He thinks he's so big now. Let him flirt,* she thought to herself. Actually, she was enjoying his attention immensely, but she wasn't about to let him know! She hated to admit it, but she was going to miss him too!

They had come out to the worksite today because Jim wanted to check on the progress the carpenters had made in the past couple of weeks. The early spring weather finally seemed to be behind them, and now that the ground was dryer, he said things should start moving along.

It shouldn't be too many weeks now before they would be making final decisions about paint colors and furniture, curtains and all the other details that had to take place before they could move in.

Jim and Sandi had decided to have the house built rather than looking for a pre-built home. That way, all of them would have a say in the design and specifics that would make it special for them.

It was getting closer to the wedding, and the plan was to have everything completed so they all could move directly into the house when they returned from their honeymoon.

Jo and Annie were going to be staying for several weeks with Bill and Mary's family and would remain until Jim and Sandi had gotten back from their trip and had the main area put together and in livable order.

At this point, there wasn't much there except the exterior walls and some of the interior framework indicating where each of the living areas were to be. It was going to be a very busy place for the next couple of months.

It promised to be a beautiful house. The living room, kitchen, dining room, office, and master suite were on the ground floor, with three bedrooms and a library upstairs. There was also a large family room and utility room in the finished basement. It had 3 ½ baths and would have walk-in closets in both the master bedroom and Jo's room. A covered patio area created the floor for a large balcony connected to the upstairs library.

Joletta's window faced a large pond, and there was a thickly wooded area behind that. The property that the woods were on did not belong to them but was conservation land so would never be available for building purposes of any kind but would remain wild and beautiful.

Jim told her that after they got settled in, he would have a barn built in the side pasture. Jim's father had said when the building was ready for use, he would have Golden Boy brought to live with them. The horse had always been Jim's, and since Joletta enjoyed riding, he felt it would be good for both the horse and his new granddaughter.

For Annie, there was to be a new puppy as soon as Sassy, one of J.R.'s prize-winning golden retrievers, had her litter in a few weeks.

Both Jo and Annie would have their own rooms, and the fourth bedroom would be for guests or perhaps someday for the extra child Jim hoped he could persuade Sandi to have. He said he wanted a little brother for Jo and Annie. Of course, what he really wanted was a little boy for himself! Sandi said she was not ready to make that decision. They would have to wait until things calmed and then they would talk about it more.

The wedding was to be on July 12, exactly 2 years since Sandi and the girls had first walked into Jim's office. It felt like it was only yesterday, and it felt like a lifetime ago.

There would only be four attendants. Jim's closest friend from college was to be the best man. Beth was serving as matron of honor with Joletta as bridesmaid and Annie would serve as "little bridesmaid."

The plans were already in high gear. Mom said she didn't want anything too elaborate but had agreed to have it at the Benning Estate. Gloria had hired a professional wedding planner who was making all of the arrangements and seeing to all the little details. It was going to be a challenge keeping Gloria and Monica from getting too carried away. They neither one seemed to understand what a simple wedding was.

It was to be held in Gloria's lovely rose garden behind the main house. There were benches and beautiful walkways as well as a large lighted fountain that would be a perfect setting later in the evening

Sandi had asked her to promise and keep her guest list to 50 or less, and there would be at least another 40 or so guests that were family and friends of Sandi and the girls. She was not comfortable in crowds and to be the center of attention absolutely petrified her.

It still seemed strange to Sandi and Joletta that they were to become a part of the Benning family. This was "a rags to riches" story that topped even her favorite childhood fairy-tale, Cinderella. Not ever, even in her wildest dreams, had she ever come close to thinking she would ever fall in love and marry a man who would someday be one of the wealthiest people in the country.

She worried that she would not know how to act around the people in this world that she knew little about. She didn't know how to dress or talk or even use the right fork at the dinner table. She didn't want to embarrass anyone, especially her fiancé'.

Not that anyone had said anything her to make her feel that way. It had now been several months since she had been introduced to Jim's dad and Gloria, and they had spoken nothing but kind words to her. Still, it was a long way from where she had started, and she still felt like she was walking on shaky ground when the family was together.

No one that did not know already would have ever guessed that he had money. Jim was a very down to earth person and a hard worker. He did not discuss finances with the majority of his friends. He felt his finances were not anyone's business but his own, and now, of course, Sandi's, and he preferred to make his own way. He had somehow been able to separate general friends and business friends.

There was plenty of money to be had but, only on occasion, had he used any of the generous allowances that came from the trust fund left by his mother. He also owned stock in his father's company, which, up to this point, had never been touched. His father had once hoped he would join him in the business but, until now, Jim had shown very little interest.

Since he would be returning to college to complete his teaching degree and was at the same time acquiring a family, at least for the time being, he planned to use some of the cash that had been building equity since he had turned 18, almost 20 years ago.

It would give them options that he had never accessed, and that Sandi had not ever known existed.

Sandi would now have the choice of working or staying at home with Annie and Jo. She could buy clothing from retail stores instead of the thrift shops and did not have to worry about the cost of groceries. She could even afford to have her hair and nails done professionally for the first time in her life. Not that she necessarily wanted someone else telling her how to dress or wear her hair. She was determined that she would never forget where she came from and not ever let the fact that they were now financially in a far better place change who she was on the inside.

Gloria did have a weekend planned for them to go into the city and do some shopping. Jim had been telling Sandi for weeks that she should go on a shopping spree, but, so far, she was still wearing the same jeans and casual shirts as always. It was going to be hard to go from the bargain basement to shopping the best stores on the strip, so to say.

She would be giving up her job at the nursing home and would miss all the friends she had made there, but even if she had wanted to continue, it was much too far to drive. The property that was soon to be her home was close to an hour's drive away.

She was still undecided as to what she would do in the long run, but for right now she would stay home with the girls. They were growing up so fast. Too fast, as far as their mother was concerned. It seemed only a moment ago that Jo had been a tiny baby, but she had now grown tall and slender and was looking more and more like a young woman instead of the sweet child she had held in her arms so long ago. And then there was little Annie, now talking up a storm and getting into everything, she never stopped for long. She was like a happy little whirlwind spinning around in joyous circles. Sandi knew this one was not like her older sister, who had been quiet and thoughtful from the beginning. This one was already quite the" tiny tomboy" with rosy cheeks and wide blue eyes.

The property that the house was being built on was an early wedding gift from Jim's father and Gloria. There were almost 20 acres of beautiful, green, softly rolling land that was only a few short miles from the family estate. "Just far enough," Jim's dad had said, with a grin, "that we won't be sticking our noses into each other's business!"

"What are you thinking about, Sweetie?" Sandi came into the room and stood behind Joletta.

"I don't know exactly. I guess, just about how much our lives have changed in the last two years. It all seems so unreal."

"I know, I think the same thing sometimes. I have a hard time believing it myself. This is going to be such a beautiful house, don't you think?"

"Yeah, but Mom, are you sure this isn't just another dream?"

"Is what a dream?" Jim came into the room carrying Annie on his shoulders, her very favorite place these days.

"Joletta is afraid this is all just a dream, and she will wake up, and it will be gone."

Jim swung Annie down from his shoulders and encircled the three of them in his strong arms.

"You bet your bottom dollar this is a dream, Joletta! But there is a difference with this dream. In this dream, you don't have to wake up. You are already awake and, you have my word, you never have to worry about it disappearing."

"THIS DREAM IS HERE TO STAY!"

DREAM RIVER, CARRY ME HOME

THE JOURNEY CONTINUES

KAREN CRAKER FORESTER

WHOEVER HAS MY COMMANDS AND KEEPS THEM

IS THE ONE WHO LOVES ME,

THE ONE WHO LOVES ME

WILL BE LOVED BY MY FATHER,

AND I TOO WILL LOVE THEM,

AND SHOW MYSELF TO THEM

JOHN 14:21

NIV

278

Contents

Chapter 1
TO YOU MY HEART I GIVE

Sandi woke to the sound of a gentle knock on the bedroom door. The sun was streaming through the sheer curtains, and it took her several seconds to realize where she was. She sat up and smiled to herself.

She had come to believe this day would never happen... most of her adult life had been a series of bad relationships, troubles, and harsh realities. Had it not been for her girls, she would have given up long ago. But now things were very different. Today, she would give her heart to the one man who would hold it tightly and never let it go! This was her wedding day!

Shivering slightly at the thought, she responded to the knock on her bedroom door. "Yes? Who is it?"

The door opened a little and Gloria peeked into the room. "Are you awake, Dear? I've brought you some breakfast."

"Oh, Gloria. That is so sweet of you. You didn't need to do that." Sandi sat up and swung around preparing to get out of bed as Jim's stepmother came into the room with a tray filled with food.

"I knew you wanted to be up early, and I thought you might want a little something to eat before everything gets too busy."

Sandi stretched luxuriantly and smiled. "Oh, Gloria, I just can't believe that it is finally here. It looks like it's going to be such a beautiful day."

Gloria smiled as she poured a cup of coffee from the carafe and handed it to Sandi. "I think it is about as perfect as a wedding day can be, as long as the groom shows up and remembers to bring the ring. I think it should all work out," she said with a twinkle in her eye.

"In case I forget to say it, Gloria, thank you for everything. You and Jim's dad have been so wonderful. You will never know how much we appreciate it all."

"You are very welcome. Now Darling, there is too much to do today for us to sit here and get all sentimental. We have enjoyed every minute of it. You had better eat a little bit and get yourself into a bubble bath. The girls will be here soon to do your hair and help you get dressed."

"Where is Annie? I didn't hear her this morning. Is she still sleeping?"

"No, no. She has been up for an hour already. She is having breakfast in the study with James. It seems he has fallen victim to the charms of your little princess."

They both laughed. "Well, I hope she doesn't create any problems; she can be a handful at times. Mary and the girls should be here by about 10:00, and they can take her off your hands when they arrive."

"Don't you worry yourself, Dear. She is well looked after. James is really eating up all the attention. It has been a very long time since there were any small children in this house. She is like a bright ray of sunshine. Now I will get out of here so you can have a little time to yourself. Let me know if you need anything." Leaning over she gave Sandi a gentle kiss on the cheek. "I am so glad Jim found you. You are going to make a beautiful bride and" ---Gloria hesitated slightly--- "I'm happy to have your friendship."

After Gloria left, Sandi walked over to the window, pulling the curtain to the side as she looked out. The big house was more than 100 years old. Built by Jim's great-grandfather around 1894, it would someday pass to Jim.

The main section faced to the east and had a scenic mountain view. Two large wings had been added a few years later, one with a south view and one looking to the north. It formed a large "U" shape which wrapped around the central courtyard at the back of the house. Gloria's

157

gardens were there as well as a large fountain and the swimming pool beyond that.

There were several people busily setting up rows of chairs in a huge canvas tent that had been erected, where the reception would be held later that evening. Colorful flowers were everywhere. The roses were blooming on either side of the twisting pathway which was beautifully festooned with garlands of flowers and many yards of tulle, wrapped and draped, softly floating in the summer breeze. Huge fluffy clouds floated in a brilliant blue sky.

More tulle was being wrapped by the decorators as they completed adorning the white metal archway where she and Jim would stand and say their vows. Sandi twirled around the room hugging herself. "It is really happening!" She laughed aloud, and as she did, the door flew open and a joyful bundle of excitement came running into her arms.

"Mommy! Annie loves you!"

"Mommy loves you too, Sweetheart! Ever so much! I thought you were having breakfast."

"I 'ready did. I want my new dress!"

"Not quite yet, Sweetie; it isn't time yet. Grandma Susan and the girls are going to help you a little later."

"No, Mommy, no! Annie wants new dress! Now!"

"Annie will have to wait. See, Mommy hasn't put on her new dress yet either."

"'K, I wait. Annie gonna' be pretty!"

Sandi's soon-to-be father-in-law came to the door and watched the interaction between mother and child. "I'm so sorry, Sandi; I turned around and she was gone. I'm not quite used to keeping up with one with this much energy!"

He smiled as he observed how much the two were alike, from the curls that refused to be tamed to the upturned noses and blue eyes. Unlike his Gloria and young Joletta, most people would

158

not necessarily think of Sandi as beautiful. Appealing perhaps would be a better word. This woman, however, had a beauty that radiated somehow from within. Her little one already had a draw that was hard for anyone to resist.

"Come with me, Annie, and I will take you for that walk I promised."

"You don't have to, you know. She can stay here with me."

"No! Want to go with Gam-pa! I want to see the horsies!"

"I don't mind at all. You'll need this time to get ready. Anyway, I promised Gloria I would help and this is the job I would most enjoy doing," he said with a smile. "Maybe it will keep us both out of trouble for a little while."

"Gam-pa, is it?" She sat the little girl down and patted her backside. "Go and walk with Gam-pa then." She looked at the clock and realized she had better get into her bath, or she would end up being late... It was definitely time for her to get started; Mary planned to be there by 9:00. The girls planned to bathe before coming, but there was still much to do before one o'clock. Jim and his friend Jay, who was to be best man, arrived shortly after 11:00. There was a lunch buffet already set up in the kitchen with fruit and bagels so anyone that arrived early could enjoy a light meal.

The girls were all having a wonderful time doing make-up and hair.

Sandi had been pampered and powdered and was now glad to sit for a moment and rest.

The musicians had arrived and the caterers were setting up the many things needed for the reception that would take place after the wedding ceremony was over.

Most of the family and close friends had already arrived, and "Gam-pa" had apparently done his job well, because little Annie had crawled onto a couch and was already napping, a good thing for it would be a long busy day.

Beth was the only one expected that was still missing. Her plane was scheduled to arrive at 11:30 and although it would be a bit of a rush for her to be ready, this was the best she could do. Because of her work schedule she had not been able arrange an anything earlier. One of Gloria's friends had offered to pick her up and was now on the way to the airport.

With only another hour to wait, Susan came to Sandi's room. Sandi held out her arms and held her dear friend close to her. "Thanks so very much for coming, Susan. I was hoping to talk with you for a few minutes before the ceremony."

"How do you think I look?" She twirled around in front of the older woman like a little girl wearing her first Easter dress.

"You are just breath-taking, Darling. I can't imagine a more beautiful bride. I am so happy for you. For all of you, of course. You don't know how much I am going to miss you."

"Yes, I think I do. I am going to miss you too. However, remember, we aren't far away. We'll never be far away, Susan. Remember that, OK?"

"Susan, I just wanted to tell you something." Sandi's eyes became soft and moist.

"What is it, Dear? Is everything all right?"

"No, no, I mean---Yes! Everything is fine." Sandi sniffed and laughed. "Susan, I just wanted to tell you how much you have meant, no— *mean* to me. You have treated me like a daughter, and I wanted you to know—"

"Darling, please." She put her hand under Sandi's chin and dabbed away a tear. "I love you and the girls. You never have to thank me, for you have done every bit as much for me as I could ever do for you." Susan was near tears herself. "Look at me! We need to stop this right now. You and all of these giggling girls had

160

better get yourselves out to the tent. It is almost time for things to get started. And I need to go and get seated or there isn't going to be a place for me to sit."

"Don't be silly, you know you are sitting in the front row with Jim's parents and the rest of the family." She gave Susan one last hug as Sandi & Susan's girls circled around laughing and chattering much like a bunch of happy little birds.

Sandi had chosen to wear a creamy-white satin dress with a tight bodice and a full flowing chiffon skirt. It was sleeveless, and the rounded neck and low-cut back were accented with tiny pearl beads. Her hair was pulled up, loose curls falling on her slender neck and around her face. She wore no veil, but a spray of baby's breath and tiny blue forget-me-nots were fastened in the back. She carried a white Bible, a gift from Susan.

Little Annie's dress had a high waist, but otherwise matched her mothers. Susan had pulled her hair into two blond curly pigtails tied up with the same blue flowers and baby's breath as her mother's. Joletta and Beth both wore slim satin dresses the same color of blue as the flowers that were arranged on the Bible Sandi carried.

At exactly two o'clock on Saturday, July 12, 2002, music began to play as a beautiful dark-eyed young woman holding the hand of an adorable little angel with golden curls preceded the lovely, smiling bride down a rose petal-covered pathway into the arms of the man that they all three had fallen deeply in love with.

"Who gives this woman in marriage?"

Jo picked up her little sister and stepped forward. "I am Joletta and this is Annie. We are happy to give our mother Sandi in marriage to Jim. Aren't we, Sissy?"

"Uh-huh! Give Annie's Mommy to Daddy Jim!" She giggled and clapped her hands.

As Joletta stepped back, she kissed her mother's cheek. Annie reached out, and Jim took her with his free arm as he continued to hold Sandi's hand. Sandi indicated to her older daughter to stand close beside them, and the ceremony continued.

"Dearly Beloved, we gather here today---"

After the wedding, Joletta and Annie stayed with Bill and Mary until the first week of August when it was once again time for Joletta and Tiffany to leave for camp. Annie would then be taken to spend a few days with Grandma Susan while Bill, Mary and Samantha made a short trip to the beach.

They were having a great time visiting the Taylor's. The older girls spent most of their time together while Sammy played with Annie and the puppy. Sometimes they went out to the movies or just spent time walking around the neighborhood. Some days they would agree to take Sammy with them, but on other days they did not want a "little girl" tagging along. Usually, they could bribe her out of going by promising to bring her a candy bar or something of the sort.

Once they even told her if she stayed home without whining that she could use their much-coveted nail polish. Other times they would wait until she was busy doing something else. Then they would gleefully sneak off without her. They knew it was rather mean but decided to do it anyway. She had become quite a pest recently and if they so much as spoke to a boy, she would report word-for-word what was said. She had friends of her own; she could just call one of them.

Tiffany had recently gotten her driver's license and the week before camp she and Joletta were allowed to take her mom's car and drive to the mall. It was the first time either of the girls had been given permission to go into the city on their own without adult supervision.

Sandi and Jim returned from their honeymoon the middle of the month, and now school was about to start. Jo was beginning her sophomore year and once again would have to adjust to a different school and new challenges.

Chapter 2
MOTHER MAY I?

"Mom, I need to talk to you about something."
Joletta spoke in a serious voice and as Sandi looked up
from the computer, she noticed Jo holding a letter from
Jillian in her hand.

"What is it, Honey? Is there something wrong?"

"No, Mom, I just wanted to ask you a question."
Joletta paused for a moment and then continued, "Mom,
I want to go—that is, Jillian and Tom have asked me if I
want to come and spend the summer in Africa with
them."

Actually, this was not the first time Sandi had heard
this idea suggested. Last Fall, not long before Jillian and
Tom left to return to Africa, Jill had mentioned that
perhaps Joletta would be interested in coming over and
spending some time helping out with the boys.

Of course, at that time school was only a few days
away, and Sandi had let it go as being just a passing
thought.

"Mom, are you listening?"

"Oh, Jo! Do you have any idea what you are asking?
Africa! Life there is completely different than anything
you have ever known. I don't even know anything about
Africa except what Jillian and Tom told us. Surely you
do not seriously want to go and spend your whole
summer—" Sandi's voice trailed as she saw the look of
desperation in her daughter's eyes.

"Mom! I do! Jillian and I have been writing back and
forth all winter about it, and I've talked to Grandma
Susan and Tiff. Everybody thinks it's a good idea. They
need me, Mom!"

"Jo! If you've talked to "everyone," why haven't you
said anything to me about it? I don't understand. What
exactly have you been writing about?"

164

"Mom, don't you remember me telling you how so many of the people don't even have the basic things they need to stay alive? A lot of people are getting sick and are even dying! There are little children that don't have any family left to take care of them. Jill says that 10 percent of babies die before they even have their first birthday! Mom, it is just awful, and I want to help."

"No, Jo, you are just too young to be going away that far. I hardly know anything about Africa. I know there are places that are not safe, and Tom and Jillian live in a tiny cottage that doesn't even have bedrooms. They don't have room for themselves and those three little boys they adopted. I don't think we could even consider—"

"Mom!! Listen to me!" A look of stubborn defiance and determination was on her face as Joletta spoke through clenched teeth, her dark eyes on the verge of tears. "Mom, I have been praying about this. I have been praying a lot, and I know God wants me to go! I just know it!"

Sandi was at a loss as to what to say. "Jo, you just had your 15th birthday. What about your friends, what about camp? I'm sorry, Darling, but—"

Jo let the letter fall to the floor and ran out the back-door sobbing, "I knew you wouldn't understand! I just knew it!"

Sandi leaned over and slowly picked up the pages and the envelope. Looking at the postmark through tear-filled eyes, she sat in silence. *Now what?* This was not the way she wanted things to be. *Joletta is still far too young to be going off, so far away from home!*

She was still sitting in the office when Jo returned a few minutes later. Her eyes were red, but she now had regained her self-control.

"Mom, I'm sorry. I didn't mean to upset you. It was disrespectful and immature of me to leave like that. I just want you to know how important this is. It is what I want.

I have been thinking about it for a long time and praying really hard. I truly believe God is telling me this is what I am supposed to do."

Sandi sighed as she drew her daughter close to her heart. "But Jo, can't it wait a couple of years."

"No Mom, I don't think it can. Please, please, won't you at least think about it?"

"Don't you think you're getting a little carried away with all this praying and "God stuff," Honey? I know you want to believe in all that, and I am glad if it makes you happy. It's a lot better than some of the thing's kids get into, but I really don't think God usually talks to us. And I still think you are too young to be going so far away."

"You're wrong, Mom. No matter what you think, I know this is something I need to do. If you don't let me go now, I will go later anyway. I am just going to keep on praying and hoping that you will change your mind. You know Mom, God sent Jesus to die for us. It was a horrible way to die, and He did it because he loves us all. His blood was shed on that cross for you and me. All we have to do is believe in Him and ask Him to come into our hearts. God wants us to accept Jesus as our personal Savior."

Sandi did not know how to argue with such sincerity and said nothing more.

"I'm different now, Mom, and I want to do what God is asking of me. It may sound crazy to you but that is how I feel."

Jo walked quietly out of the room and closed the door behind her. As she watched her almost-grown-up daughter leave, Sandi was struck by her solemn dignity.

A nearly forgotten memory came to Sandi's mind. It was the memory of when she and little Annie had huddled alone in that dark closet during the tornado nearly two years ago, and the memory of the gentle whisper in the wind. *Could Joletta be right? Could it really be possible that maybe, sometimes, He does talk to us after all?*

166

It was more than a week before the subject came up again.

Joletta spent the weekend at Susan's house. Tiffany and Samantha were going to be there, and her friend Tina had been invited to spend Saturday night and attend church with them the following morning. Afterwards, the four girls and Susan were coming out to the house as well as Jim's dad and Gloria.

It was a beautiful spring day. Jim was going to put steaks on the grill, and they would be eating outside on the patio for the very first time this season. Sandi and Gloria had spent the preceding weeks happily working in the yard.

Gloria went to the nursery with Sandi and helped her decide how to arrange specific areas for the new flower beds they were planning at Sandi's.

Gloria had taken classes and was a certified "Master Gardener," the gardens at the Benning Estate being the envy of everyone they knew.

For Sandi, it was just a lot of fun picking out which flowers and plants to use. Sandi bought some magazines and read articles on gardening and where the different kinds of flowers would be most likely to grow best.

Sandi never had a yard to garden in before, and she never had the money needed to buy books, plants, fertilizer, mulch and all the other things you need when designing a flower garden. She loved the feel of digging in the loose, moist dirt. She would work for hours and each evening she would come in exhausted, but happy. Planning the gardens also gave her something that she and Gloria could share.

Although Jim had warned her that Gloria could be stuck up, Sandi had been pleasantly surprised and found that she liked her quite a lot. Even so, it was sometimes a strain to find common ground on which to communicate with her.

There were few things they could discuss that they agreed on. Gloria, having been raised with the many privileges of the "well to do," could never quite understand what it was like to struggle just to put food on the table or to buy school clothes for your children. She was amazed when she found out that Sandi shopped at second-hand stores and thought $10.00 was too much to pay for a pair of jeans!

Sandi had never had money and could not understand how someone could spend so casually that the cost was the last thing they thought of, if they thought of it at all.

The flowerbeds were just about finished and with the new patio furniture and planters full of color and greenery, Sandi was excited for everyone to come and see the results of their labor. She was so proud of her beautiful new home and her wonderful new life.

As for Jim, he was just happy to see her happy! No longer did she have the frown lines that so often had appeared on her forehead in the months before their marriage. Now, on most
days, he was more likely to see a smile on her face and even on occasion, he had come home to find her humming or singing oldies along with a cd or the radio.

Chapter 3
THE COOKOUT

Sandi was making a salad when the phone rang. "Hello?"

"Mom, would it be all right if we brought someone else home with us today?" It was Joletta, and she sounded excited.

"Well, I don't know how many extra steaks Jim has, but I suppose it would be all right. I warn you, though, you may end up having to eat hamburgers if we don't have more steaks in the freezer."

"Oh Mom, that would be great. I can eat peanut butter if you want me too!"

"You know, Jo, it would have been better if you had let me know about this earlier. Who is it you are bringing?"

"It's Scotty Randall, Mom. Do you remember? He was the missionary that filled in for Tom when they were home last winter. He spoke during church and came in and talked to the youth group. It was so exciting, Mom; he told us all about the mission and the new orphanage they are building!"

Sandi swallowed a large lump in her throat, wishing she could take back the invitation, but it was already too late.

"Mom, are you still there? That's the reason he was here today. He was picking up a check, and some Bibles, and supplies that he will take back to the Mission a little later this month."

"Mom, I have something else to tell you when I get home." She hesitated and said, "It's a surprise; I hope you will be happy." Without giving Sandi even time to respond, she hung up.

What on earth? Sandi was a little irritated for letting Jo talk her into something that she was not sure would be a good idea. She had never had so much as a serious conversation with a minister. Of course, there were Tom and Jillian, but they were different, kind of like family. However, now Joletta was bringing one home with her.

She and Jim had never talked extensively about religion. He had once told her there had been a time, before his mother died, when he had been a regular churchgoer, but that was years ago. Other than that, she really knew nothing about his feelings about religion.

Well, one way or the other, apparently the preacher was coming to eat with them, and she still needed to mix up her baked beans and get them and the scalloped potatoes into the oven, or there would be no lunch to eat. She figured Susan and the girls invited him, so they could entertain him.

Jim came into the room as she was putting whipped topping on the dessert.

"Are you ready for something to drink?" she inquired, "Joletta called and asked about bringing the missionary that was at today's church service here to eat with us. He is the same young man that was Tom's replacement last winter. I guess he was there this morning to get some things for the Mission."

"I know; I talked to Jo a little bit ago. I told her she needed to check with you first. Oh, and yes, I would like a   glass   of   tea if you have some made."

"O--K, she didn't say she called you. Did she tell you she has a surprise?"

"She did, but I thought she should wait until later to talk to you. She seemed pretty excited about it though. I wasn't sure she would be willing to wait."

"You mean, you know what it is? Tell me? What...?"

He grinned, "No way, that is for you and Jo to talk through. I don't think I want to get in the middle."

"Jim, what is going on? I want to know!"

The doorbell rang, and his dad and Gloria opened the door and stepped inside. "Is there anyone home?"

Jim grinned and winked at Sandi as he headed for the front room to greet his dad and stepmother. "Come on in, Dad, glad you could make it." He shook his dad's hand and reached out and gave Gloria a hug. "Hope you came hungry", he said. "Sandi has been fixing food for hours."

Sandi, who had followed closely behind him, graciously gave her father-in-law a kiss on the cheek and hugged Gloria.

"I'm glad you're here. Everything is about ready except for grilling the steaks. I just put some beans and potatoes into the oven, so we still have a little while before we eat."

"Come on out back and while Jim gets the grill going, we'll walk around so I can show you the rest of the flowers."

For the moment, Sandi let the conversation she was having with Jim drop. She felt like there was a conspiracy or plot of some kind, but for the moment, she gave up on trying to find out exactly what it was. She guessed, correctly, that it would come up again later that day.

Annie woke from her nap just minutes before Susan and the girls drove into the long, paved driveway. An older van pulled in behind them. Printed on its side were the words ---

"Christian International Ministries of Eastern Pennsylvania."

The three older girls got out of the car and after a quick greeting to Sandi, headed into the house and up the stairs. This was the first time Tina had been out to the house and Joletta wanted to show her around. Samantha happily scooped Annie up into her arms and they headed out the back door toward the swing set.

Sandi called after them, "It won't be long before we're ready to eat, girls. Don't be too long."

Susan smiled. "Sandi, we have brought someone for you to meet. Let me introduce you to Scott Randall."

He laughed as he offered her his hand. "Those girls are certainly full of energy."

"I hope it wasn't too much trouble having them," Sandi said to Susan. "Joletta was so excited about them all being together this weekend."

"Oh, Sandi, you know how much I enjoy them. I must admit they have what seems to be an unlimited supply of energy. But we visited awhile and then they were happy to entertain themselves. I actually went to bed about the usual time, but I have no idea when they finally went to sleep. Don't be surprised if they give up early tonight. They may never get up tomorrow unless they get some rest!"

Laughing, they entered the house. "Thanks again, I'm just so glad she has good friends." Sandi led them through the main living area of the house as they went to find the others.

"Let's all go out back. Jim's folks are already here and I think Jim is about ready to get the meat started. It shouldn't be long before things are ready. I hope you like casual dining, Mr. Randall; we are eating outside today."

He laughed again and said, "No problem at all. I just got back to the States the other day. A good American barbeque sounds great. And please, call me Scotty. This is really a nice place you have here."

172

"Thank you so much, Scotty," she said with a smile. "I guess it is a lot different here than some places in the world."

"Jo says that the situation in Africa is really bad," Sandi offered, changing the subject.

"Sadly, she is right. For many it is a daily struggle just to live."

"Aren't there places right here in America where people are in desperate need also? I've often wondered why missionaries are sent to other countries when there is need right here in our own country."

"That is, of course, a question that I've heard before. You are right about the need being great and I am not sure why others make the decisions they do, but, as for me, I just felt it was where God wanted me to go right now and I always try my best to follow what He has planned."

It wasn't long before everyone was seated at the large wicker table, enjoying wonderful food and good conversation.

James and Gloria talked about the plans they had to take a cruise to Alaska later in the summer. Susan told them she was considering moving into a condo downtown closer to Bill and Mary.

Tiffany shared that she and Samantha were going out west to visit their other grandparents for a few weeks and would be attending camp in early August. This would be Tiffany's last year of camp and Samantha's first.

Chapter 4
PASTOR SCOTT

"Joletta tells me that you and Tom are cousins." Jim looked across the table at Scotty Randall who was hungrily devouring the plate-full of food in front of him.

The good-looking young pastor looked up and winked at Jo. "We are, but we aren't a bit alike, other than our good looks and the fact that we both like attention."

Everyone laughed at his attempt at humor. Tom and Scott had very few, if any, physical similarities.

Tom was not unattractive; he was just not what you would call "handsome." He was kind of rough-cut, not very tall with a stocky build, sandy blond hair that looked like it had never been combed, a bushy beard, and green eyes.

Scott was tall and slim, rather elegant looking, with deep chestnut brown hair and eyes to match.

"We are first cousins;" he continued to explain. "My mother and Tom's mom are sisters."

"Tom's parents were also missionaries and the year I was six they were sent to China for a year. Tom came and lived with us so he could finish out the school year and stayed until his folks were able to arrange for him to join them. He was with our family about three months, I think."

"Mom said I really got attached to him that summer. He was 14 that year and she said I pretty much followed him wherever he went. I can still remember him carrying me around on his shoulders. Since then he has always been a kind of mentor to me. I have always looked up to him and have a lot of respect for him."

"Tell them what you told us at church this morning," Joletta requested. "About when you were a teenager and how Tom helped you get out of trouble."

"That's really kind of a long story for dinner table conversation, don't you think."

"No, no," Jim spoke. "We would enjoy hearing your story."

"Well, if you are sure. . ." His listeners nodded and he continued, "As Joletta has already told you, I sat in with the youth this morning and shared with them about my experiences that eventually led me to become a Christian and later, a missionary."

"The class was having a discussion about how we, as Christians, need to take personal responsibility for everything we choose to do."

"I was a young teen, about the same age as some of the kids in class, when I became aware that my parents were having problems in their marriage."

"It started causing a lot of stress in our home and although they never argued much, at least not in front of me, sometimes late at night I would hear the back door shut and the car leaving. Other times I thought I heard Mom crying. I asked several times what was wrong but was always told that everything was all right. I didn't know exactly what was going on but sensed that it was something very serious. There was an almost-palpable feeling of anger hanging over our home. It no longer felt like the safe haven I had known as a younger child."

"I suppose that somehow I was trying to fix things going on by drawing attention to myself, and I started getting into all kinds of trouble. I'm really not quite sure myself what I thought I would gain by it, but, anyway, I was not only causing problems at home but also started getting into trouble and creating problems at school."

"I would talk back to my teachers, purposely not turn in my homework, things like that. Just being generally a smart-aleck and acting like a tough guy. At first, it was mostly little things, but then I started running with a group of very rough kids. They were older and, I thought, wiser. We would hang out at the local pool joint, smoking and flirting with the girls that came around.

A couple of the guys were real good at pool and they would hustle anyone they could, purposely losing and pretending they didn't know anything until they got a good bet on the table. They actually made pretty darn good money sometimes. Problem was, the guys they put the hustle on didn't like it one bit. A couple of times it ended up in a fight in the back alley and got really nasty. One of the guys got cut up pretty bad and about bled to death before they got him to the hospital."

"Well, long story short, it wasn't many weeks before I got arrested for breaking into several cars and stealing things."

"The police officer that picked me up happened to be a guy that had been friends with Tom and knew who I was."

"He took me to the station and called my parents, and because I hadn't been in any trouble like that before, they let me go home. I didn't have to go to juvenile detention or jail, but was put on parole for several months."

"Mom called Tom and asked him if he would come and talk to me. I think by that time they had about decided there was not a lot they could do with me."

"Tom did come, and he did talk to me. He talked to me then and for months after that he would call me just to check how I was doing. I can't say it happened overnight, but he kept in contact with me and helped me understand a lot of things. Mainly, he talked to me about how much God loves us and accepts us for who we are and he helped me realize that just because my parent's marriage was on the rocks, it was not my fault."

"Even though my parents did eventually separate, I finally got myself back on track."

176

"My family had always been churchgoers and I was baptized as a small child, so I already considered myself a Christian."

"I had not attended church for months - I didn't think it was cool - but Tom just kept talking to me about it and praying for me."

"Finally, he helped me realize what it means to be a real Christian. He explained that Jesus cares more about us and loves us more than it is even possible for anyone on earth to ever love."

"We talked about my parents' problems, and we talked about the fact that, at the time, I felt like nobody cared who I was or what I was doing."

"He said that no matter how alone you feel or no matter how many times you mess up or how many mistakes you make, God will always forgive you."

"Jesus died on the cross; He took the sins of the world upon himself and all any of us have to do is ask forgiveness in Jesus' name and ask Him to come into our heart."

"Tom also said that after you have asked Jesus to be your Savior, it doesn't end there. He will help us change, but he wants us to become personally responsible for everything we do. He said there are times we all mess up, but all of us can turn our lives around, if we are only willing to put our lives into Gods Hands. I'm telling you, my friends, to this day, I don't exactly understand why I was willing to listen to Tom. I had pretty much refused to listen to anyone for a long time, but I did ask Jesus to forgive me and after that I have tried my best to do what He expects of me."

Chapter 5
NEWS FLASH

"Isn't that a wonderful story?" Joletta spoke with enthusiasm.

Everyone was quiet for a short time and then Jim said, "Scott, I want to thank you for sharing your story. What a wonderful testimony. It has been a very long time since someone has reminded me of God's love."

Sandi looked at her husband and saw that his eyes were slightly misty.

"Do you think I should I tell them now?" Jo, looking at Jim, spoke quietly, almost shyly. Several at the table looked knowingly at the girl as others turned to her with a questioning look.

"Jo, if you feel like it is right, I would say this is as good a time as any," Jim responded.

"Mom---everybody, I, --- you all know that for the last several months I have been praying and reading the Bible. *Today at church, I got up, and I went and prayed at the altar. I made a commitment to God.*" Sandi was watching her daughter intently as Joletta hesitated.

"I am going to be baptized next week."

Sandi felt like she had been slapped in the face; she looked around the table and felt as if everyone were looking directly at her. She felt they were all waiting for her to respond. She had not been prepared for this. How could Jo put her in this position? A flash of emotion mixed with confusion caused her face to feel suddenly warm. She stood up. "Excuse me, I need to" – she turned and almost ran from the table.

"Mom? Wait, where are you going?"

Susan got up and put her arm around Jo. "It's OK, Honey. She'll be all right. Let me go and talk to her."

"No", Jim spoke, "I will go. Don't worry, Hon, I think it was just a shock."

Jim's dad stood up and cleared his throat. "Well, Jo that is a big decision for a young girl." He patted her back. "I hope it all works out. I think we should give Joletta and her folks some time to talk. Who wants to go for a walk out to the barn? I still haven't seen Golden Boy's new home."

Scott smiled and said, "A walk sounds great after all that food!"

Jo sniffed back tears. "You two can go if you want,"

"You girls go along," Susan said to Tina and Tiffany. "I'm sure Jo will be out soon."

Little Annie and Samantha were already on their way, Annie clinging to her grandfather's hand and Sammy walking beside Pastor Scott.

"Are you coming, Gloria?"

"No, I think I'll stay and start cleaning up a little."

"You can go with them, Susan," Jo said.

"No, no, I am just not up to long walks anymore," Susan replied, "and I want to stay here and talk to you and your mom, too, when she's ready."

"I don't understand. I thought everyone would be happy for me. Why is Mom mad at me?"

"Oh, Jo, I don't think she's mad at you at all. I think she just didn't quite know what to say to you. People who don't know Jesus sometimes don't understand how important it is. She wants what is best for you so I'm sure it will all work out."

"How could you, Jim!" Sandi's voice was filled with both anger and betrayal. "I can't believe you knew all along what was going on, and you didn't breathe a word of it to me! I thought when you were married you weren't supposed to keep secrets!"

"Now, Sandi, you need to calm down. I didn't know anything other than what you and Joletta had told me already, at least not until earlier today. Remember, I told

179

you that she was really excited, and she just wanted to tell someone. So, she told me."

"Well you should have told me then."

"I'm sorry Sandi but I felt it was her news and she should get to tell it. I do admit, I didn't realize she was going to announce it at the table with everyone here."

"Sandi, how do you think she feels right now? She just made what she feels is the most important decision of her life and her mother goes running off and doesn't say one word! What is it, Darling? It isn't a bad thing to believe in God!"

"Oh, Jim! I don't know. It's just that all of a sudden she seems to be so far away from me."

"First she thinks she needs to go all the way to Africa and now this! It feels like they're all plotting against me and they want to take her away!"

"Who are you talking about, Sandi? Susan, Jillian and Tom? God? Sandi, no one is trying to take Joletta away. Have you ever thought that she is just growing up? She wants to do what is right for her. You have taught her to make good decisions and now you need to decide to go out there and tell her how proud you are of what she has decided, whether you agree with her or not."

Sandi leaned her head against his side, and he took her into his arms. "Oh, Jim, I know you're right. I am so sorry. I guess I embarrassed everyone. Did they all leave?"

"I don't think so. Tell you what, I'll go out and tell Jo to come in and talk to you. Then I'll check and see what everyone else is up to. OK?"

A short time later Joletta came to the doorway of Sandi and Jim's master bedroom. "Mom, is everything all right? Can Grandma Susan come in too?"

Sandi was sitting in one of a matched set of soft upholstered chairs that had been turned toward a large arched window, giving them a view of the meadow, which was still covered with the soft fresh green of spring. From this vantage point, she could see the freshly planted flowers along the side of the new stable and she could hear the laughter and voices of her family and friends.

"Of course, Susan can come in too. You are always welcome. Come here sweet girl!"

Sandi held her arms out and Joletta ran into them.

Both were crying as Jo said, "Momma, I'm so sorry; I didn't mean to upset you!"

"I'm sorry too, Jo. I don't know what happened. Honey, it really is all right. I just don't want you to grow up too fast. That's all. I don't know if I'm ready to have a grown-up daughter!"

"Oh, Mom, that is so silly." Jo laughed. "Just because I want to get baptized doesn't mean I am grown up!"

"Are you really sure this is what you want? I mean, I just don't really see the need to join a church. I think you are all right just way you are."

"Mom, it's very important. It isn't just joining a church. That isn't it at all. It's that I want to do what God wants me to do. Mom, *Jesus said that the only way to be saved is to trust in Him. He is the only way that we can connect with God. We have to ask Him for forgiveness and accept Him into our hearts.*"

"I thought you had already done that last winter."

"Well, I did, but now I need to do this. He wants us to be born again."

"I don't understand at all."

Susan put her hand on Sandi's shoulder. "It's OK, Sweetheart. Sometimes, it takes a long time to figure these things out, but God understands everything. He loves us always, even when we don't understand."

"So, is it ok, Mom? For me to be baptized? I really do want you to want it for me."

"If this is what you feel like you need to do, then of course, I do want it. I just want you to be sure, that's all."

"Oh, thank you, Mom! Mom, would it be all right if Susan said a prayer for us? Right now, with just with the three of us here."

"Yes, that would be just fine."

Susan reached out and put her arms around the girl and her mother and prayed. *"Our dear Heavenly Father, we come before you with our heads bowed and our hearts humbled. . ."*

Chapter 6
TELL ME WHY

Later in the evening, after tucking Annie into bed and saying goodnight to Joletta who was watching a program on TV, Sandi and Jim were once again sitting outside on the back patio.

The low western sky still held onto the soft colors of the setting sun, but to the east and above them, an almost surreal deep blue painted the expanse. Soon thousands of sparkling stars would be visible filling the heavens. A single robin dipped down and perched on the trellis only a short distance from them and sang its evening song.

"Jim, after Pastor Scott finished his story this afternoon, it seemed like you were getting kind of emotional. You thanked him for what he said. I'm not sure I understood what you were talking about."

He sat quietly for several moments before he began to speak. "I guess it did get to me a little. Do you remember me telling you that when Mom was still living, we used to attend church? It was just that while Scott was talking about being saved it really brought some of the memories back from when I was younger. It has been a long time since I thought much about the commitment that I made back then to serve God."

"When I was in high school, I loved being part of church. I was very involved and thought I had a lot of faith, but when Mom got sick, everything changed."

"My grandparent's and their family were raised as Southern Baptist; they loved God and never missed church or any church-related activity."

"Mom's parents were very unhappy when they found out that Dad was not a Christian, but Mom didn't care. She was determined to marry him no matter what he believed. Since she was already over 21 there was not much they could do to stop it."

"Yes, I remember you told me that. What does that have to do with how you felt today?"

"Well, when they first got married, she completely quit going to church for several years. Dad would not go with her and she wouldn't go without him."

"They didn't attend at all until after I was born, but about that time she somehow convinced Dad that, even though he was not a believer, it would be best for me if they would start going. She said they needed to take me to Sunday School so I could be taught about Jesus. She argued that it would be an awful mistake not to give me the chance to understand who God was. I guess Dad just got tired of fighting about it."

"At first, he only went because she had begged and pleaded for so long, but after a while he got acquainted with the people in the congregation and he began to participate. For a number of years we went as a family very regularly. He even joined the church after a time and became an active member, but when she was diagnosed with cancer, it changed everything."

"For almost two years she went through so much. Surgeries, chemo, radiation treatments, you name it, she had so many procedures we lost count. Sometimes it seemed like things were getting better, but then she would find another lump, or the doctors would find more cancer on her scans and everything would start all over again. It was like being hit in the face with a baseball bat over and over again! Sometimes she was so sick and weak she could hardly hold her head up, but she was a fighter. All that time she kept on praying and fighting."

"Then finally the cancer just took over her whole body. There was nothing more the doctors or anyone else could do, no more treatments they could try for her. Nothing."

"It was a really, really hard time, for her and for all of us."

Sandi leaned against his side and took his hand. "Oh, Jim, I didn't mean to bring up such sad memories."

He squeezed her hand and continued his story. "Mom and I continued going to church until just a few weeks before she died. She was so sure that God would heal her. She had everyone in her family and many friends that prayed for her. *She always told me not to worry, that she was in God's hands. Whatever happened would be God's will.*"

"You know, I tried to believe her but, as she got sicker, it was harder and harder to watch her just fading away like that." He paused, drawing a deep breath and continued.

"At the same time, Dad drew further and further away. She would beg him, but he just said he wouldn't do it anymore. He said he was sick of pretending. So, he stayed home, and no one could convince him to come back to church."

A single tear slid down his cheek as the story went on.

"After she passed away, he never did go back. He believed God had let her down. He said he wasn't even sure there was a God. Well, I was still pretty young, and I tried believing that it was all in His will. I knew she would not want me to give up on God the way Dad had, and I did try for a while but every time I walked into that building I would completely break down. I couldn't seem to find God there, or anywhere, for that matter, anymore, and I decided it was just easier not to go at all."

Jim once again became quiet and sat looking up at the stars and the tiny white sliver of the new moon.

"Are you all right, Jim? I never had any idea how bad it was for you. Your poor mom, I just can't imagine having to go through all of that, and you and your poor dad. I'm just so sorry, Darling."

He put his arm around her and held her to him. His shoulders shook and he cried as he had not done in years. As he got himself back under control, he spoke once again. "This afternoon, having Pastor Scott here, it kind of brought it all back. I never really thought much about how far off track I have been."

"Sandi, I'm glad for Joletta. I am glad she's found God. It's where she needs to be."

"I don't know. I guess I'm glad. I just don't know much about God and Jesus and all that."

"Well maybe this is a good time to start learning. *I know God is real. He isn't just a fairy tale and I believe He wants us all to know how much He loves us.* You know, I don't think it was an accident that Scott came here today after all. Maybe he came because we needed to be reminded how far away from *Him* we really are."

He held her as they sat in silence, feeling the cool night air upon their faces. . . both lost in their own thoughts.

"Jim, there's one more thing. I don't know what to tell her about this big idea she has about going to Africa. I know she wants to go badly, but I am just not ready for her to go so far away."

"Let's give it a few more days to think about everything. School won't even be out for a couple of weeks. That gives us a little more time to check into things before making a final decision."

She took a deep breath and relaxed against his arm. It felt so good having someone with whom she could share her worries and concerns.

Chapter 7
WHAT A TANGLED WEB

It was almost the end of May, only two weeks left before school got out for summer break.

Jo was really getting excited. She liked school but she was really hoping against hope that her mom would come around and agree to her request about the trip to Africa. She was sure she could be a lot of help to Jillian. She loved kids and didn't even mind helping with housecleaning and cooking sometimes. She wanted to learn all about missionaries. She knew they were hoping to start an orphanage and wanted to be there to help. If she was going, there was a lot to do to prepare and the sooner she got done with school the sooner she could start getting ready!

Everybody seemed to be busy doing something. There was almost an electric excitement in the air. Kids couldn't sit still and concentrate and even the teachers seemed to be distracted by the coming weeks of summer vacation. The grass was growing, flowers were opening their colorful petals, the days were getting warmer, and the trees once again were dressed in tender green leaves.

The school prom had already taken place the Saturday before and all the seniors were preparing for graduation that was to be held on the first day of June. Everyone at school was excited at the thought of finishing finals and looking forward to the long lazy summer days ahead.

Joletta had just turned in her final write-up for the school newspaper, "Tales and Tidbits of Thomasville High." Missy Lesser was the senior responsible for editing all articles before giving them to Mrs. Brownsly, who taught the class, for a final check before printing. Jo was pleased that she had been given the chance to do this particular story. It included interviews with several members of the senior class. She had done an overview of how each person felt about his or her experience at Thomasville. It included answers from each person interviewed on what their plans were for the up-coming years. Joletta was proud of her work and felt it deserved the "A" she was hoping for.

Each person on staff had to turn in at least one article weekly that would be of general interest to the student body. Also, each was responsible for a minimum of two special interest stories. These were required in order to receive a final grade.

This was her second special interest article and she had finished it a full week early. As she started to leave the room, Missy stopped her. "Wait a minute, Jo, I was going to ask you if you have any plans are for the weekend - actually not the weekend, for tonight. I thought we could get together."

Jo was a little surprised at this. She and Missy had never really been particularly friendly. Not that either disliked the other; this was the only class they shared and they hardly knew each other. Not only was Missy a senior, she was a member of a tight-knit group of the "popular" girls that had lived in Thomasville their entire lives. Jo on the other hand was an underclassman who had only recently arrived on campus. Missy was captain of the cheerleading squad and the star runner of the girl's track team. To top that off she also had a steady thing going with Kenny Diller, the mayor's son and one of the most sought-after boys in school.

Joletta wondered why Missy had decided to be friendly now. "I thought I might take my horse out for a ride this afternoon, but other than that, I don't really have anything major planned except on Sunday."

"Oh! I didn't know you had a horse. That's pretty cool. Anyway, the reason I'm asking is because my cousin Donny is in town. He is spending the weekend with us and, well, you know how it is. Kenny and I have a date and we need someone to go along, so Donnie won't feel left out. He just got out of Boot Camp and he's leaving in a couple of weeks to go to Iraq. I thought maybe you would like to meet him. Kind of like a blind date. Megan was going to come with us, but her sister's in the hospital having a baby, so she can't. I thought you might do me a big favor and go instead." Missy smiled sweetly and waited.

"Well. . ." Joletta now realized she was just a fill-in so Missy did not have to break her date to entertain her cousin, but the thought of going out with an older guy, one that was in the Army, was kind of exciting. "I don't know. I've never been out with someone older. I don't think Mom would let me. She is kind of strict about who I hang out with. If she doesn't know you—"

"Aw, come on. He isn't that much older! It'll be fun with four of us. He's really cute. I promise you'll like him." She paused and went on, "Just tell your Mom you're going to the movies with me and some friends. Tell ya what, we'll be there to pick you up about 7:00, OK?"

"Well maybe you ought to call first. I really need to ask."

"Oh, don't be a baby, Jo! Just be ready on time. I promise to have you home before morning! Oh, there's the bell! We better get going."

With that, Missy waved the papers in her hand and giggled. Grabbing the stack of books on the desk, she headed down the hall, long blond hair swinging in unison with her hips, toward her next class. Jo slowly walked down the hallway wondering what she had gotten herself into. She passed several girls she knew without even speaking.

189

Several hours later, Jo found her mom curled up in her favorite overstuffed chair with a book in hand.

"What are you reading, Mom?"

"Oh, Hi, Sweet girl! It's just a novel I picked up the other day. It gives me something to do while Annie is sleeping. I thought I heard the bus. How was school today?"

"It was good, Mom. Where's Jim?"

"He's outside working in the yard. I'm not really sure. I think he had something to do in his work shed."

"I think I aced my article! I won't know for sure until Monday, but Missy thought it looked good."

"That's really great, Honey. You don't have many more days of school left now, do you?"

"No, but I just hope I don't mess up on any of my finals next week!"

"You are going to be fine. You've been working really hard this year. I'm proud of you."

"By the way, Mom, Missy asked if I could go out with her and some of her friends tonight. Do you think that would be ok? They want to pick me up about 7:00."

"Isn't Missy a senior? Is she driving?"

"Well, I'm not really sure. I think so. Oh, please Mom. I promise not to be late."

"I guess it would be all right if you go, but I'll need to know what your plans are and who all you're with."

"Oh, Mom, it's just some girls Missy knows. It'll be ok." Joletta was actually surprised that the lie had come out of her mouth so easily. It had not been planned exactly, but Jo was pretty sure if Mom knew the entire truth, the outcome would be different.

She went up to her room and refused to eat supper, saying they would probably get some popcorn or a sandwich at the movies. The less time she spent with her family the fewer chances for questions.

Shortly before seven Jo saw Missy's small red sports car pull into their long driveway. Missy beeped her horn loudly several times.

"There they are!" Jo came running down the stairway dressed in fitted jeans and a light-colored spring sweater, her hair pulled back into a ponytail. Her eyes sparkled and her cheeks were bright as she kissed her mom and gave her a quick hug. She looked every bit the teenager she was, and Sandi felt a pang of sadness. She knew it would not be very long before this sweet girl would no longer be a child. Too soon, she would be grown and gone.

"Joletta, why don't you tell them to come in and meet us?"

"Oh, Mom, we need to go. Please?"

As she opened the door, they could hear the loud music from the car's radio and Missy's horn sounded once again.

"Well, I really don't think it would hurt anyone to come to the door. Promise me you'll stay out of trouble and be home on time."

"Thanks Mom! Love you bunches!"

With that, Joletta quickly headed out to the car before her mom had a chance to say more.

Kenny was already in the front seat with Missy leaving the smaller back seat for Jo. Missy's cousin was not with them.

"Hey, Jo, I see your mom let you out of jail! Told ya she would let you go; it's all in the way you ask."

"Hi. Where's your cousin? I didn't tell her we were going with boys."

"Way to go, girl! I didn't think you had it in you! We're meeting Donny at the carryout. He had to get some cigarettes and beer."

"Beer? Oh, Missy, I didn't know anything about beer. Maybe this isn't such a good idea. I thought we were going to the movies or something."

191

"Oh, stop, Jo! You don't have to drink any if you don't want to. It isn't going to be that much, and a little beer isn't going to hurt anyone!"

"Maybe you better take her back home if she's going to whine." Kenny laughed and turned around to look at Jo. "You know, Sweetie, if you aren't old enough to play with the big kids you better go home to your playpen."

Joletta was confused and getting angry. "I don't have a playpen and just because I don't drink doesn't mean I'm a baby!"

"Come on, Kenny, be nice to her. She's a real sweet kid. She just hasn't been around much. That's all. She'll be all right. Won't you, Jo?"

"Sure, I'll be all right. Are we going to a movie or not?"

"There isn't anything on in town that's worth watching. We could go over to Cedarville, I guess, if that's really what you want to do."

"Cedarville is an hour away! I have to be home by 11:30. There's no way we could get there and make it back in time! What else is there to do?"

Missy and Kenny looked at each other and said something in low voices that Jo couldn't hear.

"Just thought we'd ride around awhile. We can go and get some sandwiches or a pizza and then we can go down by the river later. I thought Kenny and I could go for a walk while you and Donny get better acquainted."

Once again, Jo felt there was a private joke or something between the two of them. She hadn't even met Donny yet and already didn't like the way things seemed to be going.

Chapter 8
WALKING THE LINE

A few minutes later, they pulled up at the little carryout where they planned to meet Missy's cousin. Pulling in beside a black SUV, Missy honked the horn. The young man was sitting in the driver's seat with his window down, smoking a cigarette. He waved them over and said, "Get in, we'll take my car. It's bigger."

He got out and opened the door of Missy's car for Joletta. "Hi, there. I'm Don. I guess you must be Joletta?"

"Hi." Jo looked up. Well, at least Missy was telling the truth about one thing. He was good-looking. He had a dark complexion and chestnut brown hair, cut in a short military style.

She had to admit he was handsome, and she liked his voice. She was most impressed by the fact that he opened the door for her. None of the boys she knew would have ever thought to do that.

As they all got into the vehicle, she was relieved to see the bucket seats in the front of his car. It would be more comfortable if she didn't have to sit right next to him. This would give her a little space, so she could think.

He climbed in and started the car.

"Did you get the beer?" Kenny spoke from the back as they pulled out of the parking lot into the main flow of traffic.

"Yeah, I got some, but it'll have to wait till we're out of town. I warn you, though. You get yourself drunk, you better keep me out of it. You so much as mention my name, and you are dead meat! I can't believe I even let you talk me into this."

"Right, man! I wouldn't want to get a solider boy into trouble or nothing."

Kenny and Missy both laughed as Missy cajoled, "Come on, guys. Let's go and get something to eat and then we'll go down to Beaver Creek."

"Where is that?" Jo had never heard of anywhere called Beaver Creek.

"It's a place we used to go and picnic when we were kids. It's about 5 miles out on Highway 31. You can take the access road just past the railroad bridge down to the river."

"Why would you want to go there? It will be dark in an hour."

Once again, Jo was left feeling slightly foolish while the two in the back snickered.

"Oh, Jo, you are so dense! Don't you get it at all? It'll be fun; we can go for a walk or build a campfire. Maybe we'll even go skinny-dipping! I brought a blanket and a flashlight."

Joletta was getting more nervous by the minute, and she didn't know what she was going to do about it. For the moment, she sat in silence wishing she had never agreed to come along at all. She didn't exactly know what she had expected, but it certainly had not included spending the night drinking beer and whatever else they were planning. She was not completely innocent and by now had a pretty good idea of what Missy and Kenny had in mind. Nervously, she looked over at Don. They barely said ten words to each other. Surely, he was not expecting her—

"Are you sure you don't want to go to the movies?" she asked quietly.

"Naw, I said there wasn't anything any good on. Ya want to go get pizza or burgers? I'm hungry."

"Pizza sounds good to me. You hungry, Jo? I haven't eaten for hours." Don looked at her and smiled. He winked, and her heart skipped a beat. He didn't look or sound like he wanted anything except food.

"Sure, pizza would be great."

Don turned the corner and headed toward the outer edge of town where most of the fast food businesses were located.

After agreeing on a place called LuJoe's they went in and ordered two large pepperoni pizzas and drinks. It was a busy little place, phone constantly ringing, music playing in the background, and customers coming in and going out. Don and Missy talked about their shared childhoods and Don told them of some of his experiences in boot camp.

As they waited, Joletta began to relax. She started to feel like she perhaps had overreacted earlier. She still didn't much like Kenny - he was far too full of himself. He seemed to enjoy making comments that made her uncomfortable.

She learned that Don had already been out of school for almost two years. He had worked for an uncle out West the first year after graduating and then decided a few months ago that he wanted to join the military. His parents had been separated since he was small, and his mother had raised him and his two sisters on her own.

"You guys about done?" Kenny spoke over the noise. "We need to get this party going if we have to get "Baby Face" home before Momma sends the "Kiddie Cops" out looking for her."

"Shut your trap, Kenny. Stop picking on her. Maybe it'll be *you* we take home!"

"Aw, man, I was just kidding. That's all." Kenny mumbled as Missy glared at him.

"Thanks, Don." Joletta smiled shyly as he handed her sweater to her and waited as she picked up her purse. He put his hand on her lower back and gently guided her toward the door.

"Hey, he's just a loudmouth, don't let him bother you. Some people just don't know when to shut-up."

It wasn't long before they drove off the main road and down a twisting dirt path leading them under an old bridge which crossed the river. There were several other cars already parked on the rocky riverbank. They could hear laughter and loud music and smell the smoke from a large bonfire.

"I didn't know there were others coming," Don said as he pulled to a stop and put the car in park.

"It's just a bunch of kids from school. Real casual, ya know. Whoever shows up, great. Whoever doesn't, it'll be their loss!"

"Where's the beer, man? Give us a six pack; I'll pay ya back later."

"It's in the back, Kenny. I'm not so sure this is a good idea with all these people here. You should have told us Missy. You said it would just be the four of us."

"Come on, cousin, it isn't a big deal. Just give him the beer. You promised, remember? Kenny and I are going for a walk. We'll be back in a little while; you guys go and have some fun."

With Kenny carrying the blanket and beer, Missy grabbed his free hand and the two of them soon disappeared into the crowd of rowdy, laughing youth.

Don lit a cigarette, drew in a deep breath and stood looking toward where the crowd had closed in around his cousin and her smart-mouthed boyfriend...

Darn that girl, she hasn't got a bit of sense!

"Oh, I'm sorry, Joletta. I almost forgot about you."

Jo had gotten out of the car and had been watching the interaction between Missy and the two guys. How had she ever gotten herself into such a mess? She didn't have a clue what to do next. . . Don seemed like a nice guy, but she didn't really know what he expected. She hadn't even gone out with boys her own age much and now here she

196

was with an older guy! To top that off, Missy and Kenny had taken off and left her alone with him! *Stupid girl!* She almost spoke the words when he put his hand on her shoulder and interrupted her thoughts.

"Anyone in there? This is Don to Jo." He laughed, but somehow it wasn't the kind of laugh that hurt her feelings. "You look like you are about to cry. Are you all right?"

"Oh, yeah, I guess I'm OK. I was just thinking— it's just that—well, I don't know." She struggled trying to put her feelings into words. "I mean— I mean - I just didn't expect tonight to turn out to be like this."

"Well, my little friend, this isn't exactly what I had expected either. So, I guess we're kind of in the same boat."

"Missy told me that her friend was already 18 and would be graduating. How old are you anyway? Don't take that wrong now, I think you are a really sweet girl and all that...really good to look at, too, but----definitely not 18!"

"Well, I turned 16 a couple of weeks ago. I'm not the friend Missy had invited. In fact, I don't really even know Missy very well. I guess I was kind of a fill-in for her other friend who couldn't come."

"Ah-ha, sixteen, huh? Grade?

"I'll be a Junior next year. I'm sorry; I didn't know it would turn out like this."

He laughed again. "Oh, no, don't be sorry. I think I like you better anyway! Well, Sweetheart, Missy has some serious explaining to do. Little brat is so spoiled she thinks she can get by with just about anything. I will fix her pedigree when she shows up!"

He put his arm around her shoulder and gave it a gentle squeeze. "Meanwhile, you want to go down and check out the campfire and listen to some music? Guess we might as well enjoy ourselves since we seem to be stuck here for a while."

"Well, I guess it would be ok. I just hope they get back before long. I'm supposed to be home by 11:30."

"I would imagine they'll show up after a while. Between "Beach Blanket Bingo" and the fact that the beer won't last, it shouldn't take them too long. It's only a little past 9:30 now. We should be able to get you home in plenty of time." He smiled. "What say, let's go down and listen to some music?"

He took her hand and grinned at her. Jo's heart melted inside her chest, and they walked down the gravel bar along the water until they came to the open area where the huge bonfire was burning. There were perhaps a couple dozen kids laughing, talking and sitting around. A few of the faces were familiar but Jo didn't recognize most of them. Some were lying on blankets; some had drinks and were eating chips and hotdogs. Joletta didn't see anyone that appeared to be drinking alcohol, but in the firelight, it was hard to tell exactly what everyone had. The music was playing at top volume, and a few people were even dancing. No one seemed to care or hardly noticed that they were there.

If it had not been for the fact that Joletta had slowly worked herself into a panic over the entire situation and was worried sick about what her family would say if they found out what she had done, she might have actually enjoyed being there. It was a beautiful evening, warm and breezy, and the sky was full of stars so bright you felt you could reach out and touch them. At least, now that she felt Don was no longer a threat, she could relax a little. In fact, she really liked him. He was good-looking, polite and very sweet. She wished that he could be her real boyfriend.

They stood and watched the fire for several minutes and then walked down to the water's edge where they found a large rock to sit on. For the better part of the next hour, they sat listening to the music and talking.

198

Don told Joletta about his hopes for the future and his fears and concerns about going to Iraq. He told her about his younger sister that suffered from a serious heart condition.

Jo told him some of the things about her family that had happened in the past couple of years and how her mother and Jim had gotten together and fallen in love. She talked about Annie and told him about her hopes to go to Africa. She didn't bring up church. She knew she had made a bad decision when she chose not to tell her mom the entire truth. She knew she had disappointed God.

"You know; I have really screwed things up now. I shouldn't have lied about tonight and if Mom finds out she will never let me out of the house again, much less let me go to Africa!"

"It may not be as bad as you think. Your folks sound to me like they are pretty reasonable people. Then have you decided you are going to tell them?"

"Oh, I don't know! I know I was wrong--- but---I just don't know what to do!"

"Get your hands off me, you leach!" It was a very rumpled Missy and Kenny that had appeared out of the darkness. "You don't care about anything but beer and sex!" She swung her large canvas purse, hitting him hard on the back.

"Why, you little bit ----! Who do you think you are? I'll teach you a lesson!" Kenny reached out and grabbed her upper arm, but before he had a chance to go further, Don tackled him and pushed him to the ground.

He grabbed the collar of Kenny's shirt and quietly said in a slow, measured voice, "You will not touch her. Do you understand?"

"Hey, man! Don't hit me! I wasn't gonna hurt her; I wasn't!"

"Did you hear what I said? I said you are not to touch her! Not now, not ever!"

"Right, --- right, no problem." Don released the hold he had on Kenny and let him fall back against the gravel.

Several people had gathered around in hopes of seeing a good fight, but it was over as fast as it had started. Don got up and brushed off his clothes as Missy ran into his arms and burst into tears.

As he held her to him, he stroked her hair. "You little idiot! When are you ever going to learn? You are too good to give yourself to a screw-up like that. Let's get out of here!"

He guided both girls back up to where the cars were parked.

As they climbed into the car, Kenny called from behind. "Hey, wait, what about me?"

"You can find your own way home, wise-guy! Come on girls, it's time to go home. I think you've had enough for one night!"

Sandi and Jim were in the family room watching the evening news when they heard the car pull into the drive. A couple of minutes later, they heard muffled voices, and the door opened.

"Thanks, I'll talk to you later."

Jo came through the foyer, and into the room where her folks were. Sandi spoke, "Who were you talking to? I thought you were with Missy."

"I was, Mom. Listen, can we talk about this tomorrow? I'm really tired."

Her mother gave her an inquiring look but decided not to question her further. "I think perhaps you're right. Maybe, tomorrow would be better."

Jo ran over and hugged both Sandi and then Jim. "I love you guys so much." She turned and ran up the stairs without another word.

Sandi and Jim looked at one another. "That was definitely not a girl's voice."

Chapter 9
WHEREVER THE WIND BLOWS

Joletta had tossed and turned, and she woke very early feeling as if she hadn't slept at all.

She was still feeling guilty that she hadn't been completely truthful with her mom, but on the other hand, she was glad she had gone with Missy.

Otherwise, she would have never met Don. At first, she had been really nervous, but after they got better acquainted, she had grown more sure of herself, and it had all turned out great ---well, not exactly great for Missy and Kenny.

Jo couldn't help but smile when she remembered Kenny's whine calling after them. She couldn't imagine, after the way he had acted last night, how anyone could think that he was a hot catch! Thank goodness her date wasn't another guy like him! That would have been disastrous!

She smiled as she thought of Don who, on the other hand, was everything a girl could want. Cute, polite and really, really sweet! He even insisted on walking her all the way to the door. Before he left, he leaned over and kissed her on the cheek. She wished with all her heart that it had been more. She sighed, knowing that there likely would never be any other opportunity to spend time with him. Even if he weren't being sent away she doubted that he would ever give her a second thought. She put her hand against the cheek he had kissed and imagined it was still warm. It was a memory she would always treasure.

Hours later, Joletta became aware that the sun was beginning to filter through her lightweight curtains. Yawning, she sat up. It was going to be another gorgeous day. The sun was just coming up and for a few moments, everything in her room took on a golden glow. Mornings like this were so beautiful it almost brought tears to her eyes.

It would not be an easy day though because Jo had decided she must come clean with her mom. There might have been a time when she would have left things alone but for some reason, this time she just could not.

Don had told her that it sounded like her mom and Jim were reasonable people. She already knew that, of course, but for the most part, she had never given them much to worry about.

One of her main fears was that she had probably just totally messed up any chance of her spending the summer with Jillian and Tom.

It would still be a couple of hours before anyone else would be getting up, and Jo wanted to talk to Mom alone. She knew Sandi would tell Jim later, but right now she didn't think she could handle admitting her screw-up while both of them were there. Jim had been doing volunteer work in town at a shelter for teen boys, and he would be leaving early. Most likely he would be gone all day.

After trying for another 15 minutes or so to go back to sleep, Joletta realized it was not going to happen. She hadn't had time to ride Golden Boy the day before, and since she wasn't sleeping anyway, she decided she would go out and give him some exercise. Usually, she rode at least a couple of days a week as long as the weather permitted. This was a perfect morning for a ride.

She pulled the light PJ's off over her head and put on jeans and a sweatshirt. It was still quite cool in the early morning hours. Picking up her riding boots, and tiptoeing down the hall, she descended the stairs. Passing the master bedroom, she continued out the back door as quietly as she could. Sitting down on the back step, she breathed in the morning air as she put on her boots.

She felt a surge of energy, and running the rest of the way to the horse-barn, Jo pushed open the door. Golden Boy nickered in greeting. Laughing, she rubbed his velvety nose and nuzzled against him. "At least I don't have to explain anything about the error of my ways to you, do I, Boy?"

Joletta continued to talk to the gentle giant as she pulled his halter over his head. Scratching his neck, she took a blanket off a shelf and flung it onto his back. Fastening his saddle into place and tightening it securely around his belly, she pulled herself up and over his broad back. She then did some final adjustments on her stirrups. Flicking the reins, she clicked her tongue, a signal that he was to start their morning adventure.

At first, they rode slowly around and across the meadow. The sun was just rising in the east and the field sparkled with thousands of dewdrops reflecting the morning light. She then turned the horse north along the path into the woods. The smells and sounds of early morning were everywhere. As the world awoke birds flitted out of brushy areas, a doe with a speckled fawn started and fled almost before she realized that they were there, and she could hear dogs barking from a neighbor's place on the other side of their property. She let Golden Boy munch on the fresh green leaves that were growing along the edge of a little creek that rippled from a spring in a hillside a quarter of a mile back into the wooded area.

Joletta would have been happy to have continued riding for the entire day, but after a while realized she was beginning to feel a little hungry. The sun was already getting high, and the day was warming. Breakfast would soon be ready, and she decided it was time to head back to the house and "face the music."

She guided Golden Boy into the creek and let him drink his fill and then turned and rode out of the wooded area into the bright sunshine.

"Well, fella, I guess we had better be heading back. You want to run a little bit first?" Joletta flipped the reins and tapped her heals into Golden Boy's flanks. Soon they were cantering at full speed. Almost flying, they were as carefree as the wind. Jo's hair and the horse's mane and tail flew wildly behind them. She laughed aloud and urged him on. Faster and faster they went!

Then suddenly the horse faltered. Falling forward, Joletta was no longer on his back but hurtling head-ward through the air.

The last thing heard was a terrifying scream. It was hard to tell if it came from the girl or the horse. Then there was nothing but silence.

Sandi woke and smiled at her husband who was still sleeping peacefully in the bed beside her. Annie would be getting up shortly. Sandi had promised to make her pancakes for breakfast. Annie was in the middle of a growing spurt and was hungry more often than not these days. Looking at the clock, she realized if Jim were going to share their breakfast, she had better get up and start moving.

As she began to dress, she spoke gently to him. "Darling, it is almost 8:30. What time did you say you had to leave?"

Stretching and yawning, he looked at her and grinned. "Not until around 10:00." He rolled over and patted the bed. "Most of the kids won't be done with chores until closer to 11:00. We still have plenty of time to have a roll under the covers, if you're interested?" He grinned and winked at her.

"Umm— it is tempting, but not this morning, Darling." She leaned over and gave him a quick kiss then turned to finish getting dressed.

As she did, she noticed the door to the barn stood open. "Jim? Why is the stable door open? Didn't you lock it last night?"

"Yeah, I did." As he stood and walked toward the window, Sandi saw the horse. "Jim, something isn't right. Why is Golden Boy loose? He should be in his stall."

The horse was standing alone, far across the field. Sandi's heart stopped as she realized that he was saddled and rider-less!

"Jim! Something is terribly wrong! He's hurt! He's limping, and---Oh, no! no! No! Where is Jo?"

Sandi was screaming her daughter's name hysterically as they both ran for the back door. "Jo! My God! Where is Joletta?"

Once outside the house, they could see the girl. Golden Boy stood beside her with his head down, his reins dangling loosely.

"No!" Jim stopped Sandi long enough to put his hands firmly on both her shoulders. "It will be OK, Darling; you need to go and call for help!"

"Jim! I have to go to her!" She tried to break his grip, but he shook her hard. "Sandi, do as I tell you. GO! Now, Sandi! Phone for help! Tell them to get here as fast as possible!"

Leaving her standing at the back door, Jim called back, "Get Dad. He'll have to take care of the horse."

As Sandi ran for the phone, she almost knocked little Annie off her feet. "What wrong, Mommy?"

Pulling her little one close, she picked up the phone and dialed 9-1-1. "Please, please answer! Hurry! Please, God, if you are there!"

Moments later, Jim reached Joletta and fell to his knees beside the limp girl, who was lying face down, at an odd angle. One arm was obviously broken. As he rolled her gently over, her long, dark hair, which covered most of her face, was matted and bloody. He smoothed it away and saw a ragged six-inch cut running from her ear into her hairline. Her lips were blue, and he wasn't sure if she was even breathing. "Jo? Can you hear me?!"

He almost yelled as he patted her cheek. Leaning close he could feel her shallow breathing. "Hang on, Honey, help is coming." There was no response except for the slightest quiver of her eyelids. "That's right, Darling; that's good. Jo, you can't do this to us. We love you too much!" He held her gently as tears ran down his face. He prayed as he had not prayed in years.

"Father God, I never expected to have a family. Please don't take this child from us!" As he prayed and held her, the sound of a medical helicopter overhead drew his attention. *"Thank you, thank you, Lord!"* He saw people waving directions to the EMS team, and he saw Sandi, running across the field toward them.

"Jim, is she going to be all right?" she called as she ran. Reaching them, she dropped down and wrapped her arms around her precious child. "Your momma is here now, Sweetheart. Help is here; it will be all right now." Tears streamed from her face as the medical technicians gently drew her away and into Jim's waiting arms. They then turned their full attention to Joletta.

The next hours were long and cruel.

Gloria and James arrived even before the rescue unit got there and Gloria immediately took charge of Annie. She promised to get in touch with the rest of their family and close friends and told Sandi not to worry about her little one.

Shortly after, the helicopter took off with Jo and the medical crew onboard. Sandi and Jim followed in the car.

It was almost an hour's drive into Scranton where Joletta was being taken to Hope Hospital. No one knew if Jo would even be alive when they arrived.

Jim's dad took the responsibility of calling the veterinarian. He knew from his many years working with animals that it was not going to be a good prognosis. It took only a few minutes and between the two of them, they made the terrible decision that Golden Boy would have to be put down. Sadly, the horse had compound fractures in not one, but both of his front legs. They were simply not fixable. It was a heart-breaking decision, but kinder than watching the beautiful animal struggle any longer than necessary. Dr. Matt felt deep sympathy for the horse and the family as he prepared the medication. James stroked Golden Boy's neck for the last time. "It's all right, Boy. Just hold on. It'll be all over soon." Tears ran freely down his face as he bid an old

friend good-bye. How was he ever going to be able to explain to Joletta? Would she ever forgive him?

A sick feeling came over him as he realized that, at this time, he did not know what was going on with Sandi's girl. Joletta was now lying in a hospital herself. How badly she had been hurt, he did not know. He had been so busy with Golden Boy. What if---but--he refused to let his mind go there. He had dealt with too much already today. Suddenly, he felt like a very old man. His head hurt, and his body felt as if it must weigh a thousand pounds. Slowly, he walked over to a chair where he collapsed, putting his face in his hands, his shoulders shook, and he cried like a little child.

At the hospital, things were not good. Joletta had survived the fall and the flight to the hospital but, although her vital signs had stabilized, the doctors were unable to tell Jim and Sandi what her prognosis was.

Hours later, she was still unconscious and unresponsive. The ER doctor approached Sandi. "Right now, the only thing we can tell you is that she has a traumatic brain injury and there is swelling around the brain. It's not unusual in head injuries and will possibly get worse. If that happens, we may have to do surgery to relieve some of the pressure. But at this time, we will watch and wait. We simply cannot tell a lot until the swelling subsides. The brain is tough, but it can only handle so much, and that was quite a tumble she took."

"On the positive side, she is a strong girl, and that is important."

"We will be keeping her in intensive care and will continue to monitor her very closely. I hope that by tomorrow, we will know more. In addition, we'll continue to evaluate the extent of her other injuries. We have stabilized her spine and believe at this time that it is not affected, but we will keep her in traction until we get the results of the M.R.I. After that it will be one step at a time. First things first. We will need to set her arm in the next 24 hours. Other than that, it does not appear that there is any internal bleeding which, of course, is a good thing."

The young doctor smiled and shook first Jim's hand and then Sandi's. "About all you can do for her right now is to get some

rest and pray. I will continue to check on her before I leave tonight, and we will talk again tomorrow."

After the doctor left to see other patients Sandi said, "*Pray*? Did he say "PRAY?" A lot of good prayer does! Look at her, Jim! Prayer isn't going to help her! It hasn't been two weeks since she was baptized. See where prayer put her!"

"Sandi, don't be bitter. You know perfectly well that God didn't do this."

"Maybe he did. Maybe he's punishing me for not believing. Maybe he's angry with me!"

"My darling*, God doesn't work like that. God loves all of his children."* He then gently took her into his arms and tried to comfort her the best he knew how. "Hush, my love. Hush now."

Slowly, slowly the hours passed. Hours and hours of waiting and sitting. Hours that then became days.

With each passing day, Sandi sat beside Jo, holding her hand, stroking her cheek or reading to her. She now had a stack of recent magazines and books. Family and friends brought them to help her pass the long days.

She would sometimes talk to her silent child as if there was nothing wrong, telling stories about when she was a child herself or telling stories about Joletta and Annie. She was very careful only to talk about good times, never anything negative.

She would comb Jo's soft hair and put cool washcloths against her warm forehead.

When the nurses needed to change Joletta's hospital gown or the bedding, Sandi would offer to help. Sandi would do anything to pass the time. Anything— that would keep her close to Joletta. Anything— to keep her from thinking too far ahead. Thinking--- was far too dangerous, especially--- thinking about the future...

Jo lay uncomplaining with tubes to monitor every vital sign and tubes that put fluids and life-giving nourishment into her body. She now had several metal screws coming out of her right arm that was wrapped in white gauze, supported by a metal contraption that connected to her hospital bed. In addition to that, there was a long row of stitching which ran above her right ear and back into her hairline. Her doctors were pleased with the progress of her physical injuries. They would heal with time. Even the swelling around her brain had subsided somewhat, but still she did not wake.

Dr. Miller came into the room, as he did each morning. He also came in to check on her in the evening before leaving for the night. The hospital team had made the decision to move Joletta from the ICU to a private room.

"This does not mean that she is completely out of the woods," the doctor told them, "but she seems to be holding her own." He spoke gently. "We only have enough beds in intensive care for our sickest patients and since Joletta is doing well physically, this will give your family more privacy and freedom to visit." He hesitated for a moment then continued, "Unfortunately, we just cannot tell how long she will remain

comatose. I am very sorry we cannot be more encouraging, but as I have said before, it is a wait-and-see situation."

It was Sunday, a week to the day after Jo's accident.

Chapter 10
IF NOT NOW, WHEN?

Sandi reluctantly gathered her belongings and walked over to Joletta's bedside. "I won't be gone long, my Darling." She leaned over and kissed her daughter's cheek as Jim put his hand on her shoulder.

"It's all right, Sandi. Susan will be here with her, and we will come back in the morning if you are up to it."

Sandi hadn't been home since the day of the accident. She stubbornly refused to leave Joletta. However, now Jim was insisting that the time had come when she must allow someone else to stay with Jo, if only for a short while. He told her that she needed to get a full night's sleep and spend some time with little Annie.

Annie was becoming more upset with each passing day. She had cried herself to sleep the past two nights. James and Gloria had tried bringing her to the hospital one evening, hoping it would assure her. Unfortunately, the plan completely backfired, and Annie then cried because Jo would not wake up and play with her. Shortly thereafter, she became almost hysterical because visiting hours were over and they had to leave.

Jim told Sandi, "She is just too little to understand any of this, and she needs you. Right now, Annie needs you even more than Joletta!"

Sandi had started to argue but sighed. She was much too tired. She knew Jim was right. It had about broken her heart hearing Annie's cries as her grandparents left the hospital with her the night before.

Still, walking out of Joletta's room was frightening. It was really hard to leave Jo. She just lay there, so quietly, not a move or even a flutter of her eyelids.

Sandi seemed to find comfort and had now even developed a strange attachment to the routine of caring for her helpless daughter. She was always on watch for any sign of change.

"What if she wakes up? What if there is an emergency?"

Jim anticipated her thoughts. "We will only be a phone call away. Honey, you need some rest. You can't do anyone any good if you fall apart yourself."

She knew he was right, so she followed him out of the room and out of the hospital. They said very little on the drive back to the house.

Heading south under the mid-day sun, Sandi noticed that it was another absolutely beautiful day. The sky was a clear brilliant blue with only a few wisps of fluffy white clouds in the atmosphere. She had almost forgotten that Spring had come and would soon be gone. "Oh, Jim, it is so lovely." Colorful flowers meandered across the valley floor, meeting the soft green of the hills and contrasting with the darker greens of wooded areas. Still farther in the distance, the mountains turned to a blue haze. You could almost smell the coming of Summer.

This would be a long, hard summer; different than any they had ever expected or experienced before.

Arriving home an hour later, Jim kissed his wife and held her gently before going into his office to answer phone messages.

Sandi went into their bedroom and prepared to take a shower. It did indeed feel a little bit like Heaven itself. She could feel every nerve in her being throbbing, and she couldn't remember a time that she had ever been this tired before. She stepped into the shower and as the warm water flowed over her body it slowly began to melt away tension that had been building inside her since Joletta's accident.

When had it happened? It must have been a lifetime ago? Sandi honestly could not remember and for a short moment at least, it did not matter.

212

Although she had access to, and had taken, several quick showers at the hospital, this was the first to have any effect other than giving her the feeling that she was wasting away important time that she needed to take care of her daughter.

Jim planned to take Sandi home first and then would go and get Annie who was at her grandparent's house. He would bring her home after Gloria finished with lunch. That way, it would not be long before Annie would be ready for her nap. It would give the two of them time to rest together. He knew Sandi had little reserves left to play and, because Annie still napped every afternoon, it would give them that special time to snuggle and be close without overstraining his wife.

Done with her shower, Sandi wrapped a towel around herself and walked over to the window that looked directly out over the meadow where the accident had happened.

In an instant, their entire lives had changed, perhaps forever. *Could it only have happened a week ago? Poor Golden Boy!* Large wet tears slipped down her cheeks and she shivered when she remembered. *That could have been Joletta.*

She wished it were only a bad dream. Sometimes it felt as if the nightmares Jo had dealt with in the past months had become reality.

Tears welled in her eyes once again. Where they came from, she did not know, for she had shed so many tears in the previous days she thought it impossible that there could be any left. She knew this was not a dream, but very real indeed...

Why, God! Why do you let bad things happen? Why did you let this happen to my beautiful girl?!

She turned and finished toweling off, then slipped a loose satin gown over her head and picked up a comb,

213

running it through her tangled hair. Just as she put the comb on the vanity, she heard footsteps.

As Jim came into the room, he spoke, "Look whose home Momma!" Annie came running into her mother's arms.

"Mommy! Mommy! Annie wanted you to come home!" Her excited little voice told Sandi how much she had been missing her. She seemed so small and vulnerable; Jim had been right, as usual.

Sandi lifted the child into her arms, hugging her tightly, and said, "Mommy is so glad to see you, would you like to rock and sing a song, Sweetheart?"

"Uh-huh, Mommy. Mo-o-m-my, where is Jo-Jo? Jo-Jo won't wake up, Mommy. Why, Momma?"

Sandi did not answer but held her little one closely and walked over to the rocker that sat in a far corner of the room. She began humming an old familiar tune.

The old rocker had belonged to Jim's grandparents many years before. When his parents married, they gave it as a wedding gift to Sandi and Jim.

Somewhere, hidden away with old papers, Jim had told her that there was a lullaby, written by his grandmother. It was a song about this very rocker, sweet memories of rocking *her* little children many years before.

It was not hard for Sandi to imagine his grandma, and later Jim's momma, rocking and singing while holding a sleepy-eyed child in their arms.

Sandi was glad her husband's momma had been there to sing to him when he was small like Annie, and to hold him when he was hurting. It made her sad to know that he had lost his mother at such a young age.

She loved Jim so dearly. He willingly gave her his all. Without him, she would not have had the strength she needed in her time of pain and weakness.

She lifted Annie and walked over to the bed. Gently laying her down, Sandi then curled her own body around

Annie's and pulled a lightweight throw over the two of them. Within only moments, both were sleeping peacefully.

Two hours later, Sandi woke. Annie was still sleeping next to her, making up for her own missed rest of the past week.

The phone rang in the other room. She raised up on one arm, straining to listen to what was being said. Unable to hear, she got up and started toward Jim's office.

He was just putting the phone back into the cradle as she entered. "Oh, I didn't hear you come in." He stood and started towards her. "That was Susan."

"What? What is it? What's wrong, Jim?"

"No, Darling, nothing is wrong. For once something is right, Sandi." He reached out for her and continued, "Sandi; Joletta is starting to respond."

"Oh, God! She's awake? Oh, God! What do we do? We have to get back to the hospital!"

"No, Sandi, not awake, not yet, but she opened her eyes and turned her head to look at Susan." Susan said she was sure that Jo recognized her, but then she closed her eyes again only a couple of minutes later."

"Why didn't she call?! We should be there!"

"Honey, she did call! Everything is ok! The doctor was called in right away and is in there with her now. He says this is a good sign, but that's all it is. It's only a beginning. You know he has told us already that she is not likely to wake up all at once. She is sleeping again now. I don't think, unless the Doctor feels it is important, that we need to go right back to the hospital. It's an hour's drive and you just got home!"

"Mary and Tiffany are coming after a while and Mary will stay with her tonight. Tiff will go home later with Susan; she still has school this week."

"But, Jim—"

215

"No, Sandi, if there were anything we could do, we would go right now. However, there simply is not anything to do. It is just going to take time and patience. Susan is going to call back and fill us in when the Doctor leaves." Sandi was not easily convinced, but a short time later; Susan called and assured her that the Doctor confirmed Joletta was doing well, but was once again sleeping. Finally, she gave in to Jim's reasoning.

"Dr. Murdock said he will be in tomorrow around 8:30 to do rounds. If you have questions, he will try to answer them at that time," Susan said, settling the matter.

It was a long evening. Sandi was emotionally exhausted but playing with Annie was sweet relief.

Her littlest daughter had grown over the winter months. It hardly seemed possible that she was 3 ½ years old. Sandi realized that someone was going to have to get Annie some new summer clothes before long. Maybe she would ask Mary. She was sure that Gloria would try, but she had never had children, and although she had come to love the little girl, Sandi didn't think she would know how to buy play clothes. Mary would obviously be the better choice. Having raised two little girls of her own, she would know what to buy.

"Mommy, can we go outside and swing?" Annie looked up at her mother with innocent eyes.

Sandi's insides twisted and she felt a little sick. The swing set was in the back yard. She didn't think that she could go out there. Not yet. It was just too much to ask. Trying to distract Annie, she said. "Why don't we go get some ice cream instead, Sweetie?"

"No, Momma, I want to swing."

Sandi swallowed hard and tried to explain. "Annie, Mommy doesn't want to go out and play in the backyard right now. We can find something else to do, all right?"

216

Annie became solemn and looking directly into her mother's eyes, asked, "Mommy, are you sad?"

"Annie is sad, too, Mommy." She put her little hand on Sandi's cheek. "It'll be OK, Mommy; Jo-Jo will be OK. Mommy, where is Goldie Boy?"

Sandi could hardly believe that Annie was reaching out in almost a grown-up fashion and trying to comfort her, not the other way around *Poor, sweet, little girl, she shouldn't have to take care of me.* She closed her eyes and had to control the lump rising in her throat before answering the question. "Oh, Honey, Golden Boy is gone away. We won't be able to see Golden Boy anymore."

She just couldn't bring herself to try to explain the full truth to her little girl. Sandi reached down and lifted the child. "You're right, Darling, everything will be all right! Soon it will all be OK. I promise."

If only she could truly believe her own words.

Chapter 11
ABNORMAL, THE NEW NORMAL

The next weeks were unnerving, to say the least, each day different, each day the same. One minute up and the next minute back down.

There were times Joletta appeared to be waking. Sometimes she seemed to understand that something terrible had happened; silent tears would roll down her cheek onto the white sheet or her eyes would open and a look of pain or confusion would cross her face.

A few times, as if to try to get more comfortable, she had even shifted her position or moved her free arm. She would open her eyes and seemed about to ask a question, but she had not yet spoken a word. Her wakeful times had only been for very short periods and then soon she would sleep again.

The doctors were encouraged, but, since each case is unique for every individual, they were unable to give a timetable as to when, or if, any major changes might be expected.

Jo's external wounds were healing slowly and steadily, but every day they lived hoping that she would wake and be whole once again.

Hope was all they had, and they clung to it tightly, fearing the worst if they dared to lose their grip on it for even an instant.

Jo's family and Susan, Mary and even Tiffany, continued to keep vigil day and night.

Those that were believers prayed. Friends from the church had started a prayer circle the very day of the accident and continued praying day after day, week after week, believing that the time would come when Joletta would be completely healed.

Jim made sure that Sandi spent as much time at home as was reasonably possible. Although at times she would resist, she did realize by now that their ordeal would not be over anytime soon, and they would have to try and continue their daily lives as well as deal with Joletta's needs.

Sandi was truly amazed at the outpouring of love sent by friends, and from the church her child had recently joined. Cards and flowers arrived with notes of hope and love, and her room became a virtual garden of balloons, stuffed animals and floral arrangements people sent.

When Sandi mentioned how overwhelmed she was with all of this, Susan just smiled and gently reminded her of what an amazing daughter she had raised.

Pastor Jay, the church's new youth minister, had stopped in several times since the accident, just to see how things were progressing. He was a good-hearted guy (about the same age as Sandi) who had dealt with some tough issues in his own past. As they became further acquainted, he shared some of his own history about how his life had changed one summer when he attended a youth retreat with a Christian friend of his.

Jay, as a teenager, had been dealing with an abusive stepfather, and a mother who was not able to protect herself, much less her two young children. While at the retreat, he had felt the need to respond when they had the nightly altar call. He had not ever experienced anything quite like that before and on that night he had asked for forgiveness for past mistakes and sins and given his heart and life to Christ.

Pastor Jay truly cared about the young people he worked with and served them with an eager enthusiasm.

Sandi and Jim both began to look forward to his visits. He was not the preachy type, but they could see that there was something special about him. Before he left the hospital, he would always ask permission to pray.

There was something powerful in the way he spoke, not loud but with such genuine sincerity. Sandi began to realize that after his visits, she felt a sense of quiet peace.

Could it be that perhaps, God really is there? Susan, Jo and Jim all think so and of course the church pastors. Sandi knew even she had prayed when she felt most desperate. She still could not understand why, if there really was a God, like they insisted, he would allow so many terrible things to happen. Then once again, she remembered the horror of huddling with Annie in that dark closet during the tornado. She *had* experienced something extraordinary.

Whatever it was caused her to feel less fearful. Now, there was this strange, peaceful feeling when Pastor Jay prayed.

Saturday afternoon Sandi was sitting beside Jo's bed reading a book when a pretty, blonde-haired girl tapped on the door. "May I come in?"

She looked up and smiled. "Oh, hi. I'm sorry, I didn't hear you. Of course, you may. Are you a friend of Jo's?"

The girl looked nervous, and she didn't respond immediately. Looking over toward Jo's bed, she put her hand over her mouth and quietly asked, "Is she going to be OK?"

"We sure hope she is, Honey. Right now, we just have to wait. Do I know you?" Sandi asked, still not knowing the reason for the visit.

"No, we haven't met." The young girl hesitated, then hung her head. "I'm Missy. Jo was with me the night before the accident." With that, Missy began to cry. "Mrs. Benning, I am so sorry. If it hadn't been for me--"

"Missy? Oh yes, I do remember, but Dear, what do you mean? Jo was riding her horse; you didn't have anything to do with her accident."

"Yes---Yes, I did; it was my fault, and I'm so sorry! If I had only known." Her voice trailed off as she sniffed and wiped her hand across her eyes.

Sandi was trying to understand what the girl was saying. "I don't understand; I don't know how you could be responsible for anything."

Missy lifted her head and interrupted, "But I am responsible." She continued, "You see, Joletta told me she was going to ride her horse on Friday, but because I wanted her to go with us, she didn't. Don't you see? She rode Saturday instead of Friday! That's why she got hurt! If my cousin hadn't been in town, I would have never asked her to go, and she would still be OK!"

Sandi was still confused but the girl was obviously determined that she had caused Jo's accident. She walked over to Missy and put her hand on her shoulder. "Why don't you sit down over here, and we can talk for a little while. Jo likes it when her friends are here to visit. The doctor says it is good to talk to her. They don't really know if she can hear us, but just in case, we tell her what is happening, and I read to her sometimes."

Taking Jo's hand, Sandi said, "Jo, look who came to see you. It's Missy. She has been really worried about you. It's OK, Missy; she just can't respond to us right now."

The girl beside the bed stood with tears running down her face. Once again, she said, "Oh, Jo, I am so sorry."

Sandi could hardly believe that it was only the end of the second week since Joletta's accident. In ways, it seemed a lifetime ago that her vibrant young daughter had come running down the stairs, ponytail swinging. Kissing her mother good-bye, she had breezed out the front door seemingly without a care in the world. Of course, after Missy's visit, Sandi now knew that Joletta had not told the entire truth that evening before the accident.

221

If she had said no to her daughter that afternoon or made Jo bring her friends inside to meet the family before leaving. . . If she could turn back the clock and change the outcome. . . If only things could be different! Tears did not come for she had cried until she felt she had no more tears. As the days drifted into weeks, it felt as though she were living in a never-ending nightmare. One from which she could not wake. *Truly,* she thought, *this is a nightmare, but this is not a dream. It's real!*

Why? Why? Her heart once again formed the words her mouth had quit whispering days ago.

Beth and her husband Darrel traveled from North Carolina to spend several days visiting. Sandi was very glad to have her sister there.

For many years, Sandi had felt alone in a troubled world. Now it seemed unreal to have so much love and support around her.

Although, they would be spending the majority of their visit at the hospital, it would feel so good just to have something new to focus on for a while. They could spend time

talking about family and other things. Of course; the ever-present concerns with Jo would still be there, but it would be a chance to put those issues on the back burner, if only for a short time.

Over a mid-morning cup of coffee, Beth filled her sister in on what had been happening in her own life. She had only just recently gotten a much-coveted promotion. It seemed that Sandi's little sister was well on her way to a successful career.

They talked about their puppy, Puddles, and the new baby boy on Darrel's side of the family. Beth and Darrel had decided to wait a while before having children but were planning to enjoy his sister's little boy as well as little Annie whenever they could.

She also told Sandi about the most recent news she had on their younger brothers.

So far, the family had not been able to get together with all of the siblings, but the plan had been to have a reunion during summer break. The Fourth of July weekend had been what everyone had been hoping for. Now Sandi wasn't sure that would even be possible.

The men spent most of the days watching Annie while visiting at home. Jim and Beth's husband Darrel took an instant liking to each other. Even though Darrel was considerably younger than Jim, they had many similar interests, thus making conversation easy.

Beth and Darrel were hoping to buy a home soon, and they talked at length about the pros and cons of building versus buying and renovating. They were not well off but Darrel, who had lived with his parents until they married a few months ago, had been able to save a reasonable amount for a down payment. The rest they would finance.

They also both loved sports and were avid golfers.

As for Annie, within a very short time, she had her "new" uncle wrapped around her little finger. He was great fun to play with and soon the three of them were running through the house, playing games of hide and seek or chas

Grandma "Glory," as Annie called her, never let her run and make noise in the house. Nevertheless, now it was OK. To
Annie, she read good stories, gave really good hugs, and there were always really, really good cookies there, even if you did have to have lunch first.

Chapter 12
MORNING MIRACLE

Joletta opened her eyes and tried to make sense of her surroundings. It was not quite dark, and a dim light shone from underneath the curtains.

She could hear the sounds of rain splashing against a large window across the dim room. Someone pushed a clattering cart past the door of the room. Otherwise, it was quiet in the hallway outside of the open doorway.

Where was she? Everything was unfamiliar, and she could remember nothing.

She tried to turn onto her side and realized she could not move her left arm. She reached across her body and felt it. Her arm was tightly wrapped and immobilized. It didn't hurt exactly, but Jo was not comfortable in the position in which she had been laying so she rolled slightly to her right side. As she did this, she saw a lighted button hooked onto the bed rail. Then it came to her.

"Why am I in a hospital?" she wondered aloud. Even when she spoke it felt wrong. Her throat felt odd, and her voice sounded unfamiliar.

As she became more aware of her surroundings, she could hear hushed sounds coming from the hallway. *Hello? Is anyone there?* Her neck was stiff and her head felt strange. She was thirsty, and her eyes and mouth were dry and pasty. Turning her head and stretching she tried to remember what had happened. *What is going on? Where am I, and how long have I been here?* There were questions, but she could think of no answers.

Wait-- the button! *If I push the button it will bring a nurse.* Joletta maneuvered herself, with what felt like a great effort, until she successfully pushed the call button.

It had showered off and on all week and had rained again in the night. The early-morning air smelled fresh and sweet. Sandi hoped the sun would come out soon but decided she should take an umbrella with her as she went to run her errands. She had left the house shortly before sun-up to drive into the city and eat breakfast with Susan. Jim and Darrel were already off for a day of golf and Annie was at Grandma Gloria and Big Jim's.

Beth had left at the same time as Sandi. She planned to spend the morning with Joletta. This was Beth and Darrel's last day before returning to North Carolina and Sandi wanted to make a special meal for them.

With all the time at the hospital, there had not been time to do a lot of cooking. Sandi planned a special though simple meal. She had a pre-cooked ham that she had already taken out of the freezer. It had been spiral-sliced, and she planned to make cole slaw and potato salad to serve with it. While she was out, she also planned to pick up a fresh strawberry pie at the bakery.

Sandi felt somewhat silly; she was already feeling sad and Beth had not even left yet. It had been so wonderful having the support of her little sister and knowing she would be gone soon made her realize how hard it would be letting her go. Sandi shook her head and bit her lip. She would have to remember it would not be their last time together, now that they had found each other again.

Everything was very different since they had re-connected after the tornado. She and Beth visited frequently on the phone, but this time together had been special. Sandi appreciated that her sister wanted to come and share the pain of her family's crisis.

She also appreciated Darrel's willingness to give up the major part of his vacation to come with Beth. This visit earned him a special place in Sandi's heart. He was a good, stable young man, and she was glad for her younger sister.

225

As she pulled into the driveway at Susan's, the older woman opened the door and started down the steps before Sandi had even turned off the ignition.

Purse in her hand and waving her arms frantically, Susan rushed to the car.

"What is going on, Susan? Is everything all right?"

"Oh, my dear Sandi! It is more than all right! The hospital has been trying to reach you for the past hour! It's Jo! Joletta is awake!"

The color suddenly drained from Sandi's face and she sat in silence for a moment, not quite comprehending what it was Susan was telling her. "When, how?"

The word "awake" kept repeating over and over again in her mind. Sandi started shaking, and her hands felt frozen in place on the steering wheel. Her eyes looked at Susan and knew the truth, but her ears were still not sure of what they were hearing.

Susan continued, "Darling, did you hear me?" Susan was laughing and crying at the same time. "She woke up just before 6:00 this morning. They tried calling the house, but no one was there. She is asking questions and she wants to know where her mom is!" As she opened the driver side of the car, she put her hand on Sandi's shoulder. "Do you hear me, Sandi? All of our prayers have been answered!"

By now, tears were flowing freely from both women. "Scoot over, Dear. We need to get you to the hospital, and you are in no shape to drive! I'll fill you in with everything I know on the way."

As Susan pulled into the freeway traffic, she exclaimed out loud, *"Praise You, Father! Thank you Lord! I knew this day was coming! I knew it was coming, but I must admit; I was getting a little impatient with you!"*

It did not take long before Joletta's room was abuzz with not only nurses but also other people. There were people stopping just to peek into the room, and then they would walk away, smiling and shaking their heads.

Jo's Aunt Beth had arrived, her doctor was called, and she was assured the rest of her family would soon be there.

They tried to explain to the girl about the accident. They told her that she had been here in the hospital, in a coma, for almost three weeks. They told her that she had a broken arm and that she was still healing from numerous cuts and internal bruising and--- they told her it was already the middle of June!

Nothing was quite making sense to the pale girl lying on the bed quietly trying to take everything in. She was extremely exhausted and felt very weak. She had no memory of what had happened to her or of the past several weeks, but miraculously Jo understood the questions the doctor asked and was able to follow instructions when he told her to move her legs and squeeze his hands.

Shortly before Susan and Jo's mother arrived, she dozed off amid all the excitement.

Beth met them at the door trying to avert Sandi's panic when she entered the room only to find her daughter, not awake as expected, but sleeping!

"It's OK, Sandi, it really is. The Doc says she is just worn out from everything that's been happening. He says it is going to be some time before she is able to take it all in. Other than that, he said everything is looking great!"

"They have an MRI scheduled at 11:30 and also some other cognitive testing in the next couple of hours. He said he has other patients to see this morning but plans to talk with you this afternoon around 3:00."

Beth stepped aside. Her sister reached out and touched her daughter's hand. Then, as she gently pushed a wayward lock of hair across the girl's cheek, Joletta's dark eyes fluttered open and she smiled.

If Sandi had not been sure before this moment, she knew now without a doubt that there really was a God! She felt His hand upon her, and all the doubt of the past months simply dissolved. He had returned the child she loved so much to her family.

"Welcome, my Darling Girl!" Sandi stood motionless, holding Joletta's hand, as Jim and Darrel arrived. Entering the room, they heard her soft whisper- *"Thank you, Lord. . .Thank you for bringing Jo back!"*

Chapter 13
THE LONG SUMMER

The weeks and months following Joletta's "awakening" were slow and sometimes difficult.

After another week in Hope Hospital, she was transferred to PPRC Rehab in Philadelphia, one of the top rehab facilities in the United States for patients with head injuries.

While there, she would be re-evaluated and then begin an intensive therapy program. It was to become a summer full of challenges, more difficult than anything she had ever experienced in her young life.

Jo had no memory of the accident itself. She did remember waking that morning and spending time in the barn with Golden Boy. She could remember pulling on her riding boots and leading the horse out of the large double doors of the stable into the cool morning air, mounting and riding towards the woods. After that, there was nothing, nothing but a quiet darkness, until she woke, confused and disorientated in a hospital bed weeks later.

She remembered the weeks before her accident. She remembered the outing she had so hoped she would be allowed to go on. She remembered the omission left out of the explanation she gave to her mother the night before she fell.

Most of all she remembered her date that night, the tall dark stranger and her initial shyness. Much later that same evening he had kissed her so gently on the cheek that it now seemed impossible she could have ever been frightened of him.

When her family explained to her what had happened to the beautiful horse she loved so much, she felt her heart would break into pieces. Golden Boy had been her friend! He was beautiful and loyal. He was a gentle giant! Why had God spared her and let Golden Boy die?

Rehab was a daily round of different appointments. Joletta had to relearn things that had always come to her naturally, but now were simply gone. Her speech was slow, she sometimes lost her balance, and her short-term memory was poor.

On the positive side, her physical wounds were mostly healed. Her arm had been badly broken, but with work to maximize its use, her doctor expected her in time to regain its full function.

Water therapy was Jo's favorite, although it was painful at times. The therapist was a young man named Josh, not long out of school himself. He was tough but funny and sometimes he had her laughing so hard she almost forgot the discomfort.

Joletta was a determined patient and worked hard at everything her doctors and therapists expected of her, and after 3 months of inpatient treatment, Joletta was ready to be released to return home.

August 22, 2003 - Joletta sat in the large chair beside the window of her room waiting for her family to pick her up. Time seemed to be crawling as every fiber of her body buzzed with anticipation and excitement at the thought of going home.

There were times she had feared this day would never come. It felt as though she was being released from prison. Of course, the hospital was not a prison and Joletta had never been a prisoner.

She had already packed and repacked her meager wardrobe, taken her cards and pictures down, and all of the books, flowers, teddies and small gifts sent to her by well-wishers were neatly sitting side-by-side waiting along with the anxious girl. There was nothing left to do except wait. Waking up with the first ray of light, she had already been sitting expectantly for over an hour.

230

Of course she knew that everyone at the hospital tried their best to make it feel a little like home. There had been a bulletin board on the wall with many pictures and cards tacked to it, which she now had put in a gift box. There was cheerful printed wallpaper and fresh flowers in vases around the room.

However, a hospital room is always a hospital room, no matter where you are - an adjustable bed and a tray on rollers with curtains that can be pulled around a patient at a moment's notice, a wheelchair always ready and a large window looking down upon a parking lot and a world you are not allowed to be part of.

The hospital staff had always treated her well and Joletta knew she really didn't have anything to complain about. Everyone was there to help; it was only because she missed her family and friends so much. She appreciated everything; she just wanted to go home!

"Hi, Sweetheart," her morning nurse Julie came into the room. "I see you are all ready to leave us. Dr. Rhynard wanted me to tell you that he is sorry, but he is not able to be here this morning. He had planned to come by but had an emergency to attend to. He said he will see you next month when you come for your appointment. We are all going to miss your smiling face around here. You know, Joletta, that you are special. Many of our patients don't do nearly as well as you have; it is a joy when we have a good outcome. It makes working a job like this worthwhile." She smiled and gave Jo a gentle hug.

"Thanks, Julie, I'll miss everyone here also. Have you heard anything from my parents? Do you know when they are supposed to arrive?"

"I haven't heard, but it is only a little after 9:00. Didn't they have to come from the Wilkes-Barr area? That is quite a drive."

"I know, I'm just excited, that's all."

"You have every right to be excited, Honey. I'll let you know as soon as I hear anything."

231

It was almost another hour later that Sandi and Jim pulled into the parking lot of PPRC. Sandi was almost as on edge as Joletta and had nervously spent the entire trip chatting about all of the things that they needed to do after Jo got home.

"Sandi", Jim interrupted, "she is doing great! Everything is going to fall into place. You are going to have to calm down or you are going to pop a cork!" He smiled and reached over to squeeze his wife's hand before getting out of the car. "Come on, I'm sure she is waiting."

Julie came into Jo's room and brought the wheelchair over to where the girl was fidgeting with a bracelet that had been a Christmas gift from Big Jim last December, their first Christmas as a family. It had a little golden charm in the image of a horse.

"Are my folks here?" she asked. "Why do you have the wheelchair?"

"Didn't you know that all of our special patients get one final ride in their chair? Climb in; I have a surprise for you, young lady."

Joletta got into the chair and Julie proceeded to push her out of her room, down the hall and into a waiting elevator.

"Where are you taking me?"

"Now just be patient for a minute or two. I told you it was

a surprise!"

The door to the elevator opened on the first-floor level and Joletta was pushed down a final hallway and out onto the cafeteria patio where they were met by not only her parents, but Big Jim, Gloria, and what seemed to be the entire staff of Joletta's floor. Even Dr. Rhynard had finished with his appointment and had arrived in time for the surprise party.

232

Laughter, hugs, and happy tears filled the warm summer day as an extraordinary young woman was sent off into a brand-new chapter of her life

.

Jo slept most of the drive home with her mother riding beside her in the back seat of the car. "She is so beautiful," Sandi spoke softly to Jim. "I just don't think I could have lived if we had lost her."

"Now, Sandi, of course you would have lived! But now you don't have to think about it. Let's just enjoy the moment and go home to our Annie girl! She is waiting in great anticipation for her big sister to come home!"

Joletta spent the next months continuing her therapy appointments weekly and, as had been arranged, with a tutor who came daily to help her catch up on her schoolwork in hopes that she would be able to graduate with her class in '05.

At first, it was difficult adjusting to her new schedule but after a few weeks she slowly began regaining the skills that had been lost for the past months.

She related well with Laurie, the young woman that tutored her Monday through Friday.

Laurie would come to the house every morning at 8:00 since Joletta was able to concentrate better in the early part of the morning. Though Jo tired easily and needed to take frequent rests, as Fall turned into Winter, she began to be able to work for longer periods.

There were days at the beginning that they would only get an hour or two of work in, but as time went on they were able to put in a full school day's load by lunchtime. Without class breaks and focusing on what seemed most important, it didn't take as many hours as it would have in a classroom with 20 or more students. Laurie was well-pleased with the progress they were making.

233

Joletta would still sometimes forget what they had done the day before, but most of the time she did well on the subjects they attempted. Math was the most difficult and they spent many hours trying to help her re-learn skills that somehow had vanished like the sun when darkness falls.

They would take walks sometimes when the weather was nice. Joletta still had some weakness on her right side and she limped slightly. She was encouraged to get as much exercise as she felt up to in addition to her water therapy sessions.

Others might have given up, but not Joletta. She had a stubborn determination and the harder things were, the harder she worked. She hoped to be back at school by the first of the year.

Some days she felt sad and lonely. It was hard being 16 and Jo knew she was missing out on the things going on at school. Her friends were all busy getting ready for the holidays. Most of them didn't live very close so she didn't get to see them often. It really bummed her out!

Tiffany even had the leading role in the winter musical her school was doing. They were already in the middle of practices and making the sets, even though performances weren't until sometime in mid-January.

As Fall began to fade and the leaves once again floated to the ground, the cooler weather that would bring early winter began to set in and Jo became more and more restless. She was catching up with schoolwork now and her limp was becoming less noticeable. Although she would have to continue with therapy on her arm for several months, that too was showing improvement. She felt that it was time that she should be allowed to do more than just sit around the house with family.

"Mom," she spoke to Sandi the week before Thanksgiving, "do you think it would be all right if Tiffany and I invited some friends over to hang out this weekend? I thought maybe we could go to the mall over in Stoneville and then come back here to spend the night." Sandi looked down at her daughter who was stretched out on the floor with a "Teen" magazine spread open in front of her. "You know I haven't even started my Christmas shopping yet and it's almost Thanksgiving."

"I think that would be a good idea, Honey. It's been a while since you've had a sleep-over, hasn't it? Who else would you want to invite?"

"I'm not sure, but at least Tiffany and Tina, and Tina could bring her step-sister with her if she wanted. She says that I will like her; her name is Mindy. I might invite Bethany and Maddie and I thought Tiff could also invite someone."

"I had almost forgotten that Tina's dad got remarried last summer. Are you sure it's a good idea to include her sister since you haven't even met her yet?"

"I think it might hurt Tina's feelings if I didn't. I'm sure that if Tina likes her that it will be all right. Could we make popcorn and hot dogs in the fireplace?"

"Well, if Jim is willing to get it all started, it shouldn't be a problem."

"What about going to the mall? Tiff's dad will probably let her drive her car as long as the weather isn't too bad. We could go early and eat lunch at McDonalds or in the mall."

"I don't know, Hon; are you sure you are up to it?"

"Mom! I am fine. You have got to stop babying me. Please! I am so tired of just staying home and going only to church! You do know that other girls my age get to go out and do things, don't you?!"

Sandi smiled. "Yes dear, I do know that other girls get to go out, and I do know you haven't had much fun these past months. I just don't want you to over-do. That's all."

Jo rolled her eyes at her mom but said nothing more.

"Also, you can't go to the mall if you have that many girls. You wouldn't all fit. Tiffany hasn't been licensed long enough to drive with that many in her car."

"I guess I hadn't thought of that. I'll have to talk to the girls about that. But is it all right?"

"Let me talk to Jim and I have to check the calendar to make sure there isn't anything important going on this weekend. I think it will probably be OK."

Jo jumped up and grabbed her mom in a bear hug! "Thanks Mom! I love you so much!"

"I love you too, my Sweet Girl." Sandi smiled and shook her head as Jo bounced up the stairway, calling over her shoulder, "I have to go call Tiffany. We have a lot of plans to make. Thanks Mom!"

"I told you I still have to talk to Jim."

She didn't hear a word I said. Sandi sighed and shrugged her tight shoulders. *I guess it's time to start letting her go, but it isn't going to be easy.*

Jillian and Tom's family were planning to arrive home just before Christmas. They would be staying for only ten days while doctors evaluated little Jabral who had been born with a cleft palate. It was hoped that the following Fall they would return to start what would be the first of several surgeries to repair the child's deformities.

They were leaving the Mission in the capable hands of Audrey and Phillip Miller who had been living on the property the past month, training to take on the Mission leadership when Tom and Jill went on furlough at the end of the next year. It was expected that whenever the Roberts were re-assigned or the time came for them to return to the States full-time, the Millers would then take on full responsibility of the Mission.

Joletta was excited knowing they were coming. She still held on to her hope of going to Africa, although she wasn't sure now that it could ever happen.

236

She knew they had the orphanage up and operational. The last letter she had gotten from Jillian told her there were already 14 children living there, most of them under the age of eight. Jillian said they had two young women living in each cottage, serving as housemothers. Volunteers came regularly from the village to help with daily chores.

There were many more children in the area that needed a home, but until the mission was able to get more building supplies, things were nearly at a standstill.

Chapter 14
HOLIDAZE

Joletta woke Thanksgiving morning and shivered as she swung her legs over the edge of her bed. A beam of bright sunlight streamed in through the partially opened window blind, and she walked over to look at a world of glistening white! It looked as if the "Ice Cream Fairy" had waved her magic wand and covered everything as far as the eye could see. Snow glistened like diamonds and curled into peaks on top of the fence post. There were several brightly-colored cardinals eating below the bird feeder and a squirrel, hanging practically upside-down, filling his cheeks full of the delicious seeds that were put out, not for him, but for chickadees and nut hatches.

"Mom, did you see?" Jo was so excited at seeing the beautiful sight she didn't even think to notice if her family had risen yet. "Annie, come look! It snowed, and it's only Thanksgiving!"

Laughing, Sandi came into the hall, a towel wrapped around her. "Calm down, Honey. I don't think it's going anywhere for a while."

"Oh, it is just so pretty, Mom. We hardly had any snow last year. I hope we have lots this year! I can take Annie out and help her build a snowman and maybe later we can go sledding."

"Well, maybe later in the day you can take her out for a while, but for now, we have a lot of work that has to be done."

"Gloria and Big Jim will be here at about noon, and the rest of the family will be coming by 1:00."

"I know, Mom. I was just excited, that's all. I sort of forgot that everyone was coming over. Can I call and make sure Tim and Tammy bring extra clothes, so we can make Annie a snowman?"

"Sure, Honey, that would be a good idea, but after you do that, I want you to come to the kitchen and help me get things started."

"Well! Happy Thanksgiving, ladies! What's all the excitement about?"

"Jo is just happy about the weather."

"What weather? Oh, you mean that old cold yucky stuff outside? Who would want to get excited about that?" Jim grinned and gently pinched Jo's cheek. "Well, I guess if we are going to have to deal with the cold, I will have to start a fire in the fireplace, so we won't freeze to death!" He chuckled as he left them standing in the hallway.

"Mommy, mommy!" A much younger voice echoed through the morning air.

"Well, I think Annie must have discovered the snow." Sandi turned and started towards Annie's room. "You need to go get ready, and I need to get things started. By the way, happy Thanksgiving, Joletta!"

"You too, Mom."

Christmas promised to be a happy and busy time for Joletta and her family. Plans had already begun for the church youth to have a winter lock-in the first weekend in December. There were already thirty kids committed to coming.

It was going to be a lot of fun. Pastor Jay and his wife would be chaperones along with several other young adults that had only recently aged out of participating, but who enjoyed being helpers when needed. Everyone was to bring a gift, but instead of having an exchange, they would wrap and donate them to the local homeless shelter. Plans included lots of food, games, praise time and music, and in all likelihood, very little sleep.

Jo and her friends were planning the games. The boys were bringing soda, and the girls were bringing late-night snack food. Everyone would check in at 7:00, eat pizza that Pastor J. was ordering, and most would not leave until after church on Sunday morning.

The second week of the month the entire church was invited to go caroling, and Annie's 4th birthday was on the 12th. School would be out for Christmas break on the 19th, and they would be eating Christmas dinner at Big Jim and Gloria's on Saturday afternoon, the 20th.

The church program was on the 21st and on Christmas Eve, Sandi, Jim and the girls would celebrate at home and later would attend a community candlelight service.

Christmas day would be spent with Susan and the rest of her family. This Christmas was extra-special because Jillian and Tom would be with them. It was hard to believe but it had been two years since they had last been home.

Chapter 15
ANNIE'S BRRR-THDAY TREE

Jim had promised Annie a "real" tree - one that they would pick out and cut down themselves.

The day before her birthday Jim told Annie to get her coat and boots on. "Be sure to bring your hat and mittens. It's going to be a cold day."

"Where are we going?" Annie excitedly asked.

"Joletta and Mommy are going to get things ready for your birthday party, and we are going to go find the best and biggest Christmas tree any little girl ever had! What do you think of that, Miss Nosey?"

"Oh, Daddy! That is the very best idea! Do I get to pick it out myself?"

"Well, maybe you could let me help a little bit!"

"Yes, Daddy, you can help, but only a little. OK, Daddy? Can it be a birthday tree? Cause tomorrow is my birthday, right?"

"OK, Honey, if you want it to be a birthday tree, then I guess it can be your birthday tree. Mommy has made us some sandwiches and cookies to take along. Let's get going; it looks like it's going to snow some more."

Within minutes, the two of them were loaded into the pickup and off on their great adventure. Sandi had put in one of Annie's Christmas cassettes and they spent the next half-hour ride singing "Jingle Bells" and "Grandma Got Run Over By a Reindeer."

Soon they arrived and were greeted by a burly man with a wooly beard. He was wearing a thick stocking cap and heavy overalls. With a wide grin on his face, he greeted the pair. Reaching out to shake Jim's hand, he said, "What can I do for you folks today? I don't suppose this young lady is in need of a tree, by any chance?"

Annie was practically dancing in excitement. "Yes, yes!"

Jim stood with his arms crossed and a huge smile on his face as Annie explained the reason they were there. ""We are going to cut down a great big tree and then go home and put decorations on it! It's my Birthday Tree!"

"Well, I say! Everyone else that comes here wants a Christmas tree! A Birthday tree, huh? Well now let me think." Scratching his chin, he continued, "If I remember right, we did

have a few birthday trees here. Don't remember the last time someone asked for one though. Why don't we just drive on out and see what we can find for you?"

With a grin and a twinkle in his eye, he pointed to a Land Rover parked over beside the small business shack. "Want to go for a ride?"

The snow that had started shortly before they had left the house fell in large soft flakes, and the cold air turned Annie's cheeks as bright as a shiny red Christmas ball. Jim put his arm around the little girl, drawing her close to his side, and wrapped her scarf snugly around her neck.

It still amazed him that he had been so lucky to find not only a beautiful and talented woman but her wonderful little girls also. He had heard all the stories about ready-made families and the problems that often accompanied them. Why none of those kinds of issues had developed, he did not know, but he was truly thankful for that fact.

In only a short while, they were completely surrounded by a wonderland of thick snowflakes and a wide variety of pine trees. Except for an occasional bird and a rabbit that bounded from under snow-covered brush, all was peaceful. Only the sound of the Land Rover broke the silence. Even Annie had stopped her chatter and was looking outward in awe of the beauty around them.

Pulling to a halt at the top of a rise, Mr. Plummer cut the engine and climbed out of the four-wheeler.

242

"Here they are! Around on the other side of those small ones. Guess you aren't interested in a little birthday tree, are you miss?"

"Oh, No, Mister, we want a big one! Don't we Daddy Jim?"

"Well, Annie, I did say you could pick, but remember we have to be able to get it into the house!" He grinned down at the beaming little girl holding tightly to his hand.

Annie had no idea but Jim and Mr. Plummer had already consulted on the phone the day before and had pre-planned the entire adventure. Jim knew the weather was too cold to stay out for very long so had given the landowner instructions as to what size and kind of tree they would need. Now all that was left to do was to convince the little girl that she truly was the one doing the picking.

"Well, now, like I said, here are the very best birthday trees we have on the lot. These can be used for either birthday trees or Christmas trees, but the others are strictly Christmas trees only! Sure hope you can find one of these that will work for you."

"What do you think, Annie?" They stood in front of three beautiful fir trees that stood at least 12 feet high!

"Wow! Oh, yes, that is exactly what we want!"

"Now Annie, don't you think the ones over there would work better?" He pointed to several much smaller trees.

Immediately Annie's lower lip began to pucker into a pout. "NO!" Running to the tree in the middle of the row, she wrapped her small arms around it. "This is the tree I pick! You said I could pick my birthday tree, and this is the tree I pick!"

The two men immediately started to laugh. "Well, Bill, I guess I did tell her she could do the picking! Better cut that one."

Leaving Annie and Jim, Mr. Plummer returned a short time later with a chain saw. After several whacks with the ax, Jim cheerfully let him complete the job of felling the big tree.

"We will go back down and finish up business in the shack where it is warm. I bet Mrs. Plummer will make us some hot chocolate." Mr. Plummer smiled once again as he said, "I think the birthday girl is about done in. I'll have some of the boys come up in a bit and get the tree, and we'll bring it over to the house for you later this afternoon. I'll have to check their schedule, but I think

they should be able to have it over there before 4:00. They have a couple of others to take into town later so it will work well for all of us."

Jim picked up Annie and the two woodsmen walked silently to the waiting four-wheeler. Before they were even halfway back down the hill, Annie was sound asleep, wrapped in her stepfather's warm protective arms.

A few hours later, a large flatbed truck pulled into the drive of the Benning house, and two young boys got out and knocked on the door.

Joletta hurried down the stairs and opened the heavy door. "Hi, I guess you're here with the tree, aren't you?"

Before either of them had a chance to answer, Jo continued, "Oh, I know you from school! You are the Manning brothers, aren't you?"

"Right, Rich and Roland. Who did you say you were?"

"Oh, I'm Joletta. You were in my Journalism class last year. Guess you don't remember. Oh, sorry, I'll get Jim, and he can come out and help you. If you want to wait a minute, I think he's in the back of the house; I'll have to go find him."

"Sure, we'll wait out here in the truck."

Both the twins were grinning from ear to ear. They remembered Joletta as the girl that had been in the accident last Spring but hadn't paid much attention to her

244

before that. Both boys had steady girlfriends at the time, and seniors didn't usually talk to underclassmen much anyhow. However, now they were both wishing they had taken more notice.

"Man, is she ever a dish!" Roland said as they walked back down the drive to wait. "Wonder if she has any attachments."

"As if she would even think of taking a second look at you, Bro! Now I think on the other hand, I am much more likely her type!" Richard gave his brother a playful punch on the arm and sprinted toward the truck.

"What do you mean her "type?" We look just alike! I bet she couldn't tell us apart if she tried!"

"Not true, man! Besides, I am much more intelligent than you are, and it is obvious that she not only has beauty but brains as well!"

When Jim stepped out the front door, the two were still laughing and shoving one another in a friendly game of one-upmanship!

"Hi boys, what's up with you?"

Both boys quieted and sheepishly grinned as they said in unison, "Nothing sir." "Nothing at all. Got your tree for you. Dad said to bring it over and help you get it set up wherever you want it," finished Richard.

"That's really nice of you; I think Sandi has everything ready, but maybe we had better take it into the garage first. With all this snow, she will kill us all three if we end up making a mess in the house. In fact, I think we have decided with all this snow that we are going to have to wait until tomorrow morning to take it in. That way it will have time to dry out first."

Roland spoke first, "Hey, man. We could come back and help you then if you want."

"Well, I really don't think that is necessary-"

"No," Richard now chimed in. "We really don't mind at all."

Jim looked at both anxious boys and wondered exactly what was going on, but told them if that was convenient, for them to come again in the morning about 9:30.

"That will be great, man. We'll be here. 9:30 sharp."

As the boys headed back to the truck a few minutes later, Jim observed Roland slap Richard on the back and together they finished the final steps with their arms across the other's shoulder. Once again, Jim wondered what had just taken place.

Chapter 16
A COLD DECEMBER WIND

It had been a long week, and it felt good knowing the first round of holiday excitement was over.

Sandi had decided to take the morning off.

She curled her long slim body into her favorite chair and reached for the book she had started the week before Thanksgiving.

She so enjoyed this spot. Whenever things got hectic, she would get herself a cup of hot tea, a good book to read and head for this very place. It was like having her own little sanctuary.

If needed, she would wrap herself in a soft throw always kept on the arm of the chair. Some days she might not even read but sat with her eyes closed as the bright sunlight soothed her mind and body. Usually, after an hour or so, she would once again be ready to deal with all the little frustrations that were part of everyday life.

It surprised her somewhat when the doorbell chimed. Jim had left early, and the girls were both at school. This was Jo's last week before Christmas break, and Annie would be at play-school until Jim picked her up at 2:30.

She looked at the clock on the mantle; it was only 10:30. She hadn't expected anyone out and wondered who it could be. Then the doorbell once again broke the silence.

Stretching, she did not hurry as she went to the door, but as she looked through the decorative glass panel, she saw two uniformed police officers waiting on the opposite side.

Quickly she unlatched and opened the door.

"Can I help you?" she asked. "Is there something wrong?"

The male officer looked solemn and held out a badge showing his identification. "Sargent Dwayne Parker,

Delaware Township Police Department, Ma'am. May we come in?"

Opening the door wider, she stepped back and allowed them to enter the house.

"Are you Sandi Benning?"

"Yes, sir, I am. What is going on?" Sandi's voice felt suddenly weak. "Has there been an accident?"

The officer held up a picture for Sandi to look at and asked, "Do you know this woman?"

Sandi's hand came to her mouth. "Yes! Oh, God! That is my friend Jen Lucio! What happened to her? Is she— dead?" Sandi appeared as if she was going to be sick as she looked at the photograph.

Jen's hair was matted and bloody, both of her eyes were swollen. It was hard to tell if they were open or shut. There were large purple bruises on the arm that hung limply over the side of the stretcher, on which she was lying.

"She was found early this morning. Apparently, she was attacked as she was closing. So far, all we have is what she could tell us. Do you know a man named Sam? We were not able to get a last name. However, she is concerned that you may be in danger."

"Sam? He is the father of my youngest daughter. We lived together when she was a baby, but we haven't seen him in a long time. Surely you can't think he did this?"

"Where is your daughter now?"

"Annie? Why do you ask? She is at play-school." Suddenly, Sandi felt as if she could not breathe. "Oh! My God! Do you think?"

The officer continued, "We are not suggesting anything, but we need to make sure—"

Sandi was already headed toward the phone.

Before she had a chance to lift the receiver, it started to ring. Confused, she only hesitated for a moment before picking it up. "Hello?"

The voice of the young woman at the other end of the line spoke in short frantic bursts. "Mrs. Benning, Mrs. Benning! This is Bev over at Fun Stuff Playschool. Mrs. Benning, something awful has happened!"

"A man, Mrs. Benning.... there was a man who came here. He just grabbed her! I'm so sorry! He took Annie right off the playground!"

Sandi gave a muffled scream and heard no more of what the hysterical girl on the phone was saying. She simply buckled at the knees as the female officer grabbed her to break her fall. Sargent Parker pried the phone out of Sandi's hand as they guided her and helped her sit in the nearest chair.

"To whom am I speaking? This is Sargent Parker, Delaware Police. You need to tell me exactly what has happened."

Within minutes, the officer had gotten the basic details of Annie's abduction and dispatched extra officers to the site of the daycare.

Officer Dunn sat beside Sandi until she had calmed herself enough that she was able to give her phone numbers to get in touch with Jim and the family.

It was almost 10:00 when Sam pulled alongside the curb and just around the corner from the small house with the fenced-in yard. A brightly colored sign out in front read "Fun Stuff Playschool."

The day was chilly but most of the snow from the week before was gone, and the sun was shining brightly.

He had spent the last hour driving past the school and around the block and finally there were now children out playing on the climbers and swings. Two young women stood talking just outside of the doorway.

Because of a large brushy area, he could observe without being immediately obvious. He watched as several of the children played on the climber while others were kicking a big blue ball back and forth. Still others played in small groups of two or three or alone.

It only took a few moments for Sam to pick out the child he was looking for. He had no doubt this was Sandi's daughter for she had blonde hair and freckles and looked exactly like a picture of Sandi's younger sister that she had kept sitting on the nightstand beside her bed.

He figured he would just hang out and watch for a while and when Sandi came to pick up the kid, he would follow them and make her give him the money he deserved.

Reaching into the glove compartment, he took out a bottle of whiskey and took a large gulp of it. He was feeling kind of dizzy, and it was hard to concentrate, but he must find out where they lived.

When that "damned" Jen refused to cooperate, he had almost given up on getting any information out of her. But after working her over, for not giving him what he wanted, he had found her purse. Opening it and checking it for cash, he came across exactly what he needed all along.

It was an invitation to a Christmas program at this school. Made of red construction paper cut in the shape of Santa's hat, it had the kid's name on it. A note signed by Sandi said, "Hope you can come."

Sam took grim satisfaction that he had really fixed that uncooperative bitch. Even without her help, he now he had what he came for anyway! He chuckled as he thought *I bet she will think twice before she ever gives me anymore of her mouth.*

As he stood and watched, the two young caretakers were busy visiting. They had not even noticed when he stopped and got out of the car.

His opportunity came when two of the little boys got into a shoving match, and one managed to get himself knocked off the play-gym. Both women responded to the boy's loud screams and became busy with the injured child. Several of the children gathered around to see what was happening. Motioning for the children to come into the building, one woman picked the child up and carried him in while the other stood at the door continuing to motion for the children to come in. Then, she shut the door behind them.

It was too perfect! Annie continued playing. She was all alone now and in the excitement, they had not even noticed that she had not responded to the quick instruction to go inside.

Sam had not really known exactly how his plan would work out. He figured all he would do would be to follow Sandi home, and then they would willingly write him a check. All he had to do was promise them he would not bother them again.

It wasn't as though they didn't have plenty to spare. He knew the Benning family had plenty. In fact, he never dreamed there could be another way of going about it. Now, the perfect opportunity presented itself.

This would be easy and would guarantee he could get more out of them. They had money! Sam realized they would pay plenty, if he had more control of the situation!

Walking back over to the car, he reached inside and picked up the kitten that lay against its mother on a dirty blanket on the floor. Slowly, he walked toward the play area and quietly called Annie's name. When he got her attention, he put his finger to his lips and motioned her to come closer. He held the scraggly black kitten in his hand.

Carefully watching for other activity, he held the kitten out and the little girl came running over to see.

"What you got mister?"

Quickly putting a rough hand over her mouth, he lifted her over the low fence and sprinted toward the vehicle, which he had left with the ignition on. As he shoved her and the kitten into the car, the child bit him hard on the hand and managed to let out a blood-curdling scream.

One of the women reappeared at the door and heard the child's scream, but it was too late! He had Annie and was driving "like a bat out of hell "as he headed toward the outskirts of town.

Annie wailed from the back seat of the filthy old car. "Where are we going? I want to go back to school! I want my Momma!"

"Shut up, kid! I ain't gonna hurt ya. Don't ya know? I'm yer daddy!"

"No! I want my Daddy Jim!"

"Daddy Jim is it? Daddy Jim is gonna have ta give old Sammy big bucks if he ever plans ta see his little princess again!"

Once again, he took a large gulp out of the almost empty whiskey bottle and pressed even harder on the gas pedal.

Shaking his head to clear it, he continued driving. Turning a number of times, he eventually swerved down a gravel road. He slowed as he maneuvered the car around large rocks and holes in the rough unpaved road. Mud, dust and gravel billowed behind the vehicle as they traveled through a field and into a thickly wooded area.

Suddenly, the child started screaming at the top of her lungs. "Take me home! Take me home now!" She was throwing her arms around and kicking her feet on the back of the seat.

Sam jerked the car to a sudden halt and reached his rough filthy hand into the back. Grabbing the little girl by the hood of her jacket, he pulled her almost over the seat and close enough to his cruel face that she could smell the foul odor of the alcohol on his breath.

"If ya ever want ta go home and see yer momma again ya'd better shut yer mouth and shut it *now*!"

Shoving her toward the back of the seat, he roughly released her. "Damn kid! This better be worth all my trouble!"

By the time they stopped, snow had begun to fall, and the sky had darkened with the impending storm.

Annie finally quieted. Her face was white and tear-streaked. Her pigtails came loose, leaving her hair in a tangled mess. She pulled her small body into a tight ball as far back into the seat as she could get. The kitten was a black fur-ball curled against her pink parka.

After another fifteen minutes, Sam finally pulled into yet another dirt lane. He stopped and turned off the ignition.

"Well, girlie, we're home."

The small unpainted shack looked like it had not seen a living thing in at least fifty years. The porch roof had caved in and several of the windows were just broken shards of glass.

Snow had begun to fall more thickly now and the ground around them was already covered. "Come on kid. We got work to do. Come on, damn it. It's freezin' out here!"

Annie whimpered but got out of the door he opened. Mumbling something to himself, he guided her toward the back of the bungalow. "Around here."

They entered at the rear of the cabin and after shutting the door, he slid an old bolt that was near the top into place. "There! Just in case ya get any ideas about wanderin' off, that'll keep ya safe. You know; my old man used ta lock us in at night, so we couldn't run off." He grunted and continued, "Didn't ever think I would need to use it myself."

253

They were standing in the middle of what had been a small kitchen area. Other than an old drop-leaf table with peeling paint and one broken chair, there wasn't much left. On the table, there were several tin cans and a jar of peanut butter, a partially used loaf of bread, and a twelve-pack of beer.

Sam stepped into another room and started piling wood into a very old cast-iron stove. "I'll git 'er warmed up soon. Sorry 'bout the mess but didn't really plan on havin' company!"

The little girl stood with her back pressed against the wall, still clinging to the kitten that was now beginning to try and free itself from her grip.

"Better let that stinkin' cat loose, or it's gonna scratch the heck out o' you." Sam moved a step closer to the child, and she scooted further into a corner. She was shaking so hard her teeth were practically rattling. She let the kitten go free, and it ran to its momma that had followed them into the house. They crawled into a cardboard box under the table, and the kitten started to nurse.

"Aw, come on kid. I ain't gonna bite ya! Come on over here - here by the fire. Lemme take a look at ya."

A single tear ran down her cheek, but she stubbornly held her chin up and shook her head.

"Man, ya must be as stubborn as yer mother! Right now. It's warmer over here anyway."

Very reluctantly, Annie slowly crept over a little nearer to where Sam was standing. He reached over and pulled her even closer. Looking at her intently, he took her by the arm and turned her in a complete circle. An odd feeling came over him, and he

quickly released her arm. "You ain't nearly as ugly as ya were when you was a baby."

254

This time he was the one that seemed to want to get as far from the child as he could. "Man, I gotta figure out what to do with ya now that I have ya."

Sam walked back into the kitchen and opened a beer. "Let me think."

"I guess now that you here I have ta feed ya something'. Are ya hungry?" Not waiting for an answer, he picked up a plastic spoon and put a blob of peanut butter on a slice of bread. "Ain't got much, guess this'll have ta hold ya till tomorrow."

He folded the slice of bread over and reached out a filthy hand to give it to Annie.

"You stink, Mister! Don't you ever take a bath?"

"What? Well you little b—, you finally found your tongue, huh? If ya must know, this ain't exactly the Waldorf now, is it?"

"Just eat yer sandwich and shut the hell back up! I think I liked ya better when ya was quiet!"

With that, he muttered something under his breath and stumbled over to what at one time had been an overstuffed chair. The faded armrests were broken and torn, and springs poked out from both the seat and the back. An old rug was wadded and stuffed in the seat in an effort to make it usable. Flopping down into the chair, a poof of dust filled the air as Sam said to himself, "Man, I hope we git this settled quickly. Don't know what I was thinkin'!"

Chapter 17
HIDE AND SEEK

Within the hour, every police station and highway patrol unit in the state of Pennsylvania had been notified of the abduction. Television stations and radio stations blared the news.

"Be on the lookout for an older car, light green, with West Virginia plates. Male suspect approximately 40 years old wearing a dark coat. This person is wanted in the abduction of a 4-year-old child.

The young girl was last seen wearing a bright pink parka, green and white sweater, and blue jeans. She has sandy blonde hair in braids and blue eyes.

This suspect is considered armed and dangerous. Do not approach. If you have information, call the number on the screen."

Phone numbers were posted, roadblocks were set up at every major highway in the area, and flyers were being printed to be distributed around local businesses.

A call center was set up at the Benning house in case the perpetrator tried to make contact with the family and every newspaper within fifty miles carried the story on the front page.

Sam woke with a start. He could not think straight. Something had woken him and he wasn't sure what it was. It was very dark, but a glimmer of light shown around the door of the potbelly stove.

Then he saw her. It was a little girl. Oh! Now he remembered. It was Sandi's daughter Annie. She was standing only a couple of feet from the chair he was in, looking at him intently. He could not see her clearly, mostly in silhouette, but what light there was reflected on cheeks wet with tears.

"Mister, I'm cold. Please, may I have a blanket?" She paused for a moment and then continued in a small sad voice, "Mister, when are you going to take me home? I miss my mommy."

Suddenly Sam felt something strange and unfamiliar. He could feel his heartbeat and his hands and neck began to sweat although the room was cold. He sat up, trying to understand what had just happened.

"Uh, girly, uh," Sam didn't know what to say. "I'm sorry."

He got out of the chair, standing there for a moment, not sure what to do next.

After only a minute or two Sam picked Annie up and sat her in the old chair wrapping her small body in the shabby rug.

Clearing his throat, he walked to the stove. Opening the door, he threw several pieces of wood on top of the red coals, which flared almost immediately.

Turning around Sam walked once again over to the chair. "That'll warm it up. I'll look fer another bl---" He stopped mid-sentence, realizing that the child had fallen fast asleep. Sam stepped back over and held his cold hands closer to the heat.

His head hurt like hell, he was hungry and, worst of all, he still had no idea how he was going to take care of the situation. By now, he realized that he had made a major mistake when he snatched the kid.

At the time, everything had happened so quickly. He hadn't really been thinking right because he was drunk and had completely forgotten the fact that he *still* did not even know where Sandi lived or how to contact her.

On top of everything else, once he had taken the time to really look at her, he found that he almost liked the kid. Now, he had her to deal with, he still had no money, and cops would be crawling all over the county looking for them. Sam had gotten in and out of many bad messes but

257

this was by far the worst. Sure, the kid was his, but he had a feeling the law would not look at it that way. No one ever had seen things from his point of view.

The more he thought, the more panicky he felt. At first, he had thought as long as he stayed here no one would be able to find him, but now he wasn't so sure.

It had been years since anyone had been down the road and into these woods. After his grandfather had been sent to prison, his mom had packed up his 1-year-older brother Todd and Sam and had moved south.

He was only 12 at the time but could well remember her heavy drinking, the drugs, and the steady stream of men that regularly cycled in and out of their rundown apartment.

Their mom had pretty much let them do as they pleased, and the older he and Todd got, the wilder their behavior became.

At one time, his brother had been an honor student, with hopes and dreams, but all that changed when Todd died of a drug overdose shortly before Sam's 17th birthday. After that, there seemed to be no reason to stay so Sam left. As far as he knew, no one ever came to look for him and he never went back.

At first, he followed the fruit harvest in the southern states, mostly picking peaches and strawberries, or doing about any other job he could find, to keep from going hungry. It was hot hard work, but he hooked up with a group of migrant workers and stayed with them for the next couple of years. He left when he got into a fight with a guy over one of the women they traveled with. After that he worked construction until he returned to the area.

He should have realized moving here would just bring him more bad luck!

For a while, things had not been bad. Meeting and moving in with Sandi had started out pretty well. At the time, she was working at the bar with Jen and other than the fact she came with a kid attached, things were going pretty well. She was good to look at, fun in the sack, and kept him fed and in clean shirts. Unfortunately, when she realized she was pregnant it changed everything. They argued constantly. She didn't feel like going out, she didn't feel like having sex, and she thought she ought to be able to quit work and just stay home until the baby was born! That was more than he could bear. Without her check, they would barely be able to make ends meet. Sam was furious and told her so, in no uncertain words... It wasn't long after she had this second kid that she came home and caught him with Gina. That was what ended it all!

After giving her a few weeks to cool down he had tried to get in touch with her. He planned to come back home, but she had moved and told Jen she wanted nothing to do with him!

He now had to decide what he was going to do next. It was only another hour or so before sunrise and he felt trapped, like a rabbit in a fox's mouth.

Was there still a way he could get in touch with Sandi and her rich family and get the money he knew he deserved. *Damn! What am I goin' to do?* He nervously looked toward where the child was still sleeping. *There's one thing fer sure, ain't nothin' gonna happen if I don't decide ta do something'. Guess I'm gonna have ta make a trip back ta town; gotta git a paper or something' and see if old Sam made it all the way ta the front page. Maybe, I can figger out what ta do then.*

Sam decided his only safe option was to leave the girl and drive down to the coffee shop he had eaten at the past several days. There was a newspaper stand out in front and he could listen to the radio on the way there. It

259

was almost morning now and he would have to hurry. It was maybe 4 miles or so to the little gas station and cafe and he was hoping to get there and be gone again before the locals showed up for their morning caffeine fix.

As he was putting more wood in the stove, Annie awoke and sat up crying once again for her momma.

"Now listen kid, you can't have yer momma right now. Got it?"

Annie's cries became quieter as she woke up more fully and, looking at Sam in the glow of the firelight, she said slowly, "Ple-e-ase, Mister! My mommy will be so glad to see me. You could show her your kitties."

Swallowing hard, for he did not know what to say to her, Sam walked over to Annie and said quietly, "I haf ta go get a newspaper, but I won't be gone long and when I get back we'll figger out what we're gonna do. Maybe we'll take a trip and go ta Disney World or something'. Whadda ya think about that?"

"No! I just want to go home!"

Becoming angry he said harshly, "Ya stay here, I'll be back in a while!" Sam opened the door and walked out into the cold darkness, shutting it behind him with a loud bang.

As he locked the old bolt on the outside of the door, he could hear her pitiful screams at the realization that he was leaving her alone. *Damn kid just needs ta shut up and be good! Good thing we're out here; she could wake the dead.*

Driving slowly over the rough snow-covered path Sam mumbled to himself, "Don't know how I got myself in so deep. Don't know how I'm gonna get myself out. Can't just leave her there!"

He tried to think back over the past 24 hours. He could barely remember any of it before grabbing the little girl. Going over it all in his head, he remembered going to the bar to talk to Jen. *What the hell happened?*

260

Slowly he remembered them arguing and him shoving her back behind the counter. *What had happened after that?* It was all a fog in his head.

It had been almost 18 hours since Annie had disappeared. So far, they had not been contacted and there had been no information leading anyone to hope that things were going to take a turn for the better.

Sandi had finally dozed off, leaning heavily on Jim's shoulder. Big Jim was sitting across the room talking quietly with the local police chief.

There were FBI agents manning the phones at the dining room table and Jo had fallen asleep in the chair where her mother had been reading the morning before. Susan sat quietly beside her with a protective hand on the girl's soft hair.

Several vehicles from local news stations were parked along the road, as close to the Benning house as possible. Reporters waited anxiously for anyone to step outside or to try to get through the crowd for whatever tidbits of new information they might give. Jim's dad was in the process of setting up a news conference for later in the afternoon.

Once Sam got onto the main road, he switched on the radio on and turned the dial to find a local station. It took only a few moments before the speaker started beeping loudly with a news flash.

"Early yesterday a 4-year-old girl was abducted from Fun Stuff Nursery School. It has been reported that the perpetrator is the child's biological father, Samuel Frick, age 39, with brown hair and wearing a black jacket.

The FBI has reportedly taken charge of the case and can be contacted by calling the National Hotline for Missing Children at 1-800-843-5678 or call your local Police Department.

They were last seen driving south on US 288 in a light green, older –model car. Be on the lookout.

The child stands approximately 39 inches and has light brown or sandy blonde hair and was wearing a pink parka and blue denim jeans.

The suspect is also wanted in the attack of a local waitress, who was transferred to the Philadelphia Head Trauma Unit at Thorton Medical Center last night and is in critical condition.

The perpetrator must be considered armed and dangerous. We will keep you updated as more information comes into the station. This is Jimmy J at QZTV 280 on your radio dial."

My God! They make me sound like an ax murderer! Sam was still shaking when he saw the dim lights of the small gas station and coffee shop. He looked around carefully as he pulled into the parking area at the side of the building. He was glad to see that the outside lighting was poor, making it less likely that he would be noticed.

Pulling his ball cap down low over his eyes and putting the wide collar up around his neck, he wrapped his jacket tightly around him. Quickly he stepped under the building's canopy and walked toward where the morning papers were kept in a coin- operated stand just outside the restaurant.

As he dropped several small coins into the deposit slot he was startled when the door opened and a man walked out laughing, as he said goodbye to someone inside, they almost collided head on...

"Oh, sorry, I didn't see you," said the man, pausing for only a moment before heading to the shiny pickup sitting in front of the building.

Climbing into the vehicle, he stomped the snow loose from his boots and shut the door with a bang.

Standing in a cold sweat, Sam's hands shook as he put the last of the coins into the slot and pulled the morning paper out of the metal box.

As quickly as possible he headed back to his car and turning the ignition anxiously, he circled back toward the cabin. Several inches of snow had fallen overnight, and had he not known the lane into the woods so well, he would have missed it completely.

As he drove the final quarter mile down the old path to the shack, the sun turned the sky a deep pink and soon the dark night had disappeared and another day began.

Unlocking the padlock, he could hear Annie sobbing on the opposite side of the door. He entered and there she sat on the broken chair with her little arms crossed on the tabletop and her head down. "You—you left me here! All alone, and I-I didn't know where you were!" She was sobbing so hard he could barely understand her.

For some reason Sam suddenly felt as though he was going to cry too. He stood there looking down at the tiny shaking child and did what he had never in his life done before.

He picked her up and held her close to him. Patting her on the back, he could feel her heartbeat through the thickness of the heavy jacket he wore. She was shaking like a leaf but her body was soft and limp.

A warm rush of long-forgotten feelings came over him and, finally using her name, he said, "Listen, Annie, listen. I'm gonna make this right. I promise I am, but ya have ta be quiet and lemme think of a way."

"See, it's this way, I don't think anyone is ever gonna understand, and if I took you back now—" His voice trailed off as he realized she was looking intently at him and had all but stopped crying.

Clearing his throat, he put her down.

"Well, I'm glad that's settled. I guess we need ta have some breakfast."

"I need to use the toilet, sir."

"Oh! Uh—well, over there in the corner's a bucket. See it? Ya can use that."

"A bucket!" The little girl's eyes grew big. "I can't sit on a bucket! Where is the potty?"

"Uh—well, as I said, this ain't no hotel or anything like that. If ya need ta go, then just go and use the bucket. OK? You can take it over there behind the stove, but be careful, the stove is hot."

"You promise you won't look?"

"Yeah, I promise." Sam actually felt embarrassed by the child's modesty. Who would have thought a kid no bigger than she was would worry about a thing like that?

Chapter 18
READY OR NOT

It was just after 7:30 a.m. when Denny Thomas pulled into the angled parking spot in front of the Delaware Police Department.

Opening the heavy glass door, he stepped inside and walked over to the reception desk. "Hey, Jerry, is Sargent Parker here?"

Getting up and coming around the desk, Jerry Leonard reached out to shake Denny's hand. "Sorry, he is still over at the Benning house. Something I can do for you? Everything going ok with you and yours, I hope."

"Oh, yeah, kids are growing, and Gale is doing great. Baby's due in a couple of weeks, so of course she is beginning to feel like a giant watermelon, but other than that, not much happening. I think I may have something for you, though. On that kidnapping case you all have on your hands."

"Hey, man, we could sure use a break here. What you got?"

"Well, I'm not sure of anything, but this morning I stopped in at Dusty's Diner. I had been out at the farm helping Dad take care of a sick heifer and by the time we got that all taken care of it was so late I just stayed over."

"Anyway, on my way back into town I stopped to have a little breakfast before heading home to shower and as I was leaving, I practically ran smack into a guy outside on the porch."

It was still dark out but it looked like he was getting a paper. Guess that isn't really unusual but he sure did act surprised and kind of shook up when I spoke to him."

"At first I didn't think much about it, you know how some people are just not very friendly. But as I was leaving, I noticed him high-tailing it around to the side of the building to his car. Now doesn't it seem a little

265

strange, given the fact that my truck was the only vehicle there, that he parked clear around on the other side?"

"You're right, man, that does seem strange. What did he do next?"

"Well, that's the thing. I really didn't give it much thought until I got almost into town, but, after thinking about it, he really did seem shook that I came out the door. He kind of turned away and pulled his hat down like he didn't want me to see what he looked like. And another thing - do you remember old man Ruthers?"

"Ruthers? No, don't believe I do. Who is he?"

"Now, think back a few years. It was just about the time I started high school. He was caught messing with little kids. They charged him with about everything they could get by with and sent him to prison. As far as I know, he is still there. Probably the only reason I remember was because my sister went to school with some of Ruther's grandkids. Guess they moved away and never came back. Anyway, the reason I mentioned it is because my brothers and I used to go out off of Bolo Road and fish quite a bit. I'm not sure what made me think of it, but there used to be a little cabin out there, quite a ways back in the woods."

"My older brother Ethan told me it was where Ruthers had lived. I was just thinking, that maybe there could be some kind of connection. It couldn't be more than a few miles over there from Dusty's."

Officer Leonard tore a page from the notepad he had been writing on at his desk and said, "Actually, I do remember that case. It was a couple of years before I graduated from the academy, but the guys used to talk about old cases sometimes. Do you know if the cabin is still there?"

"Not really, it's been years since I've been out that way."

"I think we need to give the Sarge a call and give him this info. I'm sure if they haven't already checked it out, they will want to. I'll also pull up the old files and see what we can find out about Ruthers. Do you still remember where it is?"

"Well, it was down river quite a ways from the area we usually went to. If I remember right, we weren't catching much the day we found the place. We decided to explore the area for some new holes and hiked around quite a while --- followed the river until it split --- before we came upon it. As I said, it's been years. You got a county map showing the river? I'm almost certain if you do, I can pretty much promise you I'll be able to show you the spot."

Officer Leonard responded with a nod. "I'll get one for you and then we'll call Sgt. Parker."

Dwayne Parker stood alongside his cruiser smoking the last of the two packs of cigarettes that he carried with him in case he had a situation like this where he wasn't able to get to the market to buy more. He looked at the watch on his wrist. In only a couple of hours, it would mark a full 24 since the Benning's daughter's disappearance. Feeling slightly sick to his stomach, he thought of his own little girls.

Every minute, every hour, it became more and more likely that this would not end the way everyone was praying it would.

Only having had one other case in the past 19 years that had involved a child this young, he remembered that luckily at that time, things had turned out OK. After searching the neighborhood, police found the child playing at the home of another little boy, only a block down the road from where the family lived.

Hoping this would turn out as well, Dwayne jumped as the phone fastened to his belt started ringing. Unlatching the black leather case, he pressed the button that said "talk." "Sgt. Parker."

"Sarge, it's Jerry down at the Department. Listen, man, I have Denny Thomas here with me and he has some information that I'm thinking may be helpful to your people there."

"Shoot, man, at this point we could really use some help."

Within the hour, the search helicopters had been reassigned. A parade of law enforcement vehicles, including F.B.I. agents, a swat team, and local authorities were on their way to their destination. Following not far behind was a convoy of news reporters that had been camped out as close to the action, or inaction, as it had been, until this development.

After Sandi, when told of the new development in the case, had become almost hysterical, she and Jim were given the OK to ride with Officer Parker, but only as far as the barricade that was being put in place at the turnoff on Bolo Road.

The sound of a helicopter in the distance was the first hint of impending disaster for Sam. Hearing the whirring of the spinning blades as the chopper drew closer, Sam nervously walked over to the door. Cracking it only enough to look toward the blue sky, he watched in silence until he was sure that his nerves were not getting the best of him.

Had it been summer, the thickly wooded area would be well-camouflaged by the leafy trees and bushes. Although there had once been a small cleared area, with many years of neglect, it had long ago become overgrown. Now there was very little cover and the small, graying cabin was likely to be seen more easily.

The sharp eyes of a federal agent riding in the passenger seat of the helicopter, using high powered binoculars, scanned as much of the land below as humanly possible.

Sam turned and frantically started putting things into a plastic bag he had gotten at the small market the first day he came back to the area.

"Come on, kid, we gotta get outta here! In a few minutes there are gonna be cops crawlin' all over the place. We gotta go before that chopper can let 'em know where we are."

Annie looked up, confused. Since earlier when Sam had clumsily tried to comfort her, she had settled down and was now sitting on the floor quietly playing with the kitten and the momma cat.

"Where are we going? Are you going to take me home now?"

Sam did not answer. Acting as if he had not even heard the child, he picked up the quickly-gathered food and the old blankets they had been using in an attempt to keep warm. He then grabbed Annie by the hand. Practically dragging her, he headed toward the car that he had parked and covered with an old tarp.

Letting her hand loose, he yanked the tarp off and opened the back door. Shoving the blankets and grocery bags in, he then turned and reached for the child. Suddenly she pulled away and started running back toward the house.

"What in hell are ya doin'? Get back here!"

Annie was almost to the open door of the cabin when she turned. "We forgot my kitty, Mister!"

In frustrated anger, Sam ran behind her and grabbed her around the waist. "No! Forget about them damn cats! I told ya we haf ta go. Now!"

Running back to the car, he shoved the small girl into the back seat and slammed the door. Climbing into the driver's seat he hardly heard her pitiful sobs. All he could think of was getting away.

Jabbing the key home, he turned it as he pumped the gas pedal. The engine sputtered but it did not start. Trying again, he stomped several times on the pedal before turning the key once more. Still it only sputtered. Now Sam was in full panic mode.

Annie's pleas from the back were only background noise as he once again heard the helicopter coming closer.

"Shut up! Can't ya see I'm busy?"

"Please, why are you mad at me, Mister? I was trying to be a good girl like you told me." Her howls got louder as Sam continued his efforts to get the vehicle running.

Finally, the engine roared to life. Shifting into reverse, he looked in the rearview mirror and to his horror he spotted the dark figures of several uniformed persons moving stealthily in and out of the cover of towering trees. Not understanding how the authorities had gotten there so quickly, he shifted into drive and jammed his foot on the accelerator.

With tires spinning, he made a desperate effort to head the car away from the impending danger, down what had once been the back way off the property. He accelerated hard and the car began to move, skidding and sliding first one way and then another.

The snow that had fallen the previous day, and the condition of the gravel lane, made his attempt at escape nearly impossible. He tried to control the vehicle as he swerved in and out of rocks, scrub grass, and fallen timber.

Lurching forward, Annie was jerked and thrown in all directions. Her small body flew forward and landed hard on the floor as the car hit the sharp rocks at the edge of the partially-frozen riverbed. Terrified and freezing the little girl wrapped her small arms around her knees and drew them to herself. Only whimpering now, she waited for what would come next.

For what seemed like an hour, they plundered along until suddenly the car careened into the shallows of the creek bed. As the tires made contact with the jagged flint of the river bottom, both front wheels blew out, bringing the car and its passengers to a final jarring halt.

In his desperation, Sam had forgotten that, in order to get to the main road, you first had to cross the creek bed, which was dry only in midsummer.

Knowing that his pursuers were not far behind him, he tried to get the car to move again. Pushing the gas pedal to the floor the rear tires only sank deeper into the ground as gravel, mud and dirty snow flew wildly into the air. With the tires now useless, he could go no further.

Cursing and yelling he got out and pounded his fist on the hood. Kicking the car hard, he turned and looked behind and around them, assessing if there were any remaining options. He felt as though he had fallen into a deep pit and realized his chances had all but run out.

Annie, huddling on the floor, crawled under the blankets that had fallen beside her and tried to keep as far away from the angry voice and frightening rough hands of her abductor as possible. She hoped he would forget she was there.

He could hear his pursuers; closer and closer they came, until Sam realized there was no time left. *If he could only get across the creek—*

In a final effort, he ran on foot into the frozen creek.

The thin layer of ice cracked like a shotgun blast as icy cold water soaked through the heavy boots he was wearing. Pushing on, he only had gone a few yards when he fell onto the cruel rocks. Numbing cold soaked through his heavy winter jacket and clothing, astounding him.

Getting up, he tried to maintain his balance only to lose it again on the slick icy rock, this time cutting a large gash on his hand. Excruciating pain exploded deep within his beating chest and only adrenalin kept him going as he forced himself up once again and continued running for what he hoped would be freedom.

He had almost made it to the far side, when suddenly they appeared, coming toward him. From every direction were Federal officers with high-powered rifles pointed directly at Sam. The hunt was over and all hope was now gone.

Staggering to the edge of the water, he tried to speak but no words came out. Ice crystals hung from his unwashed hair and clothing. His normally ruddy skin was gray and his lips, blue.

With no control of his own body left, he attempted to put his hands in the air, but he fell once again, this time face first into the snow. This time he did not attempt to get up.

Officers approached cautiously, pulling him further onto the embankment and barking orders for him to stay down. A young officer hesitated. Rolling Sam over, he said, "Well, I'll be!" Calling back across the creek, he shouted, "Captain, we better get a rescue unit out here. I could be wrong, but I think this man is dead!"

As Captain Powell radioed for further assistance, he turned to a nearby officer and inquired about Annie. "Have you found the little girl?"

"Yes, Sir, we have her. Smart little thing, she was hiding all wrapped up in some blankets! Poor child was scared half out of her mind. Took a couple of minutes to convince her it was over and she was OK, but all is well. Her parents are on their way as we speak."

"Thanks, Ray, I'll let the team know!" As he holstered his two-way radio, the Captain was all smiles. Soon cheers and applause came from the officers standing in the area.

"Let's wrap things up and go home, folks."

It had been a long 48 hours, but it always made their hard work worthwhile when it ended this way. Dwayne Parker walked over towards where Sandi and Jim were sitting. A young man from QZTV had brought over two folding chairs and generously offered them to the overwhelmed couple.

"Well, Momma, are you ready to go see that little daughter of yours?"

"Oh, yes! Yes, please!"

Grabbing Jim in a bear hug, they both immediately jumped up. Heading almost at a run toward Sargent Parker both Sandi and Jim spouted, "Where is she? Is she all right! Oh, my God! Please, where is she?"

Smiling the officer spoke again. "Well, we can walk to meet them or wait here until they bring her out. It'll take about 10 minutes or so. There is some really rough area---"

"No!---I mean, yes! I want to go now!" Sandi was laughing and crying at the same time as they started down the old rock road toward the cabin.

Annie flew into her mother's arms!

Tired and cold but unhurt in any way, she still did not understand exactly what had happened, only that her momma and Daddy Jim were here and that was enough for now. She did not realize, nor did she care, that she would never again see Sam, the man responsible for her birth.

"Mommy? Can we go get my kitties now?"

Chapter 19
ANSWERED PRAYERS

"They have her!" the officer announced to the crowd waiting anxiously just outside of the barricaded area that was marked off with bright yellow tape. "She is safe and unhurt."

Immediately electric excitement filled the area. Cheers, high-fives, and laughter replaced the strained silence that had settled over them.

News reporters were ready, and the somber scene soon became one of organized chaos.

Phones ringing, newscasters, with cameras ready and microphones in hand, hoping to catch the best angle, or the best statement from anyone willing to comment or to talk to them - they waited for anything that might give them the edge over another station!

Two days had felt like an eternity. Sandi could hardly believe that finally, it was over!

"What? What kitties are you talking about, Sweetie?"

"Mister Sam gave me a kitty, Mommy. It's a boy, and his name is Blackjack. That's 'cause he is black all over. Mr. Sam said that was a good name for him."

"Blackjack is in the house with his momma. Sam said they couldn't come with us, but I think they are lonely."

"Mommy, Mr. Sam got mad at me, but I was being a good girl. Can we go and get them now, Mommy?"

Sandi looked at Jim, who stood beside them quietly listening. "I don't know, Honey. The police have to look at the house, and I'm sure they will take care of them."

Her tired little body suddenly stiffened, and she started shaking as tears flooded her eyes and freely rolled down her dirty cheeks. "No! They are *my* kitties!"

274

Annie's mother gathered the child closely to her heart as Sergeant Parker, who had been listening, walked over.

Stepping a few feet to one side from Sandi and Annie, he talked earnestly with Jim for a few moments, and then the two men walked

away, only to return with the kitten a short time later, its mother following closely behind them.

"Jim!. . ."

Paramedics soon arrived and took Sam's body away. Later, an autopsy would reveal that Sam died of heart failure. Unknowingly, Sam suffered a hereditary heart condition - the same condition that had been responsible for the early death of his father.

Sam and his brother had been just young kids. It was at that time their mother had moved herself and her boys to this property. Even back then, it was a pitiful little shack, deep in the woods near the banks of Spring Creek.

Sam always had a hard life. There had been many poor decisions, cruelty, pain, and no one had ever taught Sam compassion or how to love.

Now, there was no more time to learn. Sam literally had been "scared" to death!

"It'll be all right honey. We will take them to the vet and have them checked out tomorrow."

Annie squealed in delight as Jim handed her the black ball of fur. "It's probably cleaner than *she* is right now anyway. What do you say we go home?"

Much later, after a long bubble bath and after everyone had the chance to see for themselves that she was safe, her mother sang to Annie and rocked her until she slept.

Jo had taken on the task of bathing the cats and, after several scratches and a couple of escapes by the momma, both were now curled up next to the sleeping child. Sandi had objected, fearing they could be sick or full of fleas, but after Jim declared them healthy and after Jo bathed them, she simply could not refuse.

Finally, Jim convinced her to come across the hallway into the Master bedroom. "We need to talk, Sandi."

"What is it, Jim?"

"Sandi." Since he didn't have any other way to tell her except to just say it, Jim paused and then said, "Sandi, Sam is dead."

"No, Jim, they arrested him. They rescued Annie and arrested him. I know he's in a lot of trouble, but he isn't dead—is he?"

"When we went and got the cats, Sergeant Parker told me that he just keeled over. Must have been a heart attack or something of the sort. No one even fired a shot; he was running, trying to get across the creek, and he just fell over and died. They tried CPR but he was gone before the rescue unit even got there."

"Oh, Jim, that is just sad." Sandi looked down at her hands, trying to hold back tears, but she was just too tired. It was too hard to take it all in.

He gathered her close to him and she cried in the arms of the man she loved. "He wasn't all bad, you know."

"I know, Honey, I know, but the important thing is, we have our Annie back safely!"

The next several days the family stayed close to home. Everyone seemed to want to know all of the details of their story and the news media was determined to satisfy the public interest.

With less than a week until Christmas, they made the decision to allow an in-home interview to the local news station. The 10-minute session would be carried live on the morning news shows and would be recorded to be shown later in the day.

Jo chose to spend the night before the program with Susan and the girls. Tiff and Sammy were staying with their grandmother while on Christmas break and although Joletta had talked to Tiffany on the phone they had not been together since Annie had disappeared.

With the stress of the past days, Jim and Sandi felt it would be a good thing for Jo to have time with her special friends.

They needed to be with Annie, and they knew that Jo was always very open and comfortable with Susan who had become, to Joletta and Annie, the grandmother they had never had. Jim's stepmother Gloria was a wonderful person and friend but seemed more like a doting aunt than a grandmother.

Joletta had handled Annie's abduction with an adult-like calm assurance, saying that God would take care of her little sister and insisting He would bring her home. Even with her amazingly calm attitude throughout their ordeal, she asked her parents to let her go to Susan's and be excluded from the interview.

Big Jim and Gloria would be at the house to support them as well as several of the officers that had been directly involved with the case.

Jillian and Tom's family had arrived the night before but, because of the long exhausting trip, planned to stay upstairs until later in the day. It had taken them almost twenty hours to travel from South Africa and they were all exhausted.

Chapter 20
THE GOOD OL' USA

Jillian woke very early - it was mid-day in southern Africa - before any of the others. It felt good to be home again. She loved the Mission and all of their African friends and she loved the work they did there, but sometimes she wished they could return and just live a quiet uneventful life. Remembering they had returned only to hear the unnerving story of Joletta's little sister, she decided that perhaps their lives were not so bad after all.

She closed her eyes and softly whispered a prayer. *"Thank You, dear Father, for returning little Annie to her family!"* She yawned and smiled as she sat up in the same bed she had slept in as a girl.

The sun was streaming in the antique window; the old glass made wavy patterns on the wall beside the bed and onto the colorful quilt that her great-grandmother had made especially for Jill before she passed away some 25 years ago.

The room had always been a special place to Jillian.

She still remembered how her brothers had coveted the room at the top of the house. They wanted to make it a "Pirate Crow's Nest" but mother had overruled them.

Mom had told them the room was too small for the two of them. Jillian believed it was more than likely that their mother was afraid they would end up using the small window in the room to access the roof, and then in turn, would fall and break their necks!

It really was quite a small room, but it was warm and cozy and she loved every minute she spent in it. There was a window seat where she had enjoyed many happy hours reading her favorite books.

Ever since she was a very small child, she had loved to read and would sit for hours with her nose poked in whatever book she could find. It did not really matter what book it was; she loved all books. She loved the way they looked, the stories they told, the way they felt in her hands, and even the way they smelled.

For a while, her favorites were "Pollyanna" and "Anne of Green Gables." Pretending she was an orphan she would play that she must rebel against the many house rules and always made up exciting adventures in her imagination.

She named all the trees and flowers, the squirrels and the chipmunks that played in their big yard. She even gave a robin with a broken wing a name. He became Mr. Puffer because of the way he puffed his chest as he sat on the branch outside of her window. His wing healed and he managed to fly south in the fall. He returned in the spring for several seasons before disappearing forever.

Sometimes, she let the boys play in her room, but only if they followed her rules, which didn't always work out too well.

Finally, in order to keep the peace, Mom had told the boys that the third floor was off limits to them. Girls needed "their privacy." Jill sometimes chose to ignore her brothers completely and kept company with the many wonderful and exciting characters from her world of words.

She stretched and yawned, letting her thoughts bring her back to the present moment.

She needed to stop daydreaming and do her morning devotional before Tom and the children woke up.

She had made it her habit, even before marrying Tom, to spend a short time each morning reading her Bible and praying before the day got busy.

It had been a habit she had gotten from her mother, a habit that had served her well.

As a missionary's wife, there were many challenges with each new day and it always helped when she spent time in the Lord's presence, thanking Him for all the blessings He had given them. She always asked for His guidance, protection and continued blessings for her family and all the wonderful people for whom they cared so much.

As quietly as possible, she opened her carry-on bag and got out her Bible. Then walking over to the window, she sat down and looked out. A light snow had fallen the night before and it clung to branches of the large oak tree that had guarded the yard for so many years. For a brief time, as the sun rose higher above the horizon, the sky turned golden and the dark winter shape of the tree was transformed into a beautiful glowing work of art.

Dropping to her knees, Jillian folded her hands in prayer.

Susan and the girls, with blankets, pillows and bowls of cereal, settled into the comfortable main living area of the house and tuned on the TV. It was still a few minutes before time to start but they wanted to make sure they would not to miss a moment of the show. Finally, after the morning run-down on accidents and weather reports, they were ready.

The announcer spoke, "Good morning, friends!"

"I am Dave Woodrow and, as promised, today we have a very special program for you. It is full of heartbreak, betrayal, and happy endings. We here at QZTV have been keeping you informed of each new development as it was given to us, and now we will introduce you to the family that just experienced it. This family has just been through a terrifying time. This is a story that concerns many parents, especially those that must share their children with ex-spouses or partners."

"My friends, our subject today is "The Abduction and Rescue of Annie Breese Benning" who was taken exactly one week ago from her preschool by her biological father, Samuel Frick."

The cinematographer then turned his camera to focus on Sandi and Jim. Annie was sitting on Jim's lap. The newscaster reached out and shook hands, first with Jim and then with Sandi.

"We would like you to meet Jim and Sandi Benning."

"Thank you so much for your willingness to permit us into your home."

"This is their daughter Annie. I understand Annie has a birthday coming up. Birthdays are a lot of fun aren't they, honey? How old are you going to be Annie? She turned her face away and refused to acknowledge Mr. Woodrow's question. Smiling he turned toward the adults. "May I call you by your first names?" Nodding Jim answered his question.

Annie is turning 4 on the 23rd. She's still a little overwhelmed with everything."

"I have no doubt of that, I am sure it will take time for your entire family to recover."

"And you also have an older daughter?"

"Yes, Joletta. She wanted to spend the night with friends. She has been with us since the beginning and has been wonderfully supportive, but she is a teenager and I think she just wants things to get back to normal."

"Yes, of course. This has been a very traumatic experience for your family, I'm sure."

"I do want to say, for myself and my staff, how very sorry we are that you had to go through this ordeal. As a parent myself, I cannot imagine how frightening it must have been. Of course, we are all equally as thrilled that it is now over and you have your little Annie home again."

After asking a number of general questions, Mr. Woodrow then asked Sandi, "How did you feel when you finally had your daughter in your arms again?"

"Oh, my! Nothing can describe how happy we are to have her home. God has blessed us so much! I do want to thank everyone that has supported us and prayed, especially our family and friends. If it hadn't been for them, I don't know how we could have gotten through this."

"In addition, I want to thank Capt. Powell, Sgt. Parker and the entire police force for doing such a wonderful job. You will never know how much your determination and dedication has meant to us!"

Woodrow continued, "And what about Mr. Frick? How did you feel when you found out that he died? Were you glad that was over and done with?"

Jim put his hand on Sandi's and said, "That is a very personal question. How Sandi feels about him is not your concern."

"No, Jim, it's OK."

"Mr. Woodrow, you have to know, I was terrified when I realized that Sam had taken Annie. We didn't know where he took her or why he had taken her, but, that said, I never believed for a minute that he would have purposely harmed her. He was a pitiful mixed-up person and was obviously drinking, at the very least, or perhaps even on some kind of drugs. My biggest fear was that she was in danger because his judgment was impaired, not because he wanted to hurt her."

"But, what about the woman from the bar? We understand she is a friend of yours."

"Yes, she is a friend. She was trying to protect me and he did hurt her. She is now doing much better, but we have been asked not to discuss her in this interview and we plan to honor her wishes."

"As far as Sam's death, I find it heartbreaking. He was so alone that he felt the only way to find love was to steal it from someone else. His death is just one terrible tragedy in a world full of heartbreak."

"So are you saying that you forgive him? That is very generous of you, considering what he caused your family to go through."

"No, I am not saying that. Right now I don't exactly know how I feel but I do know one thing, and that is that I would never have had Annie in the first place if it had not been for Sam Frick. Only God has the right to judge a person. I don't have that right, no matter what he did to us."

"Annie, were you scared when that man took you away from school?" queried Mr. Woodrow.

Annie looked up at Sandi and her mother nodded. "It's OK, Honey, you can talk to him."

"I was mad at him! I wanted my Daddy Jim! He was naughty, and he smelled bad!"

Mr. Woodrow smiled and continued. "What did you do then? Did you tell him he was naughty?"

"No, I told him he should take a bath and I said 'I want my Mommy!' He told me I had to be good so he could think."

"Wow! You are a very brave little girl. Were you good then?"

"Yes--- but then he got mad again." Annie's lip quivered, "and he wouldn't let me take my kitties with me." Leaning against Jim, she turned her face into his shirt.

"I think that she's had enough."

Mr. Woodrow's voice was filled with emotion as he concluded, "Yes, we are about out of time anyway. May we at QZTV wish you and your family a wonderful and happy holiday." Turning once again to face the cameras, he said, "There you have it, friends, a Christmas gift like no other! A wonderful family and an amazing child - reunited and truly looking forward to the merriest Christmas ever!"

283

"This is Dave Woodrow with QZTV wishing you all the very best of what the holidays have to offer!"

"Wow! I can't believe my family is really on TV talking to Dave Woodrow!" Joletta made a funny face and Sammy giggled.

"Maybe Annie will become a movie star and we could all go to see her in Hollywood! Don't you think that would be cool?"

The three girls were still laughing when they heard the sound of small feet running down the hall at the top of the stairs.

"Grandma! They're awake! Can we go up and see them?"

Samantha at 11 still had not lost any of her childish exuberance and had been anxiously anticipating the arrival of her little cousins for weeks.

This time the boys were big enough to actually play; the last time she had seen them they couldn't even talk to her and were scared of their own shadows. Now things were different. They could understand her and she was old enough to help take care of them.

Uncle Tom and Aunt Jillian had adopted another baby a few months ago and the girls were going to see her for the very first time! Sammy had already picked out the nickname "Flower" for her. Jillian told Grandma the first time they saw her, she was very tiny and as fragile as an evening rose. Grandma Susan had evening primroses in the backyard.

Every night, in midsummer, just as it started to get dark, the pretty yellow flowers would pop open, one after another, until the stems were completely covered with the happy little blossoms. It was always fun to watch them as they bloomed right before your eyes. Jillian had even given the baby an African name that meant 'blossom.'

284

The boys had already been to visit one other time, when they were too little to remember. Sammy had many things she wanted to do with them. She wanted to show them the Christmas tree, because it is too hot in Africa to have real Christmas trees, and she would show them the tricks her dog Rascal could do.

She was going to show them where Grandma always kept the cookies. It was supposed to be a secret, but of course she had known their hiding place for a long time.

Most of all she wanted to play outside with them. Of course Annie would come too, and they would all have a wonderful time in the snow. She had a new sled which she hadn't even gotten to use yet, and after sledding, she was going to teach them how to build a snowman. Maybe the big girls would even help.

Since Aunt Jill and Uncle Tom's family lived in Africa, the boys had never played in snow. Sammy thought it was important for them to get the opportunity!

The older girls were already ahead of her bounding up the staircase before Grandma had time to even answer Samantha. As the three of them clamored up the stairs, Jillian opened the bathroom door and came out wrapped in the pink fuzzy robe that had been hanging on the back of the closet door since her college graduation. Pulling her hair back into a ponytail and putting a stretch wrap around it, she turned and spoke to the small boy standing behind her.

"Come on, Honey, it's OK. Come out and see your cousins."

"Hello there, girls." Samantha ran willingly into her aunt's welcoming embrace. "Oh, my goodness, girl! Let me look at you. This can't be our little Sammy, can it?"

"It is, Aunt Jilly. I sure have grown up a lot since you saw me, haven't I?

"You absolute have! I almost didn't recognize you at all. Who are these other beautiful young ladies you have here with you?"

The older girls both laughed and joined in on a group hug. "Oh, it is so good to see you again, Aunt Jill!" they chimed.

"Mommy?" The little boy standing behind his mother reached for her hand and looked up at the girls with large dark eyes. Jillian smiled and stooped down beside him. "Jabral, these are your cousins, Tiffany and Samantha, and this is our friend Joletta. Can you say hello?" The little boy stepped behind her and did not speak. Smiling, Jillian said, "Let's go get Daddy and the others up and we'll all go downstairs to see Grandma."

"Do you need help with the kids, Aunt Jill?"

"That would be great, girls, but we will have to see how willing they are. As you can see the boys have a tendency to be a little shy. They'll warm up after a while though. Now both the babies, Ajani and Zarah, will pretty much let anyone take care of them. I think Tom already has Zarah up. I need to feed her before going downstairs. We'll go see if Omari is awake and maybe you can help me get the boys dressed and ready to go down and eat breakfast."

"Can I go see Uncle Tom and help with the baby?" Sammy asked anxiously.

"Well, Honey, are you sure you want to go in there? He can be a growly old bear when he hasn't had much sleep."

"He won't growl at me. Uncle Tom loves me!"

"Well, if you are sure then." She ruffled Sammy's hair and smiled. "Tell him Aunt Jillian will be there in a few minutes after we get the boys up and around."

A beaming Samantha headed up the stair to the attic room and Jillian and the older girls went with little Jabral to wake the other two boys.

Within only a few more days, the year 2003 would be gone and a brand new year would begin. 2004 promised to be a year of new beginnings, new possibilities and new adventures!

Chapter 21
FLY, FLY AWAY

Joletta could hardly believe that she was really on her way. She and Pastor Scott were actually on a plane headed for the small African country of Malawi. She had hoped for so long to make this trip but with all the craziness of the past couple of years, it had all started to feel as if it were only another "impossible dream."

After checking in at Kennedy International Airport, there had been a two-hour wait before they could board the huge air ship, but finally the announcement to start boarding came, and now the long trip to Africa was a reality. The first leg of their flight would take 7 hours. They would be landing at Dakar, Senegal, where the plane would refuel and then the trip would continue until, after approximately 19 total hours in the air, they would touch down at Johannesburg International Airport in South Africa.

After the long flight, they would stay in Johannesburg with friends of Tom and Jillian, Able and Melissa Fullerton, facilitators at Helping Hands Orphanage, located only a few miles from the airport. Wednesday would bring a second flight, a five-hour trip taking them to Lilongwe, Malawi, after which a bus would transport them to Salima where finally they were to be picked up by someone from the Mission.

A small screen attached to the back of the seat in front of Jo showed the path the plane was taking. They were now on the second leg of their long flight, somewhere over the Atlantic Ocean off the central coast of Africa. The long red line on the screen bowed slightly across the dark expanse and showed no land mass under the wings of the small digital plane, giving Jo a slightly sick feeling. She had never before thought much about how big the world was, but now, flying thousands of miles from everyone and everything she had ever known, it made her realize how much bigger, how much more there is, to this amazing place we call earth! Never again would she think of home in quite the same way.

She was so excited and nervous, all at once she could hardly breathe! She was beginning to realize the scope of life and the opportunities it offered.

"Tell me what it's really like, Scott. Do you think everyone will like me? I know I'm going to love it, but I just don't know what to expect. I hope I've brought everything I need. Do you think—"

Scott interrupted, "Jo, you need to just relax." He smiled down at the girl. "You will love Malawi, and it is all going to be all right."

Jo had been very quiet the entire time they waited at the airport and had spoken little since taking off two hours before. Scott suspected she needed that time to get her emotions under control. The past months for Jo's family had been full of both physical and emotional difficulties. Healing was slow and definitely not complete. Scott was both surprised and proud of Sandi for making the decision to let Jo make this trip.

When Jo finally started talking, she was full of questions. Many they had already discussed, but Scott grinned tolerantly as he looked at her. "I can promise you one thing; it will be an experience you are never going to forget. Once you have experienced Africa, it gets into your blood and changes how you think about everything, and even who you thought you were."

"It is an amazingly beautiful and diverse place. Some areas are barren and dry, but others are rich, and green and tropical. The sun is like a huge ball of fire, and the stars are so bright you feel as if you can reach up and pluck them out of the heavens."

"With even the slightest breeze, Lake Malawi shimmers in the sun as though there were millions of diamonds laid out on a silver-platter. Africa has a uniqueness all its very own; it is truly like no other place on earth."

"Oh, Scott, that sounds just wonderful."

Actually, Jo had been studying the African continent for the past several months and had even done a term paper for geography class on Malawi. She now knew much more than she had the summer before, but what she had learned was mostly statistics and interesting facts that she had researched over the internet. Now, as she listened to Scott give such beautiful descriptions of a place he obviously loved, she could almost see the mysterious land unfold before her eyes.

"Go on, tell me more."

"The people in Kaikeki Village have suffered great losses but are generally a happy and loving people. They have come to love Hope Mission. Tom and Jillian have done a wonderful job reaching hearts for the Lord. In the past couple of years, church attendance has almost doubled. Jill said 23 people were baptized the week before Tom got sick."

"It's terrible that he got Malaria. I hope he gets better soon; Jillian is having a really hard time taking care of him and the kids and everything else," Jo offered.

"I know it has been a hard time, but remember Phil and Audrey are there with them now. I am sure things will improve. Tom is still weak, but he is getting stronger every day; he should be good as new before long."

"Gosh, I really hope everyone likes me."

"Tom and Jill have become an important part of the community and everyone knows you are a very special friend. I'm sure you will be welcomed with open arms. It is always a big event when someone new comes." He grinned at Jo. "In fact, it's likely that you may get too much love rather than not enough. It can sometimes be a little bit overwhelming. But, no need to be concerned. You will do just fine."

"Do you really believe that?"

"No doubt about it. I'm not saying you won't feel a little strange at first. It takes a bit of getting used to when you realize that you are now in the minority. There are other light-skinned people around and many speak English so you will get along fine." He reached over and put his hand on her arm.

"OK, thanks. I guess I'm a little nervous." Joletta grinned.

Scott chuckled. "A little nervous? I don't think so. More like a lot nervous!" Pulling the entertainment pamphlet out of the seat pocket Scott said, "Let's see what kind of movies we have here to watch. It'll help the time go faster."

"Really, it's all good. I'm OK." Soon Jo settled in and began to relax as the two of them watched a movie. The hours slowly passed and eventually the lights in the cabin dimmed and most of the passengers quieted and slept. Scott, who was restless, watched the angelic face of the sleeping girl beside him. Joletta had become a favorite of his. She had such a sweet spirt and was so full of love and life. *If she were only a few years older---* He was brought up short by his unintentional thought. Jo was much too young for him. He could not even consider her anything but a friend. Only recently had he acknowledged to himself his attraction to Joletta, and he knew it was something that could not be! She was a beautiful young woman, bordering on the verge of adulthood, but Scott realized that to even consider acting on his feelings would be a total betrayal of her innocence.

In Scott's position, working with the youth of the church, it was extremely important that he always be very careful to never take advantage of any of the young people and it had not ever been a problem before. He was

291

somewhat confused and more than a little ashamed of himself for having let his mind go places where it should have never gone. Closing his eyes he offered up a quiet prayer asking forgiveness for his inappropriate thoughts.

Jo's family trusted Scott implicitly. Joletta was only beginning to find the person she would one day become. Scott knew the only thing to do would be to honor the trust her parents expected from him. He would treasure Joletta as a special child of God and protect her with all he had. – that, and nothing more. Laying his head back, he sighed and closed his eyes.

A sharp beeping sound alerted the sleeping passengers that something was not right. Rain was pelting the windows and lightning flashed. The pilot, speaking into the intercom, announced, "We are coming into an area of turbulence and the going may get a little rough for a while. Please fasten your seat belts and secure all items. If anyone is in need of assistance, please ask your flight attendant."

Suddenly the plane jerked and felt like it was falling. Jo let out a small, terrified whimper. "What is it? What's happening?"

The Captain's voice calmly continued, "Please be assured, friends, these measures are only precautionary. We are flying through a line of storms. Changes in air pressure may cause us to experience what are, in essence, "rough roads." Please review the instruction card provided in your seat pocket in front of you, and if you have questions you may ask your cabin attendant."

"Folks, we will get through this within the hour and hopefully should arrive at our destination at the scheduled time."

Once again, the plane lurched, this time even more violently than before. Tension was palpable.

Scott had experienced rough flights before, but although he certainly did not enjoy them, he knew most of the time the pockets of air that caused the phenomenon did not cause serious problems. Keeping his composure, he did his best to assure Joletta that it would be over soon.

Scott was very aware of how fragile the cord is that holds us to this world. How quickly it can be severed. Patting Jo's hand, he closed his eyes and whispered a prayer of protection.

After what felt like, to many of the passengers, a longer period of time than it actually was, the un-nerving turbulence finally calmed, and the rest of the flight was uneventful.

It had been a long and tiring flight. Everyone on Flight 2247 was very happy to hear the pilot's voice once again. "Ladies and Gentlemen, if you look below to the right you will soon see the city of Johannesburg coming into view. We should be on the ground in approximately 20 minutes. The time is 6:20 a.m. South Africa Standard Time. It is a balmy 78 degrees here. Please stay seated until all blinking lights are off. Cabin lights will be activated and your attendants will instruct you when to disembark. Thank you for flying with Air-Tran today. Enjoy your visit to Johannesburg."

Looking below, Joletta saw a patchwork of golds, browns, and greens, and in only seconds she saw the city. Skyscrapers and buildings looked as though they were made of Lego blocks with highways and roads twisting and turning throughout the massive city. Everything at first looked minuscule, but within moments it all began to grow magically as the plane sped toward its final destination. With breathtaking speed, they were soon taxiing down the runway.

Jo grabbed Scott's arm. "Oh! My gosh! We're really here!" She was so excited she could hardly contain herself. It seemed like such a long time since she had first asked her mom about coming to Africa. Now here she was, about to step out of a plane, *not just into another country, but onto another continent!* Jo had almost given up believing this would ever happen.

   Perhaps she should pinch herself to make sure it was all real.

Chapter 22
HELPING HANDS

After getting through Customs, they went to pick up the luggage. Scott had several extra bags filled with donated items. He was delivering some of the items to Helping Hands, but other things were going to Hope Mission.

Two of the duffels had mosquito netting that children would use while sleeping to protect themselves from mosquitoes, the little vampires responsible for spreading disease. Other bags had jump ropes, soccer balls with hand pumps, and various other items not easily available in the rural location where they were headed.

Joletta also had an extra duffle filled with T-shirts and small gifts that the kids in her youth group had sent. The shirts were printed with the slogan "JESUS is our HOPE" printed across the front. The project had been her idea and she was excited about giving the shirts to the children at "Hope."

Soon Scott was helping load the luggage into the dusty old passenger van which belonged to Helping Hands Orphanage. They would be spending the night with Able and Melissa Fullerton at the orphanage.

Able and Melissa were college friends of Tom and Jillian. The two couples had continued the relationship since that time.

After Able and Melissa married, they began the ministry in Johannesburg, serving as outreach missionaries. Now, they were the senior directors of Helping Hands Orphanage." The Fullertons had now lived in Africa for close to 20 years.

Tom and Jill had later traveled to South Africa to visit their friends. It was this visit that planted the seeds of inspiration for their own ministry some years later.

Helping Hands Orphanage had at that time housed less than 30 children, but much had changed in the past several years. Now they housed and schooled more than 100 children. HH ministry also served daily meals to the many children who came to school nearby but continued to live at home with their families.

Everyone climbed into the van as Melissa explained it wasn't unusual to have short-term guests at the orphanage.

"We have several mission teams a year come through this area and it works out well for everyone. We are close to the airport and because transportation to more rural areas can be complicated. We make a good stop-over point. Smiling, she added, "Of course we always take advantage of our guests. Joletta, we thought you could help to serve this evening's meal."

Jo smiled back. "That will be fun; I was wondering what my first job in Africa would be."

"I'm sure your talents will be put to good use while you are here, Dear. How long will you be staying in country?"

"Pastor Scott will only be here for ten days. He is the youth minister at Templeton Church and has to be back, but I get to stay for five weeks. I'm a senior this fall, and I need to be back home before school starts the 26th of August."

"How exciting! We've heard a lot about you and your family. Tom and Jill are really happy you are coming."

The city of Johannesburg is huge, but the newcomers would not get to see much of it on this visit. There would simply not be enough time. They had come for a purpose, and that was to help Jill and Tom. Visiting large cities was not on their agenda.

The sun was just coming up over the horizon as the van left the airport parking area. Driving away from the early morning congestion of Johannesburg, soon they were heading out into the open countryside.

As the city grew distant, the sun spread across tall dry grasses, waving in the breeze. The open windows allowed the cool air to blow their hair "every which way" and everything appeared golden in the early morning light.

Conversation came easily and it wasn't long before Able turned the vehicle off the paved road, onto a curving drive. Red dust billowed behind and around the van as they continued for perhaps a half mile until he stopped at a metal entrance gate marked with a sign that read "International Church of God Missions." A smaller sign beneath gave a verse from the Bible, reading "Let the little children come unto me." Mt 19:14.

Scott jumped out and opened the gate, then waited until the vehicle passed through. Closing it, he climbed back in and they followed the dirt road until their final stop in front of a large block building.

Able announced, "Well, friends, here we are! Home Sweet Home." In brightly painted letters a hand-made paper banner read "Welcome to Helping Hands Orphanage."

The complex consisted of numerous buildings all made with mud bricks. The two largest buildings had corrugated tin roofing, while the remaining buildings and small cottages were roofed with long dry grasses, the same tall grass they had seen growing wild alongside the road. One huge tree, which they later learned was a Baobab tree, proudly stood guard over the main buildings, while brush and a few smaller trees kept the remainder of the grounds from being completely barren.

Within minutes, what had at first appeared to be a quiet and almost deserted place began buzzing with activity and soon they were surrounded with a lively, noisy crowd of men, women, and children of all sizes!

Laughter and welcoming greetings were called out as Able attempted to make introductions.

Joletta felt somewhat overwhelmed. Never had she experienced anything quite like this. Although some spoke English, most spoke in dialects that Jo had not, until this very day, ever heard before.

It was almost 9:00 a.m. and Able had to attend the morning staff meeting. He asked Scott if he felt like going with him. "I thought you might like to hear what's been going on around here. We are trying to decide on a couple of new projects we have in mind and your input would certainly be welcome. I know you would like to relax for a bit, but it shouldn't take too long, and I think you might learn something yourself. It is entirely up to you."

"Thanks, Tom. Sure, I would like to come and listen in. Don't know if I have any bright ideas though." The men were laughing as they walked away. Scott turned to Joletta. "Guess I'll see you a bit later."

Jo smiled and nodded, holding back a yawn as she gave a little wave of her hand.

Melissa couldn't help but notice. "I'm guessing you are pretty tired yourself and would like to clean up and rest for a while." Calling an older girl over, Melissa introduced the young woman as Tillie.

"Tillie will show you where you can clean up and where you will be sleeping. I have some things I need to take care of now. I hope you will forgive me, but the work is pretty much never ending."

"I will put you in Tillie's capable hands and will see you a little later today. Someone will come and let you know when the lunch meal is served. If you are up to helping, we start feeding the younger children about 11:00, but if you feel you need more time to rest, that is fine also."

"Thanks, Melissa. It will be great."

298

Tillie was tall and very slim with smooth coffee-colored skin. Her hair was cropped short and she had huge dark eyes. With a broad smile and speaking in broken English, she motioned Jo to follow and, as they walked, she pointed out different buildings, explaining their purpose.

They went past a garden where there were boys working alongside a couple of grown men. They passed a large group of younger children playing with a soccer ball and several women working in an open kitchen area, busily preparing food for the noon meal.

Soon the two girls came to the buildings where the children slept. The large rooms were filled to the brim with bunks, every bed no more than a few feet from the next. Each one had a colorful blanket and a pillow. Some of the covers were quilts, others knitted or crocheted, while still others were of woven material. A few appeared to be new, but most were frayed and worn. All of the beds had been made up, some smooth and neat and others wrinkled and uneven. Tillie explained that even the little children were expected to help by making their own bed and keeping the rooms clean and neat. She grinned, "It takes a while, but everyone tries hard and everyone helps."

It was quite dark in the room, but the blankets and lumpy pillows made a kaleidoscope with many patterns and colors, making it not at all unpleasant. Small cubicles covered one wall with a different name on each, one for each child.

Tillie showed Joletta the bed she would use. It was at the back of the room. She told her to put her overnight bag on the bed. Jo wouldn't need a cubicle, since she would not be staying.

"How many others sleep in here?"

"The rooms have about 50 beds in each but, if we get more kids, we have extra sleeping mats that we can use. We all take care of each other. The older kids help the younger ones, and we all clean and help out. There is a job chart over there on the wall."

She pointed to the right. "If you want to wash, there is a pan in the cabinet over here. Do you want me to go back out with you to the well? We have some indoor water, but it is in the kitchen area and the toilets. The water buckets are out by the well. We get what we need and then return the pan when we are done."

Jo smiled. "No, Tillie, thanks, but I think I'll wait to clean up. I just need to lie down for a while." Stretching, she said, "I didn't realize I was so tired. I don't want to sleep all day, so it would be great if you could let me know when it is time to help. Melissa said she would let me help at lunchtime. I want to see everything we have time for, so I'll see you later. Thanks again."

Jo stretched once more and looked around the quiet room. Smiling, she reached over and picked up the lightweight cover lying at the foot of the bed. Only months ago her own youth group had cut material squares that were to be made into quilts by the churchwomen. She wondered if any of the coverlets in this very room might have come from her own church! Joletta gratefully pulled her cover around her shoulders and lay down on her lumpy pillow. Closing her eyes, her mind drifted. She was no longer certain if she truly was in the exotic land of savannahs, or if it was all just another of her dreams.

The next 24 hours came and went quickly. Soon it was time to leave their new friends and board another plane for a five-hour flight to Lilongwe, Malawi, to be followed by a bus trip to the village of Salima, where Limbani would be picking them up. He would then drive them the final 10 miles to Hope Mission.

With hugs and good wishes, they said their goodbyes. Able and Melissa promised that they would see them again. "Thanks for all your help, Jo." Smiling,

Melissa added, "If you ever run out of things to do at "Hope," you can sure come back and help out here."

Chapter23
THE WARM HEART OF AFRICA

It would be another long day - first the flight and then a bus ride that apparently would last several hours. Jo was excited and even though she was a little nervous about flying again, she was determined to let nothing interfere with her good mood.

Scott waited until they settled into their seats and the plane had taken off before asking how she felt about her trip so far.

"Wow. I'm not exactly sure how I feel. It's kind of---like it isn't really---real! Everything is just so different. I keep thinking I'm going to wake up and realize it is nothing but one of my crazy dreams!"

She hesitated a moment and shook her head before continuing, "Really, though, everyone has been so nice; the kids are amazing. Actually, I just don't know how they can keep up with everything that has to be done! It never stops! I mean—200 kids! That is just crazy!"

"Well, the Fullertons have had a lot of experience. I'm not sure exactly how long they have been in Africa, but I do know they were already here when Tom and Jillian came for the first time."

"It is so neat how they all work together the way they do. Melissa and Able must be miracle-workers. I wish I could do something really important like that someday."

"Well, I don't know what you will do with your life, Jo, but I expect that someday you may even surprise yourself."

"Hmmm, I don't know about that. But, thanks anyway!" She grinned at Scott and he patted her arm.

"Oh, I have no doubt that you are going to charm the world with that smile and those big brown eyes of yours!"

"You are kind of goofy, Pastor Scott!" Joletta laughed and shook her head. She settled back into her seat and closed her eyes. She was tired but as happy as a songbird after an early morning rain.

Limbani had been at Hope Mission since losing his parents to AIDS almost three years before.

The AIDS virus has made death a cruel reality in this beautiful land. In Malawi, there are a great many people who are suffering or have lost loved ones to the HIV/AIDS epidemic. Other factors such as cholera and malaria are sometimes the cause of sickness and even death, but no other illness has created as much grief and heartache as the dreaded disease.

For Joletta, it was far from anything she had ever known. Of course, she had taken the required sex-education classes given at school which had included statistics and some comprehensive emphasis on the dangers of becoming sexually active, but the focus of education had been on abstinence and included very little information on safe sexual practices. Most of the young people she knew had not taken the classes very seriously because they didn't believe it would ever actually affect their lives. Until this trip Joletta had never known anyone that actually had suffered from the disease.

The many differences culturally in the way the people in Malawi believe, and how they live, made it difficult for Joletta to understand how truly disastrous the prevalence of the disease is. Limbani had lost not only both his parents to the virus, but many members of his extended family were sick or had died, even before the death of his own parents.

On the day Limbani's mother died, Tom happened to be visiting with the sick in the small village where the family lived. It was something that Tom had never gotten used to witnessing. Although it certainly was not the first time he had been present as someone bordered on death, it did not get any easier to watch the excruciatingly slow painful process.

He stood observing the woman's young son with the resigned look of someone who understood there was no hope left. Lovingly, the boy continued to minister to the his dying parent, offering her small sips of broth and gently wiping her brow with a moist rag. Pastor Tom remembered the young woman from earlier visits to her village and knew that she was probably not yet 30. She had once been a beautiful young woman, but now her fragile frame was no more than a shadow, lying quietly on a bamboo sleep mat.

The deathwatch continued until mid-day, when a weak smile came across her face and her thin hand reached slowly and touched the boy's face. She started to speak, but her words were only a whisper in the wind. Soon her hand fell silently across her lifeless body. He didn't even cry out. He simply stood and without a word walked to where his two younger sisters and a brother, only a toddler, sat waiting. Taking the hand of the youngest, he walked into their hut. The little girls followed.

Other members of the community stood by, but were helpless to do anything. With few close relatives left in the family, Brother Tom simply did not have the heart to leave the youth alone with his younger siblings.

In Malawi, when possible, family members step up to care for children left behind when a parent or caregiver dies, but the remaining members of this extended family were already overwhelmed caring for their own and numerous young cousins whose parents had also expired from the dreaded disease.

The compassionate pastor stepped into the hut and putting a protective arm around the boy's shoulder, he invited the children into his ever-growing mission family, now officially named Hope Mission Orphanage.

Limbani was almost fifteen at the time of his mother's death. Many girls in Malawi are married and having babies long before we Americans would consider them adults. It was not long before the young boy became a familiar face around the Mission complex. He seemed to be wherever someone needed help, cheerfully taking on more than his share of the many tasks of village life. He helped with the gardening, learned to milk the goats they had recently acquired, and played games with the small children. Lim could even cook. This is an unusual task for a boy in Malawian culture, but before the death of his parents, a young visitor had stayed with his family and not only taught Lim how to prepare nutritious meals but also numerous other skills.

There was one thing above everything else that was Limbani's very favorite thing to do. He loved driving the Mission's rusty truck. Scott fondly had christened it "Hunky Monkey." Everyone in the village knew about the ugly old vehicle. Faded and dirty, the original blue paint color was hardly recognizable, the muffler covered with rust with large holes along its length. It could be heard coming from a mile away! Nonetheless, everyone loved the old truck, and the noise bothered no one at all. There were few motorized vehicles in the area, making it a popular attraction.

Tom had taught Lim to drive the truck the year before so he could haul tools or the large barrels of water needed daily.

Today, Limbani would drive the truck into town to pick up supplies and transport their guests back to the mission. Tom was recovering from Malaria and still needed as much rest as possible. It had been a great help having Phil and Audrey Miller on staff for the past several months. As the number of children now living at the Mission continued to increase, the necessary workload increased as well. When Tom became ill, Phil had stepped in and taken on many of his responsibilities. He would be riding along with Lim this morning, as official greeter when Jo and Scotty arrived. Phil had agreed to let the boy drive knowing that he had grown up traveling to and from Kaikeki Village along the rutted jungle roads when his mother went to Salima to sell produce at the market. Limbani knew both the roads and the town of Salima much better than Phil.

Volunteers came daily to help with the children. Without that cooperation, Jill and Tom were aware that the Mission and Orphanage would have very likely failed. It had taken some time, as they became acquainted with the local culture, but eventually everyone came to realize the benefits when all worked together. As time went on relationships between Hope's core workers and the volunteers of Kaikeki Village continued to grow.

Volunteer workers did not always know for certain what they would be doing but cheerfully came daily to do whatever they could. They might start the week doing one job and the next day they could find themselves doing something entirely different as there were plenty of jobs to go around - carrying water, feeding chickens, planting, watering, or weeding the gardens, to name a few, while other jobs included milking the goats or perhaps helping cook and serving meals. Someone had to be available for cleanup and to do laundry. Maintenance was ongoing and constant. Help was always needed, and much appreciated.

Mishal and Caroline lived with the youngest children and served as housemothers. Both women were AIDS widows, and both had small children of their own. Realizing the Mission's need for full-time help and understanding Mishal and Caroline's own poverty, Jillian had first made the suggestion to Tom that they invite the women to come and live on the Mission campus full-time.

Two other young women, actually older girls, lived and worked at the Mission. Taona and Memory each had moved to the orphanage with their younger siblings because they had no family left to care for them. Tom and Jillian refused few.

Kaikeki Village did not have a school until Jillian and Tom came. Now Jillian had a certified teacher, an enthusiastic young woman named Tonya, and a retired professor, Mr. Paul. The three of them taught the 20 children who now called Hope Orphanage home. In addition, most days numerous other children attended, although they did not live on-site. No one was ever turned away. The needs of the children were numerous and varied.

Each school day started in the open courtyard where Tom would greet everyone, say a prayer asking God to bless the day, and teach a short Bible lesson. Besides teaching about Jesus, there were other important lessons included in each day's schedule.

The children learned about good sanitation and health practices. Another top priority was teaching the children about the AIDS virus and other sexually transmitted diseases, helping them understand how many of the traditional sexual practices were affecting their community. It was a difficult thing to teach, but there was not a person living at Hope Mission whose life had not been touched by the terrible disease of AIDS.

Frequently, Tom enlisted local artisans and other visitors who were willing to get involved. The children benefited, learning skills, some that had been passed down through many generations of their ancestors.

Currently their favorite artisan was "Old Bomani." No one knew exactly how old he was, but he had lived his entire life on Lake Malawi, supporting himself and his family as a fisherman. Early in his life, his father and uncles had taught him all things related to fishing.

Everyone respected his abilities at net-making; also, at crafting spears and beautiful dugout canoes.

Several of the "Hope" boys, all in their early teens, were now his enthusiastic students. He promised them that once they mastered net-making, he would teach them to make a canoe. His gnarled hands were still quick and sure as he twisted and tied the long strands of cord into a useable work of art, and his eyes lit up as he laughed and joked with the group of boys that watched intently and then much more slowly attempted to do the same with the cords held in their inexperienced hands.

Every few weeks, a young man of Chewa origin came and shared his musical skills. While there, he would bring several different musical instruments and play for the enthusiastic groups that always gathered around when he visited. Everyone clapped along to the beat of the drums and before long; they would all be chanting and dancing with the rhythm. Frequently others would join in with drums or whatever homemade string instruments that might be available. Azibo played with a wild, natural ability that somehow affected the very soul of his listeners. At times, he would stay over a few days and as the evenings turned to night, the rhythmic beat of the drums and soulful sounds of the "Lonely Land of Malawi" could be heard, carried by the warm tropical breezes across the land and into the forest.

It took close to an hour to make the trip from the orphanage to the town of Salima. With so few paved roads in the area and most full of deep potholes, it took talent just to keep your vehicle on the road itself. By the time Lim and Phil arrived in town, Phil decided it might have taken less time to walk, and it certainly would have been easier on his frayed nerves. Lim thought each time they hit an extra deep rut it was hugely funny. First, the vehicle wheels would drop hard into the hole and then bounce high in the air and then from side to side! Hanging on for dear life, Phil thought he would not go into town often with this wild young man.

They finally did make it safely to the market where they would take care of the Mission's shopping needs. Pastor Scott and Jo were not arriving until later that afternoon. This gave them time to finish making the needed purchases prior to picking up their guests. They wanted to return to the compound before dark because of the bad road conditions. In addition, lack of security at night made being out late unsafe.

Although it was still early, the market was bustling with people selling all kinds of items. After only a couple of hours they had purchased the needed supplies so, after loading everything into the pickup, there was ample time to explore before leaving to meet the bus coming from Lilongwe. Phil had not previously been on assignment in southern Africa, so he was pleased when he realized this.

Only some weeks before, Jillian and Tom had received notice that they were to be re-assigned, meaning they would be returning to America, at which time the management of the Mission would be given to Phil and Audrey. Although the change was still months away, Phil was anxious to learn as much as possible about the place that was to be home to his family for the next several years.

Phil treated Lim to a coke, and they wandered up and down the rows of brightly colored fruit and vegetable stands. Beans, potatoes, tomatoes, and peppers made a colorful display. There were many items for sale - handmade intricately woven baskets, clothing, and shoes. There were colorful plastic buckets and bowls, pans, woodcarvings, coal, and all manner of things. People were hawking food items and soft drinks.

The colors, smells, and sounds of the busy market took some getting used to. Some of the stands had woven awnings to protect from the hot sun, others were not stands at all but simply a blanket, or piece of material spread on the ground with the store proprietor sitting on his or her haunches, bargaining with customers.

The bus ride from Lilongwe was hot and dusty. Jo and Pastor Scott would be very glad when they finally arrived in Salima. Before the trip had started, the passengers waited for the bus's fuel tanks to fill completely. With no air-conditioning, they felt like sardines packed into a small can. Many bodies were pressed one against another and unaccustomed odors floated all around them. Although the ride was not comfortable, to Joletta it was all just a part of the adventure. Soaking everything in, she made mental notes of each new experience.

The sun shone brightly through the dust-covered windows as she watched this new exciting world pass by. She had now experienced both a sunrise and a sunset in this strange new country. Somehow, knowing that the great golden ball of fire that God placed in the heavens not only shines upon Africa but on the entire world and her home as well gave Jo comfort.

So far, she had not really had time to be homesick, but between planes, buses and the old van owned by Helping Hands, home was feeling far, far away. Through her clouded window, Joletta looked to the sky. Smiling and closing her eyes, although she heard no voice, she felt like God was speaking directly to her—

"It's OK, Jo. I have it all covered. You and all that you love are in My Hands. I am always with you. Remember, the sun is always in the sky, no matter where you go, even when you cannot see it, I am there. It was I that created the sun. Never worry, it is in My Hands."

Everything was vastly different from her American home. As the bus bumped down the road, she watched the passing landscape. The countryside was a mix of browns and golds with purple mountains rising along the horizon. Tall waving grasses and occasionally a tree or a group of trees stood like giant monuments. A vivid blue sky and fluffs of white cumulous clouds drifted in the vast expanse above. A wind that never seemed to stop sent dust swirling through the air each time they passed a vehicle or the occasional pedestrian, carrying items balanced upon their head, driving goats or walking beside an oxcart. Beautiful, wild and unknown, it only made Joletta want to see and experience more.

As the young African and an older white man approached, Scott stood up from his stooping position. He reached for the older man's hand. "Good afternoon, sir, Scotty Pearson here. How are you doing?"

"Fine here, my friend. I am Phillip Miller. This young man is Limbani Naidoo."

The young man stepped over and reached for Pastor Scott's hand. "Just call me Lim, that's what everyone at the Mission calls me. Hope you haven't been waiting long."

Turning to the girl, he surveyed her with his eyes. "Joletta? Miss Jill is going be very glad to see you." Jo had to listen carefully; although the young man spoke fluent English his words did not sound at all like the English she had always heard spoken in her part of the world.

"Hunky Monkey" is right down the road. I will help you get your things and then we better be heading home. It's getting late."

Jo smiled shyly at the tall dark-skinned boy who was about her age.

"What is a Hunky Monkey?"

Both Lim and Phil laughed. "Well, it is our transportation home," was Phil's dry reply. "Just follow us and we will introduce you."

"I hope you have plenty of room," said Scott as he turned toward the waiting pile of luggage and duffels needing to be loaded.

As the four of them piled it all into the bed of the truck already filled with the items purchased earlier in the day, Jo doubtfully surveyed the unworthy looking vehicle. "Well," she said slowly, "I hope the Mission is close by. Are you sure this thing runs? And--where is everyone going to ride?"

Scott spoke up then. "Well, looks like you and I will ride in the back.'"

Joletta looked horrified, "In the back-- of this truck? Are you kidding?"

"Honey, it is very common here to travel by whatever method is available."

"That's OK," Phil said, "there is room in the cab for three. I can ride in back."

"I'll ride in the back with you, Phil," Scott said. "Jo you ride in the cab with Limbani. Lim, you slow this thing down on those roads. You were driving like a maniac! Do you hear me, son?"

"Sure, sure, Mister Phil. I'll take it slow!" He flashed those white teeth again with a wide grin as he climbed behind the wheel of the old truck.

As Joletta got into the other side and closed the door, she decided that she was going to like this boy.

Turning to see that his passengers had gotten themselves settled between the large bags of maize, bamboo mats, vegetables, luggage and building materials, he inserted the key into the ignition. With a quick turn, the engine roared to life. Shifting into gear the vehicle lumbered across the rough dirt parking area and turned onto the paved road.

An uninvited thought went through Jo's mind that, just maybe, they still might not make it to their destination.

312

For the first part of the drive both Joletta and Limbani were quiet. Neither was sure what to say to the strange new person sitting only a couple of feet from the other.

The boy driving had skin as dark as night, making Joletta fell as if her skin was so white that she glowed. Glancing over at Lim, she was the first one to speak. Finally breaking the silence, she asked, "Why do you call it the Hunky Monkey?"

"I really don't know. That is just what Tom calls it."

"I guess it sort of fits," she replied. "Maybe you ought to call it Junky Monkey! It looks like a piece of junk."

He looked offended. "This is a good truck! Don't say bad things about it, or—" grinning, he said, "or, you may have to walk!"

"I will not! But I'm sorry if I insulted you."

He looked over at her and shrugged his shoulders. "Don't worry about it; it's not a big deal."

"I like your name. Does it have a meaning?"

"It is a Chewa name. That is the tribe of my relatives."

"Linnn--?"

"Limbani. Our village was flooded at the time I was born. The rains had not stopped, and all of the crops were ruined, and our home was washed away. My mother knew that without a miracle, there would be little food to eat during the dry time, and she worried that we would all starve to death. She said I needed a good name, one that would help me stay healthy. So, she named me Limbani, because it means "to be strong.""

"That is so cool! Oh, but I'm so sorry about what happened."

"I'm still here." He flashed a smile in her direction as he maneuvered around yet another hole in the pavement.

313

"I wish my name had a good story with it."

"Joletta, that is a good name."

Just then, they hit a deep rut, and the truck bounced hard! Jerking to the side, Lim quickly corrected the vehicle and re-connected with solid roadway once again.

"Oh, my goodness!" Jo yelled. She turned to look behind and see if their passengers were still with them. "Oh, my goodness, I thought maybe they fell out!" Phil pounded on the window and shook his fist. "Maybe they will be the ones walking, if you hit a few more holes like that!"

Lim steered the vehicle again from one side of the road to the other, and both young people broke into giggles. Once more, an insistent knock came from behind their heads, only causing another round of laughter.

Chapter 24
HOPE" IS HOME

As "Hunky Monkey" drove into the gate of Hope Mission, not only were Tom, Jillian, and the children who lived at the orphanage waiting, it appeared the entire village had come to greet them.

The Mission now consisted of a large brick building which served as both church and school. Farther back on the property were another dozen cottages built in a semi-circle, some housing Mission residents while others served various purposes.

In front of the first building stood a wooden Cross, proudly proclaiming the word "Hope" painted in capital letters across the mid-section.

Although it was late, Jill had a meal prepared for them. Since leaving earlier in the day neither Phil nor Lim had eaten anything except some fruit and a sweet potato Melissa had sent with them when they had left that morning. Tom, after eating a second serving of everything, jokingly told her he had been so hungry that even cardboard would have tasted good.

Joletta, having been a little nervous about the thought of eating food she was not familiar with, was pleasantly surprised when she actually enjoyed it.

After the meal, everyone gathered outside in an open area where a large campfire was burning. Tom said a few words to the group and then some of the locals entertained them by playing instruments as everyone joined in the singing.

Jo loved the hypnotic music but her tired body could hardly take it all in. Luckily, after an hour or so things calmed as most villagers headed out of the compound to return to their own homes. It had been an eventful day; another she would never forget.

Exhausted, Joletta followed Jillian to the small neat cottage that was the Robert's home. For now, two of the little boys would bunk together, and Jo would then use the extra bed. The orphanage had been blessed with the beds the year before when the "World Children's Outreach" donated the materials and a team to construct them.

Jillian had told her that later in the week they could discuss what she would want to do about sleeping arrangements.

Either Jo could continue to stay with the family or, if she would prefer, she could stay in one of the other cottages.

Jill and the children were up early the next morning, as usual, but Jill had scooted the little ones outside to give Joletta a little extra time to sleep. She knew from experience how long the trip was, and she knew Jo would need a little extra time to adjust to the six -hour time difference.

When Joletta woke, she opened her eyes to sun filtering into the dark corners of the room. She could hear children's laughter and wondered what time it was. Swinging her feet off the bed, she stepped outside and saw Jill and the others.

Jill had snugly wrapped baby Zarah in a colorful piece of material tied in a sling around her body and was busily washing dishes. The three little boys were busy chasing each other around a large tree nearby.

When they saw her, they ran to her. "Missy Jo! Missy Jo!" they sang in unison. She lifted Omari, who was not quite four and swung him around in a wide circle, which elicited squeals of "Me too, me to, me too…" from the other two boys.

Jillian looked up and spoke in a language that Jo would soon become familiar with, and all three boys quieted. "Good morning, Joletta," they said, as they put on their best manners. "We are glad to see you."

Joletta laughed, "I didn't mean to get them into trouble."

"You didn't, Jo, but they have been practicing how to greet a guest in the proper way. The family has already eaten, but we saved you some sweet potatoes and fritters if you are hungry."

Jo looked at Jill as the boys went back to their game of chase. "It sounds weird to eat sweet potatoes for breakfast, doesn't it?"

"It is definitely different than how we eat in the States, but you will get used to it. I think you will like most of the food; there are many of the fruits and vegetables that you will already be familiar with. I will make you some tea to drink."

"Thanks, Jill. What time is it anyway?"

"By your time, it is only about five in the morning, but it is almost 11:00 here. We knew you would be tired, so I thought you would like to sleep in a bit. We will show you around today and introduce you to everybody. Then in the next couple of days we'll try to figure out where you will best fit into our daily routine and what job you might like to help do."

"Oh, I'll be glad to do whatever you want me to."

Jill smiled, "I know you will, Jo. I appreciate that. Now go get dressed and I'll warm your food and finish up here. Afterwards, we'll go over and see what the schoolchildren are learning today. Tom and Scott will be back before long, and we'll need to get things ready for the mid-day meal."

"Do we eat with everyone here?"

"Not until the evening meal, then everyone eats together over by the main kitchen. I'll show you where it is later. The earlier meals are fixed by the housemother or a volunteer and eaten at their cottages."

Nothing in Africa was the same as home. Joletta's first few days at Hope Mission were certainly not easy for a girl who had never in her life been camping. She had never been a Girl Scout and her summer camp experiences had not been exactly "roughing it." The young people were all housed in updated cottages or comfortable dorm-style rooms. She had never slept in a tent or used an outdoor toilet! Although Jo had dreamed of coming to this place for a long time, she had never really considered how it would be to live here.

Jo's first job at the Mission was seeing that Jill and Tom's children all got ready for school at the proper time. Baby Zarah needed fed and changed. After the morning meal was over, she would take the children and they would walk together to start their daily classes.

The only water at the complex was from a well with an old-fashioned pump. Most rural villagers had to walk, sometimes several miles, to get water, so having access on the property was a blessing. Although electricity was limited, they did have access to a large generator. It was turned on for only an hour or so in the evening or if it there was a necessity for it. On nights when clouds covered the moon and stars, the sky was so black you could see absolutely nothing without a light source of some kind. Jo had always thought of herself as pretty tough, but now she was beginning to find out what "tough" really means.

What she disliked most was the lack of modern bathroom facilities. No flushing, no bathtub, and the showers that Tom had ingeniously constructed had no warm water if you did not fill the large garbage cans that served as water tanks early in the day.

Lim had taken responsibility for doing water runs. Each morning he would pump and carry water to fill the containers, and then the sun would heat it as the day progressed. It was impossible for each child to shower daily, but a chart in each cabin allowed two weekly visits.

Everyone looked forward with much anticipation to "Shower" day, similar to how children in America look forward to going to a water-park for the day.

By the time Scott was ready to fly back to the States, Jo was beginning to get the swing of things and was feeling quite comfortable in her new surroundings. She refused the invitation when he jokingly offered to escort her home.

"Nope, this is home for the next month. I've finally learned how to get to the toilet after dark, so I think I'm good!"

Jo spent the afternoon with Lim, playing with a group of the children. She loved their cheerful enthusiasm and never tired of watching them. It amazed her how resilient these kids were. Every one of them had already dealt with suffering and great loss in their lives, but still they were full of hope and their love of life could warm the hardest of hearts. She was happy she had come.

Later that afternoon, after finishing the meal of nsima (a dish made with white cornmeal and flour), fish, and batata (biscuits made of sweet potatoes), Jo and Limbani got up from the mats they used to sit on and walked over to the adults who were enjoying a break from their long day. "Tom, when Lim takes Scott to town tomorrow, would it be all right if I ride with them? It would be so much fun to see the market, and I might not have another chance to go."

Tom looked at her anxious face and paused for a moment. "I don't know, Joletta; I'm not sure what your parents would say, since no one else will be with you." He turned and looked at his wife. "What do you think, Jill? Would it be all right?"

Jill looked thoughtful before she answered. "Well, she is right. Unless something changes, I don't know that anyone will be going back into Salima for a couple of weeks. Things stay so busy, I don't see that either one of us is going to have any extra time to take her. I think she should get the chance to see as much as she can while she's here."

"What about..."
"Now Tom, you know Lim can be trusted to stay out of trouble, just as long as they promise to start back in plenty of time to get home before dark. I think you should let her go!"

He hesitated for only a moment, "Well, if you think..." Tom had no chance to finish---

"You're the best, Tom!" Joletta laughed as she hugged him tightly.

Scott's plane to Johannesburg was to take off at 1:00 P.M. so timing was important. The first bus would fill quickly and leave for Lilongwe shortly after 9:00. Once again, Able would be picking him up when he arrived in Johannesburg. Before boarding, Scott shook hands with Limbani and thanked him for being such a willing helper. Then turning to hug Jo, he said to her, "Well, Jo, I guess we'll see you in a few weeks. Keep busy and stay out of trouble."

As he kissed the top of her head, he sensed her hesitation. Putting his finger under her chin, he lifted it until her eyes met his. "Hang in there, little lady..." Turning quickly, he stepped into the bus. Without warning, Scott has suddenly experienced a strong emotional reaction. Not wanting Joletta to see his eyes, he waved but did not turn. What was it about this girl that stirred his heart and left him completely open and vulnerable?

It didn't take long before Joletta forgot about her moment of sentimentalism and refocused her attention on the day before her. Since their first meeting only a week before, Limbani and Joletta had formed a special friendship. It was not at all like the ones she had experienced in the past. Watching him as he played with his little brother and sisters, Jo could see there was much love between them. He would roll around with them and be rowdy, but although it appeared to be rough, he never once hurt them. He always included any other children who were nearby in their play. It was plain to see that everyone loved him. He was sweet and polite, and very funny. Not that she could really explain it, but one minute he seemed to be all about business and the next he had every person in the area bending over with laughter

Lim was a handsome youth with the dark skin and the eyes of his ancestors. He was tall and slim, with skin unmarred and smooth. When smiling, his beautiful teeth showed off his honest face.

Not at all like the guys back home; most of those boys were into sports, girls and cars, but not Lim, he was different. Limbani was all about pleasing people. Always up early, doing whatever needed done, he worked as hard as anyone did in the complex. Even older men that came and went from the Mission could not outwork the young man. Although Joletta had not seen much of the serious side of Lim, she knew it was there. She could see something special deep in those dark eyes.

When Jo and Lim arrived at the market, they parked in the same rut-filled area he had parked in the week before.

Jo was thrilled about the colorful displays and all the different sounds and smells. She had only started to become accustomed to hearing people speaking a language other than her own at the Mission, and now here was this place buzzing with people, both black and white, speaking many dialects and languages. She was starting to see that Malawi was a mixture of very diverse cultures. It was more than a little overwhelming.

Vendors called out to shoppers in loud voices, hawking products from beside their stands, all along the roadway and throughout the entire area. Tourists wandered around in their expensive clothing, surveying all the beautiful products and picking up this or that. Laughing and talking, they purchased whatever trinkets or other interesting items caught their eye. In contrast, many of the vendors and people milling around were very poor.

Both city and rural people had no other choice but to spend long tiring days working at the market. At their homes, they had already labored in their gardens or spent days carving and creating all the different craft items, before they even made the trip in hopes of adding to their meager incomes. Mothers or older sisters or brothers carried the babies wrapped in the colorful scarves called chitenjes. Other small children played in the dust close to where their parents were selling vegetables or whatever they had brought that day.

Those who came only to have a good time did not see the pain or poverty that surrounded them but saw only what was beautiful. Most would return to their own country or comfortable homes without ever knowing or considering the hard life faced by so many of Malawi's population.

Joletta loved the beautiful batik scarfs the women made with a special process of wax-resist dyeing. The women wore these chitenjes two or three at a time, wrapped around their waist as skirts; babies were then swaddled and carried close to their hearts while they did their daily chores. She bought three of the scarves for herself and several others to take home with her as gifts for her friends.

It was amazing to her, seeing how many of the children and young girls carried babies. She knew from her school project that girls in Malawi are forced to marry and become mothers before they are even adults themselves. Jo was learning that it is far different to read about the social problems of the world than it is to see them firsthand. She could not even imagine herself being a mother or little Annie being expected to care for babies and work like an adult. Many things in this beautiful country saddened her heart.

She was now beginning to understand why Jillian, Tom, and other people such as their friends in Johannesburg were so passionate about the work they were doing.

She walked with Lim to watch some boys he knew playing a game of Wari. He explained to Joletta that it was a very old game and that African people had played this same game for many generations. He said Tom had told him there were people that called the game African Chess, because it can sometimes last for hours or days. Explaining the game, he said either you needed a game-board, or you sit on the ground, as the boys they were watching were doing, with dips scooped out on the ground. You must have two rows for each player. Using small stones, each   player tries to capture the stones belonging to their opponent.

When Limbani introduced Jo to his friends who did not speak English, they nodded in her direction, but continued with their play. Looking up at her and grinning, one of the boys said something to Limbani, which made the others standing around laugh. She could not tell what he said to them, but Lim's voice in response sounded irritated, and soon he suggested they leave. She asked him what the boy had said, but he waved the question off and did not tell her anything.

There was so much activity and things to see that the day went quickly. At lunchtime, they bought cokes and Chippies, which are fried potatoes. Jo bought some trinkets and things to take home to her family before it was time to leave for the Mission.

"Do you think we had better start back, Lim? I promised we would not stay late."

Lim agreed that it would be good to get back early. He had told Tom he would clean the storage shed. It was where they kept extra bed mats, donated items that had not yet been used, and the few tools owned by the Mission. Thinking that if they got back he could at least get started on the project, he agreed.

Preparing to leave, they had almost gotten to the truck when Jo stopped. "Wait, what is that?" Listening hard for several moments, she had almost decided the sound was her imagination. No...there it was again. "Listen! Do you hear it?"

"What? Oh...There it is. It's probably an animal or something."

"No, Limbani," Jo was already running toward the soft mewing sound. "Over here! Oh, my God, Lim! It's a baby, a little tiny baby! Oh, no! Over here! There's a girl here."

The girl was just beyond a bush, possibly trying to get to help. She was lying on the ground in a pool of blood. Her eyes were closed, and she was barely breathing. "We have to get help!" Once again, Jo heard the soft cry. Running over to the pickup, Joletta pulled out the scarves she had purchased earlier. Turning to the baby, she wrapped her naked little body in one. Taking another scarf, she covered the mother with it.

Lim had already left and soon he was back with several other people following him.

Jo was sitting on the ground next to the young mother. She was crying as she held the tiny child tightly to her chest. One of the women leaned over the girl lying on the ground and began speaking with others that were now surrounding them. An older woman came to Joletta.

"I don't think she is breathing," she sobbed. The woman could not understand the words that Joletta was saying, but she understood the girl's face. Bending down she gently touched the tiny bundle, offering to take the child. Jo could not let go.... For only a moment, she believed that if she kept the little one locked tight against her, she would not have to know... but after what seemed like an eternity, Jo slowly released her grip.

Kneeling, the woman put the baby on the ground. Quietly opening the wrap her sad eyes told Jo what she did not want to acknowledge. Realizing there was no hope that the baby was still living, she dissolved into yet another round of tears. The woman spoke softly to her, and Jo looked at Lim, who was watching the ongoing activity. He spoke with sadness, sounding much older than his 17 years. "She says it was too early; the baby was not ready be born yet."

Hearing the sound of an emergency vehicle, Jo looked over at the young girl who had just given birth. "What about her?" The woman who had taken the baby reached over and patted Jo on the hand; she nodded her head and gave a small smile.

Limbani said, "It looks like she has lost a lot of blood, but if they get her to the hospital, hopefully, she will recover."

Most of the observers had left, and things had calmed down as the ambulance prepared to leave. Lim came over to the truck where Jo was sitting. "They want to thank you." He indicated the two women that had taken charge. "The one with the red head-wrap is the girl's grandmother." Joletta sniffed and wiped a tear with the back of her hand as she got out of the truck.

The girl's grandmother took several steps toward her and took both of Jo's hands into her own. She firmly squeezed Joletta's fingers and nodded once again. The two simply looked into each other's eyes - no other words were necessary.

Even with all that had happened in the last few hours, the young people arrived home before anyone had a chance to become unduly concerned. It was good, for there was no way they could have communicated to let them know what had been happening.

Tom and Jill listened intently as the two told the story of their ordeal. "Oh, Jo. What a terrible thing to have witnessed. That poor girl! How frightened she must have been! I'm very sorry, Jo." Jill walked over and put her arms around Joletta.

"The baby...she was a perfect little thing, Jill."

"I know, Honey. Some things are so hard to understand." Jill continued, "It was just a blessing that you and Lim were there at the right time for that young mother, though. You know, she might have died also, if you had not come along."

The weeks went by so quickly Joletta could hardly believe when she realized one day that it was already the second week of July. She would be leaving Africa in just a few more days, and she felt like she had just arrived. She was always so busy; there had been little time to think about anything except what each day would bring.

She became good friends with both Mishal and Caroline, the young housemothers that lived in cottage #1. They were both young, not much older than Jo, and even though they spoke very limited English, the three learned to communicate with each other after a few days of working together.

Mishal had a little girl named Blessing who was five, and a little boy she called Paki that would soon turn two.

326

Her husband had died after an accident only a few months before.

Caroline, the older of the two, had three boys, all of school age. When they left for school in the morning, Caroline helped do morning chores before going to supervise the volunteers who came daily to prepare and serve the evening meal. She had arrived at the mission three years before when her husband had died of AIDS. Sadly, Caroline also suffered from the virus, but for now, with daily anti-viral medications, she was in remission.

At the end of June, a visiting work team came to help build the first stage of what would be the permanent school. Because of limited building supplies, they finished all they were able to do before their scheduled return.

When a bus came lumbering down the dusty pathway that led into the Mission complex, the children had no idea what was happening and excitement grew as they began to realize that *they* were actually going to ride on the bus!

The generous church people had arranged everything, and the entire "Hope family" was traveling to the Kuti Wild Animal Preserve that was not far from their location.

It was the highlight of the year for the children. Most had never been on a bus and getting to ride one was almost as exciting to them as seeing the animals. Many of the animals living on the preserve now needed the protection of their human neighbors, because they could no longer survive living in the wild. Poachers had killed many of the large animals in Africa, and the continuing influx of humans meant their habitat became smaller every year.

Everyone was in high spirits and the weather was perfect for a road trip. Once they drove beyond the property gates and into the preserve, a group of elephants came out of a brushy area and walked right along the dirt roadway next to the bus. Everyone laughed, watching as two baby elephants tried their best to keep up with the rest of the group. A little later they saw zebras and, as the morning went on, many other animals and beautiful birds. The day turned out to be such a big success, the Preserve's "new friends" promised to do their best

to come back again the following year. Of course, the plans were made with Pastor Tom and his staff. It was not shared with any of the happy children, knowing that with fluctuating finances, there was the possibility it might not happen.

Joletta's final adventure while in Africa was a trip to the beach with Limbani. She knew that the best beach along Lake Malawi was only about twenty miles away from the Mission, but because of the many responsibilities there, it had not been possible for them to leave the compound. Tom as usual was at first hesitant to give his permission. He was somewhat concerned about how appropriate it was to let the two young people go on their own, but another reason was the fact that he was finally feeling much better physically, and he had a long list of projects that needed done. His illness had kept him laid up for weeks and although everyone had stepped up to do what they could, he still needed all the extra hands he could get. He hoped the young people would stay and help rather than "wasting" the day playing. Jill, on the other hand, felt Joletta deserved the day off. She had worked cheerfully and diligently, and had never once complained about any task they asked her to do.

Explaining to Tom that it would be a big disappointment if Joletta had to go back home without even seeing the beautiful lake, she gently persuaded him to side with her. So in the end, Tom smiled begrudgingly, and once again gave in to the women in his household.

Lake Malawi was even more than Jo had expected it to be. Its azure blue waters stretched out before them, glittering in the morning sun. She had never experienced a place like it.

Limbani served as her proud guide. He knew many interesting stories and details about the area. They spent the morning walking along the golden sandy shoreline as he told her stories about the lake, its people, and its history. He knew and shared many interesting tales of

329

local lore, some funny and some tragic. "Did you know that Lake Malawi is a National Park? It was designated a Natural World Heritage Site because, just as an example, it contains the largest number of fish species of any lake in the world: 3,000 in all!"

Jo was impressed with her friend's knowledge. 'Oh my! I've never heard of a Natural Heritage Site. What does that mean?"

He grinned and flashed those white teeth at her. "It means," he paused and let her wait for a few seconds before he finished his sentence. "It means a "lot" of people come here to vacation." Laughing at his joke and thinking himself clever, he continued, "Really, there are a lot of things to do here besides swimming and fishing. There are boat tours, kayak and sailboat rentals, bicycles, and snorkeling, to name a few. But you must have money to do many of the things."

"It's a freshwater lake and is the second deepest lake in the world. It's over 700 meters deep in places further north! The locals are mostly fishermen, but some work in the hotels and resorts."

"A missionary-explorer named David Livingstone "discovered" this lake about 150 years ago and he said the fishermen's lanterns reflecting on the water made it look like the lake was filled with shining stars instead of water. He is the one who named it the "Lake of Stars," but there are others that call it "Calendar Lake" because it is 365 miles long."

"That is neat, like the number of days in a year, I guess. I like "Lake of Stars" best. I can just imagine it at night. There must have been a lot of men fishing when he first saw it. I wish we could have seen it then," said Joletta longingly. "I know we have to be back, but I bet it is beautiful when the moon shines on it."

They walked through a small fishing village and talked to the amicable local people who greeted them as if they had been friends forever. Everyone they met was kind and patiently explained to Joletta the details of daily life on the shores of the large lake.

She was fascinated with everything.

There were many wooden drying racks made from sticks bound together with long reeds. On the racks, hundreds of silvery fish had been placed to dry in the bright sunlight. This process preserved the fish for later use. The strong smells made Joletta wrinkle her nose, but she laughed and said, "Now, this is something you would never see in Pennsylvania!" Once the drying process was finished, the fish were safe to be used for a family's meals, or to be taken and sold in local village stores or at market.

A young couple Limbani and Jo visited with invited them to eat lunch. As guests they were served first, as is traditional in Malawi, after which the husband ate and then the young wife. They all enjoyed the meal of fish and nsima. Later they bought fried potatoes from a "Chippie" stand. With their stomachs full, it was early in the afternoon when Lim told her there was still one more thing they were going to do before going home.

"OK. So, what is that?"

However, with merry eyes he refused to divulge the secret. "I'm not going to tell you, you'll just have to wait and see."

Nothing she said would get him to say where they were going, or what they were going to do. He just said she would have to wait. He was obviously enjoying her frustration as they walked along the edge of the lake, wading up to their knees in the cool wet liquid. Occasionally one would reach down and send a wide arc of glittering water toward the other, only to be returned, with equal enthusiasm and a round of laughter. With each splash, as the game continued, both Jo and Limbani were getting wetter and wetter, but neither seemed to mind. They were young and the sun was shining. The wind blowing across the lake cooled their damp bodies and for the moment neither had a care in the world.

They had been walking along for quite a while when Joletta tried again. "Come on, Lim. Aren't you ever going to tell me what you are up to?"

Grinning from ear to ear, he just shook his head and ran ahead of her.

"Wait!" She sprinted after him. Her hair, which she had not put into a ponytail that morning, flew wildly behind her. "Wait, Lim!"

Suddenly he stopped, causing her to run right into him! The two fell, laughing into the shallow water. Out of breath, the young man caught her in his arms. For only a moment, time seemed to stop, but almost as quickly as he had caught her, he let her go, and stood up. "Oh, Jo, I'm sorry-- I didn't mean—I--it isn't much farther now. Come on." He reached out and pulled her to her feet.

Shyly, he offered her his hand, and they once again began to walk. It was another 10 minutes or so when they saw several people ahead. They were obviously local fishermen, sitting beside several dugout canoes pulled up on the beach.

"Here we are," Lim announced. Calling out to them, an older man stood and acknowledged Lim's greeting. "Hello, my friend!"

It was Bomani, the old fisherman that had been teaching the village boys how to make fishing nets the week before. Jo had not actually met the old man but had helped serve meals the week he was at Hope, and remembered his cheerful voice as he talked with the others. "I thought you would like to go out and see more of what Lake Malawi really has to offer."

"Oh! Do you mean we are going in a boat?" Joletta did not know what to say. She would not have guessed in a hundred years what Limbani's surprise was going to be.

"Are you all right, Jo? I thought you would like to go out on the water. When he was at Hope last week, I asked Bomani if he would take us out today."

"Yes!--- Oh yes! I do want to go," she hesitated, "but, is it safe?"

This caused a round of good-natured laughter, although some of the men did not understand exactly what they were laughing about. "Come on, men have been fishing on these waters for hundreds of years. It will be just fine."

Only Jo and Limbani went along with Bomani for the ride in the dugout canoe. At first, she was nervous. She had never been in any kind of watercraft even remotely similar to this, and if looks counted, this hollowed-out log certainly didn't look very water worthy. Furthermore, she didn't see any sign of life jackets.

The old man chanted a song as their craft skimmed effortlessly along. The further out they went, the less she thought of her initial fears. She became fully immersed in the beauty of the crystal water and the colorful shimmering fish that could be seen flitting along just under the water's surface. Jo soon completely forgot about her water worries.

The rhythm of old Bomani's song and the gentle splash of the oars as they dipped into the water were hypnotic and beautiful. All too soon Limbani said it was time that they head back to the beach. Instead of taking them to where they met him earlier, Bomani paddled back to the area where they had begun their adventure that morning. It was only a short walk to where they had left their vehicle and soon they were in the truck and started home.

"Oh, Lim, I hope you know what a wonderful day this has been. I loved every minute of it." Joletta scooted to the middle of the seat. Stretching to reach his cheek; she kissed him gently and then scooted over once again.

The two rode the rest of the way back to Hope Mission and home in silence.

Joletta's final week at Hope Mission was busy and full of mixed emotions. She was not sure she would ever have the opportunity to return to Africa. Although she had expected to make new friends while in Malawi, she had not once thought about how hard it was going to be to say goodbye.

Mission life was always hard. It was sometimes dirty. Very often, it was sad and sometimes heartbreaking. However, there were also moments of joy and the feeling that you could make a positive difference in someone's life. It reminded her of a little story she once heard.

The story told about a little boy who was walking on a beach and tossing starfish back into the surf. Someone came along and said, "It won't make a difference. There are too many starfish to save." The little boy replied, "It will make a difference to this starfish."

Jo had sensed long ago that this far-away place was where she needed to be and she was glad she had come. "Yes," she said aloud, "I did make a difference." She smiled to herself.

Joletta had learned to love the work. She loved Jillian and Tom and the boys and little Zarah; she loved everything about mission life, the workers, the volunteers, the precious children and everyone at the Mission. How was she ever going to live without it all?! Hardest of all, she must leave Limbani, her soul mate and her "hero."

Chapter 26
SEASONAL CHANGE

Jo was as happy to see her family as she was sad to leave her new friends in Malawi, but somehow she felt like she was now completely out of her element.

It wasn't so much that things were different than they had been before her trip. It was more like Joletta was different. She didn't exactly know why she felt like a fish out of water.

She missed the structured beginning of each new day: rising and preparing everyone for breakfast, early morning prayers, cleaning and straightening the dorms and settling everyone into classes or play before beginning any of the other necessary daily activities that needed attention.

Here at home, she arose each morning with nothing more important to do than brush her teeth, figure out what outfit she might decide to wear, and if she should wear her hair loose or pull it back in a ponytail. No one seemed to need her to do anything and she felt slightly depressed. Not really seeing much reason to get out of bed, she slept in the first few days.

While in Africa, the days started and ended with activities that felt important, that *were* important. Small children needed help dressing and preparing for the day, the babies had to be diapered, fed, or comforted. Jo always helped the littler ones with their housekeeping chores, sang songs to them, read stories, and helped teach Bible verses to them. She was always a willing helper whenever there was a need.

Sandy was so happy to have her precious daughter home and little Annie was more than thrilled to once again be with her big sister.

It was Friday night and Jo had been home almost a week when she woke with a start! She had been dreaming that she was riding Golden Boy and she could see the house in the distance. Urging him forward, they were flying across the field.

Jo had never had any conscious memory of her accident and realized that while sleeping her mind had remembered that day as she was headed home to admit that she had not been honest with her family in the days before she was thrown from the horse.

Closing her eyes, she concentrated on the imagines still floating in her head. Leaning low on Golden Boy's back, he was at a full canter when he jumped across the narrow creek bed. Suddenly he faltered and Jo felt herself being flung through the air. Landing hard on the ground, she tried to make sense of what just happened. The gentle horse nuzzled her face and softly nickered. Confused, she could see blood on his forelegs and something jagged was sticking into, no, out of his leg!

Why couldn't I get up? That was the last thing she had recalled, until now! She now knew exactly what had happened that awful day two years before!

Rising from her bed and walking to the window, Jo slowly pulled back the heavy drape that covered it. The window looked onto the pasture where the accident happened. The curtains had remained closed since that fateful day.

The moon was full, and the wind was blowing the tall silvery grass in the field. The barn stood brooding and empty although there was now a dog kennel attached to the south side where her mother trained her white Samoyed pup that Jim had given her last Christmas.

But no longer did the barn house Jo's beautiful Golden Boy. Never again would she feel his strong body underneath her, never again would she put her arms around his golden neck and feel his rough warm body against her face.

Dizzy and sick, her body slid to the floor. Wrapping her arms around her knees, she let the tears come. She sobbed and sobbed. Later her mom found her heartbroken girl, quiet and still on the floor. There were new tears as mother and daughter wept together.

The summer had been a hot one but finally, by early September, the days had begun to cool. Some trees had even begun to show signs of the coming fall. The large yard now was covered with thick green grass and Sandy's flowerbeds were full to the brim with masses of colorful mums, dahlias, zinnias and other late summer flowers.

Jo had reconnected with her friends and was once again dating Roland. He openly insisted he was madly in love with her. Jo really liked Roland and they always had good times when they were together, but she only agreed to go out with him as friends. She simply was not ready to be in a serious relationship. Both she and Roland would be going off to college in less than a year and she was already enrolled in afternoon classes at Bridgetown Community College. Spending mornings at the High School and the afternoons at Bridgetown, Joletta knew she would need to stay focused on her studies if she had any chance of being accepted at Penn State next Fall.

Chapter 27
FAMILY TRADITIONS

Jo sighed and smiled as she straightened her back and looked at the stack of Christmas gifts she had just finished wrapping. The leftovers of wrapping paper and name tags lay scattered on the floor along with empty brown tubes, tape, ribbons and scissors. It had already been such a fun season and now it was only a few more days until Christmas.

Her mother's younger brothers, Tyler and Jacob, had surprised everyone when they came with Beth and Darrel at Thanksgiving. For many months they had hoped to get the family all together for a reunion, but it had proved to be a real challenge. Everyone's lives were busy and to find time when everyone was free at the same time was next to impossible and did not happen frequently. Sandy and Jim had seen her brothers while visiting at Beth's the past summer, but at that time Jo was still in Malawi and Annie was staying with Grandma Susan while her parents vacationed.

Jacob had talked Tyler, Beth and Darrel, and also Jim, into keeping quiet until they got to the house.

Beth and Darrel first came in and a short time later Jim excused himself but soon returned with Sandi's younger brothers casually walking in as if there was nothing unusual at all! "Look who I found," Jim said as he entered the room ahead of the younger men. Sandi immediately burst into tears of excitement, and after a moment of confusion was enfolded in a double bear hug from her laughing brothers. Jo, who had been out shopping with friends, came home an hour later and had the opportunity to meet her uncles for the first time.

It was just great and a lot of fun getting to know each other. At first, she wasn't quite sure about Tyler. He seemed so quiet when compared to his "happy-go-lucky" brother. But as the weekend continued, her feelings changed as Tyler proved easy to talk with, and he questioned her extensively about her experience in Malawi. It was her favorite subject and she happily told him how much she had come to love the people and the African. He was interested in her future plans, sharing some of his own experiences in college, and earlier in his family's life. He also proved to have a good sense of humor. Several times he had everyone in the room laughing and telling stories about when they were children. With his newly earned bachelor's degree he would begin medical school the following fall.

Jacob spent the weekend with Annie on his lap much of the time and flirted with Jo's friends. Beth told them, laughing, that they should not believe a thing he said! He was full of stories and obviously enjoyed telling of his adventures. He had always been active in sports and loved anything that could be done outdoors. Winning awards for swimming and track, he also played basketball and in the summer months, tennis.

His good friend, Fin, an exchange student from Switzerland, was the person that got him interested in distance hiking. Being raised in the Alps, Fin had done a lot of hiking and skiing, and Jacob, always up for a good challenge, liked the idea of a new adventure. The two of them spent most weekends for months hiking every trail they could find within a two-hour drive of home.

Fin had to return to Switzerland the middle of June after graduation, but by the time he left, Jacob was hooked. Soon he committed himself to a plan to hike the Appalachian Trail.

The more he thought of it, the more he liked the idea, so he started to seriously gather information to make arrangements necessary to do a "through-hike" of the Appalachian Trail. He knew it would be the biggest challenge in his life. Hiking the entire trail, almost 2,200 miles, was something many tried, but many never completed the trek. Jacob was determined and knew he would succeed!

There were lots of considerations and extensive training before he could make it happen, but he was sure he was up to it. He had always kept his body in prime condition, but training for long hours every day filled the months before the trip with painful overstrained muscles and little time for extra activities. Financially, he felt comfortable, having worked throughout his high school years. He had always been a bit tight with his money, enjoying seeing the numbers add up with each paycheck that he got.

By the end of February 2002, he was set to go. Tyler would be on Spring Break the first week of April and had agreed to transport him to Springer Mountain in Georgia where the hike would begin. Supplies would be sent general delivery along the route because the trail came close to small towns along the way. He would be hiking north, hoping to reach Baxter State Park in Maine by mid-October.

Unfortunately, a month and 200 miles into the hike, Jacob slipped and took a bad fall off a steep, slick section of the trail, breaking several ribs and his left forearm.

Airlifted off the mountain on a gurney suspended from a helicopter, a very disappointed young man woke up in a hospital the following morning where he spent the next two days and nights. But, still determined as always and unwilling to accept that his journey was at an end, soon he was once again training and preparing to start the hike once more the following Spring!

He told wonderful stories of the breathtaking beauty of woods and mountain, of clear rippling streams and white foaming waterfalls and the people he met along the way. He told them his "hiker's pseudonym" had been

"Tracker" and that everyone that hikes the AT uses not their given name but a trail name.

He told that he happened onto two small cubs playing in the tall grasses and realized the mother bear would be close by. Fearing for his life he was both awed and terrified! And he told them of the difficulty of hiking in heavy rain and snow, trying to sleep when he was so wet and cold, he thought he would freeze! As spring turned to summer the weather got so hot he felt he could not breathe, or take another step, or climb another mountain!

Starting the second chapter of his trip at Clingmans Dome in the Smokey Mountains National Park, a few miles south of where his accident happened, Jacob completed his hike on Mount Katahdin, Maine in late September 2003!

Always an adrenalin junkie, he was now researching the idea of becoming a Smokejumper! He was enrolled at Wayne Community College in Goldsboro, NC, taking courses in Forestry and Conservation, as well as those needed to become a licensed paramedic, since joining the Volunteer Fire Department in Goldsboro.

The Christmas tree was now standing tall and beautiful, framed by the floor-to-ceiling window in the family room. Daddy Jim had taken Annie more than a week ago to get it and after putting Annie to bed Friday night, a small group of friends came for a "decorating party." When Annie woke and came downstairs the following morning, there was the "not quite a Christmas tree" but, the "Grand Birthday Tree!" Not only was the tree covered with

Christmas décor, but on the tip of many branches were sparkling silver glass balls and large blue and silver balloons tied with silver ribbons!

Never had they seen Annie so excited! Hopping down the final steps, she ran to her mom screaming, "Mommy, Mommy! Blue is my favorite color!" She continued running around and around the tree, hugging everyone, laughing and squealing. Her party wasn't until mid-afternoon, but everyone knew that Annie's 5th birthday was already a big success!

Christmas morning came, cold and clear with no new snow on the ground. Annie was hoping to go sledding later in the day, but although there had been a light covering the week before, it would not be enough for an outdoor adventure. She hated that her sister would be disappointed, but on the other hand, with such a busy day ahead she doubted that the little one would be unhappy for long.

It was a bright and sunny morning and the smell of hot coffee and sweet rolls drifting up the stairs made it hard to feel anything but cheerful. The morning was theirs to relax and enjoy, since they had been with Grandma Susan and the family until late last evening and would not be headed to Gloria and Jim's house until around 1:00 o'clock.

Several boxes were stacked on a chair from the night before with bits and pieces of wrapping paper and ribbon still attached. Jo's gifts included pretty clothing, jewelry, make-up and a hand-crafted work of art from Annie! She loved it all! She knew the time and effort it takes to pick gifts that are meaningful to those you love.

It was so different now than when she was younger. Her mother had always done the best she could but some years if it had not been for a local "toy drive" outreach, there would have been no presents at all. Joletta remembered asking her mother one time when she was quite small, "Where are your presents, Momma?" She no longer remembered exactly what Sandi had told her but was quite sure that there had not been any gifts for her mother that year.

Picking up Annie's artwork she admired it for a moment, smiled, and then pinned it in the middle of her large bulletin board. If anyone came into the room the bulletin board was the first thing you noticed. Annie would expect it to be there!

Pushing things to the side she pulled out the pair of fuzzy booties from the stack of gifts - the tag read "To Jo, From Jim" although she suspected Sandi had purchased them - and put them on her bare feet. Then picking up a brush and a scrunchie, she pulled her hair into a ponytail and headed toward the kitchen.

Sandi and Jim and the girls had opened gifts Christmas Eve and then attended church with Susan and the family. Today was the traditional "Extended Family Feast" with Jim's dad and Gloria. Always celebrated on Christmas day in the early afternoon, Jim's aunts, uncles, and cousins had been sharing the holiday since he could remember.

Christmas services were still Joletta's favorite of the year. The celebration of the birth of Jesus always began with singing. There was always an extra-large crowd and she loved hearing all the voices harmonizing both traditional and the newest hymns. After that, a lay pastor read from Luke 2 the beautiful story of Christ's birth.

This year, a bell choir had performed a medley before Pastor Blevins gave his message. The service then, as was always the tradition, ended with candle lighting and the singing of "Silent Night."

Chapter 28
HEAVEN'S HEARTACHE

Since the girls were all out of school for the holidays, Tiffany and Sam came home with Joletta to stay a few days. They planned to make the most of their time together. Samantha went to sleep long before the others, but Jo and Tiff talked late into the night. Tiffany had just finished her first semester of college and was not only busy with studies, but had pledged a sorority, sang in the concert choir, and now spent every extra moment she could find with Connor, her new boyfriend. They met on campus the first week of November and now Tiffany said they were "head over heels" in love! Joletta didn't know Connor but was worried for her friend. She knew Tiffany well enough to know that she didn't always make the best decisions when it came to guys. This wasn't the first time Tiff had "fallen in love" and it usually ended badly, leaving Tiffany heartbroken, confused and sometimes angry.

Jo continued to keep Roland at arms-length, insisting that they both needed to concentrate on their studies. She had spent many months catching up on her academics and was determined she would be accepted at Penn State. Roland was ready to take their relationship further and she was aware of it but, if truth be told, she simply was not ready to commit to anyone. Perhaps she was not being fair; he was so sweet to her and she truly did like him. The way it was, most everyone knew she was Roland's girl, meaning she was "unavailable." It was just simpler with only one guy to consider instead of dating around as some girls did.

It was almost noon before Jo came down the stairs to get a glass of orange juice and a bagel, leaving Tiffany in

344

the middle of the bed, wrapped cocoon-like and still sound asleep.

She could hear voices in the back of the house but as she walked past Jim's office, she noticed his attention was focused on a news alert. She started to speak but paused—the newscaster was standing in the middle of a rubble filled street, and the entire area looked as if it had been hit with a bomb! "What is it, Jim?"

"Oh, Jo, I didn't hear you come in." He patted the arm of the large recliner he was sitting in and said, "There has been a terrible tsunami! They are only just beginning to get details. It was in the Indian Ocean somewhere. They know it has killed many people, perhaps thousands, but still don't know exactly what happened or how many areas will be affected!"

As Joletta sat on the arm of his chair, her throat tightened, and tears welled behind her eyes. "Oh, my gosh! That is terrible, Jim!"

"One thing's for sure, there is total devastation over a huge area!"

In the following days, the news of the tsunami grew more and more grim! What had been such a wonderful season for Jo and her family was ending with the heartbreaking news of this disaster.

As time went on the Tsunami of 2004 took the lives of more than 280,000 people and spread devastation throughout 14 countries, leaving more than one and a half million people homeless!

Jo was left shaken and angry. She tried to pray that night, but the words just would not come. She felt numb. All the "fun" of the holidays now seemed flat and out of place. *How can we sit around in our comfortable little corner of the world and enjoy our lives when there is so much suffering in the world? Why?* It was the one word that kept coming into her mind! *Why?*

It was the first time since Joletta had become a believer that she questioned her belief. *Why would a God that loves us allow something so horrible, why?!* The thoughts churned in her mind for days. Joletta just could not get the terrible news out of her head. Tossing and turning throughout the night, as she slept, her mind kept returning to the disaster. Images of shadowy figures crying and devastation in all directions! Images of children without mothers, mothers without children! She felt like she was there and she wanted so badly to help, but she was unable to move; she could do nothing!

Somewhere between waking and sleeping, she cried out! As she jerked herself fully awake, she sat on the edge of the bed, realizing it was a dream--- but it was all too real.

There was a soft knock on her door. "Jo, Honey, are you OK?" Her mother opened the door slightly. "May I come in?"

"Sure, Mom, come on in."

"Oh, Honey. Another bad dream? I thought you didn't have them anymore. I'm so sorry!"

"It's OK, Mom. I guess all the news about the tsunami has been getting to me. I just can't seem to reason it out in my head! If God made us all, and loves us all, I just don't understand how he can let things like that happen! Those were people, Mom! People just like you and me! Little children and babies! It just makes me feel--- it just makes me--- mad! That's how I feel, Mom, I am so angry, I just want to scream! I am just plain mad at God, and I don't know what to do about it!"

Tears rolled down her cheeks as her mother held her almost grown-up daughter. "I don't know what to tell you, Darling. I don't have the answers you need because I don't know the answers any more than you do. I do understand though. That is how I felt when you had your accident!"

Jo settled herself back on her pillows and said in a quiet voice, "I guess we will never understand why." Squeezing her mom's hand she said, "I'm OK now. I think I will try to go back to sleep." Sandi sat beside her, stroking her daughter's dark hair as she had months before, when Joletta lay in a hospital bed, unable to wake up.

She whispered, "I love you, Sweetheart. I really wish I had the answers, but sadly I don't."

Sandi still felt unsure of herself when it came to her beliefs. Some days she felt like she was ready to accept and believe that Christ was truly the Son of God, but on other days, doubts filled her mind. Now here she sat, with the sweetest, kindest, most loving person she knew in so much pain. Pain not for herself, but for others, people she never even knew existed before the past couple of days. *If you are really who you say you are God, you need to help this innocent girl. I love her so much. Please Jesus, if, you are up there, help those that are suffering, help her, and please, help us all!*

Tiffany and Samantha were going over to their Grandmother's to spend the night with her before returning home. Tiff would soon be returning to college and wanted to spend a little extra time with her grandma. Sammy had been sick several days before the holidays and needed to get home to finish make-up schoolwork. When they arrived at Susan's, they were surprised to find Pastor Scott visiting!

He was in town for only a short time preparing for another trip to Hope Mission. Since Jillian and Tom had not been able to come for the holidays, Susan was sending packages for the little ones and other things they were not able to purchase in Malawi.

Jo was thrilled to see him and ran into his arms laughing! "Oh, Pastor Scott, I'm sorry, you just don't know how glad I am to see you!" Her cheeks turned bright as she realized she had made a bit of a spectacle in front of her friends.

347

Giving her a quick kiss on the cheek, Scott held her at arm's length. "You're looking pretty good to me, too, Miss Joletta! I've missed seeing my sweet girl." He winked and looked at the others. "I was planning to come by the house before I headed out anyway, but this is great. I'm so glad you guys are here. I have some things I need to discuss with you and your folks." Releasing Jo, he shook hands with Jim and greeted the others before they all sat down to visit.

Jim and Joletta were not able to stay long, but before leaving, they agreed that Scott would come over and have dinner with them the following evening. Walking them to the car, Scott opened the door and waited for Jo to climb in. "We will see you guys tomorrow then."

Leaning down before shutting the door, Scott spoke, "Jo, Jim was saying you've had a really rough week. I understand how upsetting some things that happen are and I know there are things that just don't seem to have an explanation, at least an explanation that makes sense to you or me. This afternoon wasn't really a good time to talk, but Jim said it will just be your family tomorrow, and if you would like to talk about it, I think I might be able to be of some help."

Looking at her step-dad she said, "Oh, Jim! I didn't realize you were going to say anything! I told you, I really am OK! I know there are things that we can't control, and I guess we just have to accept that and keep going, no matter what."

"Your mom has been really worried about you, Hon. I know Pastor Scott here is much better equipped to help than I could ever be; it won't hurt to talk awhile though, will it? I think it might make you feel a little better."

Scott spoke, "It's entirely up to you, Jo. Whatever you decide is fine, though. Now you two better get on the road. Sandi will be thinking you got lost or something! I'll see you tomorrow." Laughing, he shut the door, stepped aside and waved as Jim pulled away from the curb.

Sandi had put a pot roast in the oven with carrots and potatoes and was making salad when Joletta came into the kitchen with Pastor Scott. "Look who's here, Mom."

"Oh, Scott, it is so good to see you. They told me you were over at Susan's yesterday. It's going to be awhile before we can eat; would you like a cup of coffee? It's already made."

"I would enjoy that very much, thank you. If I remember right, you make a pretty fine cup of joe!" Looking at his younger friend, he laughed!

Joletta rolled her eyes and handed him a cup. "Here, get your own, silly. I don't know how anyone can drink that stuff! Especially without creamer in it."

He grinned and walked over to the coffee pot and filled the cup, almost to overflowing. "Well, it wouldn't have been polite to refuse, would it?" Just then Annie came skipping into the room. He put his cup down and as she climbed onto his lap, he continued, "All these pretty ladies in this house make everything sweet!" He squeezed the little girl to him, and she hugged back, giggling. Reaching into his jeans pocket he pulled out a small wooden carving and handed it to her. It was a small figure of a monkey. "My friend in Africa made this after I told him I knew a little girl in America that was a "little monkey!"

After the meal was over Scott asked if Jo would like to go for a walk with him. Soft snowflakes were floating in the air and although it was cold out, there was no wind and it was not bitter. "It's going to be getting dark soon. I would really enjoy your company." Nothing had been said about Jo's disturbing week, but she was sure he was giving her an opportunity to have the talk that had been mentioned the day before.

349

Scott was the first to speak. "Isn't it amazing how beautiful the world can be?" he said. "There is beauty everywhere in God's creation, everything that He made is perfect - flowers, trees, animals, babies, everything. The changing seasons, the tiniest flower, even spiderwebs. There is always beauty. Just look around and even on the darkest day, there is beauty."

Joletta looked up to the sky and felt the snow gently touching her face. "Yes, I do know. It's just that there are times I don't understand things at all."

"Like the Tsunami?"

"Yes, I can't understand that. I haven't ever understood why Golden Boy had to die either. It was my fault; I'm the one that did wrong. I lied to Mom and I made Golden Boy run. I'm the one that God should have punished."

"Jo, I think you already know that it doesn't work like that. God wasn't punishing you by letting your horse die! You weren't hurt because you had done something wrong. Things just happen as they do, and in this life, many times, we will never know the reasons."

"Tsunami's, earthquakes---all kinds of natural disasters are not because God is punishing us. *His plan is perfect. But, mankind has changed that because of sin.* What we have to remember, and respect, is that *His Plan will be fulfilled!"*

"When God created Adam and Eve, he placed them into a beautiful garden. There was no sadness and no natural disasters; the Garden of Eden was perfect and everything was under God's protection. Their only job was to care for it and follow his instruction. He also warned them that *if they rejected his instructions, suffering and death would result."* (Genesis 2:17)

"He gave man free will, and because they allowed Satan to tempt them, God removed them from the Garden. (Genesis 3:1-6) *No longer were they under God's*

350

protection but now they were "apart" from God." (Genesis 3:23-24)

"Ever since that time Mankind has been under the influence of Satan. (2nd Corinthians 4:4) And we have continued to push God further and further into the background. Because we first rejected God, there is now death and suffering. Natural disasters and sickness are all because of our rejection of Him. He has simply let us have it our way. It is very important to remember the fact that we are not living in God's world, we are living in man's world."

"God can and will, at times, intervene to protect His People. He does care, and He wants us to come to Him." (Jeremiah 29:11; 2 Peter 3:9) God himself said *"For I have no pleasure in the death of one who dies, therefore turn and live."* (Ezekiel 18:32)

The wind picked up and as the air grew colder the flakes changed to tiny bits of ice that stung their faces. Joletta shivered and wrapped her scarf around her neck. As she did, she noticed that the ice crystals were clinging to the sleeve of her navy wool jacket. "Oh, my goodness, Scott! Look!" Each crystal was perfectly formed and different than the one next to it. "I've always heard that no two snowflakes are alike, but I don't think I've ever quite believed it before!"

It was the first thing she had said for several minutes. "They are beautiful, Scott! Just like you said a few minutes ago—even on dark days there *is* beauty! I know you are right. God does love us. I know that now, I guess I always did." She continued, "It just hurts so much when I see suffering."

"I know, sweet girl, I know. Just keep looking to Him, that's all He wants. There will always be questions, and sometimes we just have to accept that we won't always get answers. Especially answers that we think we need or that we understand. We just need to remember that *"He" is the answer!"*

351

"I think we better get you back to the house before we both freeze!" Just before entering the house Jo quietly said, "Thanks, Pastor Scott, I do feel better now, I really do, and I want you to know that I really think you are an awesome guy."

He laughed, "Aww! You're just saying that!" Putting his hand on her shoulder, he said, "But, I'm glad you do-- and, I'm glad we talked!"

Scott was happy that he had been given the opportunity to share with Joletta. He always believed she was special and now he felt the timing of this trip perhaps had not so much to do with his plans, but the plans of the "One" much higher up! Speaking aloud he said, "Happy to oblige!" Grinning to himself, he knew that God's hand was on this young girl he cared so much about. *You have big plans for her, Lord, I know you do!*

Sandi had coffee and hot chocolate made and after helping themselves Jo and Scott went into the family room to join the others.

Since it was getting late, Scott had to leave soon, and he still needed to talk about the new project he was working on. As he sat down, he said, "It has sure been good to see you all again and Sandi, dinner as always was great!"

"I do have something I wanted to discuss with you. I am in need of some help, actually a lot of help, and I am hoping to interest you in a new project that will involve Hope Mission and eventually other areas of Africa."

"Right now, I am in the process of recruiting a group of people willing to form a planning committee and later an advisory board. Most will be professionals, but we will also include others that are interested and would like to partner in our effort. Because our church has agreed to provide funds for the launch, Hope Mission will be the first site to benefit. Because we are familiar with Hope and already provide support, it is a good place to start. As you may or may not know, there is a desperate need across Africa for clean water and access to sanitary toilets. Our hope is to install wells and build toilets and sanitation stations to a wide area. We know that unclean water and unsanitary conditions contribute immensely to numerous serious health issues and even death."

"Obviously, this is not a one-step process. It is so new, it still has not even got an official name. We have been calling it TFWP." Grinning he added, "For "the fresh water project.""

"Jim, I was wondering if you and your father might consider heading up the planning committee? We are hoping to get about 10 or possibly 12 people that are capable of doing research for the projects and who will then make decisions concerning which are the most workable options and how to best implement them."

"Also, there are the financial concerns. We believe the Lord will provide but we need hands-on help with fundraising and I'm sure many other needs will present themselves as we get everything up and running."

As it turned out, Scott ended up staying considerably longer than planned. He left tired, but with the new "recruits" he was hoping for.

In only two more days it would be the New Year! Scott felt that he was truly blessed. He felt his prayers for guidance had placed him here, *where* God wanted him to be, *when* God wanted him to be there.

2005 would offer new opportunities, new challenges and new blessings! And, as always, he would pray for the lost and the suffering.

Chapter 29
TOO MUCH ADOO

Jo could hardly believe that it was almost the middle of May. The past several months had flown by.

She had been busy the week before finishing her term papers. This week, as editor of the school newspaper, there were extra staff meetings and she would be working daily on plans and preparing to format articles for the following week.

Prom was to be held on May 14 and after that would come finals and then Graduation. She had agreed to go to the dance with her friend Roland, who she had been dating for the last couple of months.

He was a great guy and treated her like a princess. They had a great time together, and she loved the way he respected her, but she worried that he was getting too serious. She knew she wasn't ready for a serious relationship. She had plans to continue her education and while it was fun going out with her friends, she felt she wanted to do something of significance with her life. She was not quite sure where her dreams would take her but had been doing some serious soul-searching. She knew this was not a good time to fall in love with anyone.

Not wishing to lead Roland on, she decided she needed him to understand her feelings before they could go out anymore. She worried it might embarrass him, but luckily, he didn't seem to be the least bit put off. Insisting he was perfectly happy the way things were, even though he really cared a lot about her, he laughed and promised to put no pressure to go further in the relationship, unless she was ready for more.

She leaned over and kissed his cheek. "You are the sweetest guy I know. Thanks for being you."

The dance was coming up quickly, so on Saturday Jo and her Mother drove into the city early, leaving Annie with Grandma Susan. They spent the morning shopping, and although they found some beautiful dresses, they found nothing that suited Joletta.

Sandi smiled at her daughter, who was beginning to get frustrated. "Don't get discouraged. I'm sure we will find one that will work....Let's stop and get something to eat. We can go over to The Purple Petal for lunch. It's only a couple of blocks from here, and then maybe we will drive over to Riverside. Gloria says they have very nice shops there.

The past couple of years Joletta had seen the dresses several of her friends had chosen for Prom and had spent hours daydreaming about exactly what she would wear if or when she was ever invited.

Having decided her gown would have to be full length with many yards and layers of flowing material, she dreamed of the softest pink or the palest green with a glittery finish to the top layer.

Tiffany's gown the previous year was layers of satin and chiffon and the skirt had the same finish she wanted on her own dress.

She tried several more dresses after lunch but had no luck finding "the dream dress." It was mid-afternoon when, as they entered yet another shop, she immediately saw it! "Oh, my goodness, Mom! There it is!"

On display in the window was the most beautiful gown Jo had ever seen. "Oh, Mom! It is beautiful! That is my dress!"

Sandi smiled. "Don't get too excited; they may not have it in your size." They were both getting tired and Jo's frustration was growing!

So far, everything they looked at had been wrong. Either Mom liked it and Joletta did not, or Jo liked it and Sandi did not, or the color wasn't right, the wrong material, it was too short, too tight, too sexy---

"It is a beautiful dress, but I thought you wanted green or pink."

"Oh, Mom, no, I just changed my mind! This dress is perfect!"

A stylish woman came toward them. "Good afternoon ladies, do we have a special occasion coming up?"

"My daughter is shopping for a prom dress and needs to see what you have in a size 7 or 8."

Joletta almost interrupted her mother. "Please, Ma'am, do you have the dress that is in the window in my size?"

"I thought you would—" Sandi began.

"No! I want *that* one!"

"Well, my dear, let me see what we can do for you. I believe the dress on display is a larger size, but perhaps we can find one that is similar."

"Oh, no! Are you saying you don't have it?" A disappointed Joletta looked crushed. "But it is exactly what I want."

"Hang on, Dear. Let's go over and see what we do have in your size, and I can go to the back and see what is there. Some of the styles are very much alike."

Sandi put her hand on Jo's arm. "It will be OK, Honey. If we don't find something today, we can try again tomorrow over in Middleton."

"But, Mom!"

"Jo! For goodness sake! Don't get all upset. Let's just go over here and see what else they have." Joletta followed her mother and the sales lady over to a rack of dresses toward the middle of the room. With little enthusiasm from the girl, they found only one dress that was even similar to the one she so coveted.

"I will go to the back room and check, but I really don't think there is another one there." Leaving Jo and her mother alone the sales lady headed to the back of the store.

"Could I at least try the dress in the window on, Mom? It doesn't look that big. She didn't even look to see what size it really is."

"I guess we can ask, but I imagine she already knows the size, or she would have checked. Honey, I don't want you to be disappointed, but you may have to get something else."

Within minutes, the sales-person returned with another lady. "I'm sorry, Dear, we don't have another dress in your size, but Beverly is our talented seamstress, and she tells me if you have a few days she could alter the one you were hoping for."

Sandi looked at her daughter's hopeful face, and with a doubtful voice said, "The dance is a week from today."

"Oh, my. That is definitely going to be pushing things a bit, but, young lady, let's try on the dress and see what needs to be done. Hopefully, it will be a fairly simple fix, and we can make it happen!"

Jo was practically floating on air when they returned home an hour later. She came through the door and hugged Jim. "I am getting the most beautiful dress I have ever seen! No one else is going to have a dress as pretty as mine!"

Jim laughed, "No one, Jo?"

"No, not one person!" She danced circles across the room to the stairs.

Sandi just smiled and shook her head. It was going to be a long week and *Oh my, please don't let anything go wrong with the alterations!*

The week came and went as time always does and promptly at 5:30 Thursday evening they picked up "the" dress.

Roland and Richard were there at 6:00 on Saturday, and they would go from there to pick up Rich's girlfriend

Shelley at 6:30. She had not been able to get off work early, so to give her extra time they had made dinner reservations for 7:15. Although people would be arriving at the school any time after 7:00, the dance would not officially start until 8:30.

Jo's prediction about her dress was not far from wrong. Not only was the dress itself beautiful, but the girl wearing it made a lovely picture to behold. Her skin glowed above a sweetheart neckline, and the beaded cap sleeves showed just a hint of perfectly shaped shoulders. She wore her dark hair in a soft thick braid swept to one side and the full, flowing, pale blue skirt trailed behind as she descended the staircase.

Around her neck, Joletta wore a necklace Jim and Sandi had given her - a gold chain with a single teardrop-shaped pearl that fell close to her heart. It represented the tears shed during the months after her accident, her love for Golden Boy, and the wonderful tears of joy that were shed when she recovered.

She had chosen to wear simple pearl-colored slippers with no heel since she was almost as tall as Roland was. The young men looked handsome in tuxedos with cummerbunds to match the dresses the girls were wearing.

Putting a sweet corsage on Jo's wrist, they went outside to do the traditional photo shoot. After some strict words on safety and appropriate behavior, with hugs and laughter, the three young people were off for what promised to be a very special night out "on the town."

Sandi worked outside in her flowerbed while Annie played on her swing set, and Jim worked on the new lawnmower he had recently purchased. As evening turned to night, they went inside and Sandi went to run a bath for Annie and prepare her for bedtime.

After bath was over the little one climbed onto Jim's lap and, hugging him, said, "Oh, Daddy Jim, you are the

"Best-est" daddy I ever had! I love you. Did I ever tell you that?"

"I don't know that you ever told me exactly like that, but I already knew that you loved me." Smiling down at Annie, he grinned and squeezed her little body to him.

"Will you read to me tonight?"

"Well, doesn't Mommy usually do that?"

"Mommy wants you to do it! You can read to her, too! Please, Pretty plee-se!"

Sandi walked into the room in time to hear the pleading child. "Annie, Daddy Jim is tired."

"No, Hon, that's OK. She said you want me to read to you also."

"Oh, really? Well what do we want Daddy Jim to read?"

Hopping down and running to her room, Annie immediately pulled a book off a shelf and within a minute was back on Jim's lap. "This is the right one!" It was a copy of Disney's *Cinderella.*

"Why is *Cinderella* the right book?" Sandi asked.

"'Cause of Joletta, Mommy! Joletta is like Cinderella. See, her dress is blue! Just like Cinderella's!"

"You are right, Annie-poo. Joletta is just like Cinderella."

Opening the book, Jim began to read.

Later, with Annie sound asleep, the adults sat on the swing outside of their master bedroom and watched the stars sparkling from far away.

"You're very quiet."

"Just a little melancholy, I guess. Time just seems to be passing so quickly. Joletta is going to be grown and gone, and I'm not ready.

Jim squeezed her hand, "Honey; she will always come home."

Chapter 30
TOMORROW, JUST AROUND THE BEND

It was finally here! June 5th, 2005! Today was the day she would actually walk across a graduation platform! Today was the beginning of the "rest of her life!"

Jo got out of bed and headed for the shower. There would be no time today for sitting around doing nothing. She would spend the next hour getting herself ready for the day ahead. She had to shower and do her hair and nails. Mom would insist on her eating some breakfast, and she still had to iron the sundress she was wearing under her graduation gown.

Roland would be coming at 11:30 to pick her up. Although they had practiced the day before, Mr. Thomas insisted they be there before Noon to get last-minute instructions. Everyone would then line up in alphabetical order so the processional could enter the football stadium just before the National Anthem began to play. After everyone had been awarded their diplomas, there would be a short reception in the Gym so everyone could share hugs and good wishes and do photo shoots before they all headed to their own homes or, in many cases, graduation parties.

Preparation for these upcoming celebrations had already been evident the past couple of weekends as one noticed large party tents and tables with folding chairs being set up on front lawns and back yards of homes throughout town.

Joletta's graduation party would not be until the following weekend. That way she would be able to attend Roland and Richard's party on graduation day and they would then be free to come to hers.

The week before there had been an honor's banquet for all the graduating seniors and their families. It had been quite an affair with personal introductions of each student. College scholarships and grants were awarded to numerous deserving students, and Joletta had been very happy to accept several of her own.

She had been afraid that after her accident her test scores would not be high enough to win any of the awards being handed out, but she was very mistaken. By the time the family left for home, Joletta had excitedly accepted a significant amount of cash assistance to use towards her chosen college career.

She had already received acceptance letters from two of the schools she had applied to but was still anxiously waiting in hopes of hearing from Penn State, the college she truly hoped to attend.

It was not too far away, in her home state, and had an excellent pre-med program. Joletta was still unsure exactly what her career choice would be, but the medical field was what interested her most, especially following her visit to Africa the summer before.

After going to Malawi last summer and watching the devastating effect the AIDS virus was having on so many lives, she had been considering possibly medical research or perhaps something else in the medical field, maybe becoming a nurse or even a physician! She knew it would be a long road, if indeed that was the direction she was headed. Math and science had always been her favorite subjects, and until her accident she had been a straight "A" student in all related classes, whether it be biology, chemistry or calculus.

The months after her accident she had struggled and had to work extra hard playing catch-up, but with the help of her wonderful tutor and a lot of encouragement, she now felt she could keep up with or exceed the best of the competition.

"MOM! It's here! Mom-- Mom! Where are you?!"

The front door slammed loudly and Joletta came flying into the kitchen where Sandi was making sandwiches for lunch.

"What on earth is going on, Joletta?"

"Are you listening, Mom? It's the letter, Mom! The one from Penn State. It's here."

Joletta fumbled in a frenzied attempt to open the envelope. "Oh, Mom, I'm afraid to read it. Here! I can't even open it! You do it, read it to me!"

Sandi took the thick manila package and, with hands shaking almost as badly as her daughters, tore it open. Clearing her throat as she unfolded the pages, she began to read aloud the formal-looking document to Joletta.

On behalf of the administration, faculty, and staff of Penn State. the Provost is proud to inform you,

Joletta K. Breese,

of the acceptance of your application to attend Pennsylvania State University. Our compliments to you on your personal and scholastic achievements.

We were impressed by your application and enjoyed our interview with you. We feel that you have fulfilled the stringent enrollment criteria of this institution and are ready to meet the challenges of college life on our campus at Penn State Behrend, Erie, PA.

We were very impressed with your application essay for the "Behrend Extreme Challenge Scholarship" and are pleased to inform you that you have been chosen as the recipient of this award!

362

This yearly scholarship in the amount of $10,000 will be renewed each year that you attend this university, provided that you continue to meet all requirements.

Also find enclosed maps, phone numbers, staff names and other helpful brochures that we hope will assist you in getting further acquainted with our campus and staff.

We will be happy to answer any questions that you may have by simply calling the number listed on the bottom of this letter.

To reserve your place on our list of enrollees, you must send a non-refundable deposit of $600 by June 30.

Again, we congratulate you on your high school accomplishments and wish you continued success in your college endeavors! We look forward to seeing you on our campus this fall.

Sincerely, Kevin Person, President
Pennsylvania State University

Jo flung her arms around her mom and danced her around the kitchen until they were both dizzy! Laughing and crying at the same time, Jo sang, "I did it, Mom! I just can't believe it! I actually did it! I am going to College at Penn State!!"

As they were both catching their breath, Jim walked in the door. "What's all the ruckus about? I could hear you two a block away!"

"Oh, Jim, that isn't true," Sandi laughed, "but Joletta has some really exciting news---"

Sandy didn't have a chance to finish before Jo, still breathless from their impromptu dance, was telling him everything the letter contained.

Jim, in his usual fashion, grinned and shrugged his shoulders. "So, OK? Is there any *important* news?"

Rolling her eyes and laughing, Jo turned as Annie who had been asleep on the couch came into the room stretching. Jo ruffled her curls, skipped and started up the stairs. As she went, she was singing to herself, "I'm going to Penn State! Joletta is going to Penn State!"

"I have to call Tiffany I have to call Tina! They are going to be so happy!" Up the stairs Joletta went!

SOMETIMES DREAMS DO COME TRUE!

Hello, my name is Karen Forester,

I was Born number six of seven children. We had wonderful, loving parents and our maternal grandmother lived with us. I share my birthday with my twin brother and our birthday month of September with two other brothers. We were all four born within three years and were called "the little kids" by our older siblings who shared the status of "big brother and sisters!"

Our early years were spent running through fields, woods and splashing in the cold clear streams of our SW Missouri Ozark home. We later moved and I became a "small town girl." Although I never lost my love of the "country life" I have remained a "small town girl."

I married a special man and we will soon celebrate 54th anniversary. We are privileged to be Parents, Grandparents and now Great Grandparents.

We also shared our home with foster children. An experience that kept us very busy for almost 20 years!

We moved our family to NW Ohio and bought the little house we continue to reside in 45 years later.

I have been blessed beyond measure and I am so very grateful to all my friends, my family members, our church family, and so many others, that have contributed in so many ways.

Joletta's story has been an ongoing project that has taken years to complete. The story includes bits and pieces of my own dreams and experiences and my prayer is that whoever reads it will find encouragement and hope as they follow Joletta and her family through the twist and turns of life.

I will soon be working on the next part of Joletta's story.

May God Bless You as He has Blessed Me.

karenforester@yahoo.com
Store.bookbaby.com
iBooks
Amazon Kindle
Barnes & Noble
Kobo
Baker & Taylor
Copia
Gardners
eSentral
Scribd
Goodreads
Ciando
Vearsa (Overdrive, Playster, Hoopla